The
Measby Murder
Enquiry

ANN PURSER

BERKLEY PRIME CRIME, NEW YORK

THE BERKLEY PUBLISHING GROUP
Published by the Penguin Group
Penguin Group (USA) Inc.
375 Hudson Street, New York, New York 10014, USA

Penguin Group (Canada), 90 Eglinton Avenue East, Suite 700, Toronto, Ontario M4P 2Y3, Canada
(a division of Pearson Penguin Canada Inc.)
Penguin Books Ltd., 80 Strand, London WC2R 0RL, England
Penguin Group Ireland, 25 St. Stephen's Green, Dublin 2, Ireland (a division of Penguin Books Ltd.)
Penguin Group (Australia), 250 Camberwell Road, Camberwell, Victoria 3124, Australia
(a division of Pearson Australia Group Pty. Ltd.)
Penguin Books India Pvt. Ltd., 11 Community Centre, Panchsheel Park, New Delhi—110 017, India
Penguin Group (NZ), 67 Apollo Drive, Rosedale, Auckland 0632, New Zealand
(a division of Pearson New Zealand Ltd.)
Penguin Books (South Africa) (Pty.) Ltd., 24 Sturdee Avenue, Rosebank, Johannesburg 2196,
South Africa

Penguin Books Ltd., Registered Offices: 80 Strand, London WC2R 0RL, England

THE MEASBY MURDER ENQUIRY

A Berkley Prime Crime Book / published by arrangement with the author

PRINTING HISTORY
Berkley Prime Crime mass-market edition / May 2011

ISBN: 978-0-425-24156-1

BERKLEY® PRIME CRIME
Berkley Prime Crime Books are published by The Berkley Publishing Group,
a division of Penguin Group (USA) Inc.,
375 Hudson Street, New York, New York 10014.
BERKLEY® PRIME CRIME and the PRIME CRIME logo are trademarks of Penguin Group
(USA) Inc.

PRINTED IN THE UNITED STATES OF AMERICA

10 9 8 7 6 5 4 3 2 1

Titles by Ann Purser

Lois Meade Mysteries

MURDER ON MONDAY
TERROR ON TUESDAY
WEEPING ON WEDNESDAY
THEFT ON THURSDAY
FEAR ON FRIDAY
SECRETS ON SATURDAY
SORROW ON SUNDAY
WARNING AT ONE
TRAGEDY AT TWO
THREATS AT THREE

Ivy Beasley Mysteries

THE HANGMAN'S ROW ENQUIRY
THE MEASBY MURDER ENQUIRY

In loving memory of my Grandma

Acknowledgments

The Professional Gambler's Handbook—
Beating the System by Hook and by Crook

by Weasel Murphy

A Paladin Press Book

One

"IF YOU ASK me," Ivy Beasley said to Roy, as she sat down and carefully straightened her serviceable tweed skirt, "the fees in this place are daylight robbery! And what do we get for it? Bed and board, and not a lot else!"

She had lived at Springfields Luxury Residential Home in the Suffolk village of Barrington for over two years now, exiled, as she said, to Suffolk from her native Round Ringford, where she had lived for most of her long life. "All Deirdre's fault," she said often. "Made me agree to it when I wasn't meself. That flu was very weakening, and before I could say knife, she'd booked me in."

Deirdre Bloxham was Ivy's only cousin, much younger, rich and bossy. She was a widow, and had inherited her wealth from her husband, Bert, who had built up a network of car sales showrooms all around the county. Ivy was a bit of a tartar herself, used to organising Round Ringford to suit herself. But times had changed, and when Deirdre had suggested the move, Ivy was perceptive enough to see that in Ringford she had been reduced to an awkward old woman who lived in the past. Newcomers had taken over, and she was ignored. Added to that, she had reluctantly agreed to having help in the house from New Brooms, a cleaning business run by a Mrs. Meade in Long Farnden, not far away.

"Now Ivy, see sense," Deirdre had said. "You're in your eighties, and the only friends you have left are a couple of old women no longer able to get about, and you're not too frisky yourself." And so Ivy had agreed.

Deirdre herself was very frisky, and, well positioned in her oddly triangular-shaped home, Tawny Wings, she had renewed a friendship with Theodore Roussel, the squire of the village, who lived in the Hall. He was still a bachelor, possibly even more frisky than Deirdre. Both of them were in their early sixties and well preserved. Plenty of money in the bank allowed Deirdre to buy the best designer clothes, and her apricot gold curls were kept immaculate by the best hairdresser in Thornwell, the nearest big town.

Soon after Ivy had moved to Springfields, she had been persuaded by a newcomer to the village, Augustus Half-hide, a thin, bony man with a charming smile, to join him in an agency entitled Enquire Within. They began in a small way, and the two of them, along with Deirdre bank-rolling expenses, and Roy Goodman, another Springfields resident, supplying local knowledge, had played a large part in solving a very nasty murder in the village.

Augustus Halfhide was still something of a mystery, even after some while living in Barrington. Ivy was at first convinced he was an undercover agent, now retired, either from choice or expediency, and was keeping his hand in with Enquire Within. But now she was not so sure.

The fourth member of this oddly assorted group, Roy Goodman, had been a farmer, and had been resigned to boredom in Springfields for the rest of his days. Apart from the inevitable wearing away of his wiry frame, he had all his marbles intact. He had taken to Ivy at once, partly as a fellow prisoner, as he described their incarceration, and partly because she stirred in him feelings which he realised were unaccustomed affection, and occasionally as—could it possibly be?—love. Though Ivy had never actually said as much, he suspected and hoped that she returned these in some measure at least. When Roy had taken a recent tumble and retired to his bed for a few days, it was noticed by everyone in Springfields that Ivy Beasley spent most of the day in Roy Goodman's room.

"He's having a whale of a time," said Mrs. Spurling, the home's manager, sourly. "We shall have to stop Miss Beasley visiting him so much. His ankle is quite better now, and he should be downstairs with the others." She need not have worried. As soon as Ivy judged it was time, she told Roy that she would see him downstairs for breakfast next day, and he duly obliged.

Now, on this blustery day, he had come down saying he was quite restored, and sat close to Ivy in the residents' lounge. She had told him that something important had come up, and began to speak in hushed tones. "Time to convene," she said. "Gus just phoned and said he's got another case for us. Meeting tomorrow at Tawny Wings. Two o'clock sharp."

DOWNSTAIRS IN HER office, Mrs. Spurling was talking to a smartly dressed woman who introduced herself as Bronwen Evans. "It's about my mother, Mrs. Wilson Jones," she said. "A lovely person, but now sadly unable to look after herself, even with help from my sister, who fortunately lives a couple of streets away from her. I am afraid I myself am much too busy to be of help to Mother. The dear soul understands this."

I wonder if she does, thought Mrs. Spurling. And what about that sister? Did she understand that Mrs. Evans was too busy to help? She sighed. It was such a familiar story. Widowed mother, no longer of any use to her family, so must be comfortably installed somewhere where they could hand over responsibility.

"I quite understand, Mrs. Evans," she said, remembering the empty room not earning anything in the Green Wing of the house. "And I'm sure we shall be able to welcome her into our friendly home here at Springfields. There are, of course, a number of official matters to deal with first, but I am sure we shall be introducing your mother to new friends here in the very near future."

Ivy and Roy were finishing their breakfast when Mrs. Spurling came into the dining room with her usual mirthless smile.

"What does she want?" said Ivy. "She never comes in when we're eating. Much too sensitive to see a lot of old parties dribbling over their food."

"Ivy!" said Roy. "You know that's not true. We are a very genteel lot in Springfields, minding our manners along with the best."

Mrs. Spurling stood in the centre of the room and cleared her throat. "Ahem! Could I have your attention for a few moments, guests?"

"Get on with it, then," muttered Ivy. "My toast is getting cold. I do hate cold, leathery toast."

"I know you'll be delighted to hear that we are to have another guest joining us very soon. Mrs. Alwen Wilson Jones has been living in Thornwell for many years, and has now earned a period of rest and quiet in our midst. I know you will welcome her with your usual warmth," she added, looking nervously at Ivy. She looked around at the residents, some faces expressionless, others frowning suspiciously, and then walked quickly from the room.

Silence reigned for a moment, and then a babble of talk began as the residents aired their views about giving a warm welcome to Mrs. Alwen Wilson Jones.

"Never heard of her," said Roy, who had grown up on a local farm and knew everybody worth knowing.

"We shall see," said Ivy. "If you ask me, it's best to stand back and see what the woman's made of, before we clasp her to our bosoms."

Roy chuckled. "Good for you Ivy, right as ever," he said.

Two

THE ARRIVAL OF a new resident was always a welcome diversion in Springfields, and by lunchtime all had gathered in the dining room, spruced up in their best outfits and ready to assess Mrs. Alwen Wilson Jones.

"Here she comes," Ivy said to Roy. "Walks with a stick, I see."

"And leaning on her daughter's arm," Roy said, and sniffed. "At least, I suppose that's her daughter. You can see the likeness."

"Don't stare, Roy. Let her go to another table, until we see what she's like."

"Too late. Old Spurling is bringing her over. Look, her daughter's kissed her good-bye. Can't get out of here fast enough. Here she comes. Smile, Ivy dear."

"Miss Beasley, Mr. Goodman," said Mrs. Spurling bravely, "I am delighted to introduce Mrs. Wilson Jones, our new resident here at Springfields. These two lovely people," she said to the sullen-looking newcomer, "are our liveliest guests, and I'm sure you will all be great friends."

Ivy glared at her. "Not if you don't bring the poor woman a chair to sit on," she said.

Mrs. Spurling had decided to start Mrs. Wilson Jones off at the deep end, seating her at Ivy's table. She could always move her to sit with less challenging companions, but when first introduced to Alwen Jones she had sensed an unwillingness to be moulded into shape, and decided another strong woman was needed. Perhaps Ivy would oblige.

"Of course, my dear," she said, and called to the buxom waitress to bring over an extra chair. Then she settled Mrs. Wilson Jones down, said a small prayer and went back to her office.

Roy was a kindly soul, and immediately began to talk about the old days in Thornwell, turning on his undoubted charm, finding acquaintances they had in common and generally attempting to cheer up the woman and make her feel at home. Ivy, on the other hand, for the first time in her life felt something like jealousy. She and Roy had become close friends, and she had begun to regard him as her property.

"That was your daughter, was it? And by the way," she added, "is it all right if we call you Mrs. Jones?"

"If you must," she replied, and changed the subject back to her daughter. "Yes, Bronwen is a very successful businesswoman, and always busy, unfortunately." There was a sour tinge to this answer, and Mrs. Jones hastily went on to assure Ivy that she was very proud of her clever daughter. "Though like the rest of us, she has her problems," she added.

"Any other children?" asked Ivy. Who did she think she was, boasting about her genius offspring? Perhaps her son was a binman.

"Another daughter, living in Thornwell. A sweet girl, but not the calibre of Bronwen. No, Bethan is a home-maker, and dedicated mother of two. They live close by my house, and are always popping in to see me." Then she remembered that her house was on the market and her face fell.

"Don't fret," said Ivy firmly. "We've all been through it. You'll get used to it here, and I've been told there are worse places."

"Ivy! Don't frighten poor Alwen. May I call you Alwen, my dear?" Roy said with a smile. "Dear Ivy's bark is much worse than her bite," he added. "Now then, do you play pontoon?"

Mrs. Jones brightened. "Oh, yes," she said. "I love it. I love all card games, and often play with the grandchildren."

"Ah," said Ivy, somewhat mollified by Roy's declared "dear Ivy." "Mrs. Spurling ain't too keen on noisy kids. But I expect one at a time would be all right."

Mrs. Jones raised her eyebrows and looked coolly at Ivy. "Oh, they wouldn't be at all noisy. I was a teacher you know. Fifty years dealing with young children, and I'm still able to guarantee good behaviour!"

Roy smiled. "Goodness, you must have many stories to tell us, Alwen," he said. "Where did you teach?"

"I was head teacher at Thornwell Primary. And I certainly could tell you endless stories, I can assure you! But by the time I was due to retire, education had changed so much—"

"—that you felt like an old dinosaur?" interrupted Ivy with a bland expression.

Oh, lor, thought Roy, trouble ahead.

Three

GUS, AS HE liked to be known, sat in the sagging armchair provided by his landlord, the Hon. Theodore Roussel, and looked through the *Guardian* obituaries. Nobody of interest to him today. Then his eye was caught by one of the mini-obits at the foot of the page. "George Jones—brewer extraordinaire," he read. He had heard of him, of course. These days any single owner of a brewery was extraordinary. Most of the small ones had been swallowed up by conglomerates or brewed cult beers for the connoisseur. But as Gus read on, it was apparent that George and his family had maintained a successful brewery in Thornwell, producing beer by old methods and trading on a local reputation for providing a consistently good pint.

"Poor old George," he said aloud. "What will happen now? Save the brewery!" he said loudly to his dog Whippy, sitting obediently by his side.

Miriam Blake, living next door in Hangman's Row, was hastily taking in her washing as the skies darkened. Gus had opened a window earlier, before the rain had begun to bucket down, and now Miriam heard his shout. Never needing an excuse to rush to the rescue of her attractive neighbour, she hurried to his back door, clutching her washing basket.

"Gus? Are you all right?"

Oh, sod it. Gus had more or less trained Miriam not to call unless invited, but now here she was, with anxious brown eyes like a worried spaniel. Whippy bounced out to greet her best friend. No amount of training had taught *her* that Miriam was anything more than a wonderful woman who fondled her velvety ears and threw a ball for her up and down the lane.

"Of course I'm all right," Gus said, and added belatedly, "Thanks. It's just that I've discovered that George Jones, brewery owner, has just died. It's a tragedy."

"Are you thinking of taking over, then, Gus?" Miriam asked fondly, creeping into his porch to get out of the rain.

"What with, Miriam? As you know, my ex-wife takes all my money. I have barely enough to live on."

Miriam had heard Gus plead poverty before but did not believe him. He seemed to have plenty of money when needed. Trips to London, a new suit for an old friend's funeral. Sometimes she wondered jealously if he might be supported by his friend Deirdre Bloxham of Tawny Wings. A kept man! Well, he certainly needed rescuing from that woman's clutches. And this ridiculous agency he'd set up with a lot of old fogies. That cannot have earned him much so far! As far as she knew, the only case they'd solved was the murder of her late and unlamented mother.

Miriam at once invited him to supper, saying that by a strange coincidence she had a couple of bottles of Jones Brothers Best in her larder. She hadn't, of course, but she knew that the new shopkeeper, James, sometimes had a few bottles, and she had plenty of time to walk up and buy supplies.

Gus thought rapidly. "Sorry, dear," he said kindly, "already booked for dominos at the pub. Can't disappoint old Alf. Another time, maybe. You'll have to excuse me now. Due at Springfields to do my bit for the old dears." He shut the door and closed the windows, made a mental note to ask at the pub for Jones Brothers Best and set out to visit his partner in detection, Ivy Beasley.

"MORNING, GUS. MORNING, Deirdre, my dear." Roy Goodman beamed. "Ivy is on her way. Seems our gaoler wanted her to have a chat with our new resident, Alwen something-or-other Jones. Apparently the poor woman had some complaints about this and that at Springfields, and Mrs. Spurling thought Ivy could help."

"Shall we start the meeting, then, Gus?" Deirdre had a hair appointment at one o'clock in Thornwell, and was anxious not to miss it. Theo Roussel was having a drinks party this evening and she wanted to look her best.

"Not if you know what's good for you," Gus said firmly. "If we start without our Ivy, there'll be hell to pay."

Roy nodded in agreement, and the conversation revolved around Mrs. Alwen Jones and whether she was related to the brewery Joneses in Thornwell.

"There's dozens of Joneses in town," Roy said. "I remember my dad telling me about the Welsh drovers who used to travel on foot with their cattle to market. The drovers' roads had inns along the route where they could stop on the way and leave their cattle in keep overnight. So there's loads of Joneses and Owens and Davieses around here. Good beer, though," he added thoughtfully. "I hope it don't get taken over by one of them giants."

The large black iron knocker on Tawny Wings' front door banged loudly three times, and Deirdre went to admit Ivy. Her stiff, dark blue raincoat had been bought from a Round Ringford jumble sale with the waterproof guarantee that it once belonged to the village policeman, and she had pulled her black felt hat well down over her ears. She removed the coat, shook off the raindrops onto the parquet floor and lifted her black hat carefully, flattening down any wayward strands of hair. She said not a word.

"Why didn't you ring me?" Deirdre scolded. "I could have popped down to pick you up."

"Or I could have collected you both on the way," Gus said.

"Well, you didn't, did you?" snapped Ivy. "Anyway, I was delayed by that ridiculous Spurling woman. She seemed to think I would reassure the new prisoner. Tell her what a wonderful place Springfields is. Huh! I didn't take to this Mrs. Jones from the start, but I did my best." She smirked at the apprehensive faces watching her.

"That's that, then," said Roy, chuckling. "Come and cheer us up, Ivy. We wouldn't start without you. Couldn't, actually, could we, gang?"

My goodness, thought Gus. He knows how to handle the old thing. Maybe I should take a few lessons.

"Well, then, over to you, Gus," Deirdre said. "We're all ears."

Gus settled himself more comfortably in Deirdre's leather library chair. "We have a real commission this time," he said, reminding them that their first case had been successful but not lucrative. There had been no paying client, and they had kept going to satisfy their own curiosity and interest.

"I've had a call from an old colleague, Martin," Gus continued. "He asked me if I had heard anything about the death of an old man over the other side of the county. Apparently there were rumours of blackmail alongside local suspicions about the actual cause of death. Graffiti found in the old man's house. That kind of thing. Martin knows my background, of course, and asked me to keep my ears and eyes open for other cases of extortion or fraud." Gus had been intrigued, and, more importantly, was sure the old firm would still pay for information. He had decided it would be a good investigation for Enquire Within to pursue.

At the mention of Gus's background the others exchanged

glances. Although now they knew each other pretty well, none of them had been able to find out anything substantial about Gus. They knew he was married and possibly divorced, possibly retired from MI5 or something similar, or possibly none of these things. Ivy said occasionally that she suspected he made the whole thing up and had never done anything more risky than keeping his total earnings from the tax inspector.

"So how are we supposed to help?" asked Deirdre. She, like the others, felt let down. After all, what was a vaguely suspicious death the other side of the county when they had tackled a much nastier case close at hand?

"There is another factor," Gus said, sensing their lack of enthusiasm, and paused dramatically. The others looked at him expectantly.

"Well?" said Ivy.

"There was a slogan painted in blood on the kitchen door."

"Ah, that's more like it," Roy said, his old face alight with interest. "What did it say?"

"'YOU WERE WARNED!' Or something like that."

"Ugh! How horrible!" Deirdre said. "I'll go and make coffee. That is, if anyone fancies any."

"Where was this dreadful crime?" Ivy said. "I haven't seen anything in the papers."

"No, it was hushed up. I told you it was a very confidential matter. Ramifications, you know," Gus said, and tapped the side of his nose.

"So where was this village? Surely we must know, if we're to help?" Ivy was beginning to wonder if Gus was wasting their time.

"A village outside Oakbridge. The other side of the county," Gus said.

"Name of the village?" Roy said. He and his family had lived in the county for generations and local knowledge was his department.

"Measby. About three miles outside Oakbridge. Know it?"

Roy nodded. "Oh, yes, I know it, all right."

"Why do you say it like that?" Gus asked, frowning. What did the old boy know about Measby?

"Ah ha," said Roy. "Confidential, you know. Ramifications . . ." And he tapped the side of his nose.

Four

IVY AND ROY sat at the lunch table, waiting for their first course. "Here she comes," Roy whispered. "Don't look up, then maybe she'll sit somewhere else." But he spoke in vain.

"May I join you?" Alwen Jones said.

Roy was tempted to say they weren't coming apart, but he had used that old joke of his father's several times to Ivy, and she'd probably think up some crushing remark. Not worth risking.

"Now, then," Alwen continued, as if addressing an attentive class of five-year-olds, "what have we been doing with our morning?"

"Getting wet," said Ivy. "How about you? Did you sort out the pillow problem?"

In reply to Alwen's request for at least four pillows, Mrs. Spurling had mentioned a shortage and an order not yet received.

"Well, I made sure the woman has ordered some really good feather pillows as of this morning." Alwen beamed. "Start as you mean to go on, I always say."

"I'm allergic to feathers," Ivy said. "I hope they don't find their way into my room."

Allergic to feathers? Roy frowned at her. He was sure she had a special cushion for her back, brought all the way from Round Ringford, and stuffed full of the finest goose down. Then their plates of pork and beans were brought steaming to the table, and conversation was interrupted for a while.

When the rich sauce had been commented on as being too indigestible for old stomachs, Roy asked politely if Mrs. Jones had any connection with the well-known Thornwell brewery, Jones Brothers?

Ivy watched her face closely, and was intrigued to see a shadow fall, wiping out Alwen's distinctly smug expression left over from licking her lips and thanking God for a good strong stomach.

"Distant connection of mine," she said. "Jones is a very common name. That's why we always use Wilson, my maiden name," she added pointedly, looking at Ivy.

"No other Joneses in Springfields, so no need for Wilson here," Ivy assured her.

"And your husband, Alwen? Was he a teacher, too?" Roy asked in his kindest tones. Ivy was certainly giving the poor woman a hard time.

"If you'll excuse me," said Alwen Jones, "I think perhaps the sauce was a little too rich, after all. I'll just stretch out for half an hour. See you later? Perhaps a hand or two of bridge?" She pushed back her chair and stood up. A fine figure of a woman, thought Roy, and then caught Ivy's eye and lowered his gaze.

"It's pontoon this afternoon," Ivy said. "Our friend Augustus Halfhide is coming along to play. A real gambler, that one. You have to keep a close eye on him, else he'll have the shirt off your back."

Roy couldn't help thinking that this might be a sight worth seeing, and watched Alwen Jones walk with a slight limp that was somehow appealing, out of the dining room and up the stairs to her room.

* * *

GUS HAD ARRIVED on time, as always. He was at once trapped by Mrs. Spurling, who, he suspected, lay in wait for him. She had a clear view of the front gate from her office window, and there was no way for visitors to sneak in without her knowing.

"Ah, Mr. Halfhide!" she said. "So nice of you to come and cheer up our dear guests," she said. Although he had announced his intention of becoming a Friend of Springfields, she was well aware that the only people he talked to were the dreaded Miss Beasley and dear old Roy Goodman, who was becoming rapidly corrupted by Ivy and her henchman, Mr. Halfhide. Springfields was a part of a chain of old folks' homes, and if her superiors discovered she was allowing gambling, there would be a severe reprimand. They had been forgiving when husband Spurling had run off with the cook five years ago, leaving her as sole manager. Another transgression might mean dismissal for her, and Springfields had become her life.

Her assistant, Miss Pinkney, had told her this morning that the two Polish girls, Katya and Anya, had asked about the possibility of a rise, hinting that they had been headhunted by a rival retirement home in Thornwell. It was one of those mornings, she decided, as she fluttered her eyelids at Gus and said that Mrs. Worth, now bedridden, would love to have a talk with him if he could spare the time. No visitors or family, not much longer to go. Could he oblige?

"Of course, Mrs. Spurling," he said, patting her lightly on her shoulder. He was at least a couple of heads taller, and she felt at once small and feminine. No wonder little Katya had had a serious crush on the man! She had at least saved that from becoming a seriously desperate situation.

"When our card game is finished, I will find my way to her room. Number five, isn't it?" He couldn't think of anything more boring than attempting a one-sided conversation with a poor old thing who was aged and probably senile, and reminded him of graveyards. But maybe this was the price he had to pay for a safe passage to the hereafter.

"I hope this card game—pontoon again, is it?—won't be too tiring for Mr. Goodman. He is not too strong, you know."

Gus knew that Roy was a wiry old devil who was as fit and well as his great age would permit, and who, in any case, was determined not to die of boredom at Springfields. "Oh, the game is pure enjoyment, Mrs. Spurling. You can rely on me to prevent over-excitement!"

At this moment, Ivy appeared and rescued him. "Come along, Augustus," she said. "We are waiting for you. Oh, and by the way, Mrs. Spurling, did you sort out the dripping tap in Mrs. Jones's room? Nothing worse than a dripping tap. We used to call it Japanese torture when I was a girl."

Mrs. Spurling took a deep breath as she watched them disappear into the small room reserved for private interviews with prospective guests. They had not asked her permission to use it for a gaming den. Just taken it over! And Miss Beasley and Mr. Goodman seemed to get younger and fitter every day. Ah, well, she supposed it was a feather in her cap that her guests thrived so well in her care.

DEIRDRE BLOXHAM, MEANWHILE, was sitting in the smartest hairdresser's in town, watching as the young man with magic fingers tweaked and snipped and smoothed her shining hair.

"A new shampoo, Deirdre," he had said. "Do you want to give it a try? Lovely perfume—here have a sniff."

It was a pleasant lemony smell, and Deirdre reckoned it was just the thing to help things on their way with Theo. They had had regular assignations in his bedroom for some time now. Sometimes in her bedroom, too, but he seemed to prefer his own territory. He probably wouldn't want the county set who were his friends to see his car parked outside Tawny Wings too often.

Lately, he had made an excuse or two, cancelling dates

they had made and saying he would be in touch. She hated that phrase. People used it when they had no intention of being "in touch." Perhaps she had begun to take him for granted.

"Mmm," she said, "that's lovely, Terry. Yes, I'll have some of that."

"Guaranteed to bowl over the hardest heart," he said, gaily mixing his metaphors. Deirdre was a longtime client, and there was very little she hadn't told him about herself. A listening ear was as important as a good training in hairdressing, he always said.

"How is your cousin at Springfields?" he asked, as he massaged her scalp with exactly the right pressure.

"Oh, she's fine. They've got a new inmate there. A Mrs. Jones, retired teacher and getting beyond it. Not that far beyond, apparently, and looks like being a match for our Ivy!"

"Jones?" said Terry. "I looked after a Mrs. Wilson Jones for many years. She actually taught me! Could be the same one. She talked about it being difficult to get into the salon in the future. Big woman, walks with a limp?"

"Sounds like her. I have yet to meet her, but Ivy is definitely on the defensive."

"She's well-heeled. Came from a moneyed family, I believe." Terry heard most things, and was a mine of information. Though he declared secrets were safe with him, he had no compunction about revealing them to the next client to arrive in his chair.

"There we are, then, Deirdre," he continued, standing back to admire his handiwork and holding up a mirror for Deirdre to confirm. "Really lovely, though I do say it as shouldn't." He smiled and handed her over to pay an unbelievably large sum to the girl behind the desk.

Five

THEODORE ROUSSEL WAS not happy. After the disastrous end to his long association with former housekeeper Beatrice Beatty, he had engaged a woman from the village to take her place. Although Noreen Price kept herself to herself, and this was a welcome change from the domineering Beatrice, she did not run his household with the same sense of what was right, or, come to that, the same efficiency.

"I have people coming for drinks next Tuesday," he had said to her at least a week ago, and as far as he could tell she had made no preparations. And now it was Tuesday. He looked at his watch. It was three o'clock already. Perhaps he should find her and check.

"Noreen? Are you there?" He peered into the kitchen and saw the big larder door was open. "Noreen?"

She emerged, looking flushed. "Bit of a failure, I'm afraid," she said. "I made some bits and pieces this morning and they're disgusting. That's what comes of cooking something from a recipe you've never used before. Now what are we going to do?" She looked helplessly at him, and he was tempted to say *he* was going to do nothing, but she had better find a way of dealing with it or else take herself off and not return.

Instead, he heard himself saying he would take her into Waitrose in Thornwell and buy quantitites of those ready-made mini-snacks. Not the same, but a very useful substitute, he had heard Deirdre say. He told Noreen to get her bonnet on and received an uncomprehending look from her, and the two of them drove down the drive and off towards town.

During the half an hour it took to make the trip, Noreen kept up a running commentary on the events, good and bad, that had occurred in Barrington during the previous week. After a while, Theo stopped listening. At the mention of Springfields and a new resident, he had begun to think of Katya, the Polish maid there. Such a pretty little thing, and always so helpful and willing. Just how willing, he had yet to find out! But now he was reminded of a vague plan he had formed some time ago. He would persuade her to come and work for him at the Hall, and once she was on the premises he could get to know her better. How much more would he have to pay her to tempt her away from Springfields? She could assist Noreen for a few months, and then he would find an excuse to fire old useless here, sitting next to him and keeping up a monologue all the way to Thornwell. Katya would be in charge, and then . . .

His speculation was interrupted by a raised fist from a man backing out in front of him in Waitrose car park. He had not noticed the reversing lights, and had to stand hard on the brake.

"Oops, Mr. Theo!" Noreen said. "Now, are you coming in to help me choose?"

Theo shuddered. He would not be seen dead in a super-market and said no, he had an appointment with his bank manager. He would see her back at the car promptly at half past four.

DEIRDRE HAD PUT her car away, put the food shopping in the fridge and settled with a cup of tea in front of an afternoon rubbish programme when she heard her telephone.

"Blast! Who the hell can that be?"

It was Ivy, and she sounded oddly quavery. "Deirdre, can you come round straightaway? No, I'm all right. No, it's the new woman, and for some reason she's latched onto me, and old Spurling is out and Miss Pinkney is hysterical, and you're the only person I could think of to help. Get here as quick as you can."

Deirdre sighed. The one thing she had tried to avoid had happened. When she persuaded Ivy to come to Springfields, she had made it clear that she did not want to become involved in Ivy's private life, or the daily happenings in the home. So far, Ivy had been only too pleased to establish herself in her own way, and had life at Springfields pretty well sewn up to her own satisfaction.

And now this. Was it serious, or was Ivy panicking? No, Ivy never panicked. It must be important. She locked up her house and began to walk swiftly along to Springfields. As she approached, she remembered Ivy's words. It's the new woman, she had said. Must be Mrs. Jones, the possibly mysterious Mrs. Wilson Jones.

What could have happened that was so serious that Ivy had to call for help?

Miss Pinkney was waiting for her at the door. "Oh, I'm so glad you could come down, Mrs. Bloxham," she said. "Poor Mrs. Jones is very upset, and Miss Beasley was sure you'd be the person to help."

"What seems to be the trouble?" said Deirdre, like a visiting doctor of the old school.

"Best if you talk to her," Miss Pinkney said. "They are both together, with Mr. Halfhide, in the interview room. Mr. Goodman was there, too, but Ivy sent him away.

"Why?"

"Goodness knows why Miss Beasley does anything!" Miss Pinkney did indeed sound on the verge of tears, and Deirdre said not to worry, if she could be shown where the interview room was, she was sure she could sort it out.

* * *

IT HAD ALL been very distressing, Ivy said, on greeting her cousin. "If you ask me," she pronounced, "the silly
woman's been conned."

The room was sparsely furnished, with four reasonably
comfortable chairs, small tables dotted around for soothing
cups of tea, a seedy-looking plant on the corner of a desk
and an overhead fitting that reminded Deirdre of torture by
spotlight. Ivy was sitting upright, as usual, Gus had slumped
down and had the desperate air of someone needing to be
elsewhere, and Mrs. Jones was a deflated version of her
usual solid self. She peered over the top of a large handkerchief obscuring most of her face, and said, "Who's this?"

"My cousin," said Ivy, who had clearly regained her
confidence. "Deirdre, this is Mrs. Jones."

"I'm Mrs. W-Wilson Jones." The anguish in the woman's voice reached out to Deirdre's kind heart, and she sat
down next to her and reached for her hand.

"Now then, what is all this about? Take your time, Mrs.
Jones. Whatever the problem is, I am sure it can be solved."

Mrs. Jones lowered the handkerchief and said weakly,
"Not unless you've got twenty thousand pounds to spare."

There was a shocked pause. "You never said it was that
much," Gus said, looking admiringly at the ex-headmistress.
He was always impressed by wealth, and had no idea a
teacher's salary could deal in such sums. Must be family
money. Brewery money? He'd had a pint of Jones Brothers
Best at the pub at lunchtime, and it was certainly good beer.

"Tell me more," Deirdre said. She was not letting on,
but she did in fact have twenty thousand pounds to spare,
and much more, but her Bert had not worked hard all his
life to subsidise careless old ladies.

It was a sorry tale that Alwen had to tell. A few weeks
ago, a smooth-talking young man had knocked on her
door, armed with sheaves of convincing documents revealing how by investing even a small sum, she could double it
in no time at all. Of course, he had added with a friendly

laugh, if she decided to invest a larger sum, then the return would be even more exciting.

"I can guess the rest," Deirdre said. "You gave him the money, and have heard nothing since. No such invest-ment exists, and you now have no hope of getting anything back?"

"Absolutely right, Mrs. Bloxham," Alwen Jones said. "Ivy here said you'd be the one to ask, having been in busi-ness and, er, well, being comfortably situated yourself. I remember your husband, you know. Such a nice man, and always so good at cars. We bought all ours from Bert. It was Bert, wasn't it?"

Deirdre confirmed that her husband's name had been Albert. She did not miss the woman's patronising attempt at slotting her into the gradations of Thornwell society. Bert was good with cars, was he? Yes, he was, and he was also good at making money, lots of it, and would never have given twenty pounds, let alone twenty thousand, to a smooth-talking stranger.

She stiffened and said there was very little she could do. Had Mrs. Jones told her daughter? She could go to the police with what sounded like a straight up and down case of criminal extortion.

"Naturally we asked Mrs. Jones if she had told Bron-wen. Not on your nelly, she said." Ivy's face was bland.

"Not quite in those words," Alwen Jones said. "But Ivy is right in that my supremely capable daughter Bronwen would be the last person I would tell. She would explode. And what is more, she would immediately assume power of attorney and give me a weekly pocket money allow-ance!" She frowned, and shook her head sadly. "No, I'd rather lose the twenty thousand pounds than have Bronwen in charge of my money."

"You'd have to agree to putting power of attorney into effect, Mrs. Jones, so you've no need to worry about that," Deirdre said. Voluntary work for the Citizens Advice Bureau had taught her this. Worried sons and daughters of senile old parents, seeing their inheritance at the mercy of unscrupulous marauders, were frequent visitors to the CAB waiting room.

"The police, then?" Deirdre said.

Alwen shook her head. "That would obviously bring in Bronwen and Bethan, and the whole tribe of rabbits' friends and relations."

"Rabbits?" said Ivy, confused. Had the shock knocked the silly woman off her perch?

"Oh, sorry. That's what Bronwen calls the Jones extended family. Beatrix Potter, I believe."

"Including the brewery rabbits?" Gus said. He could not believe that there was no connection between this woman and the brewery. Where else had the wealth come from?

Alwen sidestepped this question and looked at her watch. Her financial situation was her affair. She had spent nearly a lifetime teaching unruly infants and saving enough money from her family bequests to make herself feel safe. "Do you think you would be able to help? I know you conduct enquiries for people, and I'd be very happy to pay for your services. Enquire Within, did you say, Augustus? Are you busy with a case at the moment?"

"Have you got plenty of money left?" said Ivy baldly. "We're not a charity, you know."

Gus stepped in quickly. He had immediately thought of Martin's request, and sensed that Ivy's dislike of Alwen might prejudice their chances of making a few more bawbees. "It may be," he said in measured tones, "that this attempt at fraud is related to another investigation involving extortion that we have been asked to handle. If preliminary research suggests that this is the case, then we would certainly be happy to take on what we realise is a very unfortunate situation for you and possibly other people in the area."

"In other words, yes," said Ivy, who began to see what Gus was getting at. Rumours of death and extortion in Measby, and now Alwen's twenty thousand pounds apparently vanished down the drain. "And for goodness' sake, Mrs. Jones," she added, "be more careful in future."

Six

THE COCKTAIL PARTY, now a more or less obsolete social occasion, still had its uses. Theo Roussel kept up the old tradition at Barrington Hall, and although he no longer sent out invitations, it was an unwritten rule locally that drinks and nibbles would await the select few on a given evening between six thirty and eight o'clock. For anyone who arrived late, it was a quick drink, a dry-tasting nibble and then good-bye. In order to get the full quota of drinks and nibbles they felt was their due, most guests arrived on time. Those who stayed too late and talked too long were not asked again.

Theo stuck to this tried and tested formula because he was quickly bored. Boredom had been a constant companion for most of his life. He was bored at school, doing badly not because he was stupid, but because he could not concentrate on anything that did not immediately grab his attention. After school, he had led the life of a rich man's son, dutifully riding to hounds, escorting debutantes to hunt balls and all the boring round of socialising faithfully recorded in society magazines of the time.

Then he met Deirdre. The daughter of working-class, respectable folk from the terraced streets of Thornwell, she was what his father called a bobby-dazzler. Red hair and green eyes, a peachy skin and a fabulous figure, all combined to make her a target for eligible bachelors for miles around. Theo had fallen for her, attracted even more strongly because of the competition. She seemed to prefer him, and had shown him a life that seemed to him infinitely more interesting and worthwhile. Then one day his father had called him into his study, and lectured him on marrying out of his class. He could not believe it. In these enlightened times, he had assured his father, nobody mentioned class. It was a taboo subject.

"Not here it's not, my son," old John had said. "Have your wicked way with whomever you please, but marry a sensible girl of good breeding."

"Deirdre's not a dog!" Theo had exploded. "And I'm of age, and make my own choice. In any case," he had added, suddenly alarmed by the unsmiling face in front of him, "I have no intention of marrying anyone at the moment."

"That's all right, then, but just remember what I say. The Roussel estate is a valuable inheritance. I would hate to see you forfeit it."

And so Theo had left it too late to make up his mind, and Deirdre had without warning announced her engagement to Bert Bloxham, a young and ambitious car salesman and garage owner in Thornwell. The Bloxhams had done extremely well. Deirdre and Bert together were a pigeon pair, and both worked hard to achieve a very satisfactory financial and civic status in the town.

Although subsequently they had known that they were living in the same village, Theo and Deirdre had not at first renewed their friendship, but when circumstances changed and Deirdre became a widow, they had found the bond still held, and a pleasant middle-aged affair had begun.

Now Theo looked at his watch. Five minutes to go. Those rather dreadful people from the brand-new Dower House were always first. Their luxury dwelling had been built on the site of the old one and at one stage became the subject of a planning controversy. The original farmhouse had been perfectly sound, but mysteriously collapsed in the middle of one dark winter's night. Neighbours said they had heard bulldozing noises in the small hours but had not liked to interfere.

Sure enough, the doorbell sounded, and Theo heard light steps going to answer it. He was ready with the smiling welcome, and was once more delighted that he had asked Katya from Springfields to help out with dispensing the cocktail fare. She was so pretty! Such an asset! Ah, now here they came, Mr. and Mrs. Dower House, and he could not for the life of him remember their names.

THE PARTY WAS in full swing by the time Deirdre arrived. She never arrived on time, considering that it was a waste of time making an entrance if there was no one there to appreciate it. This evening, she was entirely in black. A slim black dress with absolutely no frills, and worn with no jewellery except for a very sparkly diamond flower brooch which Bert had given her for her fortieth birthday. With plain high-heeled shoes that showed off her still exceptional legs, and hair shining, every curl in place, she was a picture to behold. Stupid old Pa! Theo thought, as he went to greet her. She is every inch the elegant matriarch. We could have made such a splendid couple, and by now there would be tribes of children around us and the estate would be secure.

"Wotcha, Theo," Deirdre said, deliberately puncturing the image. She was no fool, and knew exactly why he had failed to pop the question all those years ago. Well, they were having fun now, and without tensions that would probably have scuppered the marriage.

"All going well?" Deirdre continued, looking around the room and noting the delightful Katya dishing out drinks. He'd never change, she decided, and that was another good reason for having chosen dear old Bert.

"Much better now you've arrived. You are looking ravishing, as always," he said gallantly.

"Thanks. Have you got a minute after this lot have gone?"

"More than a minute for you," he said, smiling lasciviously.

"Come off it, Theo," she said. "It's a serious matter. So stay sober, you loose-living old gent. And you can get me a glass of what passes for champagne. At least it'll see me through tales of high jinks on horseback. Anybody interesting here?"

Theo went off chuckling. What would he do without her? A sudden picture in his mind of his tenant Augustus Halfhide with his hand confidently on Deirdre's shoulder appeared before him. He'd have to watch that carefully. He supposed he could always evict the man, but he'd have to think of a better reason than lustful jealousy!

At last the Dower House pair departed, full of promises of future invitations for Theo to see their lovely home. Lovely home, indeed! Nothing could be better than the lovely old farmhouse, restored for a previous Grannie Roussel. Theo had sold it at a time when he urgently needed cash to keep the mounting debts down to a reasonable level, and was now paying the price.

"Phew! I thought they'd never go," he said to Deirdre. "Why don't you go up to my study and we'll have peace and quiet for a while. I'll get Katya to make us some coffee."

"Better let her go," Deirdre said firmly. "She'll be wanted back at Springfields. And Noreen will want to go home, too. I'll make the coffee, and we can have the house to ourselves."

"For the serious discussion?" Theo said, drawing her close into his arms.

"That as well," she said, and burst out laughing in the uninhibited way he loved.

SETTLED IN A comfortable armchair in Theo's study, Deirdre opened the subject of Mrs. Wilson Jones. She intended only to see what Theo knew about the family in general. Gus had said it was necessary at the moment to keep to themselves all mention of the fraud.

"Ivy's got a new resident at Springfields," she said casually. "A Mrs. Alwen Jones. Ex-schoolteacher, apparently, and looks like being a rival for Ivy. Forthright woman, used to being obeyed. Loud voice. You can imagine."

Theo laughed. "Only too well!" he said. "Had one of those at my prep school. Foiled many a budding revolutionary. . . . Miss Chinnery, that was her name."

"Well, this one is Jones. Common name, but you might know the family in Thornwell?"

"What? The brewery Joneses? Certainly do! At one time they were one of the most important families in the town. Jolly good beer, too. The old boy, Grandfather Jones, was a pillar of the Methodist Church, you know. He made sure with hefty donations that they overlooked his connection with strong drink! He was mayor, of course, and a genuine philanthropist. Youth guilds, Boy Scouts, sports clubs, all that. Gave land for playing fields, built a new church hall. Made his mark in Thornwell, and is still held up as an example to miserly businessmen in town today. And now can we go to bed?" he added. "Duty done?"

"Not yet," Deirdre said. "What about the present generation. What are they like? Who was Mrs. Wilson Jones's husband? She claims to be a widow, but I always read the local obituaries and don't remember any Jones appearing. She also says she was only distantly connected to the brewery lot."

"Ah, now I have to think," Theo said, sighing and looking at his watch. He was hungry, and not just for supper. "There were two brothers, George and William. George inherited the brewery, and has run it ever since his father died. There's talk now of a takeover, so I suppose he's intending to retire."

"He's dead," Deirdre said. "Recently popped his clogs. In the local paper."

"Ah. Right. Yes. So, if this Mrs. Jones is a widow, but

not of George, who's only recently died—her husband could have been William. She'd have been very closely connected if he was the one. Can't remember much about him. I think he was a solicitor or accountant, or some such. Maybe financial director of the brewery, or something like that? You could find out easily enough. Now can we go to bed?"

Deirdre shook her head. "Did William marry a Wilson woman?"

"And did she drop poison in his beer? And was there a scandal with one of the bottle-washers in the brewery? I know your game, my lady," he added, rising to his feet and taking her hand. "Enquiring within? Well, I'll think some more, and let you know if I come up with any juicy morsels. And now, off to bed!"

Much later, as they say in romantic fiction, Deirdre awoke from a pleasant doze.

"Theo," she said.

"Yes?"

"Are you hungry?"

"Um, hungry, yes. Capable, not sure."

"No, fool. Shall we raid the larder? I could murder a ham sandwich."

Seven

GUS POURED HIMSELF a cup of coffee and opened the last letter of a pile of junk mail. He had not slept well. Images from the past had floated repeatedly into his half sleep. A rain-soaked city street in total darkness, with shadowy figures scuttling from doorway to doorway. Nights spent in a shepherd's hut halfway up a Greek mountain. Bare rooms furnished with dubious-looking recording devices and unshaded lightbulbs.

At half past three, sweating with fear, he had drunk half a glass of water and reached for a book. He needed something to redirect his thoughts but knew from bitter experience that this did not always work. If the book was a spy thriller, his favourite reading, his dreams would be a jumble of experiences, and he would wake up doubly exhausted, unable to sort out fiction from reality.

Coffee helped to improve the morning, he now decided, as he spooned brown sugar into his breakfast mug and downed the strong brew. He slit open the envelope. At least this letter was addressed in handwriting, but it was familiar and unwelcome. He read it quickly. It was brief and to the point. On a matter of personal obligation, would he remit the aforementioned sum by the end of the month without fail. Or else.

He had met his persecutor years ago, and he had seemed a good sort, reliable and trustworthy, but he had turned out to be none of these things. He had led Gus into a world of gambling and deceit, from which he had still not broken free. This was his last unsettled debt, but with the relentless accumulation of interest at a high rate, it had now mounted to a total which Gus had no hope of finding.

His telephone rang. "Shut up!" he shouted, his nerves jagged. Why had he thought living in a remote Suffolk village would be peaceful seclusion? It continued to ring, and he finally answered it.

"Hello? Oh, good morning, Ivy."

"What's up with you, Augustus?" Ivy said.

"Nothing."

"Don't be ridiculous. Of course there's something wrong. I am not stupid."

"Sorry, Ivy. Didn't sleep well. I'll tell you later."

"Unquiet mind," she said, more perceptively than she knew. "Nothing like a clear conscience for peaceful nights."

"Yes, well. Anyway, had you something special to ask me? Has Alwen Jones gone into a decline?"

"No, but you will, if you don't get over here in good time. You've not forgotten *again* your talk with old Mrs. Worth? Mrs. Spurling will have your guts for garters if you don't turn up."

Gus had forgotten, but now he assured Ivy he would be there on the dot of eleven o'clock. He had to pick up bread and milk from the village shop but would come on from there. He only hoped he had the energy to keep up a one-sided conversation.

"I'll come to see her with you, if you like. Mrs. Worth won't have any idea who I am, or you, for that matter, but any visitor is better than none. See you later, then. And don't be late." Gus groaned. He desperately wanted another coffee but dared not risk the heart flutters and racing pulse that would inevitably go with it.

THE SHOP WAS crowded with children who had the day off from school because there had been a power failure. They were excited and noisy with the heady knowledge that they had an unexpected day off. The new shopkeeper, James, smiled at Gus over the heads of milling children. James knew he had no hope of spotting the odd chocbar finding its illegal way into a jacket pocket, and allowed for this in his budgeting. He was learning fast.

"Form a queue, you lot," he said good-humouredly. "Now, girls first. Where's your manners, boys? Susan Rampling, were you first?"

Gus found his milk and a brown loaf, and waited his turn, filling in time by reading the front pages of the newspapers on the stand by the door. The nationals were full of economic doom and gloom, and he moved on to the Thornwell morning paper. This was usually good for an entertaining story.

Sure enough, the brewery story still made headlines. The takeover had been completed, and the new giant brewers were promising that nothing would change.

Inevitably there would be redundancies, but this would be achieved in the most sympathetic way possible. Early retirement, reallocation to other allied companies, that sort of thing, said a spokeswoman. Gus saw her name and peered more closely. Mrs. Bronwen Evans. Bronwen? Wasn't that Alwen Jones's daughter's name? The clever one, the one Alwen had positively ruled out as confidante?

"Your turn at last, Gus!" James called out. "Sorry about the wait. It's best to get rid of them as quickly as possible, before they filch the entire stock of sweeties. Hope you're not in a hurry?"

"As a matter of fact, I do have to be at Springfields by eleven." Gus glanced at the big wall clock behind James.

"Still five minutes to go. I'll just have these, please. Then I'll be in later for more supplies. Oh, and have you any idea what I can take a poor old thing with few faculties left?"

James did not hesitate. "Juicy Jellies," he said. "Always acceptable. Fastest selling item in the shop. And when you bear in mind my customers' average age, I rather dread the first packet put into my own shaking hand."

"Oh, come on, James, you're only a boy. What about a pint at the pub tonight? I've discovered Jones Brothers Best. That'll cheer you up. Darts match at eight, isn't it? Steady hand and eagle eye, my boy. See you then."

Gus took his purchases and started off at a trot for Springfields. He was not looking forward to the wrath of both Spurling and Ivy, so he kept it up until he reached the gate of the home, gasping for breath.

"You needn't have hurried," Ivy said critically, seeing his red face. "Mrs. Worth is in the bath. They're changing her bed, too, so we've got a reprieve for ten minutes or so."

Gus banished thoughts of soiled beds and scrubbed-down old ladies, and asked Ivy if she'd heard from Deirdre this morning.

Ivy nodded. "She phoned. Said Theo had been helpful. He told her about the brewery Joneses. George had a brother William who was married, but he couldn't remember his wife's name. Now the lovely Deirdre is lying low after the drinks do up at the Hall last evening. If I know my cousin, she won't have gone to bed until the early hours."

"Or, alternatively, will have had a very early night," said Gus mournfully. His threatening letter this morning had kyboshed any hope he had of competing for Deirdre's favours, and he sighed.

"Oh, for goodness' sake, cheer up!" Ivy said sternly. "How would you like to be incarcerated in here? At least you've got your health and vigour, and, what's more, your freedom from gaolers like this one approaching."

"Morning, Mr. Halfhide!" Mrs. Spurling was wearing her most cheerful face, and beamed at Gus. "Dear Mrs.

Worth will be receiving guests in five minutes. She's so looking forward to meeting you."

"Don't be ridiculous," Ivy said. "She don't know chalk from cheese, poor old thing. Still, I'm going with Gus, and the two of us might raise a smile at least."

"I don't think that will be necessary," Mrs. Spurling said. She frowned. Why couldn't Ivy Beasley mind her own business? It had been nothing but interference and criticism since she arrived. She just hoped the new resident, Mrs. Jones, could deal with her and modify her influence. After all, the ex-teacher had dealt with unruly classes of small children for years. Ivy should be child's play for her. She watched them go upstairs to Ivy's room, and thought sadly that Mrs. Jones didn't have a chance. "I'll give you a call when Mrs. Worth is ready," she shouted after them.

Ivy turned on the stair. "Don't bother," she said. "We'll go when we're ready. Shouldn't be more than ten minutes."

Gus smiled apologetically at Mrs. Spurling. "Ivy knows best," he muttered, and followed on behind the upright figure.

IT WAS HARD going. Mrs. Worth appeared to be fast asleep, and so Gus and Ivy talked idly of this and that and waited for her to surface.

"I tell you one thing, Augustus," Ivy said, sniffing. "This home always smells nice. Most of 'em smell of pee, and I couldn't be doing with that. But old Spurling is a stickler for keeping us clean. Not that I need her help—yet!"

Gus remembered his purchases, and withdrew the box of Juicy Jellies from his shopping bag. "Here, Mrs. Worth," he said to the comatose figure, "do you like these? Juicy Jellies?"

At the magic name, the old lady suddenly opened her eyes and stretched out her hand. "My favourites," she said quite clearly. "Joe always brought me them, every Friday."

Gus and Ivy exchanged glances. Perhaps they could keep the old thing awake now.

"Was Joe your husband, Mrs. Worth?" Gus said, leaning forward and helping to open the box.

"Fifty-three years we was wed," the clear voice said. "After I got bedridden, he brought me Juicy Jellies every Friday. Did I tell you that? Have one, go on."

Ivy extricated a green jelly from the box. "I'm Ivy Beasley," she said. "I live here, too."

"I know who you are," Mrs. Worth said. "The girls who help me—are they my daughters?—talk about you. The one called Katya is always on about you. Says you shouldn't be in here. Much too clever, she says. Are you? Are you clever?"

"No, of course not. And the girls shouldn't gossip."

"My Joe," said Mrs. Worth, "he worked at the brewery, you know. Brought me Juicy Jellies every Friday. Did I tell you that?"

"Jones Brothers brewery?" Ivy said. "What did he do there?"

"Don't ask me, dear. Always stank of hops when he come home. Mr. William was his favourite. Two bosses, there were. Mr. George and Mr. William. My Joe used to do gardening at weekends for Mr. William and his bossy wife. Did I tell you my Joe used to bring me Juicy Jellies every Friday?"

Gus was about to ask more questions, but Mrs. Worth's eyelids suddenly closed like blinds being lowered, and in seconds she was snoring deeply.

"That's that, then," Ivy said. "Not a waste of time, after all. Come on, Augustus, let's go and ring Deirdre. I'll tell her to come here this afternoon, and we'll see what she picked up at the Hall."

Gus stopped halfway along the corridor. "Ivy," he said. "What's up?"

"Did it occur to you to wonder how Mrs. Worth's husband, who worked at the brewery and did gardening at weekends, could afford to pay the fees here at Springfields?"

"Oh, yes, that occurred to me, no mistake," replied Ivy, who had in her armoury a lifetime of speculating on village events from behind lace curtains in Round Ringford. "The likes of Mrs. Worth and her Joe don't usually end their days in a private residential home charging ridiculously large fees." She paused, then walked to the top of the stairs. "There's something odd there," she said, turning back to look at Mrs. Worth's door. "Money like it costs to be in here don't come from nowhere. If old Joe worked at the brewery and gardened for Mr. George's brother William, old nuisance back there might well remember who his bossy wife was. Come on, best foot forward, Augustus. You're looking more cheerful already!"

Eight

ROY HAD BEEN somewhat snitched to be sent packing yesterday from the mission to rescue Alwen Jones. He suspected Ivy had noticed his appreciative twinkle as he talked to Alwen, and in her characteristic way had taken immediate action. Nobody must rock the Enquire Within boat! Still, a chap couldn't help reacting to a well-endowed bottom with a wiggle as it walked.

Now he sat talking to his old buddy, Felix Galloway. They had arrived at Springfields at the same time, and had comforted each other in their misery. Roy was at first determined to be miserable, and Felix always agreed with everything he said.

"Seen your daughter lately, Felix?" Roy said. He knew she was a regular visitor, and demonstrably very fond of her father.

"She's coming in this afternoon, bless her," Felix replied. "Always brings me something nice, but I tell her nothing's as nice as herself, and that would do, without presents."

Roy nodded. "I should've married years ago. Nothing like a family, when you're old. Mind you," he added, thinking of Alwen Jones and her bossy daughter, "they can be a mixed blessing, so I'm told."

"It's never too late, they say. Mind you, I can't see the patter of tiny feet coming along at our age!"

Both men roared with laughter at the ridiculous thought but stopped suddenly when they heard a voice coming up behind them.

"So, what's funny, Roy? Share the joke, won't you?" It was Ivy, and she touched his arm lightly.

"Ah, there you are, Ivy," he said, ignoring her question. "Are you ready for a wee drink before lunch?"

"Not time for that, Roy. Gus is here, and we've phoned Deirdre. Meeting in my room in a quarter of an hour. Be there, please."

She disappeared up the stairs, and Felix smiled. "Under starter's orders, my boy," he said. "Best have a pee before you go. Looks like it could be a long meeting."

"SO WHAT'S THIS all about?" said Deirdre crossly. She had a headache this morning, and knew it was her own fault. Still, it had been worth it! Theo back to his old loving self.

"First of all," Ivy said, "how was it last night?"

"Wonderful!" Deirdre said dreamily, and then saw Ivy's face. "Um, well, I told you on the phone about Theo and what he said. But before that the party was a good one for once. Some quite interesting people. As I said, Ivy, I did have a chance to talk to Theo about the Joneses, if that's what you're asking. He knew them, of course. Apparently there were two brothers—"

"George and William," interrupted Ivy. "We already know that. Did you sort out which was which?"

"George was the boss, and William possibly company secretary, or finance director, or some such. He was an accountant, Theo said. He also said if he thought of anything else of interest he would let me know."

Gus nodded. "Very useful, Deirdre," he said.

"We got some useful stuff, too," Ivy said. "Daffy old Mrs. Worth—you know, Roy, the one who yells in the middle of the night—she had a few lucid moments this morning when me and Augustus went to see her. I shall see her again, to see what else she remembers."

"She made sense for once?" Roy said in surprise.

"Briefly," Gus said. "It looks like the most interesting Jones brother who might've had something to do with our Alwen is the younger one, William, who had a bossy wife. We wondered if you, Roy, could remember anything about a Jones/Wilson wedding way back?"

"Do we think Alwen *is* connected, then?" asked Roy. "I thought she said she wasn't, or only distantly? And does this have anything to do with her trouble yesterday?"

Ivy smiled at him. "Yes, we do, and yes, she did say that, and yes, it might have. Remember what we're supposed to be looking out for? As well as digging around in Measby for more on the old man's death, we are to keep our ears open for other cases of extortion or blackmail? Well, that means money. Alwen has lost twenty thousand, supposedly, and Daisy Worth is in here, paying out a fortune in fees which she ain't likely to have in her Post Office savings account. Two and two make . . . ?"

"You're not suggesting Mrs. Worth is blackmailing Alwen, surely, Ivy?" said Gus, smiling broadly.

"Don't be ridiculous!" Ivy said crossly. "It'll be more complicated than that."

"Only teasing," said Gus. "Anything you'd like to add, Deirdre?" He felt it necessary occasionally to remind the team he was unofficial team leader. Or was he? He couldn't remember what the initial meeting of Enquire Within had decided. He had a nasty feeling Ivy had just taken over, although the private enquiry agency had been his idea.

Deirdre shook her head. "I remember the brewery, of course I do. But in Oakbridge the Jones family weren't much talked about." Deirdre had spent her formative years in the town across the other side of the county, moving to Barrington after her marriage to Bert.

"Well, I remember the lot of 'em," Roy said. "Sniffy lot. Do-gooders, every man jack of 'em. Very disapproving of people enjoying themselves, though what they thought their beer was for, I don't know. Methodists, they were. Po-faced lot always sat in the front pew with their noses in the air. What do you want to know?"

"Well, that's pretty good for a start," Gus said, suddenly cheered, as always, by Roy's resilience and good humour. "Tell us about the brothers, George and William."

"Ah, now wait a minute. There was something strange, I do remember," Roy continued. "George was always the one in the news, o'course, with his large donations and good works. Then he was made mayor, and his picture was in the paper every week, cutting ribbons and kissing babies. Young William was scarcely mentioned."

"Can you remember anything at all about William?" Ivy smiled encouragingly.

"Nothing much. He got married, I believe, but I don't remember the name of his bride. There was something, though, later on. Just can't recall it at the moment. Don't worry, Ivy," he added, "I'll remember it later."

"Don't forget to tell us then, or write it down before you forget it again," Deirdre said, and continued, "and meanwhile, Gus and I can go to the newspaper archive and find William's wedding notice. That'll give us his wife's maiden name."

"Good idea," Gus said, sitting up straight and smiling at Deirdre. "It's worth remembering a brewery statement I read in the local, put in by spokesperson Bronwen Evans. Bronwen? Remember? Alwen Jones's clever daughter? That might give us a lead. When shall we go?" His good mood increased at the thought of spending some time with Deirdre. Maybe he could ask her out for a meal at the pub this evening, instead of always waiting for an invitation to Tawny Wings. Then he remembered he had promised James at the shop a game of darts, and he gave up.

"It'll have to be tomorrow," Deirdre said. "Volunteers' meeting at the Oxfam shop in Thornwell this afternoon.

They want to open a separate bookshop, and I think it's a rubbish idea. If we're left with only secondhand clothes and a few bits of old china, it's not going to attract the most interesting customers, is it?"

"Never mind about Oxfam," said Ivy irritably. She wanted a bit of the action for herself and Roy, and thought rapidly of something useful they could investigate. "Why don't we two ask Alwen if she'd like to walk down to the shop with us, Roy?" she said. "A gentle stroll and a casual question or two might catch her unawares. She obviously don't want to talk about her late husband. If he *is* late," she added darkly.

Roy nodded. "Something dawning up here," he added, tapping his forehead. "Bells definitely beginning to ring." Maybe he had been wrong about Ivy and Alwen. A walk with two pleasant companions would be just the ticket.

LUNCH HAD BEEN late, the potatoes not quite cooked and the gravy too salty. There had been complaints, and it had taken much tactful assurance of improvement before the residents settled down to their afternoon television. Mrs. Spurling and Miss Pinkney sat in the small office with its observation window newly cleaned by Katya, and stared in defeated silence as three of their residents set off in the autumn sunlight down the path and out of the gate.

"They might just as well be in a hotel," Mrs. Spurling said. "There are some hotels, you know, Miss Pinkney, that specialise in old people who are able but want companionship. Those three are nothing but trouble here, and Mr. Goodman has been like a dog with two tails since he got that buggy. Can go for miles now, instead of a gentle walk around the garden. I had high hopes of Mrs. Wilson Jones being quite grateful for what we offer, but now she's fallen in with bad company, and I suppose the next thing will be that daughter of hers coming here to accuse me of neglect."

"Neglect?" said Miss Pinkney. "Not never ever, my dear. Nobody could accuse you of that! No, my advice is to let them get on with it. We are not a prison, after all, though I have heard Mr. Goodman refer to us as, er . . ." She remembered in time that Mrs. Spurling wouldn't see the joke, if it was one, and changed the subject.

"That nice daughter of Felix Galloway is due to visit this afternoon, isn't she? Such a pleasant person. But then Felix is a dear old man, isn't he. Like father, like daughter!"

"Oh, do shut up, Pinkers," Mrs. Spurling said. "Just go and see to something, and leave me alone to brood."

Miss Pinkney smiled. She knew her boss so well, and felt sorry for her sometimes. It couldn't be easy to remain working in a place where your husband had run off with the cook.

"LOVELY AFTERNOON. WHAT a good idea of yours, Roy," Alwen Jones said. "Are you sure you're all right in that vehicle? I must say your steering is pretty nifty!"

The electric shopper, a motorised vehicle for disabled people, had been the best thing, next to Ivy, that had happened to Roy. Although able enough to get around Springfields easily, he could not manage on rough pavements, nor go too far. He had quickly learned the shopper's little ways, and was extremely deft at negotiating potholes and kerbs all round the village. Dropped kerbs providing a smooth crossing for wheelchairs and pushchairs had not yet reached Barrington, though Deirdre had said she would talk to the right people and get them fixed in no time.

"It's a revolution, Alwen," Roy said. "Saves Ivy from pushing an old fogey along in a wheelchair."

Ivy smiled fondly at him. She knew how much it meant to him to be independent and in charge of a wheeled vehicle again. That was the rotten thing about old age. It changed the way you felt about yourself. Well, she did not intend it should happen to her, or Roy. If you ask me, she said to herself, you have to keep up the fight to the end.

"And you've got a lovely big bag for your shopping," Alwen said. "What shall we buy this afternoon, Ivy?"

Ivy was tempted to say maybe Alwen should watch her pennies after the recent debacle, but she was sure there were plenty more tens of thousands in the Jones kitty.

"We usually keep supplies of our favourite chocs or biscuits in our rooms," she said. "Nothing like a chocolate digestive if you feel a bit peckish in the middle of the night. Of course," she added, "I expect when your husband was alive, he'd go down and make a nice hot cup of tea to help you back to sleep?"

Alwen's face closed up. "I've never had trouble sleeping, Ivy," she said.

"Lucky you," said Roy. "My dreams wake me up sometimes. 'Dreaming, oh my darling love, of thee,'" he sang in a soppy voice, and Ivy looked at him sharply. Surely he was not referring to her? Well, it had better not be anyone else.

"Watch out, Roy!" said Alwen. "Oh, sorry, I thought that cat was going to run right in front of you. Now, here we are. Can I help you alight?"

There's no doubt about it, thought Ivy. She clammed up the minute her husband was mentioned. Definitely something funny going on. "Roy can manage," she said sternly.

Nine

BRONWEN EVANS, NEE Wilson Jones, had received bad news in the post. She and her husband Trevor were having their customary gins and tonics in the smart drawing room of their new house on the outskirts of Thornwell. The builder had described the houses as executive dwellings in the best part of town, but in spite of exterior additions such as coach lamps and a Doric pillar here and there, they were pattern-book estate houses with little space between them. Bronwen had expected more, at her time of life, having lived at home with her mother in a large Victorian villa with kitchen garden and greenhouse until she met Trevor, who had swept her off her feet with practised ease.

Trevor was a salesman, as good at selling houses as he was at selling himself. He was an up-and-coming competitor in the residential property market, and had negotiated a good deal from the developers on the purchase of his own house, although now there was a financial slump—temporary, he hoped—and he was not in the best of tempers.

"What's the matter with you, Bron?" he said. "It's me

who should be looking grim. Haven't sold a house for two weeks now, but staff have to be paid and expenses met."

"Well, at least you've got a job," she said dully. She handed him a letter she had stuffed in her handbag this morning, waiting for the right moment to show it to him.

"Bloody hell!" he said. "This is a bit sudden, isn't it? They've only just taken over!"

The letter said in shockingly brief terms that in view of the economic climate, the new owners of the brewery were having to cut down on staff numbers, and regrettably Bronwen's post as public relations officer would no longer exist. They would be using a central department within the group. They thanked her for past service and wished her well for the future.

Bronwen watched him read through it again and waited for his reaction. He looked at her for a full minute, and then said, "You know what this means, don't you."

She nodded. "We're going to have to extend our loan. I suppose we'd better make an appointment with the bank."

"Some hopes!" he said bitterly. "We're up to our limit, and beyond what most people would get, thanks to my weekly games of golf with our friendly neighbourhood bank manager."

A flash of fear crossed Bronwen's face. "So what will we do? Don't tell me we'll have to sell up our home, after all the work and loving care I've put into making it half decent?"

"And the rest. It'll have to be your mother," he said baldly. "She's the only alternative. Rich as Croesus, if all indications are correct."

"Not from the Joneses! It's all dribbled away over the years."

"Not just because of your father?" He knew he was on thin ice here, as Bronwen would not allow any mention of her father, and he had always respected this. But now things were dire, and he needed to know as much as he could about his mother-in-law's likely pot of gold.

"Give me another gin," she said. "And if Mother has what you hope for, it's Wilson money from her own family.

And," she added with emphasis, "she's not telling. Nor, I'm afraid, would she in any circumstances lend us more than twenty pounds. If that. Scrooge is her middle name, and she's renowned for being a lifelong miser."

Trevor stared at her. "Then you're going to have to play Tiny Tim Cratchit, my dear," he said. "I'm off to the club."

"It'll be too dark to play a round," she objected.

"I don't intend to play golf. More important things to discuss."

She heard him slam the door and rev up his car, skidding off down the drive and disappearing at speed.

"Fool," she said, and poured herself another gin.

NEARLY SEVEN O'CLOCK, Gus said to himself. Just time to ring Deirdre and make a date and time for their visit to the newspaper archive. Then off to the pub for a convivial pint of Jones Brothers Best and a game of darts with James the Shop.

His eye was caught by the envelope he had stuck behind the dusty clock with a broken spring that stood on the mantelshelf. That letter. He supposed he should think seriously about it. Perhaps his persecutor would settle for monthly repayments? Thank God he'd agreed to a retainer from his previous employer. "You might be the only person who can help us," they had said. "Naturally we would not wish to disturb your, um, retirement, but we'd like to think we could call on you in an emergency. A small retainer, Gus? Would that be acceptable?"

He could just about spare a small regular sum, which would allow him to pay off his debt in one hundred and fifty years. He sighed. "Worth a try, anyway," he said to his ever-faithful Whippy, who lay curled up on the best of a bunch of shabby chairs. "Maybe you'll have to make a sacrifice, too, little dog," he said, and an ear twitched to show she was listening. "No more luxury dog feasts made with best cuts of beef and lamb. Back to evil-smelling tripe blocks in packets impossible to open."

A knock at his front door interrupted his conversation, and he peeped from behind the curtain to see who it was. Miriam Blake, of course. Ah well, he had the perfect excuse for getting rid of her.

"Hello, Miriam! Nice to see you! Can't ask you in, as I'm due at the pub. Meeting James for a game of darts."

Her face fell. She had come bearing a neatly arranged basket of salad items from her garden. She thrust them at him, and said maybe he'd like to come to supper tomorrow? She'd got lovely lamb chops from the butcher and wanted to try a recipe with white wine and herbs.

"Yum," said Gus. "Lovely! Can I confirm tomorrow? Good-o. Must fly now." He eased the door shut as politely as he could, and watched her droop past his window. Oh dear, if only he fancied her, how easy it would be. She might even lend him a few bob. . . .

"MONEY IS THE root of all evil," said Ivy, pushing a small pile of matches over to Roy. They were having a leisurely game of cribbage in Ivy's room, an arrangement hard fought by Roy and only recently won.

"You're right, Ivy," he said. "Thank goodness I've never had any."

She squinted at him, and said that she really must make an appointment with the optician. "Can't even see the numbers on the cards now," she said crossly. Ivy did not like to lose, and Roy went along with the fiction that it was trouble with her eyes that accounted for him winning.

"Another game?" he said. "Or would you like to listen to that play about two blokes living together and wanting a baby? It's all about how they manage it, apparently. Using a surrogate mother, of course," he added hastily.

"If you ask me," Ivy said stoutly, "a baby needs a mother and father of the usual kind. What sort of a childhood is it going to have?"

"Better than some regular ones, they say," Roy said mildly.

"Well, I'm glad I don't have to think about it," Ivy said.

"Let's have another game of crib." She reached for her spare pair of specs. "These might do the trick," she said, and Roy shuffled the cards.

"I wonder what Gus is doing," he said. "I thought he was a bit down today?"

"Playing darts at the pub with James the Shop," Ivy said.

"How do you know that?"

"I know everything," Ivy replied, and burst into a very rare shout of laughter.

They concentrated on the game, and Ivy duly amassed a respectable number of matches. The room was quiet, broken only by a couple of doves cooing appropriately outside the window. Suddenly Roy thumped the table, giving Ivy such a shock that she dropped her hand of cards.

"What on earth was that about?" she said, scrabbling on the floor with difficulty.

"I've remembered," Roy said triumphantly. "That thing I couldn't bring to mind about the Joneses. About William, to be precise. I still can't remember his wife's name, but I do remember that he went missing."

"*Missing?* What d'you mean?"

"It was in the papers. Without any warning, he just didn't come home one evening. It was all hushed up, of course. George had influence in so many places, including with the local newspaper owner. The story just disappeared, like William. I heard no more, and not being in the charmed circle of the mayor and his entourage, I completely forgot about it. But there it is, Ivy. He could've returned, but by the time I read about it he'd apparently been gone for a couple of months. The original story was leaked out by William's gardener, if I remember rightly."

"Gardener?" Ivy said sharply. "Did you say gardener?"

Roy confirmed he had said gardener, and wondered if her hearing was going. But no, Ivy didn't waste words. He would no doubt be enlightened in due course.

Ten

"I'VE THOUGHT OF a possible snag," Deirdre said as she and Gus cruised along in her big cream-coloured car. Gus was always a nervous passenger with Deirdre, irrationally anxious in case he suddenly vomited on the cream leather seats, or had Whippy's best on his shoes.

Now he looked at her in alarm. "What snag?" he said, rather more sharply than he intended.

"Oh, it's only a possible," she said, turning to smile at him. "Just my enquiring mind churning away."

"Go on, then. What is it?"

"Well, if we're looking for a wedding notice and hopefully photograph, we might be heading for the wrong newspaper. Most girls are married in their hometown, not their husband's. We don't know where Alwen lived before she was wed, do we?"

Gus was silent, trying hard to remember if Alwen Wilson Jones had said anything about her early life and times. He thought not. She was unusually reticent about anything to do with her past. All they knew was that she had been a head teacher in Thornwell Primary School until her retirement. She had never talked about her husband, and had in fact deliberately avoided mention of him.

"Do you remember her saying anything directly about him? And has she ever actually denied having anything to do with the brewery Joneses?" Deirdre said.

"Says she was distantly connected, I think. We must ask Ivy and Roy. They see more of her than we do. Maybe their walk to the shop yesterday will have turned up something. Anyway, we're nearly there now, so we might as well have a look in the archives."

THE RECEPTIONIST IN the newspaper office was helpful and interested in their request. "Looking for William Jones's wedding, are we?"

Gus nodded. "It would be about forty years ago, we guess," he said. "Sorry we can't be more specific."

"Don't worry. The Joneses are a well-known local family, always in the news, so we're sure to find it. Who did he marry?"

"Well, possibly it was a girl called Alwen Wilson. We don't know if she was a Thornwell girl. We just hoped that because it was the brewery family, there might be a mention or a photograph. Could have been quite a big wedding."

The receptionist, a pleasant-faced woman in her forties, said that this was not necessarily the case. "Now, if you'd asked for George Jones's wedding, that would be easy! But his brother William was always in the background. Seemed to like it that way. Some said he was actually the clever one, too, clever by half, said some. But George had a better business head. Anyway, I mustn't stand here gossiping. There's a queue forming! If you'd like to sit down over there and help yourselves to coffee, I'll see what we can turn up."

Bronwen Evans had just joined the queue. She had decided to comb the jobs vacant pages in back numbers of the newspaper, and as she stood waiting, she was sure she heard her father's name mentioned at the desk. She watched Gus and Deirdre cross to the coffee machine and was certain she had seen one or both somewhere before. Why were they enquiring about her father? She could tell them all they needed to know, but she certainly did not intend to. Maybe the new brewery owners had commissioned a history of the brewery? She could help with that, but saw no reason why she should assist in glorifying a company that had just sacked her! The history idea had occurred to her once or twice. Good public relations, she had said to Uncle George, but he had scoffed at the idea. Everybody knows the story of Jones Brothers Best, he had insisted, and turned down her suggestion.

"Good morning, Mrs. Evans," the receptionist said. "Can I help you?"

"I doubt it," Bronwen said, "unless you can tell me who is enquiring about my father?"

The receptionist offered to recall Gus and Deirdre, but Bronwen said very firmly that it would not be necessary. Then she said that after all she would not take up the receptionist's time and walked off. As she left the building, she glanced back, but could see nothing now but a group of people standing in reception. Never mind, she said to herself, I can ask mother. She would want to know, anyway.

Unaware that their conversation had been overheard, Gus and Deirdre settled down with their coffee. "How's the romance going?" he said, making it sound like a joke, though he was quite serious.

"You mean Theo? Oh, he's fine, thanks. Great fun to be with. Still a roving bachelor at heart."

"Not intending to settle down, then?"

"Who knows?" Deirdre shrugged. She hadn't thought that far, and certainly had not imagined herself as mistress of Barrington Hall. She was much too comfortable in Tawny Wings to consider life in a draughty old mansion with few mod cons and a five-mile trek from the kitchen to the dining room.

"I hear he's approached little Katya to take on the housekeeper job," Gus said casually.

"What? Ridiculous idea. The girl would have no idea how to run an English stately home!" Deirdre's voice grew louder as she considered the news.

"Hardly stately," said Gus quietly. "Not compared with some. Anyway, I think Katya is a very intelligent little thing. And her English has improved no end. She'd probably be a great asset to the Hon. Theo with his posh friends."

"Huh!" said Deirdre, and relapsed into a sulky silence.

Neither said anything more until the receptionist called them back. "Miss Upson will be down shortly," she said. "I think she's found something for you."

ALWEN WILSON JONES had elected to stay in bed. "I'm sure I have a cold coming," she said. "It may even be flu. I was shivering all night," she complained to Katya.

"Oh, you poor thing! I will find a nice soft blanket to put over your bed."

"You are so kind. Do you like working here? Why don't you sit and talk to me for a while? I am still feeling a little lonely after leaving my own home and neighbours, and the grandchildren popping in . . ."

Katya was used to seeing old people in tears. This place must seem like their last stop before the grave, she thought. No wonder the poor old thing is sad. "Is your daughter coming in to see you this week?" she said, hoping to cheer her up.

"Bethan phoned yesterday," Alwen said. "She's got to see to all the beginning of term things this week. But she promised to come in next week, and bring the children after school."

"Oh good! That's something to look forward to, then," Katya said soothingly. She perched on the edge of a chair. "Mrs. Spurling doesn't like us to waste time gossiping," she said, "but she's gone to the wholesale food place, so I can stay for a chat. Why don't you tell me about your early days. You were a teacher, I believe?"

Alwen nodded, and dabbed at her face with a tissue. "Yes, for many years," she said.

"And your husband, too?"

"No, he was an accountant. Tell me about your family in Poland," she added, making it sound like an order. Katya duly obliged. She loved to talk about her family, and by the time ten minutes had passed, Alwen was much cheered. In fact, she said she felt so much better she thought she would get up.

"Ivy and Roy will miss me at lunchtime otherwise," she said. "They're an odd pair, but quite friendly. At least, Roy is friendly. Not so sure about Ivy Beasley."

"Oh, don't be deceived by Miss Beasley's stern face," Katya replied with a smile. "Her heart is made of gold, I am sure."

Alwen did not comment, being far from sure, but asked Katya to fetch her clean laundry. "I shall have a bath, and be quite restored," she said.

Katya left her then, and went back to the kitchen, where she told her friend that she thought Mrs. Wilson Jones would settle in well, once she and Miss Beasley had become firm friends.

DEIRDRE AND GUS decided to have lunch in town so that they could discuss what they had discovered at the newspaper offices.

"I never guessed anything like this," Deirdre said. "I'd thought maybe William Jones had an affair with his secretary and Alwen divorced him, something like that."

"No, this is much more interesting," Gus said. "Especially when you remember that the poor old thing has possibly been defrauded of twenty thousand pounds. Who was this mysterious financial adviser who persuaded her to part with it? And what is the real reason she won't go to the police? I mean, Deirdre, if you think about it, a possible spat with your daughter wouldn't stop you bringing in the cops, would it? I know you're loaded, bless you, but *twenty thousand pounds*!"

Deirdre nodded, not denying that she was loaded. In

fact, it had occurred to her once or twice that Theo might be after an injection of cash into his impoverished estate, but as she had no intention of letting him get his hands on her money, she had pushed the idea aside. Now she said that however much more she had in the kitty, twenty thousand was a lot by anybody's standards. "Have you got that photocopy the woman gave you? We'll get Ivy and Roy together this afternoon and tell them what we've discovered."

"And meantime, I'll give my old colleague a ring and see if I can find out more about that strange case in the village near Oakbridge. You remember, the one where the man was found dead at the foot of his stairs. Extortion was mentioned, and it might be connected with a racket working the territory in East Anglia. That kind of thing can lead to violence, as my former colleague was suggesting."

Deirdre made a face. "Very nasty!" she said. "Wouldn't want that happening to our Alwen, would we?"

"La Spurling and Miss Pinkney would be a match for any midnight intruder," Gus said, laughing.

Deirdre did not laugh. "They're not there at night, Gus. And I reckon it would be child's play to get into Springfields under the cover of darkness."

"But it's all alarmed from top to toe!" Gus protested.

"Alarms were made to be foiled," Deirdre said. "I lost half my jewellery when a couple of evil professionals got into Tawny Wings when I was away. Nowhere is a hundred percent safe, if you ask me. . . ."

"As Ivy says. So we will ask her. Come on, give her a bell and tell her we're on our way."

Eleven

ONCE MORE THE interview room had been commandeered by Enquire Within, and Ivy had imperiously ordered tea for four to be brought in immediately.

"You'd think she owned the place!" Mrs. Spurling had complained to Miss Pinkney, who, although always obedient, privately loved the idea of this extraordinary variation on the dull routine of Springfields. It made a welcome change from well-meaning volunteers organising sing-songs of old tunes, and wary-eyed children performing carols at Christmas. Even the whist and bingo faltered at times. But who in their right minds would want to play whist and bingo every day? And more residents were in their right minds than Mrs. Spurling cared to acknowledge.

"So what is this important new revelation?" Ivy said when they were settled.

"You tell," said Deirdre to Gus. "With all your experience in the field of undercover enquiries, you'll do it better than me."

Gus looked at her closely. Was there sarcasm in her

one? No, surely not. Just a little green-eyed envy, he told himself, and began.

"They were very helpful at the newspaper archive," he said, "although there was not that much about William Jones. Not at first, anyway. Much more about George and his achievements. George took care of that, apparently, being a brilliant self-publicist. No, over the years there was a mention of William's coming-of-age party; his success at university, listed alongside others; and then the notice of his engagement." He paused for dramatic effect.

"Who to?" Roy said, thinking it was time to get to the point.

"One Alwen Rosemary Wilson, of the parish of Oakbridge in the county of Suffolk."

Gus leaned back in his chair, folded his arms and looked triumphantly at Ivy.

"Yes, well, we guessed that much," she said, refusing to be impressed. "But what about the rest? The marriage, for a start. Were they actually married? Lots of engagements get broken off. And if they were, what after that?"

"Hold your horses, Ivy," Deirdre interrupted. "There's more, but at least we know for a start that Alwen was Mrs. William Jones, of the highly regarded Jones family. Go on, Gus."

After that, Ivy and Roy sat quietly whilst Gus told them what else had been found. The marriage was a quiet one, and Bronwen had been born "prematurely" six and a half months later. They discovered this from marriage and birth notices.

"Then we found the real treasure," Gus continued. "It was quite a big splash. William Richard Jones, brother of Mayor George, had disappeared. Although no confirmed reason emerged, it was strongly believed that William, then company secretary of the brewery, and responsible for all financial matters, had got into debt and absconded with a sizable sum."

"But surely George would have suppressed such a story?"

"Oh, he tried," said Deirdre. "Categoric denials, threats to sue the paper, assurances that he was in touch with William, who was merely taking a sabbatical, all of that. And then suddenly it all went quiet, and in time the whole thing was forgotten."

"And William came back?" said Roy, hoping for a happy ending.

Gus shook his head. "Oh no," he said. "He never came back, and the last mention of him in the local paper was a report of his death in Australia. He'd been bungee jumping, according to report, and the springy rope had severed. Killed instantly, said the official report issued by the public relations office of the brewery."

"So that was that? And Alwen was left a widow, but no doubt supported by the ever-generous George?" Ivy said, her eyes wide and incredulous. "Well," she continued, "if you believe that load of cobblers, you'll believe anything. Bungee jumping indeed! What rubbish!"

There was a stunned silence, and then Roy cleared his throat and said perhaps they could all do with another cup of tea. "I'll ring the bell," he said.

ALWEN JONES WAS intrigued. She was now, as usual, sitting at the supper table with Roy and Ivy, and they both seemed oddly abstracted. She regaled them with stories of infants and their useless parents, and in the end tried on them her best school story. It was when the children had written daily news books, she said, and described one entry that had made all the staff chuckle. "One little boy," she said with a grin, "had written, 'Dad killed the dog last night and buried it in the garden.'" This anecdote, a favourite one amongst teachers, had always gone down well, but Roy and Ivy had scarcely smiled.

"Poor dog," Roy had said, and Ivy had merely nodded.

"Oh well," Alwen shrugged. "I think I'll watch some television. Are you coming, you two?"

"Um, what? What did you say?" Roy seemed to have

difficulty concentrating. Was it something to do with her? Then a cold shiver struck her. Surely they couldn't have been enquiring within too deeply?

"Oh, by the way," she said, on a sudden impulse. "Um, there's no need for you to worry anymore on my behalf about the money. All a mistake, and it's back safely once more in my bank. But thanks for listening, anyway," she added with a grateful smile.

Ivy stared at her. "Well, that's all right then," she said. "Let us know if you need any help in the future. Oh, and by the way," she added, with not very convincing non-chalance. "Did your daughters ever go bungee jumping? I've just been reading that it's all the rage for students on their gap year, whatever that is. If you ask me," she added, "they'd be far better off finding a proper job and earning their living."

Alwen's face drained of all colour. "I think I'll catch that wildlife programme on the box," she said, and got up quickly from the table. Ivy and Roy watched her limp rather more unsteadily than usual out of the dining room.

"That hit home," said Roy. "More coffee, Ivy?"

Twelve

"SO WE NO longer have a paying client?" Gus said. How had Ivy managed to scare off Alwen Jones so early in their investigation? Well, he told himself, that'll teach you to work with old ladies who should be doing nothing more arduous than knitting for charity.

He had been surprised by Deirdre appearing at his door soon after he had showered and dressed, and now they sat with cups of instant coffee in Gus's cheerless sitting room discussing the latest development. Ivy had telephoned Deirdre first thing and told her about Alwen's sudden freeze up. "It wasn't anything me or Roy said," Ivy had assured her. "Maybe we were a bit quiet, still thinking about what you and Gus found out, but we didn't say anything about that to Alwen."

Now Deirdre looked at Gus and asked whether he thought they should give up, or continue without any hope of financial gain.

"Sod it all," Gus said. "That's what happened last time! I don't mind telling you, Deirdre, I need the money." This was strictly true, but when he had paid off the gambling debt in installments, and so long as he kept away from racetracks and bookmakers, he hoped to be able to manage his present lifestyle. This last was the real sticking point. What lifestyle? he asked himself. Living in a scruffy cottage, out of touch with all his old rakish friends, who were fun, always fun. And then there was his demanding ex-wife . . . and fending off Miriam next door.

"I do understand about that, Gus," Deirdre said sympathetically. "If there's one thing I do understand, it's money. Bert taught me that, and it was a good lesson. So I'm not offering you loans or anything, but if you'd like to take expenses out of an Enquire Within account I can set up, then we'll treat it as a kitty for all of us."

"And who's going to fund it?"

"Me, at the moment, until we get going properly." This was not philanthropy on Deirdre's part. She had felt more alive since working with the other three than she had since Bert died. And, she had to admit, she was quite fond of old Gus. He was really quite attractive in his own way.

"So are you saying we should carry on?" Gus looked at her, and began to suspect that the companionship of this pleasant, affluent blonde was the most compelling reason at the moment for staying with what he hesitated to call a lifestyle—more a way of life.

"Yep," she said cheerfully. "There's still your friend who wanted us to help on the Measby death. If we come up with the goods on that one, he'll pay us, you said. It's possible that Alwen Jones's problem was nothing to do with that, but on the other hand it seems a strange coincidence. Two cases of extortion in a small area? Let's get together this afternoon with the other two and plan what we do next. And do you mind if I tip this disgusting stuff down the sink? We can go to Tawny Wings and get a decent cup of coffee for a start."

"GOOD MORNING, MRS. Jones!" Katya had almost collided with Alwen as she came out of her room, and she put a gentle hand on her arm. "I do hope you are feeling fit and well this morning?"

"Oh, yes, I'm fine," Alwen said. "I'm just off to find Mrs. Spurling. I wish to have a word with her about dining arrangements."

Katya frowned. "Nothing wrong with the cooking, I hope?" Her friend Anya was now in charge of the kitchen, and in general produced what residents agreed were delicious and interesting meals.

"No, no. I feel I should perhaps have a table of my own, or join up with other residents. Ivy and Roy seem very good friends, and I'd hate to be playing gooseberry! And anyway, I should get to know other people a bit more. I was rather thrust into the company of Ivy and Roy straightaway."

"I am sure they love to have you with them!" said Katya. "After all, they have all the time in the world to be together privately if they want it. Don't you think they might be offended?"

"That's neither here nor there," Alwen said more sharply. She had no qualms about offending those two. Unless she was very much mistaken, they had taken altogether too much upon themselves, nosing into her affairs. She wished she had never been persuaded to mention the missing money, and she was having second thoughts about how far their so-called investigations might go. Bronwen had called her to report hearing her father's name mentioned at the newspaper reception desk. Her description of the couple was vague, but the woman could have been Ivy's cousin.

"Ah, there you are, Mrs. Jones!" It was Mrs. Spurling, half running along the corridor. "Isn't your telephone working? There is a call for you in my office. Your own line is not answering, apparently. Let Katya help you down the stairs, and then you can use mine. I'll go back and make sure the caller waits for you."

By the time Katya and Alwen had reached the office, Mrs. Spurling had assured the caller several times that Mrs. Jones was on her way. The voice, a man's voice, had assured her he would wait. "Tell her it's Max," he said. He had some good news for Alwen, and was looking forward to talking to her.

At last Alwen, walking much more slowly than usual, arrived in the office, and Mrs. Spurling settled her in her own chair. "Come along, Miss Pinkney," she said, "let's leave Mrs. Jones to have her call in private. We shall be next door in the store cupboard if you need any help, dear," she added.

After they had gone, and the door was firmly shut, Alwen picked up the phone gingerly, as if it would explode when she touched it. She put it to her ear and listened, saying nothing, but clearing her throat to indicate she was there. A few seconds passed, and she still said nothing. Then, quite suddenly, she banged the receiver down, cutting off the call. She stood up, and realised she was shaking, so sat down again.

"Mrs. Spurling!" she called in a croaky voice. "Help! Please come back!"

In seconds, both the manager and her assistant rushed back into the office. They took one look at Alwen's face and went to comfort her.

"He said it was good news for you, my dear," Mrs. Spurling said. "I am so sorry. Did I get it wrong? Was it something bad that has upset you?"

Alwen made a big effort and pulled herself together, brushing off their helping hands. "It was nothing," she said. "Just a wrong number."

Mrs. Spurling said nothing more, but she was sure the man had used Alwen's name. It could hardly have been a wrong number, could it? Anyway, it was none of her business, so long as the poor woman had recovered herself and no harm had been done.

"I wanted to see you, anyway," Alwen continued, "on a matter concerning seating arrangements in the dining room."

"OH, LOR," SAID Roy. "She's got a table to herself, Ivy. I think we've frightened her off! We shall be unpopular with the others. Not so easy to ask her questions now."

Ivy shrugged. "Too bad," she said. "And anyway, we'll not be doing anything more for her, will we? Assignment cancelled. And if Gus doesn't like it, he can lump it."

Roy looked doubtful, and lowered his voice as he replied. "But there's this other case, Gus's rumours of blackmail, et cetera. Might be a connection there? After all, whatever you call it, conning an old lady out of twenty thousand pounds is extortion. Could be the same dodgy operator, like Gus's friend said. After all, Measby's not that far from Barrington."

"I don't think our Alwen's been straight with us about that. I'm not saying there's no connection with the Measby business, mind. We shall just have to wait and see what comes up. No, if you ask me, either she panicked or she's playing some game or other. O'course, it could just have been a delay with confirmation. Something like that. It's always happening these days. I blame computers," she added. "The work of the devil, if you ask me."

Roy smiled at her indulgently. "Like mobile phones?" he said teasingly. He knew that Ivy was very attached to hers, which had been a Christmas present from Gus and Deirdre. Ever since Katya had given Ivy lessons on her own mobile, and this had helped in the last case they'd been on, Ivy had never been without her gift. She had mastered text messaging, and dropped jargon words into the conversation with ease. Roy felt nothing but affection for this unlikely side to Ivy's nature. It was a tiny chink in her armour, and he knew there were others for him to work on if his slowly growing plan came to fruition.

Ivy's eyes met Alwen's across the room, and Alwen was the first to smile. She raised her hand and gave a small wave, just to say there were no hard feelings. Ivy managed to smile back, and on their way out of the dining room she and Roy stopped and asked Alwen if she'd be playing pontoon with them this evening. "For matches, of course," Ivy added.

"Gus is coming along," Roy said. "Deirdre's got a meeting, and you'd be most welcome. It's quite a fun game."

"I'm well aware of the rules of pontoon," Alwen said, and frowned. "And I swore I would never play it again. But if you can't beat 'em, join 'em," she instructed herself, and continued. "Very well, as long as it's matches."

After they had left her sitting in solitary state eating her lunch, she had felt miserable on her own and couldn't eat much. Irritated as she was with Ivy and Roy, she missed them. Especially Roy. He was such a jolly little man, and she failed to see what on earth attracted him to Ivy Beasley. And no harm could come from a game of cards played for matches, surely?

Thirteen

THEO ROUSSEL LOOKED across his parkland and saw heavy rain driven by a strong wind until it was almost horizontal. His horned sheep were huddled in one corner by a thick hedge, sheltering from the storm, and his thoughts were gloomy as he thought of his continual struggle to keep at bay the ravages of weather on the Hall.

"I really should spend some money on the old place," he said aloud to his faithful Labrador curled up under his desk. "If only I had some money to spend," he added wryly. The Hall was cold and draughty, and most of the rooms smelled of damp. Rising damp, damp rot, every possible kind of damp had attacked the neglected fabric of the building. He could poke his finger through the window frames in places where the wood had become a crumbling sponge.

"But how can we top up the kitty enough to finance it all? No good going to the bank. I am their most unreliable client already. So no loans. Grants from some well-disposed heritage organisation? What do you think, Wullie?"

The dog opened one eye and looked at him. Theo sensed that he was bored with his useless life, and would much rather be out hunting rabbits. A short stroll around the park was about as much as he had to look forward to, and he was out of condition and much too fat.

All this went through Theo's head as he gazed out of the window. He remembered his good intentions after that dreary old mother of Miriam had been murdered in her cottage. He was going to hire another worker to help young David on the farm, and generally take things in hand. But he had drifted without doing anything much to improve the estate.

What did other friends in his situation do? Conduct tours round the house and grounds, with entertaining stories of the adventures of their ancestors? Maybe a coffee shop in the stables? Perhaps David would have some ideas. A children's farm, with small animals to see and touch?

As if reading his thoughts, Wullie lumbered to his feet and wagged his tail enthusiastically. There were always rabbits on children's farms. Theo straightened his back, rubbed his hands together, made his way down the wide staircase, found a waterproof and green wellies and, with Wullie at his side, set off to find David, his farm manager.

As he trudged through the rain, he thought of Deirdre Bloxham. Grand girl, that one. And her head screwed on very firmly. She and that *garagiste* husband of hers had amassed a fortune, so people said. Maybe she could give him some tips next time they met. He could even consider asking her to . . . But no, he had decided to remain a confirmed bachelor. Women were marvellous, but let them get too close, and anything could happen! Remember Beatrice Beatty, he cautioned himself, and opened the gate of the cottage where David and his young family lived.

DAVID BUDD AND his wife Rose lived in the same row of cottages as Miriam Blake and Gus, and, because theirs was at the end, they had a much bigger garden, where they grew fresh vegetables and fruit for the family and had installed a swing and sandpit for their two little ones.

When Theo knocked at the door, he could hear the children's television channel accompanied by Rose's cheerful voice yelling at her offspring to switch it off. Then she was opening the door, wiping her wet hands on her apron and smiling apologetically.

"Hello, Mr. Theo," she said. "I'm afraid it's a bit of a mess in here. Do you want to come in and risk a broken ankle?"

He laughed. She was such a lovely girl. He hoped David knew how lucky he was. "No, it was David I wanted to speak to," he said. "I just thought he might have popped home out of the rain." He knew perfectly well it was most unlikely, but Rose always cheered him up.

"Um, no, he's out on the tractor, down the fields by the lake. He's fed up with the constant rain making the job heavy, but he said it's got to be done and went out quite early with sandwiches in his pocket. He'll have eaten them in his cab and carried on. Shall I tell him to come up to the Hall when he gets back later?"

"No thanks, Rose. It'll do me good to walk down and find him. Wullie here is desperate for a good run. Do you think he's getting fat?"

"Well, maybe a little," she said tactfully, and reflected that Wullie's master was also getting a bit thick around the middle.

By the time Theo found David doggedly ploughing through the rain, he was himself soaked to the skin. So much for the waterproof! Then he remembered he'd had it since he was in his twenties and thought it hadn't done too badly.

"I've been thinking," he shouted up to David, who dutifully switched off the tractor engine. "How about setting up a children's farm here on the estate? It would bring in some much-needed resources, and might be great fun for us all. A coffee shop, maybe, with Rose in charge?"

And another job for me? David knew that he had more than enough to do, but he nodded, and said maybe they could discuss it in more detail in the dry somewhere. How about if he came up to the Hall after tea?

After Theo had tramped off, his leaky boots squelching in the mud, David clambered back into his tractor cab and thought about the suggestion. It wasn't a bad idea, but he couldn't possibly manage it all, on top of everything else he had to do around the farm. Theo's promise to get him an assistant had come to nothing, and this idea would probably go the same way. Still, he had to indulge the boss. Jobs weren't all that plentiful at the moment. He had a friend over near Oakbridge who had set up a similar idea, and would be able to help with advice on how to start and pitfalls to avoid.

MEANWHILE, THE FOUR investigators were sitting in warmth and comfort at Tawny Wings, sipping hot coffee and waiting for Gus to take a lead.

He had given some thought as to how they would proceed, and now he smiled at Ivy and said, "Perhaps you'd like to tell us just what Alwen Jones said, and maybe give us an inkling into what upset her?"

Before Ivy could reply, Roy jumped in. "It was reverting to type, I reckon," he said firmly. Although he knew it had almost certainly been Ivy's remark about bungee jumping that had scared Alwen off, he also thought it had been quite useful. The very fact that she had been disturbed enough to shun their company in the dining room showed that bungee jumping was still a very worrying memory in her mind. If it was true, then any woman whose husband had been killed in such circumstances would bear the scars. But he shared Ivy's scepticism. He just could not picture a sober, responsible accountant in his middle years bouncing up and down on the end of an elastic rope, all by himself in Australia.

"How do you mean, Roy?" Gus said. He looked at Ivy's beetroot coloured cheeks and knew that Roy was covering for her. "Was it something somebody said?"

"Of course it was," Ivy said. "It was me, and I reckon there's no harm done. She'll be back. Sat there at lunchtime like Lady Muck, looking as miserable as sin and picking at her food. You wait, she'll be back with us by tomorrow. In any case, she's joining the pontoon school tonight."

"Oh, Ivy," sighed Deirdre, "what exactly did you say?"

"Asked if her daughters had ever gone bungee jumping in their student days. There was no mistaking her reaction, was there, Roy? She wasn't going to talk about bungee jumping or her husband. No, I reckon we'll have to get out the thumb screws before we get Alwen Jones to tell us the truth. That is, of course, if she knows it."

"So what next?" Deirdre said. "Are we still looking for the truth about Alwen Jones and her possibly still missing twenty thousand pounds, or are we off to Measby to sniff around the case of the old man?"

"Anyway, let's take a vote," Gus said. "Those in favour of ditching Alwen and getting on with the suspiciously dead old man?" No hands were raised.

"Well, those in favour of ditching the old man whose death sparked rumours of blackmail, but carrying on with Alwen's twenty thousand pounds, though she has already said she's got it back?" No hands.

"Well, what *do* we do?" he asked irritably.

"Both," said Ivy firmly. "I don't believe a word Alwen Jones says, and if the two cases *are* linked by an extortion racket, we might do more good by investigating both. Deirdre has told me about the Enquire Within expenses kitty, and when we get paid by Gus's friend, we can top it up." She actually had little faith in being paid by any of Gus's friends, but that could wait for the moment.

Fourteen

BETHAN JONES WAS the exact opposite of her sister Bronwen, and although there was only a three-year gap between them, they had never been close. When they were children, Bronwen had been the undisputed boss. She decided what games they would play, what stories were read at bedtime, and, because their mother was a teacher, Bronwen was quick to grasp letters and numbers and was deputed to teach Bethan.

The younger sister was not stupid, but she was slumberous where Bronwen was quicksilver. When they were in their teens, it was Bethan who drew the boys. Her older sister frightened them off with her razor-sharp tongue and mocking jibes. Also, most importantly, Bethan had curves in all the right places, and although Bronwen was not unattractive, she was angular and sharp-elbowed. According to legend, Uncle George had been heard to say of his clever niece that he felt sorry for her husband. It would be like going to bed with a bicycle, he had said.

Now Bethan, with her two young sons aged five and two, prepared for a visit to Grandma Alwen at Springfields.

It was to be a surprise visit. Bethan had noticed that if she fixed a date with her mother, the ground had been prepared by the time she got there. Tea and orange juice for the boys had been ordered, and even the conversation had been skilfully guided by her mother so as to avoid any uncomfortable questions. It had always been the same. Mother was fine, her life was in perfect order, the girls would get the best possible education, and if they had any problems they were to go to her and she would deal with them.

So now, anticipating a more spontaneous reception, they drew up outside Springfields, and Bethan went through the lengthy business of getting the boys out of their car seats and harnesses. It was worse than preparing for an arctic expedition, she thought, and every time she set out she was tempted to dump them straight onto the backseat to enjoy themselves tangling in mock fights and throwing things out of the windows.

"Good afternoon, Mrs. Ardley!" Mrs. Spurling had spied them coming up the path and was out of her office ready to meet them. "I don't believe your mother is expecting you? She said she would have a rest and listen to a play on the radio this afternoon."

"She'll be awake then," Bethan said, smiling warmly. "Do give her a call, and we'll wait in the lounge. Come along boys," she added, shepherding them along, "and don't push Freddie like that, William. He's only little, you know."

As they gathered in the lounge, Ivy looked over the top of her spectacles at the group. "Oh my goodness," she whispered to Roy, who was reading the paper. "Bang goes our peaceful afternoon. I wonder who they are? Must have come to see someone."

"Lovely boys," said Roy, beaming as the little one approached holding out a sticky hand and offering him a toy tractor. "What are their names, my dear?" he asked Bethan as she came to rescue him.

"This little one is Freddie, and his big brother is William, named after his grandfather. Ah," she added, turning to the door. "There's mother. Look, William! Here's Grandma!"

"Thought so," said Ivy, and clamped her lips together disapprovingly.

Alwen Jones, perfectly composed, marched in, sat down and lifted her grandsons onto her lap. She smiled at her daughter and received a dutiful kiss on the cheek.

"Every inch the headmistress," Ivy said. "Poor little chaps."

AFTER ALWEN'S VISITORS had been escorted out of the lounge and up to Grandma's room, conversation buzzed around the residents, who had taken a close interest. "That one looks nothing like her mother," one said. "But those boys have the look of the Joneses, no mistake," said another. Ivy and Roy pricked up their ears, and pretended to carry on reading.

"Poor girl never knew her father, of course." This was a comparatively young resident, still in her sixties, but sadly disabled by arthritis. "I remember it well, that business at the brewery." Her companions urged her on, and she told the story that Ivy and Roy already knew. Then she said something interesting which they had not learned from Deirdre and Gus.

"My sister used to work in the accounts department at the brewery, you know. Said that William Jones was a right moody bloke. You never knew which way he would jump, she said. One day he'd be on top of the world, with praise for everyone and compliments all round, and the next he'd find fault all round the office and insist on people doing jobs again and staying late to finish. Then there was that story about him and his secretary!" They laughed, and she continued, "They all thought his family was well rid of him when he went off. All a great scandal at the time. But it died down, like these things do."

All agreed that Mrs. Jones had led a very useful life, and now had two adorable grandsons, not to mention the other daughter who was so efficient and helpful to her mother.

The residents decided that on the whole, the affair had had a happy ending. They liked happy endings, and returned to their favourite afternoon soap on the television.

UPSTAIRS, ALWEN JONES was trying to look at her watch without her daughter noticing but failed.

"Time we were going, Mother," Bethan said. She had brought games and drawing books to occupy the boys, but these had been used up in no time. Now they were occupied in fiddling with everything that Grandma had in her room.

"No, William! Not Grandma's handbag, please!" Alwen automatically went into teacher mode, and her authoritative voice stopped the little boy in his tracks. Bethan looked at her in surprise. "What have you got in there?" she said, amused at the idea of her mother with a private life in her handbag.

"Never you mind," Alwen said. "I must have some secrets to keep to myself. Most of my privacy has been taken from me in this place."

"Right, time to go. Come on, you terrors," Bethan said, and after the usual affectionate pecks on cheeks, she manoeuvred the two boys out of Grandma's room and down the stairs. Alwen waved to them from the top stair, and then returned to her room.

"Phew!" she said to Katya, who had appeared to see if she was all right. "What those two need is a firm hand. Bethan is much too soft with them. I'm sure if my other daughter, Bronwen, had had children, they would be quite different. She is much more like me."

"And does Bethan take after your husband?" asked Katya, straightening the covers on the bed where the boys had bounced.

"To look at, maybe, but I sincerely hope not in any other way." She seemed to be talking almost to herself, and Katya nodded quietly, thinking Mrs. Jones would probably rather not have said that aloud.

Bethan, on her way out, had been intercepted by Mrs. Spurling. "A little word, my dear, if you have a minute?"

Ushered into the office, Bethan held on to the boys' hands and asked how she could help. Mrs. Spurling said she wondered if Mrs. Jones had had any complaints, and did Bethan feel that her mother had settled in happily.

"Oh certainly," said Bethan, anxious to get home. She had no intention of embarking on a long assessment of her mother's feelings so far. "She seems very well looked after and not at all unhappy. She's even made friends, so she said. A very nice gentleman called Roy? Apparently he is very much on the ball and they have good conversations. They're playing cards this evening, Mother said, and she was looking forward to it."

"She has a very active brain still," Mrs. Spurling said. "I do hope she finds enough to keep her interested in daily life here. Miss Beasley and Mr. Goodman are a very lively pair, and should be good companions. I hope your late father wouldn't have objected to a game of pontoon for matches!"

Bethan shook her head. "I don't think so," she said. "Of course, he wasn't around by the time I was old enough to notice. Mother doesn't talk about him much, and we don't push her. She brought us up, really, and held down a responsible job at the same time. A great character, my mother!" she added, and made for the door. "I must get these wreckers out of here. Say good-bye to Mrs. Spurling," she instructed, and they departed quickly down the path and out to her car.

ONCE MORE THE interview room had been opened up for a use not envisaged by the owner of Springfields Residential Home. The evening was chilly, and Miss Pinkney had found an electric convector heater which Ivy had insisted on switching on an hour before they were due to play.

Now all were settled round the card table, Ivy and Roy,

Gus and Alwen Jones, the latter immaculately dressed, powdered and scented with lavender toilet water. Ivy wrinkled her nose. The smell reminded her of her mother, and she would rather not be reminded. Perhaps they could give the old thing a bottle of the stuff Deirdre used. Ivy had to admit that smelled very nice, and not too strong. She made a mental note to mention it.

It was soon apparent that Alwen was no stranger to the game. Gus briefly set out the rules, but he need not have bothered. A respectable pile of matches grew in front of Alwen, and Ivy scowled. She was used to winning herself, remembering well the lessons her father had taught her.

The door opened a crack, and Miss Pinkney's head appeared. "Ready for halftime snack?" she said. This had not been authorised by Mrs. Spurling, but she was now off duty.

"We're not playing football," Ivy said acidly. "Still, if you ask me, a cup of tea and a plate of biscuits would be a good idea. What do you think, Alwen? Not slimming, are we?"

"Good gracious me, no," Alwen replied. "I don't know about you, Ivy, but I've long given up worrying about an inch or two extra around the waist!"

"You're both of you perfect as you are," said Roy soothingly.

Gus looked from one to the other, and suddenly thought of his ex-wife. She was tall, slim and elegant, apparently without trying. But the bills from hairdressers, beauty salons and health farms told a different story. He smiled to himself. If she could see him now! His companions were two old bats and a little gnomish man in his eighties. Ah, but more often than not there was also Deirdre up at Tawny Wings! She could give his wife a run for her money.

They stopped playing to have their halftime snack, and conversation continued about this and that, until suddenly, without warning, Alwen Jones announced portentously that she had something to say. The others stared at her, noticing that her hands were trembling as she set down her cup.

She seemed to have trouble beginning, and so Gus asked

pleasantly how they could help. Anything at all, however small, he said, could be dealt with by Enquire Within.

"Well, it's like this," she said. "This morning I received a telephone call which upset me considerably, and I had difficulty concealing it from Mrs. Spurling. The fact is, I am being harassed by some character who refuses to give his name or number, and when I try to identify him, the operator says, "The caller did not leave his number." Each time, he addresses me by my Christian name, and asks the same question, saying that if I give the right answer I shall avoid an unpleasant encounter."

"What could he mean by that?" Gus was intrigued, and Ivy adjusted her glasses in order to hear more clearly.

"Just a stupid threat, I hope," Alwen said, more confidently now.

"So what's the question?" Ivy said, leaning forward in her chair.

"He says," she began, and hesitated. "It sounds awfully silly. But it's the same every time. He says, 'Eeny meeny miney moe, where did all the money go?' Then he cuts off."

There was complete silence. Roy and Ivy stared at each other, and Gus was looking stunned.

"Sounds like a practical joke," said Ivy finally, and forgetting that Gus liked his private life to be very private, and his past life a mystery, she continued, "Augustus, couldn't you find out a bit more from your old colleague, Martin? And time to open up with us, Alwen, before Enquire Within takes on what I suppose you want us to do."

"Which is?" said Gus. He was beginning to have worrying thoughts. He supposed there could be no harm in Ivy's ill-considered remark. Until that recent call, it had been a very long time since he had seen Martin, let alone worked closely with him. It had been a bit odd. Perhaps this was his old colleague's idea of checking up on him? There had certainly been disagreements in the past, but nothing serious. Maybe it was time to arrange a face-to-face meeting, always supposing he could get through on that telephone line.

"Why, we have to discover who poor Alwen's tormentor is and get rid of him, of course," Roy said, taking Alwen's hand. "It could be the extortion racket having another go at getting money out of you. Don't you worry, my dear, we'll sort him out."

"And in the meantime," said Ivy, "if he rings again, you'll know his voice by now, and just put the phone down straightaway. Now drink up your tea, and let's get on with the game."

Fifteen

DAVID BUDD PUT his finger on the bell at the kitchen door of the Hall, and kept it there for some time. Noreen had gone home, and he knew Theo would probably be in his study, half a mile away from the kitchen. But there was nothing wrong with the boss's hearing, and so he prepared to wait.

In due course, he heard footsteps crossing the tiled kitchen floor, and the door opened.

To his surprise, the pretty Polish girl from Springfields stood there, smiling broadly at him.

"Ah, Mr. Budd. I was asked by the Honourable Mr. Roussel to see who was ringing the bell. He said he was expecting you, and you are to go into the drawing room, where he is awaiting you."

Her stilted English had certainly improved since they'd last had a conversation, but she still managed to make everything sound like a formal announcement. "Thanks, Katya," he said. "Are you still enjoying working at Springfields? It takes a special kind of person to get on with most of those old fogies, doesn't it? Still, there's always

Ivy Beasley! Something of a legend in her own lifetime, that one!"

"I am very much attached to Miss Beasley," Katya said, marching ahead of him, "and most of the others are very nice people. It is not always much fun for them there, Mr. Budd."

Duly rebuked, David followed her to the drawing room, and was startled when she slid in ahead of him and almost shut the door in his face. He heard her voice saying that Mr. Budd was here and was the Honourable Mr. Roussel ready to receive him? Then the door opened again, and Katya beckoned him in.

"Mr. Budd, sir," she said, and left the room, quietly shutting the door behind him.

Theo approached and held out his hand. "Come and sit down, David. Sorry about that, but I'm giving her a confidential tryout. Between you and me, Noreen is not a huge success, and I'm hopeful that I can tempt Katya away from Springfields, to come and work for me.

"Is she interested?" said David bluntly. He could not think of a more boring job for a young woman than housekeeping for an old lecher like Theo Roussel. She'd have to spend half her time running up and down stairs and round corners to escape him!

"But surely she will be going back home shortly? She's been at Springfields for some while."

"I'm sure something could be arranged," Theo said expansively. "Now, shall we talk about setting up a children's farm? Several of my old friends in the county have done this sort of thing. Now, under my present circumstances, I think we should make use of the estate in every profitable way we can."

"It's a good idea," David said reluctantly. "You could combine it with other things, my Rose says. Maybe open the house to the public, say at weekends, with escorted tours. Then the coffee shop in the old dairy building? My Rose is a trained caterer, and she could do drinks and snacks. Perhaps have a couple of craftspeople working in the stables to draw in the public?"

"Oh, my dear chap! All of that would be a last resort! I may have to, one day, but please God not yet."

David shrugged. "Well, we could start with the children's farm. You could talk to one or two of your friends, and get some advice on how to avoid pitfalls an' that."

"There should be no pitfalls, David," Theo answered. "If I put my mind to a project, I am quite capable of carrying it through with maximum efficiency."

"Well, as you know, I'm no schoolteacher," said David, who was going off the idea of anything that would mean more work for him. Theo's track record for hiring extra help had so far been pretty useless. David's good-humoured intention of going along with the boss was evaporating rapidly. "So the first thing," he continued, "might be to advertise for someone, maybe a retired biology teacher, to introduce the animals to the children. I could just about manage to do the farming side of it."

Theo's tone was chilly. "I will certainly bear in mind the teacher idea. But I am sure you could cope. After all, it would just be a fun thing to do at weekends, not an extension of school. Anyway, thank you for coming along, David. You know the way out. Oh, and by the way," he added, as David reached the door. "The business of employing young Katya is strictly confidential at the moment. Please keep it to yourself. Best if no one knows, not even dear Rose. Thank you."

Huh! David wanted to answer that he kept nothing from dear Rose, but in any case could not think why anyone should be remotely interested in Theo's little schemes. He kept silent, and since Katya did not reappear, he let himself out of the kitchen door and strode off down the drive to be home in time for the television news.

DEIRDRE'S MEETING HAD gone on much later than she expected, and when it finished one of her old friends asked if she fancied a drink before she went home. He was actually an old friend of Bert but had kept in touch with

Deirdre, making sure she was managing everything by herself after the death of her husband. Now, when it was perfectly clear that Deirdre was more than capable of running her life, he still called her occasionally, and on one or two occasions she had gone to his house where he and his wife entertained the great and good of Thornwell. There was always a spare man, and Deirdre suspected they might be attempting matchmaking. But she was proof against that and always enjoyed a jolly evening and a meal she did not have to cook herself.

The pub was a smart hostelry in the market square in town, and they pushed their way through crowds to a small back room where there were free seats. Colin went off to fetch drinks, and Deirdre looked around, deciding that she knew nobody and was really out of touch with Thornwell society.

But, ah, there was somebody she knew. That tall, sniffy-looking dame standing at the bar was surely Bronwen Evans, nee Jones, elder daughter of Springfields' latest resident, Alwen? As she watched, Colin, carrying two glasses, stopped to have a word with Bronwen and the man who was probably her husband. Then he came on to their table and sat down, putting Deirdre's gin and tonic carefully in front of her.

"There we are! I think we've earned a couple of gins! It was quite a sparky meeting tonight, wasn't it?"

"Um, yes," Deirdre replied, still staring at Bronwen Evans. "Hey, Colin, do you know that woman? The one you were talking to?" She had a sudden flash of memory. Hadn't she been standing in the queue at the newspaper office? Deirdre had watched her walking out, but it hadn't registered then. But now she was sure. Bronwen Evans. She must have heard something of what she and Gus were asking about. Yes, well, worth mentioning to the others.

"Well, I don't usually talk to women I don't know, my dear," Colin said. "Yes, my goodness, I've known Bronwen since she was a small child. Bronwen Jones? You must have met her. Daughter of one of the brewery brothers. That's her husband, the estate agent in the marketplace, Evans & Jones.

"Of course," said Deirdre. "And which Jones brother was her father? I should know, shouldn't I, but we didn't exactly move in the same circles!"

"You didn't miss much. In spite of George's success, the family was somehow unlucky. Things didn't go right on a personal level, even though the brewery flourished. Oh, and Bronwen's father was the younger brother, William. And don't ask me questions about him. The less said about that nasty piece of work the better! Mind you, I shouldn't speak ill of the dead, but . . ."

"It's no good telling me that, Colin! Now of course I want to know about him. Go on, do tell."

"It's a long time ago," he said. "But I still remember wondering how George managed the scandal so efficiently. His brother William had always been trouble. He was bright enough but couldn't be bothered to work. If there was an easy way of making money, William would take it."

"But what was the scandal?" Deirdre persisted. She guessed what was coming but hoped for a small snippet of extra information that might help in their investigations.

"He gambled away everything he earned," Colin said, and sighed. "Shame, really, as he was a clever bloke. George gave him a job in the brewery, and why it had to be in charge of finances I'll never know. Needless to say the books were cooked. There were unpaid bills all round town by the time George got to know about it. My folks' business was one of the victims."

"But what happened? The brewery survived, after all."

"Fortunately," Colin said, "it was a very profitable year for them, and George made sure all bills were settled. Then things went quiet, and the next thing we knew, William had gone. Kicked out, everyone said."

"And his wife?"

"Wife and daughters," Colin said. "Well, Alwen Jones was a wonderful woman. Just buckled to and remade her life. Brought up the daughters and ended up head teacher in Thornwell Primary. Wonderful woman," he repeated.

Deirdre drained her glass. "Gosh, that was just what the doctor ordered!" she said. "Well, it sounds like it was good riddance to bad rubbish. What happened to William?"

"Vanished. Never heard of again. Never mentioned by any of the Joneses. It was just as if he'd never existed."

"But his daughters? They must have wanted to know about their father?"

"Maybe," said Colin, rising to his feet. "But if they did, and Bronwen Evans had set about finding him, you can be sure she succeeded. Chip off the old block, that one. And, of course, later on she worked in the brewery. Brilliant publicist, apparently. She'd know exactly how to find William Jones, but I doubt if any of the family wanted to. You could put money on it."

"Perhaps not, under the circumstances! Anyway, thanks for the drink, Colin. Would you and Dorothy like to come over for dinner sometime soon? I'd like you to meet some new friends of mine."

"Love to," said Colin. "We'll be in touch."

Sixteen

"DID YOU HAVE a good weekend, Ivy?"

"Weekends are much like any other days in this place," Ivy said, looking round her room. "Except for the excitement of going to church, of course. How about you?"

Deirdre put her hand over the phone and mouthed to Gus that Ivy was in a bad mood.

They were in the kitchen at Tawny Wings, where the dishwasher toiled in the utility room next door. Gus pulled the door shut, and motioned Deirdre to continue.

"Oh, my weekend was about as boring as yours," she said. "Gardening, writing letters to my distant daughters, that sort of thing."

"You should be grateful you've got daughters, Deirdre Bloxham," the sharp voice replied. "Anyway, have you rung up just to pass the time of day, or do you want something?"

"I want something. I would like you and Roy and Gus to come to lunch next Sunday to meet some old friends of mine from Thornwell. Are you free?"

"Of course we're free! What else might we be doing? It's

very kind of you Deirdre," she added, her voice warming
up slightly. "But I expect you've got an ulterior motive?"

Deirdre rolled her eyes to heaven, took a deep breath and
said that her only motive was to have some good friends to
a jolly lunch, and that included her cousin Ivy and Roy and
Gus. "Would you like to have a word with Gus? I think he
wants to fix a date for our next EW meeting?"

"Our what?"

"Enquire Within. It's a bit of a mouthful, so I thought I'd
shorten it to EW. Here's Gus."

"Morning, Ivy. How's things? Ah, yes. You've already
told Deirdre how things are. Right, well, I'll get down to
business. Can we fix a meeting for tomorrow morning?
Up here at Tawny Wings? Would you like Deirdre to fetch
you? The forecast isn't good."

Ivy said shortly that a little rain wouldn't hurt them
and any excuse to get away from incarceration would be
welcome. "About eleven o'clock, in time for coffee? We
haven't got anything new to report, but maybe something
will come up before tomorrow. Me and Roy are pursuing
lines of enquiry. Isn't that what the police say?"

THESE LINES OF enquiry were in fact enjoyable
sessions between the two of them and Alwen Jones. Roy
and Alwen delved into their memories of the local past, and
Ivy prompted them with skilfully directed questions.
After Deirdre's call, Ivy joined Roy and Alwen in the
lounge. They had more or less claimed a corner as their
regular territory, and the other residents steered clear of
them.

"Morning, Ivy," said Alwen. "Did you sleep well?"

"I always sleep well," Ivy replied, "owing to a clear conscience and a cup of warm Horlicks."

Roy smiled at her. "I bet you look lovely when you're
asleep, Ivy dear," he said daringly.

"Cold cream on me face, and a couple of hairnets to
keep neat and tidy," Ivy replied acidly, but she could not

keep from smiling at him. "Guaranteed to put off anybody thinking of taking a look!" she said.

"That's enough of that, you two," Alwen said. She was becoming used to the sparring couple, and could see that a deep attachment was growing between them. She felt a pang of jealousy, and chided herself for bothering with such things at her age.

"Deirdre's invited us to lunch next Sunday, Roy," Ivy said, taking a biscuit from the plate on a small table at her side. "Is that coffee cold, Alwen? Perhaps I should order some more."

"Let me do it for you," Roy said. "This has been here some time. You were late down, Ivy. Titivating, I expect. I know what you ladies get up to. And how kind of Deirdre. I shall look forward to that. Now then," he continued, "where were we? I think you were telling us, Alwen, how you managed to train as an infant teacher and look after the girls and run a house at the same time?"

Alwen settled back into her chair. They were on safe ground here, and she happily launched into a story she edited as she went along. "It was a case of necessity, Roy," she said. "As you have discovered, my husband had left us and emigrated to Australia. I have to admit that the marriage never really worked, although we both tried hard." And that's a lie for a start, she said to herself. William had never tried because he was hardly ever at home to attempt a reasonable relationship with her and the girls.

"Why did you marry him, then?" Ivy put her head on one side and smiled a false smile.

"I fancied him," Alwen said baldly. "He was very good-looking and could be extremely charming. It was purely a physical attraction."

"It happens," Roy said, and risking a sharp rebuke, patted Ivy's hand.

"Roy!" said Ivy, but she did not move her hand. She returned to her questions. "Hadn't you got anything in common, then? Tennis, or bridge, or Young Conservatives?" Ivy's ideas of how the well-off middle classes lived were mostly gleaned from romantic fiction from the travelling library.

Alwen laughed. "Not really, Ivy," she said. "William spent most of his evenings poring over his accounts in the brewery office." At least, that was what he told me, she added to herself. It was only later that she discovered he'd been seen one evening with his secretary in the restaurant at Ozzy's Casino in town.

"Ah well," Roy said, "he was probably augmenting his income in order to support a family."

It's not worth answering that one, Alwen thought, and changed the subject to concentrate on how when left alone she had studied hard, attended day classes when the girls were in a local nursery group, and been helped by one good friend who looked after them when there was no alternative.

"Who was that, then?" Roy said. There was a chance he might know this friend, and then he and Ivy would have another lead to follow up. He quite fancied a trip to Thornwell to do a bit of research. He and Ivy occasionally took a taxi into town and amused themselves drinking coffee and looking out of a café window at the passersby. Then they would ask the returning taxi to go a different way back, and Roy would point out to Ivy the farm where he had been brought up and other places of interest. Ivy was always quiet, absorbing Roy's memories and getting to know what kind of a person he had been before she met him.

Alwen smiled at Roy's question, and said her friend had been the only person who really understood what Alwen had undertaken. "She was my sister-in-law, George's wife Jane. They'd had no children, and she would have loved them."

"And George didn't mind the constant reminder of his disgraced brother?" Ivy could see the difficulties, and thought this Jane person might be an interesting line to pursue.

"Oh, we had to keep it secret from him," Alwen said. "The subterfuge! You wouldn't believe how good we were at it, Jane and me. She invented the most ingenious excuses for her frequent absences from home."

"And yet he gave Bronwen a job in the brewery?" Ivy said.

"That was much later, of course, and another story. Now, it looks like we're being summoned for lunch. We have it much too early, don't you think?"

"It means the staff can have a reasonable break in the afternoons," said Ivy. "If you ask me, Katya and her friend, and poor old Pinkers, as Roy calls her, deserve a few hours free. Not from us," she hastened to add, "but from Mrs. Spurling's iron rule. It beats me why those girls stay on here. They could easily get jobs somewhere more congenial."

"SO WHAT DO you remember about Jane Jones?" Ivy asked. It was early afternoon, and Roy was guiding his shopping scooter down the uneven path of Barrington's main street, with Ivy walking at his side. "I suppose she's not still around?"

"If you mean has she died, yes, it was a sad business. Yet another piece of ill luck for that family. Years ago, of course."

"What happened? And don't tell me she fell into a vat of fermenting beer and was drunk and drowned?"

"How did you know!" Roy stopped his vehicle in astonishment. "You can't have known that? You haven't been here long enough!"

Ivy swallowed. "You mean it's true? She really did?" Sometimes she frightened herself with her uncanny perceptive skills.

"Well, she wasn't drunk. Nor was she drowned, apparently. But she did get into one of the fermenting tanks when showing a party of schoolchildren round the brewery. The workers had ladders to climb up and see how the fermentation was going. One of the boys had climbed up when nobody was looking, slipped in and was holding on by his fingernails. Mrs. Jones went in after him. They got them both out, but the shock gave her a heart attack and she died in hospital later that day. It was a terrible business. They say George never got over it. Blamed himself for letting her take the children round, but the man who usually did it was off sick and she persuaded him."

Ivy was very quiet until they reached the shop. They stopped outside, and Ivy sat down on the Hon. John Roussel memorial seat. "You know what I'm thinking, Roy," she said.

He nodded. "That Jane Jones was a very compassionate, brave woman, and possibly much too good for pompous old George?"

"No, not that. I'm thinking we need to do a lot more digging into pompous old George's past life. Nobody's as faultless as he was. At least, as his public face claimed to be. Got any ideas how we could find out a bit more?"

Roy thought for a moment. "If I remember rightly," he said, "his wife Jane came from a farming family over Oakbridge way. My dad used to talk about them sometimes. Very successful farmers, rich as Croesus my dad said. Partly inherited money, and part income from a couple of big farms. I'll have to check my memory for this, Ivy, but I'm pretty sure one of the sons went to the same school as me, but in the bottom class when I was in the top. He might still be around. Certainly went into the family farms. I do remember that. I could think of some reason to get in touch, I reckon. What d'you think?"

"I think a trip to Oakbridge might be just the ticket. We could kill two birds with one stone, Roy, visiting your old acquaintance and also taking a look at the village where that poor old man was murdered. You remember, the one Gus described in gory detail. Just in case it has anything to do with Alwen's mystery caller." She sounded really excited now, and helped him out of his scooter, saying she would treat him to his favourite Turkish delight if he managed all the steps by himself.

Seventeen

"HERE WE ARE, gathered together in the sight of Deirdre," intoned Gus.

"Don't blaspheme, Augustus," said Ivy sharply. Roy looked at her questioningly. He hadn't caught the reference, not yet having been through the marriage service himself, but he knew it was religious from the way Gus said it, and he made a mental note to suggest he accompany Ivy to church next Sunday. Might be useful, he thought, smiling to himself. Although she found fault with the vicar, his church choir and the form of the service, Ivy was predictably a regular attender.

"Settle down," said Deirdre firmly. "First of all, welcome once again to Tawny Wings." She looked at her watch. "I'll make coffee at eleven, so that gives us a good hour to pool our ideas and thoughts."

"Are you bringing us to order?" said Gus, amused at Deirdre's formality.

"Yes," she said. "And about time, too. Now, who will report first? I have a little something I've discovered to add to what we know already."

"So have we," said Ivy, looking smugly at Roy.

"Sorry," said Gus. "Nothing from me at the moment."

"Right, then, I'll go first," said Deirdre, and related the conversation she had had with her friend Colin in the pub in Thornwell. "He was quite vitriolic about William. When he cooked the brewery books, apparently Colin's family business was one of the casualties. They were owed thousands. Also, he confirmed that William was kicked out—I quote—by his brother George."

"I don't think there's anything new there, Deirdre," Gus said kindly. "But very useful to have it all confirmed."

Deirdre bridled. "Well, perhaps this is more interesting! Do you remember when we went to the newspaper office, there was a queue behind us and guess who was standing in it, quite close to us and no doubt overhearing our conversation?"

"Do tell," said Gus patiently.

"Bronwen Evans, daughter of Mrs. Alwen Jones. I saw her again in the pub with her husband, same night as I went in with Colin. I asked him who she was, that's what started us talking about the Joneses."

"That could be important," said Ivy, frowning. "Especially if she talks regularly to her mother. Yes," she added, "that was well remembered, Deirdre."

"My turn," said Roy, unwilling to be left out. "We've got something new. Me and Ivy were going over the old days with Alwen. She's more friendly again, and loves to talk about bits of the past that are not taboo."

"You mean not William, or anything to do with him?"

"Yes, well, she even gave us a few hints about him and George." He then filled them in on Alwen's confidences on the subject of George's wife. "Jane Jones, it was. She helped Alwen a lot after William went missing. Had to keep it secret from George, of course, but they managed."

"Jane Jones?" Deirdre said. "I think I remember her, don't I? I was only young, of course, but her family over near Oakbridge used to buy their cars from Bert, and have them serviced and so on. I've forgotten their name, but Bert thought a lot of them. Nice people, he used to say, as well as good customers."

"Mowlam, that was the name. Jane Mowlam she was. It just came to me, just like that."

Ivy beamed. "What would we do without you, Roy?" she said, with undoubted affection in her voice.

Deirdre got up to make the coffee, and the three were left to chew over what had been said. They agreed that Roy should definitely have a try at getting in touch with the current generation of Mowlams. "There might even be an oldie like me left among 'em," he said.

Ivy said that if Roy wangled an invitation to the Mowlam farm, she was definitely going with him. "He's not safe without me," she said, and he nodded gratefully.

KATYA AND HER friend and workmate Anya were also drinking coffee, powdered instant, of course, and not in a leisurely fashion. They were snatching a few minutes in the kitchen whilst Mrs. Spurling had gone to the village shop. The topic of their conversation was Theo's offer to Katya of a well-paid position as live-in housekeeper at the Hall.

"He has asked me to keep the matter confidential at the moment," she said, "as he does not wish to upset Noreen."

"Why doesn't he keep her on?" Anya's English was more colloquial than Katya's, mainly because she had a regular local boyfriend and was out with him most evenings. It was tempting when just she and Katya were together to speak in their native tongue, but Anya insisted it would be good to practise their English.

"Because she is not satisfactory. I noticed several dirty corners needing attention, Anya, and apparently her cooking is not good."

"Nor is yours," said Anya flatly. She was now promoted to catering for Springfields, and prided herself on her skills.

Katya bridled. "I make very good cookies," she said.

"And that's all," Anya said, grinning. "Mr. Theo can't live on cookies, you know."

"All I shall need is a recipe book from my mother. And a few lessons from you," she added placatingly. "Anyway, I haven't decided to accept the position yet. It's a great huge chilly house, and might be very lonely for me."

"From what I hear," said Anya, "Mr. Theo will be only too pleased to warm you up! I'd think very carefully, Katya, before deciding. We're both far from home, and my boyfriend says we're vulnerable to unscrupulous men."

"What nonsense! He's just trying to frighten you, so that you do not flirt with other men. And there's always Mrs. Spurling to protect us," she added, hearing footsteps approaching.

"Not if you go to the Hall," whispered Anya. "Here, give me your mug. We must get on."

When Ivy and Roy were back at Springfields, waiting for their lunch to be served, Katya approached their table carrying plates. She placed them down carefully, and then hovered behind Ivy's chair.

"What's up?" Ivy said kindly. She had become very fond of the girl, and knew at once Katya was worried about something.

"May I speak with you after lunch? In your room, privately?" Katya's voice was low, so that only Ivy could hear.

Ivy nodded. "See you there," she said, and turned to greet Alwen, who was hurrying in to take her place.

"Where have you been this morning, you two?" Alwen was carrying a large handbag, as always, and opened it to find her eating glasses, as she called them.

Roy wondered, not for the first time, what on earth she had in there that was essential to her life at Springfields. "Looks like you have all your worldly goods in that bag, Alwen," he said with a good-humoured smile. He was taken by surprise by her answer.

"It's none of your business," she snapped. "What's for lunch? And you haven't answered my question. Where've have you been all morning?"

"None of your business," said Ivy, raising her eyebrows. "And its fish. Again."

Eighteen

KATYA KNOCKED SOFTLY on Ivy's door, hoping the old lady had not dropped off for her afternoon snooze. But she need not have worried. Ivy had not forgotten, and was sitting straight in her chair in her favourite spot, from where she kept an eye on comings and goings along the village street.

"Come in," she called, and swiveled round to smile encouragingly at Katya. "Sit yourself down, child. You're off duty now, aren't you?"

Katya nodded. "Yes, I am. Thank you very much for letting me come in to talk to you."

"Well, now, why don't you begin at the beginning?"

"Yes, that is a good idea. First I must ask you very respectfully if you could possibly not tell Mrs. Spurling what I am about to say to you."

"Of course. You know perfectly well that if there's anyone you can trust in this place, it's me. Come on, now, what is it? Boyfriend trouble?"

Katya shook her head vigorously. "No, no. Not that.

At the moment I have no boyfriend. Anya says I am too snooty! Is that right?"

Ivy said that she wouldn't really know about that. She was beginning to see her afternoon snooze disappearing into the distance. She always met Roy at three o'clock in the lounge, and found a little shut-eye beforehand very refreshing.

"No," continued Katya, "it is a job that has been offered to me. The wages are higher than here, and I am—how do you say?—tempted?"

"What's the job?" said Ivy.

"The Hon. Mr. Roussel at the Hall has asked me to work for him as housekeeper. Resident housekeeper," she added, since it was that part of it that worried her most.

"No," Ivy said firmly.

"What do you mean, Miss Beasley? No what?"

"No, refuse the offer. Don't even consider it, Katya."

Katya looked crestfallen. In her daydreams she saw herself smartly dressed, acting as hostess for Mr. Theo at parties, perhaps stewarding in the drawing room when they opened up the Hall to visitors, supervising the stable units let out to craftspeople. She had been chatting to David Budd's wife Rose, and the two of them had agreed that it would be an excellent way of making extra money for the estate.

The whole village knew that Roussel was strapped for cash, and they had begun to fear that he might sell up, and then anything could happen. Over Oakbridge way there was a similar estate, and it was now a luxury hotel and golf course, and the heart and traditions of its nearby village had vanished.

"Oh dear," Katya said. "Would you please tell me why you say that, Miss Beasley? You are my best friend and perhaps my second mother in this country, and I need good advice on this matter."

"You have it," said Ivy, a little shaken at the idea of being anyone's mother. "Don't touch it with a barge pole. If you want me to spell it out, my dear, Mr. Theo is a confirmed bachelor, and because of his position in society is used to having his own way. With any luck, he's the last of a dying breed, but there he is, selfish, aging and loves pretty women, especially young ones. You are a pretty girl, and his intentions won't be honourable! Do I need to say more?"

Katya was silent for a few moments. Then she said softly that perhaps Miss Beasley did not realise that she could be very tough, and knew how to look after herself.

"I doubt it," Ivy said. "But if you ask me, it's your decision and, as my mother used to say, in this life you make your bed and then you have to lie on it."

Katya frowned. She was not sure what Miss Beasley meant, but she had made very plain her advice on the problem of Katya's temptation.

"Best thing you can do," Ivy said, smothering a yawn, "is tell him you are thinking about it. Think some more, ring your mother and see what she thinks," she added with a sudden inspiration.

Katya's expression cleared. "Yes, of course. That is the best thing. Thank you very much. You are a dear person," she said, getting up and blowing Ivy a kiss as she quietly left the room.

"I may be a dear person," Ivy muttered, turning to look along the street as far as the church, "but I ain't a sleepy one no more. Might as well read until it's time to meet Roy. If this is what it's like being a mother, I'm heartily glad I'm not one."

AT DEIRDRE'S INVITATION, Gus had stayed on at Tawny Wings for lunch. Deirdre had produced a fluffy mushroom omelette, and they had tucked in, Deirdre watching Gus wolfing down his large helping. The man didn't look after himself properly, that was for sure. She began enthusiastically telling him her plans for her lunch with her friends Colin and Dorothy, but after a while she stopped talking and looked closely at Gus.

"What's the matter? You're very quiet. Aren't you feeling well? Whippy's looking worried."

"I'm fine," Gus said. "It's just that you others are beavering away uncovering clues and coming to possible conclusions, and I'm not doing anything."

"But aren't you going to contact your friend about the circumstances surrounding that old man's death?"

"He's not really my friend. Not one I've kept in touch with. More an acquaintance from the past. I'm not at all sure, now I've thought about it, that I want to get involved with him again. In some ways, Deirdre, our little gang is playing at detectives. Anything to do with Martin is the real thing, and almost certainly dangerous. I don't mind so much for myself. I'm used to it. But with the others, well, for God's sake, two nice old people and one lovely rich lady who doesn't need danger in her life."

"I wouldn't call our last case playing at it!" Deirdre protested, ignoring his description of her. "After all, there was murder, intrigue and blackmail. Doesn't that count as the real thing?"

Gus sighed. "I suppose so," he said. "Well, I should try again to contact Martin and ask for more details. Do we still suspect Alwen Jones's mystery voice is connected in any way?"

"Seems very possible," said Deirdre. "But until we know more from your Martin—Martin what, by the way?—it's not easy to guess. So at it, lad! Gird your loins and get busy on the phone. Now, do you want some of this ice cream? It's rich and bad for you, but delicious and irresistible."

"Just like you, then," said Gus, cheering up rapidly. He reached out to grab her as she went by, but with practised ease she avoided him and went off to the freezer, laughing happily.

WHEN HE RETURNED home, Gus unlocked a small tin box he kept at the back of a cupboard and extracted a dog-eared address book. He turned the pages until he came to *M*, and then ran his finger down the list of names, not sure that Martin would be in it. "Ah, here we are," he said, and repeated the number over several times, committing it to memory. Then he replaced the book, locked the box and put it back behind a pile of files in the cupboard. He was about to dial the same number as before, hoping it would now be working, when a call came in. It was Martin, and Gus said, "You must be telepathetic, old chap! I had my thumb ready to dial your number."

"Ah, what odds would you take that that could happen twice?"

"None of that, Martin," Gus said. He added that a meeting was a good idea. They could catch up on the past, as well as discuss the Measby mystery. Then Martin gave him instructions where to meet, and the call ended. Gus reached for the Thornwell train timetable. Opening it at connections to London, he noted down a morning train and, feeling a gentle nudge on his leg, he said apologetically to Whippy that he would take her for a nice long walk now. "I shall be out all day tomorrow, so we'll make up for it this afternoon," he said, and clipped on her lead.

For once, the walk was longer than a quick trot round the playing fields, and Gus headed over the stile into the parkland surrounding the Hall. Although not an officially designated footpath, it had been used for as long as people could remember as a quick route for itinerant farmworkers from Barrington to the next village. Most of its winding way was over Roussel land, and Gus reckoned that as a tenant of the estate he would have a special right to roam at will.

Whippy was delighted. She lagged behind, investigating interesting sniffs, and then shot past him like a little grey shadow as she spotted rabbits in the distance. Wild cherry leaves landed on them in a scarlet shower as the fresh wind stirred the trees, and as the path took them into an ancient wood, a grey squirrel darted up an oak tree and sat on a branch staring down at them, chattering threateningly.

Gus noticed none of these rural delights, lost in thought and anticipation of his trip to London. Without Deirdre's confident presence beside him, his own reservations returned.

"We could get in too deep," he told Whippy, who was now sticking to her master's heels, unaccustomed to the sounds of invisible dangers in the dense undergrowth. "Do I really want to go through all that again?" He scarcely remembered Martin, and had not recognised his voice at first. Well, they were both a good many years older now. He wasn't sure what Martin's present connections were with the old firm. Perhaps he was on a retainer, too. Anyway, if his own was to continue, and he certainly needed it, he must expect to make an effort now and then.

"Sod it, Whippy!" he said, kicking at a pile of leaves like a small boy. "They've got me by the short and curlies, and they know it!"

"I *beg* your pardon?" said a voice behind him. He turned rapidly, and was relieved to see it was only Theo Roussel approaching him, a smile on his face. "I do hope you won't think I was eavesdropping," he said. "Perhaps I might join you for a short while? I'm on my way to find David Budd. Wonderful chap, David. Have you met him?"

Gus replied that they had exchanged greetings over the garden fence, and that he had once or twice helped Rose with the eldest child. "He's an escaper," he said. "And at the moment, though not for much longer, I'm faster than he is! Lovely family, anyway."

"Absolutely," said Theo. "And I'm so lucky to have such a good worker. Are you still a working man, Mr. Halfhide? Not that I imagine agriculture was your trade?"

"Not exactly," Gus replied. "I was mostly abroad. Spying was my trade, Mr. Roussel, but I'm retired now."

It always worked. Nobody ever believed him. "Oh, very good, Mr. Halfhide, very good!" chortled Theo. "We must find some jolly mysteries for you to solve with your chums in the village."

"Keeps my hand in, and we didn't do too badly with our last case," Gus reminded him. "I'm sure you've not forgotten old Mrs. Blake and the Beattys?"

"Quite so," Theo said dismissively, unwilling to be reminded. "Ah, there's David! Have a good walk, Mr. Halfhide. Lovely dog. Runs like the wind."

Nineteen

GUS HAD WORKED out that if the train to London took about an hour, he would need to leave Barrington after an early breakfast and a quick dog walk round the playing field. He had met Miriam talking to Alwen Jones in the shop yesterday, and had asked if she would mind saying hello to Whippy over the garden fence a couple of times, just to stop his little companion pining. He was off to his dentist, he improvised.

Miriam had agreed with enthusiasm, and true to form, asked for all the details of his trip. Which train was he catching from Oakbridge? He could drop Whippy in on his way to the station. Was he taking a bus to the station? So how long would the journey take? Perhaps he and she could have a day in London one day? He could show her the sights? Oh, and could she take Whippy for a walk, and would he remember to give her Whippy's red lead? Eventually, the shop had been empty except for the three of them. Alwen had said it was Miriam's turn next, and Gus smiled at her gratefully.

Now, Whippy duly dropped off with Miriam, he saw

that the bus had got him into Oakbridge in good time, and the station platform was crowded with commuters. He pushed his way with the others into an already packed carriage. He saw a single seat and quickly sat down, abandoning all gentlemanly politeness in offering anyone else first choice. He had bought a newspaper from the kiosk, and now held it open in front of his face. He had no desire to talk to strangers, and was already regretting his decision to arrange a meeting with Martin. Deirdre was to blame. If she hadn't fired him up with her mushroom omelette and several glasses of good white wine, not forgetting her warm smile and low-cut blouse, he would have returned home and concentrated on finding the perpetrator of nuisance telephone calls to Alwen Jones.

"Is that Augustus?" A hand appeared at the top of Gus's newspaper and lowered it. Across from him, a middle-aged woman in city clothes stared at him in surprise. "It is, isn't it? Augustus Halfhide, to the life!"

He stared back. He had absolutely no idea who the woman was, and as far as he could remember, he had never seen her before.

"You don't remember me, do you? Well, that's no great surprise," she said. "I suppose it must be twenty years since we played in a mixed doubles tennis tournament in that hideaway in the Pyrenees?" She stuck out her hand invitingly. "Margaret Fortescue I was then. How nice to run into you again!"

Gus's heart was in his boots. This was all he needed. He managed a small smile, and said of course he remembered that place. He was sorry he couldn't recall her name, he said, but it was a long time ago, wasn't it? He glanced at her hand but saw no wedding ring. So Fortescue had not been a maiden name, but one of her several names, just as Augustus Halfhide was one of his.

"Where are you living now, Augustus?" she asked. "I saw you getting on at Thornwell and thought you looked familiar."

"Oh, I'm between houses at the moment," he said, his

antennae waving madly to pick up any signs of danger. "And you?"

"Oh, I'm a confirmed Londoner," she said. "Been visiting an old friend, and now going back home. Are you up for the day?"

"The other way round for me," he said. "I'm visiting an old friend in London, and as for whether it will be for one day or several, I am not yet sure." He laughed. "My old friend is also my dentist," he said, sticking to his story. "If he can't fix my tooth straightaway, I'll have to stay on for a few nights."

"Still the same dentist, in Wimpole Street?" she asked. "My flat is just north of that, so perhaps we can share a taxi? Oh look, there's a buzzard! Isn't it beautiful? They're very widespread now, I believe."

She rattled on about birds of prey and new legislation, and Gus examined what she had just said about his dentist. How did she know about Wimpole Street? He had had a dentist there for many years, but was it likely the woman would have remembered a chance reference to a once only tennis partner's dentist, even if he had made such a reference? No it was not. The sooner he got away from her the better. He nodded his head in reply to a question about ospreys, and raised his newspaper once more.

As the train drew into Liverpool Street station, most passengers were on their feet and ready to run for taxis and tube trains. Gus stayed in his seat, and was dismayed to see the woman who claimed to know him was also still sitting.

"Not in a hurry, I hope?" she said, reaching for her handbag and sliding over ready to stand up. "I have a taxi booked, so stay with me and you'll be fine. Wimpole Street in no time, Augustus!"

Oh my God, what am I to do? Gus was thinking rapidly. He hadn't much time. *I could lose her in the crowds, but she didn't look easy to lose. I could say I'd changed my dentist, but she'd probably invent a reason why she had to go to wherever I said.*

"I had really thought a walk would be the thing," he

said. "It's awfully good of you, but I have plenty of time. So nice to have met you again," he added, and got to his feet. She was still struggling with her coat, and he did not offer to help. The carriage was almost empty now, and he walked swiftly to the door, not looking back. Phew! A lucky escape, he hoped, and walked out of the station and along the road towards the café where he had arranged to meet Martin. It was much too early, but he intended to dive into the network of back streets to be sure that Margaret Fortescue had not followed him.

In a narrow lane, he stopped to tie his dangling shoelace, and in the reflection in a shop window he saw a taxi stop behind him, and the woman got out. Real fear hit him then, justifiably, as his arm was caught in a vicelike grip, and he was marched firmly to the taxi's open door.

"Get in!" she said, and he felt something sticking into his back. Oh no. He thought he had left all that behind, he moaned to himself. The taxi took off at speed, and a strange man sitting next to the driver turned around.

"Hello, Gus," he said. "I thought that café we chose was a bit public, so we're going somewhere safer. Much safer, eh, Margaret?" he added, and laughed. Then she joined in and the taxi driver, too. Gus did not laugh. He felt sick, and could see no way out.

Twenty

IVY SAT IN her room, dozing before it was time for supper. Roy snored companionably in the extra armchair Mrs. Spurling had supplied on demand from Ivy, who, soon after arrival, had said she would need to entertain her visitors in private. As it happened, Ivy had few visitors apart from Deirdre, and just lately Roy had taken to popping in and staying for the odd half hour.

Today was the first time he had fallen asleep, and Ivy found herself surprisingly happy about it. It was restful, somehow. She was reminded of happy Sunday afternoons, when her father would doze off after a good lunch. Mother would go up to the cemetery to put flowers on family graves, while she sat by her father, reading her favourite book. It was always the same book, read over and over again: *The Pied Piper of Hamelin*, by Robert Browning, and illustrated by the great Kate Greenaway. She could recite it off by heart when she was only ten. "At last the townsfolk in a body, to the town hall came flocking, 'Tis clear,' cried they, 'our Mayor's a noddy; and as for our Corporation—shocking!' " she began aloud, and Roy woke with a start.

"What's shocking!" he said, rising to his feet in alarm.

Ivy put out her hand. "Nothing, nothing. I was just saying some poetry out loud. Something I remembered from when I was little. Sorry, Roy, if I startled you."

"No need to apologise, Ivy," he said. "Just so long as you're not in any trouble. I must confess I closed my eyes for a minute or two, and do you know, I dreamed a terrible dream!"

"Not much of a dream in that short time," said Ivy.

"About you, as a matter of fact," said Roy tentatively.

"Sounds more like a nightmare," Ivy said. "What had happened to me, then?"

"You'd been taken off by a stranger. He was riding a great white stallion, and scooped you up into the saddle and galloped away."

"Oo-er," Ivy said. "Was I screaming?"

"No," said Roy sadly, "you were laughing with delight."

"Oh, Roy!" Ivy burst out into deep chuckles, a little cracked from lack of use. "Nobody makes me laugh like you do."

He took her hand, and she blushed like a teenager. "Well," she said. "That's enough of that nonsense. Come along, time for supper."

Roy thought maybe he had gone too far too soon, but then he realised Ivy was still holding his hand. "I'd like to hear the rest of that poem one day," he said. "You've got such a lovely voice."

This was patently so untrue that Ivy laughed again, and the two descended the wide staircase side by side.

Miss Pinkney, standing by Mrs. Spurling at the dining room doorway, watched them. "I say, Mrs. Spurling," she said, "do you think we might have a romance amongst us soon?"

"Don't talk such rubbish," replied Mrs. Spurling. "I have quite enough trouble with this lot, without romance!"

Ivy and Roy had settled themselves at their usual table when Ivy's mobile phone rang. It was Deirdre, and she sounded worried.

"Ivy, have you heard from Gus at all?"

"He went to London, Deirdre. Of course I haven't heard from him. Did he say what time he'd be back?"

"Well, yes, he said he hoped to be back in time for Whippy's tea. She always has it around five o'clock without fail."

"But Deirdre, he could have got held up anywhere. There's always tube strikes and rail strikes and rush hour traffic jams. He'll be back soon, I'm sure. Anyway, if you ask me, he'll have decided to stay with one of his mysterious friends. You know our Gus!"

"Mm, I'm not so sure. He loves that dog like she was a child. I think he'd do his best to be back by five."

"Well, maybe Miriam Blake knows something. I saw her from my window going down the street with Whippy on a red lead. Why don't you give Miriam a ring?"

"Okay, Ivy. I'll do that. Sorry to bother you. Anyway, I'll be in touch tomorrow."

As they sat at the supper table, with Alwen now making up a permanent threesome, Ivy told the others about Deirdre's call. "Making a fuss about nothing, if you ask me," she said.

"Sounds like it," said Alwen. "It's typical men, though, Ivy. He'll turn up late tonight, I bet, full of the joys of spring." Her words were encouraging, but her expression was oddly one of concern.

IN A DINGY back room of a small café not far from Liverpool Street, Gus thought nostalgically of having supper with his friends in the protected atmosphere of Springfields.

The man and the woman, Margaret, had shoved Gus through the café, upstairs and into this smelly room, locking the door behind them when they left him with assurances of their swift return. There would be developments, he knew, but he tried not to think about that. His fear had gone. He was now the old Gus, living on his wits and never allowing distractions to prevent him from concentrating on the one important thing. In this case, it was escape.

He looked around. There was very little in the room. A few rickety chairs and a small table propped up on three legs with a pile of old telephone directories for a fourth. A window with one filthy pane looking out over a tiny backyard, stacked high with cardboard boxes and anonymous rubbish. There was no means of opening the window. He began to walk slowly round the skirting board, kicking it carefully for hollow sounds. A cupboard door was hanging half off its hinges, and he looked inside. Nothing, except for signs of an abandoned mouse nest. Not even a resident mouse. Not very promising, he admitted to himself. He would have to rely on the locked door. He sat down on the least rickety chair to wait and to think. Most urgent, he knew, was to find out why they wanted him, and why they thought he might run away when they told him. It was unlikely to be the unsavoury death of an old man at Measby.

"HELLO, THEO?" DEIRDRE was now trying long shots to find out where Gus had got to. It was nearly ten o'clock and dark, and Miriam Blake had taken Whippy into her own cottage with her bed and feeding bowl.

"Deirdre, my darling! How can I help at this hour? Well," he continued before she could answer, "I can think of lots of lovely ways, but don't suppose that's why you're ringing?"

A little of Deirdre's panic subsided at the sound of Theo's confident tones. "No, though that does sound very inviting. No, Theo, it's about Gus Halfhide. I was wondering if he'd mentioned to you anything about being away in London for more than a day? He's not answering his mobile. It's dead as a doornail, and Miriam has taken Whippy into her house, and because of, well, you know, because of Gus's past, we are all a bit worried about what might have happened to him."

Theo's answer was a hearty laugh. He said he had no idea where Gus Halfhide was, but guessed he was living it up with friends in London. "I do hope he hasn't deserted us completely," he said in a more sober voice. "He is an excellent tenant, always prompt with the rent and no complaints."

"For God's sake, Theo, never mind about the rent! The man might be in danger! Haven't you any useful connections or ideas about how we could get hold of him?"

There was a moment's silence, and then Theo said he probably still had Gus's details from his application for the cottage. "I'll look out the files in the morning, see if I can find his address at that time," he said. "Meanwhile, darling Deirdre, why don't you get into your car and speed up to the Hall, where I'll help you forget all about the mysterious Augustus Halfhide?"

Deirdre cut off the call without saying good-bye.

IVY WOKE WITH a start, and sat up. She put on her bedside light and looked at the alarm clock beside her. Midnight, the witching hour. She rubbed her eyes and listened for any noises in the home that might have awakened her. Sometimes, there were shouts and screams as the residents fought with their dreams. But tonight it was silent. Nothing but an old tomcat yowling in the garden outside. She lay down again, adjusting her hairnet over stray strands of hair. Her eyelids began to close, until suddenly they shot open again, and she sat up once more.

"Of course!" she said aloud. "I bet Deirdre hasn't thought of it. That's where he'll be. With his ex-wife!"

Twenty-one

"THAT'S ALL VERY well, Ivy," Deirdre said, "but how do you propose we should find Gus's ex-wife's telephone number or even address?"

"You've got a key to his cottage, haven't you? And if you haven't, I should think Theo Roussel has. You can bet old Beattie kept duplicate keys to all the cottages."

Deirdre had called Ivy soon after breakfast with the news that Gus had not shown up, and Miriam was still looking after Whippy. She had heard nothing, and both of them were worried sick. Gus's mobile was still dead, and he seemed to have vanished without trace. All this would not in any way have looked suspicious, but when he had left Whippy behind, and with no instructions as to her welfare if he should be delayed, they knew something was wrong.

"It's just not Gus, and no, I don't have a key to his cottage," Deirdre said, sounding offended and ending the call.

At coffee time, when Roy, Ivy and Alwen met in the lounge, they agreed that it was totally out of character for Gus to behave in this way. Even Katya, who had been taken into Ivy's confidence, said she thought maybe they should think about going to the police. Perhaps there had been an accident, and maybe Gus had not been carrying any means of identification.

"Good point," Ivy had said, remembering Gus's insistence on keeping himself more or less anonymous.

Now Deidre marched into the lounge, and Ivy ordered another coffee for her. "A council of war, you said, Ivy, so here I am," Deirdre said, flopping down into a chair drawn up to make a circle with the other three. In this way, they shut out curious eyes and ears, and felt they could talk freely, if quietly.

Deirdre reported that at Ivy's suggestion she had asked Theo for a spare key to Gus's cottage, and she would pick it up later.

"Good," said Ivy. "Now, any more suggestions or comments. I reckon we'll need plans A, B and C."

Roy looked at her proudly. There was no doubt about it. In an emergency, Ivy came into her own. No wonder she had commanded the village of Round Ringford for so many years. Various stories had filtered through to him about his beloved's record in her home village, including one about the little school, threatened with closure, being rescued by Ivy's sizable donation.

"I had this idea in the middle of the night," Ivy continued. She told them about her plan for contacting Gus's ex-wife, but Alwen was sceptical. "Last place he would go, I should think," she said. "If I know anything about ex-husbands, they stay away from you as much as possible. Especially if they're short of cash."

Deirdre looked at her in surprise. "Speaking from experience, Alwen?" she said.

"Not an unusual situation," Alwen replied, purposely vague. "I do have one thing we might try," she added. "We could go over to Oakbridge station and see if they remember selling a ticket to London yesterday to anyone looking like Gus. If they do, then at least we'd know he'd actually gone there, and not anywhere else."

Roy was doubtful. "There's a hell of a lot of commuters

catch the London trains first thing in the morning," he said. "I think we'd be wasting time."

"But most of them have season tickets," Ivy said. "I think it's a good idea. Deirdre could go and ask. No harm in asking."

At this point, Katya came over to them, and said there was a call for Mrs. Wilson Jones. Perhaps she would like to take it in Mrs. Spurling's office, to save her going upstairs to her room? Alwen said she was expecting a call from her daughter Bronwen, and limped off to the office.

The others asked Katya to bring more hot coffee to help them think, and Roy said cookies were known to be good for the brain, so could she put a few more of her specialty on a plate for them? While they waited, they discussed other ways of finding Gus, and Deirdre remembered Theo's offer to look out for any previous address he might have in the files from when Gus first applied to rent the cottage.

It was only a matter of minutes before Alwen was back, helped by Mrs. Spurling who was holding her firmly by the arm.

"She insisted on coming back to you three," she said caustically. "She should really take a rest, but as I say, she insisted." She helped Alwen, who was looking whey-faced and shaky, and then turned on her heel. Sooner or later this lot would go too far, and then she would be the one to carry the can.

"Alwen, my dear," Roy said, stretching out his hand to take her trembling one, "what has happened?"

"It was another of those calls, wasn't it?" Ivy said flatly. "The anonymous caller?"

Alwen nodded. "Yes, it was. I put down the phone, but not before he'd said something really horrible."

"Which was?" prompted Ivy. She looked at the two entwined hands, and began to think Alwen was spinning it out unnecessarily.

"It was the same voice, but the message was different. He said that if we wanted to see our friend again, I should arrange for ten thousand pounds to be delivered in banknotes to an address which would arrive in the post tomorrow."

"Oh my Lord," said Deirdre. "So did you cut him off then? Did he give you a deadline?"

"Yes, he did," said Alwen, her colour returning. "I thought I should keep him talking, to see if I picked up any clue to who he is. He then said that I shouldn't try telling the police, or it would be curtains for Gus Halfhide. And he said the money should be at the address by midnight, the day after tomorrow. Or else. Then I knew he wasn't bluffing."

"Never mind about that," said Deirdre firmly. "I am going home right now to phone Inspector Frobisher of Thornwell police. We are out of our depth here, chums. Hands up those who agree?"

She thought the result would be a foregone conclusion, but it wasn't. No hands were raised. "But Ivy!" she said. "This is really serious stuff now. We're not playing games," she added, unconsciously echoing Gus.

"Nor were we in the Beatty case," Ivy said stiffly. "Gus trusted us, and he's probably stuck somewhere where he can't come home, crossing his fingers that we don't go to the police."

"So you think his ex-wife has him tied up at gunpoint, demanding alimony or else?" Alwen had had enough. She began to rise to her feet, but then sank back into her chair. She had just remembered that she herself had every reason not to want the police sniffing around. Especially with Bronwen coming to see her this afternoon.

"No, of course not," Deirdre said. She sighed. "Well, I'll go along with what we plan to do for another few days, but after that, the police. Is that clear?"

"Another few days might be too late, if that caller is serious," Ivy said. "Personally, if you ask me, I suspect he was bluffing, Alwen. He must know that stuck here in Springfields we're unlikely to be able to do what he asks. Did he say he'd call again?"

Alwen shook her head miserably. "No. It was all I could

do not to spill it all out to Mrs. Spurling. She was not far away, needless to say. I'm afraid that he is not bluffing, Ivy. I feel it in my bones."

Ivy shifted in her chair until she was sitting upright in a commanding position. "Right," she said, "here's what we'll do. First, Deirdre has to go into the bank in Thornwell and stay there for as long as possible, then come out smiling. Doesn't matter what you do in there, Deirdre, but just make it look as if you've settled a lengthy transaction."

"Why?" said Roy.

"Just in case somebody's watching."

"You mean *following* me?" Deirdre gasped.

"Of course," Ivy said. "We're not dealing with a one-man band here, you know. There'll be several of them. Now, after that, Deirdre, you can go on to Thornwell station and ask if the ticket office remembers seeing Gus."

"What shall *we* do?" Roy was anxious not to be left out, and rather fancied the idea of taking on Theo Roussel. "Shall I go with Ivy up to the Hall and see if himself has found any papers?"

Deirdre agreed reluctantly, but then cheered up when she remembered that Theo was not taking her at all seriously last night. Perhaps Ivy and Roy would have better luck.

"And I'll wait here," Alwen said firmly. "I'm expecting Bronwen to call to confirm this afternoon, and anyway, that man might call again." She frowned, looked at Ivy and said, "D'you know, I reckon he's disguising his voice. It sounded odd, like it would be if he was . . . sort of strangulated. Now why would he do that?"

"Obvious," said Ivy. "He knows you'd recognise his real voice."

Alwen looked at her closely. It was such a sensible remark, but there was something about the way Ivy said it. And the way she returned Alwen's gaze, steadily and perhaps with a warning? Ivy had spent a lifetime behind lace curtains, picking up clues from village life going on outside her windows, sorting the evidence, jumping to conclusions, often proving to be correct. Not to be under-estimated, thought Alwen. One to watch.

I WONDER IF Deirdre's ears are burning, Gus said to himself. He had been thinking about her for a long while. He'd been told straightaway that a ransom had been demanded, and knew that only Deirdre would be able to raise that amount of cash at will. Did she care enough? He knew that she fancied him. But then she fancied Theo Roussel, and had enjoyed high jinks in his bed for some while. Could he compete with the local squire? And, more importantly, did he want to? Now he had time to examine this question honestly. Answer: yes, he did, and if he ever got out of here he would take positive steps in that direction.

The door to his prison opened, and Martin and Margaret locked themselves in with him. While he had been left alone, Gus had become sure that "Martin" was not the colleague he had been expecting to meet. It had been years, and now he saw that he looked nothing like the Martin he had known, even accounting for the passage of time. That Martin had been small and wiry, and was losing his hair at a relatively young age. His gaoler must be in his early sixties, and was tall and thickset, with close-cropped thick grey hair and old-fashioned heavy-framed glasses.

He was more or less convinced that Margaret's story had been a pack of lies. She was clever, and the way she had accosted him had made him uncertain. But that had been an unexpected meeting, and he was prepared to admit that his memory was not that good. But now he was sure. She was a complete stranger, and a dangerous one. And, if he was not mistaken, she was the boss of the duo.

"Are you hungry, Gus?" she said with apparent concern. "Sorry there's no time to talk now. We'll be back later for a discussion."

"What discussion? Just get out of my way, and let me out of here. You don't fool me. Neither of you have anything to do with the person I was supposed to meet. I don't know what you're up to, apart from blackmail, but you must know that my lunch friend will be making enquiries when I don't show up. He is a top man in his field, and I don't give much for your chances when he finds you."

"Nice try, Gus," said the woman. "And don't worry about your top man. He's certainly not worrying about you."

Twenty-two

"I'M DUE TO see Mother at half past two," Bronwen said as she stacked the dishwasher.

"It's nearly two now," he said, "so you'd best be off. And don't forget the big question this time."

Bronwen had not yet had the courage to approach her mother for a loan, which she was almost one hundred percent certain she would not get. It was a waste of time, she had said repeatedly to Trevor, and what was more, they had little chance of paying it back in the foreseeable future.

"What makes you think she has reserves enough to lend us?" she said now. "After all, the fees at Springfields are horrendous. It won't take long to make a huge dent in her savings, and compared with some of the old biddies there, she is quite hale and hearty."

"I don't know why she wanted to go there in the first place," Trevor replied. "She could have managed in her own home, with carers coming in and Meals On Wheels and all that jazz."

"Can you imagine Mother accepting personal help

from a ragbag of local authority women? As for Meals On Wheels, well, I ask you!"

"She managed to eat school dinners all those years. I think you misjudge her."

"Oh, no I don't! I know exactly what she'll do to save money when it's to her own advantage. And the fact is, none of us in the family know just how much she has in the kitty all together, investments and savings bonds and so on."

"It's a pity she's not gaga," Trevor said gloomily. "If you had power of attorney, then we could really go to town."

"Not these days, boyo," she snapped. "Takes about six months to finalise, and then there are all kinds of checks and balances to make sure her money is secure."

The grandfather clock in the hall, a purchase that had set Bronwen back several thousand pounds, struck two. Trevor picked up his laptop and headed for the door. "That clock's slow, as usual," he said. "See you tonight." He did not even wave a hand to say good-bye.

"HELLO, DEAR!" ALWEN was sitting in the lounge by the window, and had seen her daughter approaching. Good heavens! She had a bunch of roses in her hand! First time in living memory, thought Alwen. Must want something. Her expression was serious, but apart from that she looked her usual slim, youthful and businesslike self. Customary tailored black suit with crisp white shirt, neat haircut so that her dark shiny hair fitted her head like a cap. Glossy and hard, Alwen said to herself.

"Hi, Mother. How are you today? Is the leg feeling any better?"

Alwen had osteoarthritis in her knee, and some days it was so painful she felt like crying and took too many painkillers from her capacious handbag, and gave herself a stomachache. Today was a good day, and she accepted the roses and a peck on the cheek with a smile.

"Come and sit down," she said. "I'll order some coffee

for us." She waved a hand towards Katya, who was ministering to an old lady who was in tears because she was convinced she had peed herself.

"In a minute, Mrs. Wilson Jones," Katya called across the room. "I just need to make Ethel here comfortable. Good afternoon, Mrs. Evans!" she added. "Lovely roses!"

"What a pleasant girl that one is," Bronwen said. She supposed this was what her mother was paying for. Coffee on demand, polite care assistants who never made the residents feel a nuisance. She found herself hoping that by the time she came to it, Trevor would have salted away sufficient funds for her to do likewise.

"Shouldn't you be at work?" Alwen said with a frown. When her daughter ceased making an effort, she could see there was something troubling her.

"Ah, well, thereby hangs a tale," said Bronwen. "I have had bad news, I'm afraid. Made redundant by the new owners, along with about twenty others from the administrative staff in the brewery. The usual story. Falling sales have forced them to reduce costs, and apparently I'm a cost that can be done without."

"Bronwen! But I thought you were doing so well? All those new retail outlets and supermarkets stocking the beer? What on earth has happened?"

"Maybe you missed it, Mother, but the whole country has been hit by recession. We're all in the same boat. Poor old Trevor hasn't sold a house for weeks."

Alwen heard alarm bells. She began to wonder about the roses. Bronwen's next words confirmed her suspicions.

"Trouble is, Mother, as you know, we've taken on a lot of loans to get the house and things just as we want them. You know our financial position only too well! Now, of course, we shall find it nearly impossible to keep up the repayments."

"You'll have to get another job," said Alwen quickly. "With your qualifications, that shouldn't be too difficult."

"Plenty of people out of work with better qualifications than mine, I'm afraid. I shall be trying hard, of course, but until I find another post that pays as well as the brewery, we are a bit desperate for cash."

Alwen sighed. Why didn't Bronwen come out with it straight? All this pussyfooting around was irritating, when Alwen knew perfectly well they were hoping she would offer financial help.

"Bronwen," she said firmly. "I'm not a fool, as you know. You might as well ask me straight out for a loan, or even a gift, and the sad truth is that I have to say no for a number of reasons, as you well know. I have worked it all out, and by the time I snuff it here from natural causes, my savings will just about be at an end. I have never made demands on my children, unlike some of the residents here, and I intend to go on the same way. I shall pay my way here, but only just, if my calculations are correct."

She ignored Bronwen's angry expression. "So I'm afraid you will have to go home and tell Trevor that it's not on," she continued. "You'll have to sell the house, if necessary at a bargain price. It's much too big for just the two of you anyway. Look how well Bethan manages in that small house with her boys!"

Bronwen stood up with a jerk. "Bethan, Bethan, Bethan!" she said. "Bloody Bethan could never do any wrong in your eyes, could she? Oh, yes, you were proud of me because you could boast about my achievements. But Bethan had your love, all of it."

By now her voice had risen, and all the others in the lounge looked across at her in alarm. This was something strange and new. Nobody ever shouted at them in Springfields. Even relations who had shouted at them at home put on hushed, sympathetic voices when they visited.

"Now, now, Mrs. Evans!" Mrs. Spurling marched across the room and tapped Bronwen on the shoulder. "I can't have you upsetting my residents, now can I? Won't you come with me into the office and have a nice cup of tea? There are a number of matters I wish to discuss with you, and then we can come back and settle down with Mother again. Come along," she added, and with such authority that Bronwen meekly followed her out of the room.

AN HOUR LATER, there was a tap on Ivy's door.

"Come in," she said, expecting Katya to appear with a reminder that it was time to go down for tea.

But it was Alwen Jones who pushed the door open with her stick and limped into the room.

"Good gracious, Alwen," Ivy said. "What's up with you? Has our gaoler been getting at you?"

Alwen shook her head. "No," she said. "As a matter of fact, Mrs. Spurling has been rather diplomatic. No, it was my daughter Bronwen. Can you believe it, Ivy? She brought me red roses and asked tenderly after my health, and then asked me to lend the pair of them, her and Trevor, enough money to get them out of debt! Can you believe it?" she repeated.

"Oh, yes," said Ivy, who had always thought the worst of everybody, "I can believe it." She wondered whether to remind Alwen that she had been quite ready to hand over twenty thousand pounds to a dodgy stranger. Ivy was still not convinced that this foolish step had been put right. But she looked at Alwen, pale and shaky, and decided not to mention it. "Sit you down, girl," she said, "and let's talk about something else. Like how we're getting on with tracing Gus."

TREVOR CAME HOME from the golf club around six o'clock, and Bronwen could see at once that he was half cut. He smiled foolishly at her, and failed to walk the straight line between the front door and the kitchen. "Put the kettle on, lovey," he said. "I think I might need some black coffee. How'd'ya get on with your Ma?"

Bronwen shook her head. "Nothing doing," she said. "In fact, we had a bit of a scene. That Spurling woman gave me a lecture on not rocking the boat."

Trevor sobered up remarkably quickly. "You mean she won't lend us any money at all?"

Bronwen nodded. "She said she's got just enough to see her out in comfort, without being a burden on her family. That was when I lost it, I'm afraid."

"Then you'd better go back and try again, hadn't you. There's one weapon we haven't tried yet. You know what I'm talking about, don't you, Bronwen dear."

"Blackmail," Bronwen answered baldly. "You want me to blackmail my own mother to pay for your golf subscription and your nights out with the boys, not to mention funding a few relationships on the side. Well, sod you, Trevor Evans! You can forget it."

He looked at her with contempt in his eyes. "I am not the only big spender here, am I? Think on, Bronwen."

Twenty-three

THEO ROUSSEL WAS still puzzling over this morning's mysterious call from Springfields Residential Home. He vaguely remembered a Miss Ivy Beasley who had played a somewhat heroic role in the Beatty tragedy. Apparently, if it hadn't been for her unlikely skill with a mobile phone, he might have been at this minute having a celestial gin and tonic with his illustrious ancestors. And now she and her fellow inmate—a Mr. Goodman?—had asked to call on him in half an hour's time. They would have a taxi, the old dame had said, and would not stay long. He could think of no valid reason to refuse.

Useless Noreen had gone home, so Theo left his study and went downstairs to the kitchen. He rustled up a bowl of soggy crisps and cheese straws, and took them into the drawing room. A tray of glasses stood by the drinks cabinet, and he held one up to the light. It was disgustingly smeary, and he wished once more that Katya would make up her mind about working for him. He was confident of succeeding, but it was taking longer than he had hoped.

The doorbell rang, and he went to greet his elderly

guests. The minute he saw Ivy, he remembered. No two old women could look as fearsome as Ivy!

"Good evening, Mr. Roussel," she said. "I am Miss Beasley, and this is Mr. Goodman."

"Come in, come in," Theo said kindly. "Come through and have a drink." He led the way to the drawing room, and turned to Ivy. "What can I offer you, Miss Beasley?" he said. "A gin and tonic, or sherry?"

"Never touch alcohol," Ivy said, and behind her back Roy winked at Theo.

"Ah, then luckily I have ginger beer in the cellar, made by my former housekeeper."

"Her!" said Ivy. "It's probably exploded by now. Anyway, that might be acceptable, thank you."

"And how about you, Mr. Goodman? A gin and tonic to fortify you when the explosion buries us all in rubble?"

Roy laughed, and even Ivy could hardly suppress a smile. When Roy was duly fortified, Theo disappeared, and there was silence for a few seconds. Ivy looked around the room, and said, "Last time we were here, it weren't this peaceful, was it, Roy?"

He shook his head. "No, my dear, it wasn't. But now we have another crisis on our hands. The longer poor old Gus stays away without contacting us, the more serious things begin to look. We'll get a key from Theo, anyway, and then tomorrow Deirdre can have a hunt around for clues as to what might be afoot."

"Afoot?" said Theo, coming back with a dusty bottle in his hand. "How very *Boy's Own Paper*, my dears! I haven't heard that word since I was a lad. Trouble afoot, Captain! Oh, yes. Wonderful stuff."

"It is trouble afoot that has brought us here this evening," said Roy stiffly, suspecting that Theo was laughing at him.

Ivy explained, and of course Theo already knew from Deirdre that Gus had gone missing. He couldn't himself see what all the fuss was about. The man had gone to London and was probably enjoying himself in the gambling dens of Soho. He had quite by accident discovered from an old betting friend that Augustus Halfhide had been a familiar figure on racecourses and casinos in the past, though not for quite a while.

"I'm sure Mr. Halfhide would appreciate your concern," he said. "But there is no reason why he should hurry back to Barrington, is there? After all, he is a completely free agent, as far as I know."

The word "agent" clicked with Ivy, and she said they all realised that a great deal of Gus's private life was very private indeed, but the most important reason why he should be back home by now was Whippy.

"Ah, the whippet," Theo said. He had had many dogs, and had been soppily fond of them all. He began to see that perhaps there was some substance in the anxiety quite clearly felt by Miss Beasley and Mr. Goodman. And, of course, Deirdre, too, though he suspected that she was more interested in retrieving Gus for her own pleasurable pastimes than rescuing a dog.

"If you ask me," announced Ivy, "if he had meant to stay away for several days, he would have asked Miriam Blake, or, more likely, Deirdre Bloxham, to look after Whippy for him until he returned. He would not have trusted to luck that they would do so anyway. Not in a million years, Mr. Roussel."

"So how can I help?" asked Theo, looking surreptitiously at his watch.

"We'd like to look in his cottage for any helpful clues," Ivy said. "And we're hoping you have a key and will approve of our plan."

Well put, thought Roy. She don't beat about the bush, our Ivy.

"Of course, if you're sure he wouldn't mind," Theo said, going over to a small desk by the windows. "Here we are. For all her faults, Miss Beatty was most methodical, fortunately. Because I'm afraid I am not!"

"Then the sooner you replace the Noreen woman with a proper housekeeper the better, Mr. Roussel," said Ivy, and in a balloon above her head Theo could read "And stay away from little Katya" in big red letters. He changed the subject.

"Have you thought of trying his ex-wife?" he said help-fully. "A friend of mine who had played cards with Mr. Halfhide at the Carlton Casino remembered there had been a wife. That was at the time I was letting the cottage, and tried to research Mr. Halfhide's background for my own satisfaction. I could find out very little, except for this one chance remark from my friend."

"Oh, yes, I thought of the ex-wife immediately," said Ivy. "We're hoping to find contact details in the cottage." She put the key in her handbag and stood up. "That was delicious ginger beer, thank you, Mr. Roussel. Pity that woman didn't stick to brewing."

Theo Roussel saw them out and into their waiting taxi. He waved a hand as they departed down the long drive, and went thoughtfully back into his peaceful drawing room. I suppose I could give old Freddie a ring, he said to himself, and see if he remembers anything more about Augustus Halfhide.

GUS WOULD HAVE given a lot to be in the Carlton Casino with Freddie Armstrong right now, instead of con-fined in a scruffy café in east London.

"Don't try any funny business," Margaret had said as they opened the door after a while to bring in a glorified camp bed, its mattress stained and sagging. He had con-templated pushing past her and Martin and out, and had moved slowly to position himself behind them and nearer to the door. But Margaret had swung round, and he saw she was holding a gun in a disturbingly experienced way. She had waved him back, and he retreated to stand by the window.

What could they possibly want with him? What made them think anyone would be prepared to pay a ransom to get *him* released? He held no secrets now, nothing that would be of any use. Then, who exactly had these two contacted for ransom money? He had no personal details of any kind on him. Years of experience had taught him the folly of carrying an address book! He felt a sudden shiver of alarm when he wondered if they knew he had an encyclopaedic memory, and carried all he needed to know in his head. To get at that, they would have to try persuasion, and he was only too well aware of the kind of persuasion they would use. So who had they contacted? Obviously somebody with money, someone who would *care* enough to shell out on demand.

Oh sod it all! Why hadn't he stayed quietly at home with Whippy, instead of playing detective in cases of supposed fraud and blackmail? It was way out of his field, and he admitted to himself that it had been vanity. He couldn't give up the glory of solving a puzzle, the high of being in action again, however lowly the case.

"Any news of a sucker willing to pay good money for the release of a man who is worth nothing?" he said now. "And who did you ask?"

"As a matter of fact, we are still waiting, but the deadline hasn't expired yet, you'll be pleased to hear. The person we contacted is perfect for the job. Rich, vulnerable and most unlikely to go to the police."

"Why?"

"Because the person has something to hide, and we know what it is."

Gus relapsed into silence. He tried to guess who they meant. Not his ex-wife, of course. She'd be only too glad to have him out of the way. Nor his old gambling friends. No money there! That left the most recent of his acquaintances, Mrs. Alwen Wilson Jones, who had money in the bank and appeared to be no stranger to attempts to get it away from her.

And then there was Deirdre. He hoped it was Deirdre, because if he was right in reading the signs, she would be keen to have him back. Then he remembered that it was extremely unlikely that she had anything to hide from the police, and his heart sank ever deeper.

Twenty-four

AT TEN O'CLOCK, Deirdre called with her car at Springfields to pick up Ivy and Roy. They were sitting in the hall, coats on, ready for her to take them to Gus's cottage. When Ivy rang Deirdre first thing to suggest Deirdre go by herself, she had refused.

"No telling what I might be blamed for," she had said. "No, Ivy, you must come with me." So, of course, Ivy had said she wanted Roy to protect her from possible intruders lurking in Gus's cottage, and he must come, too. Although Deirdre did not rate Roy's abilities as bodyguard very highly, she agreed.

"You'll both be back for lunch, Miss Beasley?" Mrs. Spurling asked sourly. She had had a bad night, kept awake by hooting owls. She knew if she mentioned it to Miss Pinkney, she would get a gushing rebuke for her lack of appreciation of wild birdlife, especially birds whose habitat was under threat, like owls. If only she could get at them, she promised herself, she would strangle the lot.

"Naturally," Miss Beasley said. "We would have informed

you if not. Come along, Roy," she added, and the two went out to Deirdre's waiting car.

As they stopped outside Gus's cottage in Hangman's Row, Ivy immediately spotted Miriam Blake's curtains twitching. "She'll be round for a cup of sugar, mark my words," she said to Deirdre. "That sort can't resist poking their nose in."

"Cup of sugar?" said Deirdre, looking puzzled.

"Figure of speech," Roy said. "My mother used to say it about the wife of one of our farmworkers in the old days. Always coming round borrowing things and never returning them."

By this time, Deirdre had unlocked Gus's front door and they followed her inside. Shrill barking came from next door, and sure enough, a tap at the door signalled the arrival of Miriam Blake with Whippy at her heels.

"Is he back?" she said urgently. "No? Do you expect him back soon? Poor little Whippy here is pining for her master, aren't you, doggie?"

Whippy whimpered pitifully, and began sniffing all round Gus's cottage, looking for traces of him.

"We'd better be methodical, Deirdre," Ivy said. "You go upstairs and see if you can find any documents in that little room he used as an office. Me and Roy will get going downstairs. We'll start with that little desk over there, though that looks more ornamental than useful. And we'll say good-bye for the present, Miss Blake. We'll be sure to let you know if we hear anything, and I'm sure you'll do the same for us."

Miriam bridled at being shunted towards the door, but went off muttering that if Miss Beasley was so keen on keeping Gus to herself, perhaps she would like to take a turn at looking after his dog.

"Be careful to put everything back in its place," Roy said. "Of course, when Gus comes back, we'll have to tell him we've been here, but at least he'll find everything in its right place."

"*If* he comes back," Ivy said quietly, so that Deirdre would not hear.

Roy stopped opening drawers and looked at her. "Do you mean that, Ivy?" he said.

"It's possible," she answered, and then pointed up the stairs and put her finger to her lips.

They continued searching in silence, and Ivy moved on from the small desk, having found nothing but a tatty piece of used blotting paper and an incongruous bow of blue ribbon. She wondered what past owner of the desk had kept this souvenir of a loved one.

"I'll try this cupboard by the fireplace," she said, and tried to open the door. It was stuck, and as there was no keyhole for locking it, she concluded it had swollen with damp. She shivered. "Shall we have a cup of coffee?" she shouted up the stairs to Deirdre. "It's damp cold in here. I'm not happy about Roy being in this atmosphere."

Deirdre came down, and looked at the pair of them. She was suddenly appalled at the ridiculousness of their quest. "Come on, both," she said as cheerfully as she could manage. "We're not going to do any good here. If you think about it, Ivy, a man like Gus with secrets to hide is not going to leave anything where an intruder could find it, is he? I mean, there was that time when that awful man broke in and whopped him one over the head."

"Good thinking, Deirdre," Roy said, and made for the front door, only too pleased to be let off guard duty.

"No, wait a minute," Ivy said. "Let's remember why we're here. Gus has gone missing. We've heard nothing, and he's probably been taken where he can't get in touch. God knows why, but that's the fact. We want a contact, like his ex-wife, so we can get to him as soon as possible. After all, he is a colleague, isn't he?"

Deirdre nodded. "And a friend," she said. "But then you two don't need to be here. Why don't you go and sit in the garden in the sunshine while I have a quick search round the most likely places?"

"You could start with this cupboard," Ivy said, taking

hold of the knob and yanking hard. It gave way suddenly, and she tottered, rescued from falling over by Roy who was standing behind her. Straightening up, she put her hand inside, reached to the back and pulled out a small tin box.

"Ah," said Deirdre, "that looks promising. But is it locked?"

Ivy tried the lid, but it did not move. There was no sign of a key, though she searched the entire contents of the cupboard. "Nothing but a pile of old paperbacks," she said.

"Give it here, Ivy," Roy said, and fumbling in his pocket brought out an unbent paper clip. "Never without it," he said. "Not much use for it in Springfields, 'tis true," he added, "but I'll have a go."

The two women looked at him sceptically. Silly old fool, thought Deirdre, and even Ivy could not keep doubt from her eyes. Still, let him try, she thought. There's a lot I don't know about Roy, and maybe picking locks is one of his skills.

After Roy fiddled about with it for a minute or two, there was a tiny clicking sound, and he looked up. "There we are!" he said triumphantly. "Who's going to look inside?"

"Well done, Roy!" Deirdre said, and Ivy nodded in agreement.

"You'd better look, Deirdre," Roy said. "Your eyes are better than ours."

Deirdre opened the lid and took out the dog-eared address book. She looked at Ivy. "Not a waste of time, after all," she said. "Sorry. Now, what shall I look under? Do you think his ex still uses his name?"

"That's all we've got," Ivy said. "So at least start there. Halfhide. Can't be many of those around."

THEO ROUSSEL WAS also looking up telephone numbers. He had been browsing through his father's old books about rare breeds when he remembered to ring Freddie Armstrong. It took him some while to find the number, and when he rang, it was engaged. He put in a ring-back request, and started to doodle on a piece of paper on his

desk. Not much like a horse, he decided. There had been
no trace of artistic talent in the Roussels, and Theo was no
exception. He tried a dog, but it looked more like a cat, and
he screwed up the paper and threw it into his wastepaper
basket. Then the telephone rang.

"Hello, Freddie! Theo Roussel here. Yes, Theo from the
past! What are you doing with yourself these days? Still a
racing man?"

Freddie Armstrong was delighted to hear from someone
who had been a close friend in the giddy round of hunting,
horse racing and gambling in casinos years ago. "Wonderful
to hear from you, Theo!" he said. "Coming back to us, are
you? Things have changed, old chap, but we'll keep an eye
on you until you're back into the ways of our wicked world!"

Theo laughed. "Can't afford it anymore, Freddie. Cares
of the estate, I'm afraid. No, this is a small plea for help.
Not too serious, as far as I'm concerned, but a dear girl
is worried about the disappearance of her friend Augustus Halfhide. Yes, I'm afraid that *is* his name. What? You
remember him? Well, that's marvellous! Left his wife,
apparently. Oh, you knew her, too? Don't have a contact for
her, by any chance? Oh, wonderful. Yes, pen at the ready.
Fire away." He scribbled down a name and address, and
after fond farewells, ended the call.

Noreen knocked at his door and came in with a mug of
coffee balanced precariously on a tin tray, with a plate of
biscuits sliding from side to side. "No brown sugar, Mr.
Theo," she said. "Still, I always say white's much cleaner.
You never know where that brown stuff has been. Anything else you want?"

Yes, said Theo to himself. I want to see the back of you,
Noreen, and have little Katya filling the house with sunshine and efficiency. But aloud he said there was nothing,
and waited until she had gone before dialling Deirdre. She
was out, and he left a message to say he had some information for her, and why didn't she come up for a drink
this evening? He put down the phone and forgot all about
Augustus Halfhide.

Twenty-five

GUS HAD SLEPT fitfully on the uncomfortable camp bed. Noises from the café and surrounding streets had woken him almost immediately after he began to doze. He was cold and hungry, and already there were strong smells of spicy meat being cooked below. He desperately wanted to shower and shave, and clean his teeth. The inside of his mouth felt gritty, and he craved a glass of pure water. Well, that's something new for Gus Halfhide, he said to himself wryly.

"Morning, Gus!" Keys turned in locks, and the time it took to open his door made him think this wasn't the first time his disgusting room had been used to confine a prisoner. Martin slid in, going once more through the elaborate locking process. He was carrying a plastic carrier bag, which proved to contain a generous chamber pot. "Use this," he said. "It'll be emptied now and then."

I could kill him easily, let myself out of here and escape, Gus thought. But good sense prevailed, and he decided to say absolutely nothing for as long as he could keep it up. That way he was bound to learn more from them.

They would give themselves away, sooner or later, and he intended to be around when it happened.

"I expect you'd like some breakfast? And, by the way, you may as well call me Max," the man said. "I am, of course, familiar with the real Martin." He laughed, and Gus thought it was one of the ugliest sounds he had heard for a long time.

"Not answering this morning?" he continued. "Shall we just have a little chat about this and that now?" He began asking questions. How did Gus like Barrington? Had he made many friends? What did he do with himself all day?

"Well, if you won't even give me your order for breakfast, I can't bring you any, can I?" Max said after a while. "We shall just have to see if you've found your voice in time for lunch. Of course, before that we shall need some answers to more questions we've prepared. We'll be back later." He left, this time fumbling impatiently with the locks. Gus remained silent.

Ah, so that's it, thought Gus. Starve the prisoner until he's so hungry he'll tell you anything for a slice of bread. Well, I suppose these idiots have no way of knowing that I can go for days on nothing but deep gulps of fresh air. Not that the foetid air in this room could be called fresh, by any stretch of the imagination. Anyway, real Martin will embark on a hunt for me soon, I hope. But maybe not. Maybe he'll shrug his shoulders and think Gus Halfhide is as unreliable as ever, and forget him. It was so long since he'd seen him that he was not at all sure Martin would still have the clout, or, more seriously, the desire, to rescue a retired colleague who had lost the knack of keeping himself out of trouble.

Well, the one thing he had time to do now was to think about why an apparently innocent victim had been found dead in his cottage in the village of Measby, and what it had to do with his present imprisonment. It must be dangerous and widespread for the department to have bothered with it in the first place. Maybe the imposter Martin and the woman Margaret wanted to question him to get one jump ahead of an undercover investigation into whatever they were up to.

And then he had another thought. It was possible they suspected Enquire Within's involvement, and needed to find out exactly what the four of them had discovered.

BACK HOME IN Springfields, Ivy and Roy suggested Deirdre come in for coffee and a discussion on their next move. They had found no Halfhides in the address book, but then, as Ivy said, you wouldn't expect Gus to need more than a Christian name to contact his ex-wife.

"The trouble is," Deirdre said, as they settled in Ivy's room with comforting hot coffee and Katya's cookies, "there are a good few women's names without surnames right through the address book." She fished it out of her pocket and began to turn the pages. She stopped at *D*, and was embarrassed to see her own name, without Bloxham attached.

"No probs," said Ivy blandly, daring the other two to comment.

Roy did. "No probs, Ivy? Where on earth did you hear that expression?"

Deirdre laughed. "It's obvious, Roy," she said, riding to Ivy's rescue, "it means no problems. And Ivy's right. We shall just have to go through the whole lot. If we don't get the right answer, we'll just say it's a wrong number and ring off." Mindful of the cost involved, she added that she would go through them on her mobile right now, and they could tell her the numbers.

"There'll be no need for you to try the one under *D*," Ivy said with a smirk.

Ungrateful old trout, thought Deirdre, but she said there was no time like the present, and they should make a start with *A*.

"Right, this one's called Anita, and here's her number." There was no reply, so Roy made a note, saying they could try later. "On to the next, then, Ivy," he said, and soon they had a system going, but with no luck until they reached *K*.

They had just passed by Katya, with tut-tutting from Ivy, and had found a Katherine, with a London number.

"Hello? Oh, my name is Deirdre Bloxham, and I am sorry I don't have your name, except for Katherine. I don't know if you can help me, but I am trying to contact a person called Augustus Halfhide—"

She got no further. There was what sounded like an explosion at the other end of the line, and then the woman's voice said Mrs. Bloxham must be out of her mind wanting to contact that rotter!

"Oh, so you know him?"

"Know him? I was his wife, and I could tell you more than you'd want to know about Augustus Halfhide! Except, of course, where to find him, and that's par for the course. I hear from him from time to time, but only when he wants something. Anyway, have you tried his mobile?"

"Yes," said Deirdre, her voice growing chilly at this woman's reaction. "It's dead. And there's a strong possibility he may be dead, too," she added.

"Deirdre, don't say that again!" Ivy mouthed at her cousin, who was still talking. But evidently the rash remark had caused the woman to calm down and be a little more helpful. She gave Deirdre three possible telephone numbers, and said that if all else failed, she could try a number he had given her to use in emergencies. Deirdre recognised it at once. It was her own.

BY THE TIME Deirdre was back home at Tawny Wings, she had three messages on her answerphone. Two were trying to sell her car insurance, and the other was from Theo. She rang his number, and when he answered with an invitation to go for a drink, she accepted with alacrity, glad of the chance for a little light relief. There was no getting away from the fact that even Springfields, well run as it was, had occasional moments of unhappiness and decay. Perhaps she was being oversensitive, but she realised that if Ivy and Roy had not become friends, and found much to talk about and views in common, not to mention an obvious growing affection, their lives would have been very different. And, of course, if Gus had not gone missing, everything would be different. She busied herself with the garden, sweeping up leaves that the gardener had missed, storing garden furniture ready for the winter and picking remaining golden plums that hung like grapes on the old tree she and Bert had brought from Thornhill as a tree sucker from his parents' garden. Gardening usually relaxed her, but she still felt very much on edge. Perhaps it was the approach of autumn, with its cold nights and blustery days.

Time to go in and clean up for Theo. She put away her tools, and went to have a hot shower. Maybe that would brighten her up. But when it didn't, she got into her car and set off for the Hall. As she drove past Hangman's Row and Gus's empty cottage, she admitted to herself something she had up to now kept at bay. She was missing Gus himself, mysterious old Gus, and she shed a tear.

Twenty-six

BETHAN ARDLEY SHOUTED to the boys to turn down the sound. She couldn't hear what the voice on the phone was saying, although she knew it was her sister Bronwen.

"What? Sorry, just a minute. I have to go and turn down the sound."

Bronwen sighed. Why didn't her sister just turn the wretched thing off? Those boys spent far too long watching the flickering screen. She had said so to Trevor, but he had answered that kids learn far more from the telly than they ever had from school. So what did he know about kids? She thought this was nonsense, but gave up, as she did so often these days.

"Hello? Bronwen? Still there?"

"Yes, oddly enough. As you know, I'm a very busy person, and not used to the tantrums of two small boys."

"Not tantrums. Just their point of view needs to be respected. Anyway, is this a sisterly chat, or do you want something else?"

"It's Mother," Bronwen said. "She's being very cagey about money and her will, and all of that."

"You mean she won't lend you any?"

"No need to be nasty," Bronwen said. "Trevor and I were wondering whether we wouldn't get together with you two, and Mother, and in the nicest possible way thrash out some sensible course of action for the future."

"Like power of attorney, for when she gets gaga?"

There was a silence, and then Bronwen said, "Yes, possibly something like that. For all we know, she may be chucking away her savings right, left and centre! There's plenty of no-goods around trying to get old folks' money out of them. And we'd never know, Bethan, until she . . . well . . ."

"Until she dies? And since you mention it, there's other people besides no-goods trying to get money out of old folks."

There was a pause, and then Bronwen said, "Well, yes. So wouldn't it be best to organise something now with the four of us. Or, more properly, between you and me. Don't you agree?"

"No, Bronwen, I do not agree. If our mother was gaga already, then you might have a point. But she's got all her marbles, and as far as we know she is managing her own money satisfactorily. She's got a good brain. Has had to have over the years, bringing us up on her own, as even you must accept. If she's spending her savings—*her* savings, hard earned over a long career—on drink and gigolos, then good luck to her. Does that answer your question?"

There was no reply, and the call cut off. Bethan returned to her boys, turned up the sound on the telly and went to make herself a cup of tea. What a shame, she thought, that Bronwen is so tricky. It would have been nice to be close to my only sister over the years. But there it is. And now Bronners is out of a job and she and her slimy husband are in debt and facing hardship.

"What'ya laughing at, Mum?" called her elder son.

"Nothing, love," she replied. "Just something Auntie Bronwen said."

* * *

"WE SEEM TO be going round in circles," Deirdre said, as she sipped a large gin and tonic in Theo's tranquil drawing room. The sun was low in the sky, and he had half drawn the blinds to shield their eyes from the glare. The room was full of the scent of late-flowering lavender from a bed outside the open window, and Deirdre slowly relaxed. Theo had told her the result of his conversation with Freddie Armstrong, and the telephone number he had been given was, of course, the same as Deirdre and the others had found in Gus's address book.

"Not quite circles," Theo said. "Since I spoke to Freddie, I have been thinking back to the old days, when I was a gambling man myself. I never came across Gus Halfhide, but I do remember a cheating scandal in one of the poker schools set up in a London casino that no longer exists. Freddie and I often played there, but the stakes were high and one or two friends ruined their lives. It can become an addiction, you know, Deirdre. If Halfhide was also a regular there, he may well have been one of the victims.

"But not the cheat! Don't tell me he was the cheat, because I don't believe it. Unwise he may have been, but not a cheat."

Theo raised his eyebrows at the vehemence in Deirdre's voice. Did she fancy his stringy-looking tenant? He smiled. Good luck to her, he thought. At our age we take our pleasures where we find them, and as he felt a pang of jealousy he reminded himself of his plans for little Katya.

"No, no," he reassured her, "it wasn't Halfhide. The cheat was discovered, and duly punished. He wasn't a Londoner, and I have no idea of his name. Came from the provinces somewhere. Never heard of again, as far as I know. Anyway, it's probably not relevant to your search for Gus."

Deirdre was silent for a few minutes, and Theo got up to refill their glasses. "What was Halfhide's wife like?" he said idly, filling in the gap in conversation.

"Brisk," said Deirdre, smiling back at him. Things were

not good, but meanwhile, here was Theo, looking particularly attractive this evening, twinkling at her over the edge of his glass. "She hadn't a good word to say for her exhusband, but when I said he might have been kidnapped and shot, she softened up. Became quite helpful, in fact, and asked us to let her know if we found him."

Theo walked over to the window and drew up the blind. "Come over here, Mrs. B," he said. "Just look at that glorious sunset. It's just possible Gus Halfhide is on the other side of the world enjoying a fantastic sunrise coming up on his horizon. More things in heaven and earth, Deirdre love."

"I have no idea what you're talking about, Theo," she said, taking his arm.

"No matter," he said, not all that sure himself. He turned her round from the window, and suggested they go upstairs, where he would explain everything.

Except how to find Gus, Deirdre thought, and followed him slowly up the stairs.

IN THEIR PRISTINE, soulless house, the Evanses were clearing up after lunch. Trevor was taking the afternoon off, planning to work over the weekend to see if he could force a few sales.

"Do you fancy going to the Friday market this afternoon? We might pick up some fresh veg at half the price of the supermarket," Bronwen said. She had decided to warm up her relationship with Trevor. It had been sorely tested since she had failed to persuade her mother to lend them money. Now they scarcely spoke to each other, and she needed to talk to somebody. Her sister had been distinctly cool, and her mother was taking refuge behind the wretched Spurling woman.

Bronwen was feeling lonely, and, she had to admit, along with losing her job she had lost a sizable amount of self-confidence. Trevor had changed, too, and now that she wasn't bringing money into the household kitty, he had been treating her like an unwelcome dependent. She would not be at all surprised if he suggested divorce. Would she miss him? She had considered it a number of times, when she had discovered his lies and secret assignations. But what else was there in her life? Only one other preoccupation, and that was now under threat.

"The market? Is that what we've come to?" answered Trevor, not taking his eyes from a tired-looking quiz show host going through the motions with obvious boredom.

"What do you mean? Other people swear by the fruit and vegetable stall. Much fresher and all local, instead of the stuff supermarkets import from God knows where."

"Can you see me with a shopping basket over my arm, bargaining with some ignorant stallholder in Thornwell market, where I might bump into any of my clients. I do have an image to maintain, Bronwen. I am aware that yours has crashed, but all the more reason why I should continue to be the best estate agent in town. No, no, no. You go, if you want to. Mingle with the peasants, by all means. This afternoon I'm having a well-earned rest, and for the rest of the weekend I shall be busy selling houses, with any luck, and bringing in at least enough to keep us in fruit and vegetables, from wherever you choose to buy them. And now," he added, turning up the sound, "can I be left to enjoy the telly in peace?"

Bronwen said nothing. She got up from her chair and left the room. Upstairs in their bedroom she put a small overnight bag on the bed and threw some clothes into it.

Then she scribbled a note and put it on the dressing table, picked up the bag and her waterproof coat and crept down the stairs and out of the door without disturbing Trevor, who, she could see through the open door, had gone to sleep with his mouth open and the television blaring out, covering her departure.

Twenty-seven

SOON AFTER BRONWEN had left home, a warning light winked on her dashboard, signalling that she was running low on petrol. "Blast!" she cursed. She had not planned on filling up for another week, when her bank balance would be a little healthier with income from a small investment. It would have to be a credit card, and she prayed that she was not over her limit.

She headed out of town and stopped at the next filling station. She held her breath as the card went through the machine. Approved, thank goodness. As she walked back to her car it suddenly struck her that this was how a lot of people lived all the time, up to their ears in debt and living on yet more credit whenever they could. No wonder some women turned to shoplifting! She found herself wondering what would happen if after she had filled up, she just drove away without paying,

Turning into the side road that would take her to the village of Measby, near Oakbridge, she began to relax. She would stay away for a couple of nights and then return to Trevor, hoping he had been sufficiently alarmed to think again about the way he was treating her. If not, well, that would be that, and as she thought about her future, she quite fancied the idea of a completely new start.

The house was not in the village itself, but down a rutted track and set amongst a cluster of ruined barns, too small to be used for modern farming equipment. It had previously been rented by an artist with a taste for solitude and a love of crumbling relics of the old farming ways. But he had soon had enough of rural delights, and disappeared without paying the rent.

The house had not stood empty for long. The low rent had attracted tenants in no time, and as Bronwen bumped along over the ruts she wished they had chosen somewhere more accessible. She knocked several times at the front door, and then trudged round the back through scratchy brambles and high grass. Still no reply. She had not bargained for this, and returned to her car. The sun had warmed the interior, and she leaned back in her seat, closed her eyes and considered what to do next. Now that they weren't here, she realised that asking for help from them would have been a stupid mistake. She must have been desperate even to think of it.

She was about to drive off, when she heard a dog barking loudly. It was too late to make a getaway, and she sought rapidly for an excuse for being here. But it was not them returning. It was a man with a gun and a growling Labrador wearing a muzzle.

"Gone away," he said abruptly.

"What, for good?" Bronwen said anxiously.

"No. They said they'd be back in a few days, maybe a week. Shall I give them a message?"

"No, no thanks," Bronwen said. "I'll catch up later. Thanks," she repeated, and drove back slowly over the ruts to the road, where she turned to go back to Thornwell and Trevor.

It had certainly been a silly idea. Those two could not possibly have helped her. She could see that now, and tried to order her thoughts and come up with a more sensible plan. Best to go back home, think of some convincing explanation for the note and the overnight bag, and try another approach.

It proved to be easy. As Bronwen went quietly through the back door into the kitchen, she heard the familiar blaring sound of the teatime soap opera. She went through the hall and peered into the sitting room. Trevor was where she had left him, head lolling back, mouth open and snoring for England.

She turned and went upstairs, screwed up the note and flushed it down the lavatory and then unpacked the bag, returning her clothes and toothbrush to their proper places. Then she walked slowly downstairs and into the kitchen, where she filled the kettle as tears streamed down her cheeks.

ALWEN JONES, HAPPILY unaware of her daughter's misery, joined Ivy and Roy after supper for a game of pontoon in the lounge. Without Deirdre and Gus, they could easily pass a quiet hour or so before bedtime in there without disturbing the other residents. In the event, it was another resident who disturbed them. A piercing shriek came from upstairs, just as Roy was dealing out the cards.

"What on earth?" Alwen said. "Where's Pinkers? Mrs. Spurling went home hours ago."

Then Katya rushed in and up to Ivy. "Miss Beasley! I must go quickly to attend to Mrs. Worth, and please will you come with me as I know she likes you and you can calm her down. I cannot find Miss Pinkney anywhere. I expect it is another of Mrs. Worth's nightscares."

"Not the right word," Ivy said calmly, "but quite a good alternative. Come along then, lead the way."

Mrs. Worth had slid from her pile of pillows and her head was half-submerged. She was still screaming and shouting. Katya and a care assistant who had joined them heaved the old lady back until she was resting comfortably once more.

"There we are," said Ivy, in her best attempt at a motherly

voice. "Now tell Ivy what you were dreaming about? Nasty dream, was it?"

The old lady stared at her. "Who are you?" she said suspiciously. "Are you the one that flirted with my Joe? I'll soon put a stop to your nonsense!"

"No, I'm not that one," Ivy said through gritted teeth. "I live here at Springfields. I'm your friend. Tell me why you were so upset."

Mrs. Worth looked at her craftily out of the corner of her eye. "What's it to you?" she muttered.

Ivy turned to Katya. "I'm doing no good here," she said, and walked towards the door. Katya nodded, and dismissed the care attendant. "I'll stay with her for a bit, thank you, Miss Beasley. I expect she'll soon go back to sleep."

Ivy was halfway down the corridor when the office telephone began to ring. Katya came flying out and called her back. "I must answer that," she said. "Would you mind, Miss Beasley? Just until she's gone back to sleep?"

Ivy sighed and went back into Mrs. Worth's room. She sat on a chair beside the bed and looked the old lady straight in the eye. "Now then," she said. "I haven't got time to listen to your rubbish. You don't fool me. I bet you were one of them women who always demand attention. I feel sorry for your husband Joe. Probably waited on you hand and foot."

Mrs. Worth's chin quivered. "My Joe brought me Juicy Jellies every Friday," she said defiantly.

"Poor man," said Ivy dismissively. "Now, do you want to tell me about your nightmare, if there was one, or shall I go and get on with my card game? My friends are waiting for me."

Mrs. Worth frowned. "You can bugger off, if you like," she squeaked. "You'll not be missed. And anyway, I did have a nightmare an' it was the one I always have. My Joe had toppled into the beer an' he was drowning. That daughter of Mr. William's was standing there, laughing her head off, pushing him under when he tried to get out. Can't remember her name. Works at the brewery. So there, Miss Ivy Beasley, put that in yer pipe and smoke it!"

"Did he get out?" said Ivy matter-of-factly.

"I always wake up before I find out," Mrs. Worth replied. "But I seen her again, that girl. Can't tell you where or when," and she broke into a cracked singing voice, " 'but I know we'll meet again some sunny day!' "

"My Dad used to sing that," Ivy said. She reached forward and patted the old lady's hand. "Go to sleep now, gel. You won't have no more nightmares."

It was as if someone had switched off a light. Mrs. Worth's head fell to one side on her pillow and her eyes shut tight. As Ivy tiptoed out of the room, she heard a muttering and stopped.

"He did, my Joe did bring me Juicy Jellies every Friday, he did." Mrs. Worth's voice tailed off into silence, and Ivy retreated softly along the corridor and down the stairs to rejoin the pontoon players.

"And one for his nob," said Roy triumphantly, counting up his score. "First time I've won against you two. Ivy, you were miles away, and Alwen's half-asleep. Pity Gus is not here to keep the pair of you concentrating on the game."

"Sorry," Ivy said, frowning. "It's just something Mrs. Worth said. Keeps going round and round in my head. I'll tell you later, Roy, when we have our bedtime hot drink."

Alwen looked at her suspiciously. "Why not now, Ivy?" she said. It was more than likely something to do with Gus's disappearance.

"Shall we play some more, or watch the telly?" Roy could see that things would not improve with his gambling companions. Alwen yawned widely, and Ivy shuffled the cards and began to put them back in their case.

"I think I shall go up to my room," Alwen said. "I can't keep awake this evening. Must be all that teaching and running about after the children."

Ivy stared at her. "Are you all right?" she said. Alwen's eyes looked watery, more than usual.

"Yes. Just joking," she replied with a sniff. "I'll say good night. Good night, Roy. Good night, Ivy. See you tomorrow."

Ivy and Roy watched her limp away, and were silent for a minute or two. Then Roy said, "Poor old thing. Must be grim for her after such a busy life."

"Huh!" said Ivy. "Life is what you make it, Roy. We could all feel sorry for ourselves in here. But you don't and I don't, and even Mrs. Worth doesn't. She's an old schemer, you know. All that shouting. Just to get some attention. Well, I told her straight."

"What was it she said that goes round and round in your head?" Roy said.

"She was having a nightmare, she said, and it was something about her husband working at the brewery. She mentioned William's girl. Now, who was that, I wonder?"

"We don't need a Horlicks to think this one out," Roy said. "It was Bronwen, of course. Come on, let's retire to your room and have a brainstorming session, as Gus would say."

"If only he was here," said Ivy.

Twenty-eight

ALWEN HAD DOZED off after her morning coffee, sitting in the best and most popular armchair in the lounge. She awoke with a start when Katya gently touched her arm.

"Mrs. Wilson Jones? It is only me, Katya. Take your time."

"What is it? Where is he?" Alwen looked wildly round the room.

"It is just a telephone call for you. Shall I ask the caller to ring back?"

Alwen began to shiver. "No, no. Give me a minute, and I'll come. But I will take it upstairs in my room, if you could give me a hand, my dear."

Katya dashed out to tell the caller to hold on for a few minutes, but the hoarse voice said he couldn't wait, and could she please remind Mrs. Jones that it was Saturday, and midnight was the time. Then he rang off. Katya frowned at this strange message, and went back to tell Alwen Jones. Alwen was already on her feet, and Katya was aware that she was much more wobbly than usual. She was also aware that other residents were poised at the ready to take over the vacated chair.

"He couldn't wait, I'm afraid, Mrs. Wilson Jones," she said. "I am so sorry. Perhaps it would be good if you asked your daughter to obtain a mobile telephone for you?"

"Oh. Right. I'm sure it was nothing important." Alwen sank back into her chair, breathing hard, and three disappointed ladies muttered about some new residents being much too pushy.

"I am to give you a message," Katya continued. "The caller asked me to remind you that it was Saturday and the time was midnight. I think he must have been mistaken, because it is certainly not midnight! I was about to tell him it was only half past eleven in the morning when he ended the call."

Ivy had heard the telephone ringing in Alwen's room as she and Roy came downstairs. When they entered the lounge she went straight over to where Alwen sat with her eyes closed. "Did you take that call, Alwen?" she said.

"No, he left a message," Alwen replied, still with her eyes closed. "It was a reminder that the deadline is midnight tonight. Where on earth is Deirdre Bloxham? She should be here."

"As a matter of fact, she told me she thought she would go over to Measby, as she has every right to do," said Ivy defensively. "The poor girl is more worried about Gus than she lets on, and wanted something to take her mind off what might have happened to him. A preliminary recce, she said, might be useful to us." Nobody but she was allowed to criticise her cousin, and that included Alwen Jones. "And anyway," she continued, "she promised to be back well before deadline time. I must say I begin to think the threat is an empty one. If you ask me, we are up against a small operation, maybe just one man. And if he's after money, and that's all, he won't gain anything by doing away with Gus. What d'you think, Roy?"

"Well, I'm sure you're right, Ivy, but I do think we should try to get hold of Deirdre, just in case."

"In case of what?"

"Well, that's the problem, isn't it," he said mildly. "We are rather stuck here, and there's very little we can do."

"I've got my mobile. If you think I should get hold of Deirdre, I could try that?"

"Well done, Ivy," Roy said.

"It's in my drawer upstairs. I'll make a call up there. There are too many nosy old biddies in here to be private."

"It's Ivy's birthday tomorrow," Roy said, when she had gone. "Deirdre's getting something special for me to give her. I do hope she will like it and not think I am taking a liberty."

He's soft on Ivy, thought Alwen. How blind the old fellow must be! Still, there was no telling about men, she reflected, no matter how old they were.

"Are you going to let me into the secret? What is the present for Ivy?" she asked.

Roy shook his head. "I thought everyone knew, except Ivy," he said. "Never mind, you'll see tomorrow."

He could see from the expression on Ivy's face as she returned that she had had no luck talking to Deirdre. He looked at his watch. Nearly twelve hours to go. He had a sudden mental picture of Gus, his wispy hair standing up on end as he roared with laughter at one of Ivy's best quips. Roy was not a religious man, but thinking it worth a try, he said a small, silent prayer for Gus's safety.

DEIRDRE FELT HER mobile vibrate, but by the time she had it in her hand, it had lost the signal, and she put it back in her pocket. She had parked her car outside the village shop in Measby, and now stood looking in the window. This was taken up largely by notices of items for sale, dog-walking services, baby-minding and house-cleaning contacts. There were fixture dates for the junior football team, and an offer of six ducklings, free to a good home.

Not much help, thought Deirdre, but then she saw a small piece of paper pinned to the corner of a noticeboard.

The writing was in red pen, and it offered a cottage for sale, due to family bereavement. "Needs a lot of work on it," it said. Not estate-agent-speak, then. It was signed "Doris May Osborne," with a telephone contact number.

Deirdre made a note in her address book, and then walked up the steps into the shop.

"Yes?" A burly old man with crooked spectacles and thinning hair looked at her suspiciously.

"Um, have you got any Green and Black chocolate?" Deirdre asked, knowing before he answered that it was extremely unlikely.

He looked at her suspiciously. "Are you anything to do with Mrs. Osborne?" he said.

"Never heard of her," said Deirdre briskly. "Why do you ask? Has it anything to do with chocolate?" She was beginning to feel irritated with this unsavoury character.

"As a matter of fact," he said portentously, "it has. Mrs. Osborne is my boss, and she is the only one in our village who asks for that particular brand of chocolate. I get it in specially for her. And that's why I asked."

"Well, do you think you could bring yourself to sell a bar of it to me?" said Deirdre, wondering why she didn't just walk out. But she needed to check on Doris May Osborne, and wondered if she and the old man's boss were one and the same person.

Grudgingly, the old man reached under the counter and brought out a chocolate bar which he slapped down in front of Deirdre. "That's the last one," he lied. "Was that all you want?"

"No, not quite," said Deirdre. "I'm interested in the cottage for sale. I saw the notice in the window."

The change was remarkable. At once half a head taller, and with a leery smile on his pale face, the old man said that he might be able to help her on that one. His boss Doris May was at this moment out in the back room looking at the accounts. Without delay, as if Deirdre might change her mind and vanish from the shop, he called in a loud, anxious voice, "Mrs. Osborne! Can you come through, please?"

Doris May was a surprise. She was small and trim, with well-cut hair and neat pearl earrings. Her navy blue coat and skirt were clearly expensive, and as she approached, Deirdre caught a whiff of the exclusive scent that she used herself. There was nothing flashy about her, but Deirdre recognised the signs of money and good taste.

"Yes? Can I help?" Doris said coolly.

Deirdre answered, "I've seen the notice in the window about a cottage for sale. Can you tell me a bit more about it?"

"Are you looking to buy a cottage in this village?" Doris May enquired.

"Might be," said Deirdre.

"I suppose I could show it to you, then."

It was an attractive village, with ornamental plasterwork on some of the houses, painted all shades of Suffolk pink and other not so traditional colours. Doris May looked at the parked Rolls, and asked if was Deirdre's. On hearing that it was, and being told Deirdre's name, she chatted in a more friendly fashion, every now and then asking a personal question about Deirdre herself.

The cottage was clearly a wreck. Tiles were missing from the roof, windows cracked and broken, paint peeling from the front door, which was stuck fast. Doris May had not bothered with a key, explaining that nobody would want to go in. Then she put her small shoulder to the door and with surprising strength gave an almighty shove, and it creaked open.

"Not frightened of spiders and mice, I hope?" she said, and Deirdre swallowed. She was actually frightened of both, but would not admit it to this confident little woman.

"How long since anyone lived here?" she asked.

"About six months, I suppose. There's still some furniture, but it's all rubbish."

As they walked carefully through the detritus which can collect in a house that has been empty for months, especially in one never locked, Deirdre noticed some interesting items. In the main room, an old desk stood by the window. On it, she saw a well-thumbed book and picked it up, puffing off an evil-smelling cloud of dust. The cover was discoloured, and so blotched with damp that she could scarcely read the title. *Profes—al Gamb—rs H—book Beating the Sys—m by Hook and by Crook*. The author's name, which surely could not be his real one, was Weasel Murphy.

A gamblers' handbook? And not just a moral pamphlet on the evils of gambling for amateurs, but what looked like a how-to-do-it book for the professional. Must tell Gus about this, she thought, and then remembered there might not be a Gus to tell.

She looked at her watch, and saw that it was not long before the deadline expired, and her plan might have to be put into operation. She had to get back soon to have a word with Alwen Jones, and looking round, saw that Doris May had rounded the corner halfway up the narrow stairs. She quickly slipped the book into her handbag, zipped it up and followed her guide upstairs.

"Who lived here before?" she asked, as they inspected the two bedrooms and totally unacceptable bathroom. A streak of rust led from a tap to the plug hole, and spiders had woven an intricate web from one side to another. The lavatory had no seat, and no water in the pan. Deirdre gulped, and said she thought she must go now, as she was running short of time.

"You asked me who lived here before," Doris May said doubtfully. "It was very unpleasant. Did you hear about it?"

Deirde said no, she had heard nothing, and concentrated hard on not throwing up as she continued on her way downstairs.

Unaware of Deirdre's discomfort, Doris May continued. "An old man. He was found dead at the foot of his stairs, blood everywhere. At least, they thought it was blood. It's all been cleaned away now, of course."

Deirdre fled. Once out in the garden, she apologised, and said she was a little squeamish. Gathering her wits, she asked if there was any doubt about the cause of death.

Doris May did not answer but said sharply that she

guessed Mrs. Bloxham would not be interested in buying, after all.

"Well, I'm not sure about that," Deirdre said, her colour returning. "I would like to bring a friend with me and have another look?"

"If you like," said Doris May. "But I wouldn't advise it."

"Where do you live, then?" asked Deirdre.

"Measby Manor. Over there, behind the trees. It is private land," she added, and walked away smartly towards the church. As she went, Deirdre saw her take something out of her pocket and hold it to her ear. Now who was Doris May so keen to talk to?

Twenty-nine

GUS WAS NOW very hungry. For some reason, he supposed to keep him alive, Margaret had kept him supplied with a minimum amount of water. He was now hallucinating with images of sausages and bacon, toast and coffee frequently before his eyes. Café smells added to his yawing stomach pains. But he had been through all this before, and he knew he could hang on for a while longer.

He was still trying to work out exactly why they were holding him. Ransom money, of course. Possibly they had been in touch with the real Martin and were threatening to extract valuable secrets from their prisoner and sell them to interested parties, unless the department paid up. What a waste of time, and possibly his life! He no longer held any secret information of any value to anyone, and none of his former colleagues would pay tuppence to save him. He had broken his silence to tell his captors this, but they did not believe him. In fact, they had shown very little interest in the real Martin.

"Spicy chicken for lunch," said Margaret, coming silently into the semidarkness. She carried a jug of water, and half filled his glass. "Can I order some for you?"

He did not answer. He could see that she was losing patience with his silence, and this was just what he wanted. She began to pace around, saying that if he was sensible and answered their questions, and provided his chums came up with the lolly, he could have all the food he wanted and walk free. One other important condition would be that he gave no information about who had held him, or where he had been held. They would know if he talked, and the consequences would be dire, if not fatal.

Who did she mean by chums? He said nothing. She raised her voice. "For God's sake, man!" she shouted. "What have you got to lose? Do you want us to pull your fingernails out? Okay, okay, I know that's stupid, but we do have other, more uncomfortable ways of getting you to talk. I like you, Gus! *Please*, don't make us do that. . . ."

He still said nothing but could sense that she was weakening. He did not have to pretend to feel giddy. Objects, including Margaret, began to shimmer and waver, and he sat down heavily on the camp bed.

She looked hard at him. "All right. I'll get you something to eat, but for God's sake don't tell Max. He'll kill me. Literally, Gus. Hang on, and I'll be back in a few minutes."

He watched her leave, and saw that in her anxiety about her rash decision, she had pulled the door shut, relying only on the Yale lock to keep him safely imprisoned.

He moved like a streak of lightning, and could hardly believe his luck. Like everything else in the room, the lock was damp and rusty, and the lever had stuck.

Out on the landing, he hesitated. He could hear animated voices speaking in a foreign tongue in the café, and knew it would be useless to try getting out that way. In desperation, he headed towards the back of the building, down rickety stairs, and found himself in the cluttered backyard he had seen from his window. He ducked down and sped past a kitchen window, finally clearing a low wall and finding himself in the busy street outside the café.

He turned and ran for his life down the street. He was soon breathless and knew that a sustained chase would eventually catch him, so he entered the first of the many small hotels in the area, and secured himself a room under a false name. He asked that he should not be disturbed, and the burly receptionist winked at him, and said, "No questions asked, mate. You look done in. Best get some rest." Then the reception telephone rang, and he answered, directing Gus to go on upstairs to his room. This he did gratefully, and collapsed on to a clean, neatly made bed, breathing hard.

DEIRDRE WAS ON her way back from Measby. It was lunchtime, but she was not hungry, and headed for Spring-fields, where she could get handover details of the black-mailer from Alwen Jones. The silly woman had been cagey about this, reluctant even, but Deirdre was certain she had details, and probably knew more than she had told the others. For a start, why hadn't *she* gone to the police?

But Deirdre was not concerned with that now. She had already arranged for the ransom money to be available, and, if all else failed, had decided without a qualm to pay for the release of Augustus Halfhide.

A tiny rabbit ran in front of her car, and she braked hard, coming to a standstill while it leapt into the verge. At that moment, her mobile chimed. Her heart raced as she put it to her ear.

"Deirdre? Gus here. Don't say anything. Just listen. Do not pay the ransom, not on any account. And for God's sake don't go to the police. It won't help, and could mean danger for us all. I shall be—" The phone was disconnected, but not until Deidre heard raised voices and the sound of distant traffic.

She was shaking violently but immediately dialled for the number of the latest incoming call. An infuriating woman's voice said, "The caller withheld their number," and Deirdre slammed her mobile down on the seat beside her, and drove slowly forward. Gus must have had a few minutes' freedom and found a telephone. That wretched automatic message was just bad luck.

So she must not hand over money. It wouldn't help, he had said. What else was he going to say, before his kidnappers had caught up with him? And what would they have done to him now as a result?

So, first to Springfields, and then back home to think.

"WHAT THE BLOODY hell did you think you were doing?" Max said to Margaret as they sat in a waiting room at Liverpool Street station. They had no wish to be recognised, and it was an often-proved strategy with them that there was nowhere safer to hide than amongst an ever-moving crowd.

"I'm sorry. I don't know what else I can say. I felt sorry for him—I know, I know!—and I must have forgotten to do all the locks while I went to get him something to eat. Only bread and water, Max, only bread and water."

"I suppose you realise we'd have been in deep ordure with the boss if our friendly hotel receptionist had not tipped us the wink?"

"Gus had hardly finished dialling," she lied. "In any case, the hotel had one of those 'number withheld' messages, so Bernie said. I snatched the phone from Gus, and we grabbed him. No problem about holding on to him. Bernie's not lost his bouncer's skill. So Gus is safely back in his own little room again."

"I'll strangle him with my bare hands if he doesn't talk soon," Max said angrily. He looked at his watch. "Time for a last call to the old folks' home. So let's hope we're about to find out what needle-sharp Enquire Within are up to, and make a bob or two in the process. But for God's sake, don't feel sorry for him again, else you'll foul up everything, and then I can't answer for the consequences."

He took up his mobile and dialled a now familiar number.

* * *

"SIT DOWN, DEIRDRE, do! You're all of a do-dah," Ivy said firmly. "I'll get some coffee sent up."

"Not just for a minute, thanks, Ivy," Deirdre said, slumping down heavily. After several false starts, she gave as cool an account as she could manage of Gus's call.

"He's alive, then," said Ivy matter-of-factly. "And we're not to pay the ransom money. Mind you, Deirdre, I had no idea that you were even thinking of doing that. Was it wise?"

"Yes, Ivy, it was. Because we can't get the police onto it or else Gus's life, and maybe one of ours, will be in danger. So how could I ever forgive myself, knowing that I had money in the bank, and if we never saw Gus again, and . . . and . . ."

". . . and he was murdered?"

Deirdre nodded miserably. "Oh, Ivy, what are we going to do?"

"First of all, we find Roy and Alwen . . . well, maybe not Alwen . . . and you can tell us exactly what you found out at Measby. That was where you went, wasn't it?"

When Roy was sitting comfortably in his chair, and Deirdre had perched on the edge of Ivy's bed, the Measby story was told in a much more leisurely fashion, and at the end of her report, Deirdre took out the gambling book and put it on Ivy's bedside table.

"There we are," she said. "Bedtime reading for you, Ivy."

"Where on earth did you get that? And what is it, anyway?" Ivy said.

Roy picked it up. "Gambling Handbook," he read, and began to leaf through it. "Great Scott! This is hot stuff, Ivy. Better not read this, girls, else I shall have no chance at the pontoon table!"

"I have no intention of reading it," Ivy said, handing it back to Deirdre. "But it might be important. Well done, Deirdre. It might help us to make sense of some odd things we already know. An old man died in that cottage, possibly with blackmail involved. Full stop. Then there's Alwen. I don't believe she got that twenty thousand back, and nor do you, Roy."

"If she ever lost it," said Roy quietly.

At that moment, there was a tap at the door and Alwen Jones poked her head round, asking in a trembling voice if she could come in.

Ivy sighed. "This is one of them days," she said wearily. "Come in and tell us what you want. There's nowhere to sit, but you can perch next to Deirdre if you like. It's only my bed, and fortunately I sleep the sleep of the just, rumpled or not."

Alwen perched. Then, as the others were all waiting expectantly, she said that she had had another anonymous call. Same man, same hoarse voice. He warned that the deadline was very soon, and then gave her an address where he said she must take the money. If not, he had said, Gus Halfhide would be extinguished. Never heard of again, he said. And no good telling the police, he repeated several times. He would know, and nobody would be at the address. But Gus would be no more."

She looked anxiously at the others, and Deirdre put her arm around Alwen's shoulders, comforting her with an edited version of her conversation with Gus.

"Pull yourself together, Alwen," Ivy said, quite kindly. "We have to come to a decision now. Does one of us go to the collection address, or do we call the police right away?"

"Not the police, Ivy! No, I think we do as Gus said," Deirdre said slowly. "That is, do nothing, and wait to see what happens?"

The silence seemed to go on for hours. Then Alwen rose to her feet and seemed quite agile now. She took a deep breath. "I suggest we do nothing," she said. "That is, *you* do nothing, and I go to get some advice from my daughter, right now. I can order a taxi."

"How will that help?" said Deirdre, still undecided whether to do nothing or pay up, whatever the others said. She had noticed Alwen Jones's quick recovery from collapse, and began to wonder if she was maybe a really good actress?

"I can't tell you that," answered Alwen. "I can only ask you to trust that what I am going to do will be for the best."

"The best for who?" said Ivy suspiciously.

"All of us," Alwen said. "But chiefly for Gus. It is his best chance."

"Go on then," Ivy said. "But come straight back and tell us what's happening. And don't look like that, Deirdre," she added. "There'll still be plenty of time to meet the deadline, if necessary."

Thirty

THE TAXI ARRIVED half an hour later, and Alwen Jones left word with Miss Pinkney that she would be out for an hour or two but would get back in time for supper. She had decided not to warn Bronwen that she would be arriving to see her, as almost certainly her daughter would invent a reason why she would unfortunately not be at home.

As the taxi drew up outside their house, Alwen could see two cars in the drive and knew that both Bronwen and Trevor were at home. Good, she thought, and hoped it was a good omen for the rest of her mission.

The front door opened, and Bronwen stood there, looking alarmed.

"Mother! How lovely to see you! But is everything all right?"

"Ye Gods," muttered Trevor behind her. "Don't say she's coming to live with us! Has she got any luggage? Why did I come home for those papers?"

Alwen limped up to the door and said briskly that she

had come to see them about an important matter, and could she please come in. And she could do with a cup of tea, she added.

"Now then," she began, tea on a side table and Bronwen and Trevor facing her. "This is an urgent request, and if you can help me, as I know you can, I shall show my gratitude in due course by giving you—Bronwen, that is—the financial support I know you need until things look up for you both." She looked Trevor in the eye, and said, "I'm no fool, Trevor Evans, and it will be in your interests to make sure your marriage survives."

Bronwen and Trevor glanced quickly at each other, and then Bronwen said that if she could help her mother in any way, of course she would be delighted to do so.

"I thought you might," said Alwen drily. "Right. Trevor, you can go now, out of earshot, please. And Bronwen, listen closely to what I have to say, and don't interrupt. This is an important matter for us and for several other people I care about."

DEIRDRE HAD REMAINED in an uncertain frame of mind. Now it seemed they were all trusting Alwen Jones to work a miracle. This was nonsense, of course. That cagey old woman would do exactly what suited her, and Deirdre had no faith in her ability to save Gus, nor did she think Alwen cared a fig what happened to him.

She had noticed that if neither Roy nor Ivy were in the lounge, Alwen always sat alone, not talking to any of the other residents. Too superior by half! Then why had she come to Springfields in the first place? Of course, it didn't take much to see that neither of her daughters visited more than duty required. And Enquire Within should not forget that the mysterious brewer William had left her to bring up their two children, never to return. Alwen had been a schoolteacher, Deirdre recalled, and they were renowned for treating their own families like wayward children. A difficult woman to live with, then? And possibly rather a chilly mother, coping on her own.

And what was the miracle that a mere conversation with daughter Bronwen—she presumed it was Bronwen—could work?

Thirty-one

THE HOURS DRAGGED by, and Deirdre had not been able to settle to anything. In the end, she decided to return to Springfields and wait out the time with Ivy and Roy. For once, she didn't care whether her jacket matched her skirt, and she grabbed the nearest on her way to the front door.

She found Roy and Ivy watching television in Ivy's room, and they turned in surprise as she came in. Ivy took one look at her face and said kindly, "Sit down, Deirdre." They watched the end of the programme and then switched off. Before they needed to find some topic of conversation that wasn't the incarcerated Gus, there was a feeble knock at the door and in came Alwen Jones, stern-faced and with such a weary limp that Roy struggled to his feet to help her, forgetting that he needed a helping hand himself. In the end, it was Ivy who found the strength to take Alwen's arm and settle her next to Deirdre, who was looking anxiously at her watch.

"Well? What's the miracle answer?" she said. "Is Gus going to be released? Is he safe? And what about the ransom?"

"Let the poor woman draw breath," Roy chided. "You can see she's exhausted. Deirdre, you could call for Katya to bring us a hot drink."

"We've had our hot drinks," said Ivy. "Doubt if the budget will run to a second. Now, Alwen," she added, "get it off your chest, whatever it is. Deirdre has decisions to make."

"Right," said Alwen, pulling herself upright and speaking as if she was addressing an unruly class of mixed infants. "Now listen carefully. You are going to have to take me on trust again. I can tell you only that Gus will be all right. He won't necessarily be released just yet, but neither will anything bad happen to him. I can guarantee that. I have sufficient influence over events to set your minds at rest on that. As for the rest, I shall be as anxious as you to have the whole thing cleared up, anonymous phone calls and all."

"What about the ransom?" Deirdre's face was white, and Ivy saw her fists clenching and unclenching. Poor Deirdre, she thought. She loves him, silly girl.

Alwen shook her head. "No need. Final details to be worked out, but the ransom will be paid."

"So where do we go from here?" Ivy said. "And why on earth should we trust you, when so far we don't believe a word you've said about getting your twenty thousand back, nor a lot of that stuff about bungee jumping and your ex-husband."

Roy groaned softly. Straight in with both feet, he thought. Had Ivy blown the whole thing?

Alwen stared at her, and passed a weary hand over her eyes. "Believe what you like, Ivy, but what I have said about Gus is the truth. The ransom will be paid and he will be released, but it will take a short while to sort everything out. I can only suggest you take a vote between you, and then Deirdre will either accept it or not. I have done my best," she added, "and now I'm off to bed. I shall see you in the morning. Good night."

Silence fell, and Deirdre slumped back into a chair.

Finally Ivy said that if anyone asked her, she would say taking a vote was a good idea. Or, if not a good idea, at least it was better than any other she could think of.

"She wasn't going to tell us the address for the ransom, anyway," Roy said. "So what do you say, Deirdre?"

"Take a vote," muttered Deirdre reluctantly.

Ivy got to her feet and faced the other two. "Right," she said, "those in favour of accepting what Alwen said, and not doing anything rash at the moment?"

Roy put up his hand, and very slowly Deirdre followed. "That's it then," Ivy said. "And now, as acting chairman, I suggest Enquire Within retires to bed and awaits further developments."

Roy smiled fondly at her, and said she must concentrate on getting her beauty sleep, because he hadn't forgotten that tomorrow was a special day, a birthday day, and plans were laid to make sure she would enjoy it, especially now that reprieve for Gus looked likely.

Thirty-two

ROY WAS UP with the lark, to the amazement of Mrs. Spurling, who was sitting behind her desk filing her nails in the office. She always did this job early Sunday mornings, sure that she would not be interrupted, and could look at her e-mails at the same time.

When she saw Roy approaching, she quickly slipped the file into her drawer, and picked up a pen. That was one good thing about being in charge of a bunch of oldies, she thought. None of them could move fast enough to catch her unawares. She was wrong, of course.

"Have you got it?" Roy said, peering anxiously round the office door.

"Certainly have, Mr. Goodman," she answered, with as much warmth in her voice as she could manage when dealing with a project of which she heartily disapproved. She noticed that Roy was dressed in his new jacket, with a snowy white handkerchief folded neatly in his breast pocket.

"I thought after breakfast would be the best time," he said. "We can gather in the lounge. Mrs. Bloxham has promised to come up about half past nine, and we can look at cards and open presents before church. Ivy is determined to go this morning. I tried to persuade her that the Almighty would be sure to wish her a happy birthday, without her having to go to church to listen for it."

Mrs. Spurling could not help smiling. "What did she say to that?" she asked.

"Told me not to be blasphemous, and said that if anyone asked her, she would say that she had so much to be thankful for already, without presents, and wanted to go to His house and say thank you to her Maker. An answer for everything, our Ivy!"

"Well, let's hope she is thankful for this one." Mrs. Spurling looked towards the corner of the office, and said that she would stand by the lounge door and wait for Roy to give her a signal to bring it in. "Probably best to leave it until the last," she said.

To Ivy's surprise, Alwen turned up for breakfast, still pale and slow, but with a big smile and a quavery version of "Happy Birthday to You" as she sat down.

"That's very nice, and by the way, we took your advice," said Ivy. She saw a look of relief cross Alwen's face, and added, "You could have had an extra hour in bed this morning, you know."

Alwen shook her head. "Can't miss such an important date," she said. "If I'm as tough as you at your age, Ivy, I shall be more than pleased."

"Never give up hope, Alwen, that's the secret," Roy said, checking that a certain small box was safely in his pocket. He looked fondly at Ivy. This birthday morning she had been persuaded to take great care with her appearance. Katya had coaxed her thick grey hair, usually confined under a net, to lift into feminine waves, and Ivy had selected her best dark blue dress with white collar and cuffs. Neat but not gaudy, she had said approvingly, looking at herself in the mirror.

A special breakfast had been prepared by Anya, and Katya set it down on the table with a flourish. She kissed Ivy on her cheek, wished her a happy day and lifted a silver cover from a dish which she had found at the back of a cupboard, tarnished with neglect, and hastily cleaned early this morning. Revealed were curly slices of bacon, perfectly poached eggs, sizzling small sausages and stuffed tomatoes topped with crunchy fried bread crumbs.

"Wow!" said Roy. "Our lovely Anya has done you proud, Ivy." He looked closely at her and saw her chin quivering. He patted her hand, and said, "Will you be mother and pour the tea, my dear? Katya will serve breakfast, I'm sure."

After they had left the dining room and were comfortably settled in their lounge corner, Katya—who should have been off duty but had turned up anyway—brought in a large washing basket full of presents wrapped in birthday paper, and a pile of cards. "You have many friends, Miss Beasley!" she said.

A good many of the cards had come from old friends in Round Ringford, and Ivy was visibly moved, muttering that she was glad she hadn't been forgotten. One of the cards wished her a happy Father's Day, and she roared with laughter on seeing the spidery writing. "It looks like old Ellen Biggs!" she said. "In her dotage, the old thing. I could have sworn she had gone before. Still, nice that she remembered the date."

At last the pile of wrapping paper had been removed, the cards were set up in a row along the tops of low bookshelves, and Mrs. Spurling had stationed herself by the door.

Ivy was very happy and cheerful, of course, but she had not missed the fact that there had been nothing from Roy. Ah well, she thought, perhaps his family didn't bother with birthdays much. Certainly her own mother and father had scarcely remembered hers, even when she was quite small.

She looked across at him, and was surprised to see him waving his hand towards the door. Then, to another chorus of "Happy Birthday to You," sung by all residents who could more or less remember the tune, Mrs. Spurling entered, carrying a neat basket with a lid. She handed it to Roy, and retreated.

He stood up, cleared his throat, and announced that there was one more present for Ivy, and it was from him, with—he hesitated—his best wishes. He put the basket down on her lap, and she stared at him, not daring to think what might be inside.

Finally, she twisted the fastener and gently opened the lid. And now she could not stem the tears as she lifted out a small black kitten, mewing in a tiny voice and looking straight at her with huge blue eyes in its heart-shaped face.

Everybody clapped hard, and several residents mopped their eyes. Mrs. Spurling signalled to Katya to fetch the coffee trolley, and Ivy took the kitten from the basket, cradled it in her arms and got to her feet.

"I . . . I . . ." she began, and then started again. "I am not usually lost for words," she said, and several people cheered. "But now I want to thank you all for a lovely start to my birthday, the best I can remember. And, of course, a special thank you to Roy, who has remembered how much I missed my Ringford cat. . . ." She paused, took a deep breath and then leaned forward to kiss Roy's cheek.

"Oh my God," whispered Mrs. Spurling to Katya, who was standing with her at the door, waiting to bring in coffee. "Look at his face! I reckon we shall have everybody in tears if this goes on much longer. Come on, wheel in the trolley."

"What will you call her, Ivy?" said Roy, beaming from ear to ear.

"Tiddles, of course," Ivy said. "That's a proper name for a kitty. I once knew a cat named Posy Moon, and the poor little thing looked permanently embarrassed. But Roy," she continued in a whisper and with a surreptitious look at Mrs. Spurling, "how on earth did you get permission for me to have a cat?"

"Not easily," he replied. "But Katya and I arranged a residents' petition. Only one person refused to sign it, and that was old Mrs. Worth, who's gaga anyway. The rest all voted for you to have Tiddles, so long as you make sure you house-train it so's it won't pee on their shoes."

"On their *shoes*?" said Alwen, who had been very quiet up to now.

Everybody laughed, and they did not notice that Alwen suddenly jerked around in her seat to look out of the window at the path leading to the road. Coffee was served all round, with plates of Katya's special cookies, and Ivy looked at her watch. "Soon have to get ready for church," she said.

"Not this morning, Ivy, I hope," said a voice from the door. They all stopped talking and stared. A tall, stringy figure with whispy hair blown in all directions by the strong breeze stood smiling at Ivy.

"Gus," she said, and walked slowly towards him. "What kept you?"

Thirty-three

GUS PUT HIS finger to his lips. "Shhh," he said. "I'll tell you later, Ivy. Pretend I've been on a mercy dash to a dying aunt in Outer Mongolia."

"A likely story!" Ivy replied. "Who's going to believe that? Anyway, come on in and have some coffee. You look terrible, if you don't mind my saying so. I'll get Katya to bring you something to eat. By the way, this is Tiddles."

Gus put out a finger and tickled the kitten behind its ear, and a ridiculously loud purr from the tiny creature made them both smile. Deirdre, sitting transfixed in her chair next to Alwen, watched Gus take Ivy's arm and escort her back to the birthday corner.

"Gus has just got back from an urgent trip abroad," Ivy said in a loud voice. "His poor old aunt kicked the bucket in, er . . . Cape Town, wasn't it, Gus?"

He nodded, and took a vacant chair next to Alwen. She looked at him without speaking, and he saw fear in her eyes. "It's all right," he said quietly. "No casualties."

Deirdre pulled herself up shakily. "If you'll excuse me, Ivy, I have to go outside and make a telephone call. I'll be back in a couple of minutes," she said. Twenty minutes later, she had still not returned.

"Do you think she is all right?" Alwen said.

"I'll go and check," Gus said. "She's probably trying to get through to someone on her mobile. The signal is useless in Barrington." He walked quickly out of the lounge, and Ivy watched him as he passed the window in the direction of the summer house.

DEIRDRE HAD BEEN sitting in a damp canvas chair, staring into space. Fallen leaves swirled about the neglected summer house, and the wind was chilly, but she was unaware of them. How had he escaped? And why had he not even looked at her?

"What's up, Deirdre?" Gus appeared from round the corner and took her hand, which was icy. "Aren't you pleased to see me?"

Deirdre came to life. "Of course I'm bloody well pleased to see you! But how did you do it?—and why ignore me when you did finally show up?"

"Answer to your first question, they let me go. And to the second, I have to keep up the old private, unemotional Halfhide image. Wasn't sure I could do that if I looked at you first. Sorry."

"Ah, there you are!" It was Mrs. Spurling, all smiles. "Do hurry back. We've persuaded Ivy not to go to church, and Miss Pinkney is going to lead us in singing our favourite hymns. Special requests from Ivy, of course."

"Right-o!" said Gus, taking Deirdre's hand. "We can't miss that, can we, Mrs. Bloxham?"

Deirdre stepped out onto the path, still holding Gus's hand, and said, "I bet I know what Ivy's first choice will be."

"'Abide with Me'?" suggested Mrs. Spurling. This was the hymn most familiar in her line of business. "'Rock of Ages'?"

"Nope," said Deirdre.

" 'Jesus Wants Me for a Sunbeam'?" Gus was having trouble keeping a straight face.

"Nope," answered Deirdre.

"What, then?"

" 'Onward Christian Soldiers,' I'm afraid."

AFTER ALL THE jollity, everyone was invited to stay for lunch and Alwen said she would retire for a siesta to her room. Roy said he thought Ivy should do the same, but she said that was rubbish, and she could not have felt more wide awake. She wanted Gus and Deirdre, and Roy himself, of course, to come up to her room.

"You haven't had my present yet," said Gus, when they were upstairs with small glasses of port—courtesy of Mrs. Spurling's private store—and a large box of chocolates.

He felt in his pocket, and drew out a small package. "Not much, I'm afraid, but I've been unable to get to the shops lately. I had this ready for you in the cottage, fortunately."

Ivy set down Tiddles, now fast asleep in a furry ball, on a cushion beside her, and unwrapped the parcel. "Oh, that's really thoughtful, Gus!" she said, and peered at it closely.

"Well, tell us what it is," said Deirdre impatiently.

"Here, have a look," Ivy said and handed it over.

"Nice little photo," Roy said, as Deirdre passed it to him. "Where is it?"

"Round Ringford," said Ivy. "And that's Victoria Villa, my home. And that's me standing outside, with my dear old Tiddles. She used to do that. Wrap her tail round my leg, I mean. Goodness me, Gus, where on earth did you get that?"

"Aha! I don't run a detective agency for nothing, Miss Beasley. Anyway, glad you like it."

"I like it very much," Ivy said. "And now perhaps you'd like to explain to us what's been happening to you. We've been worried sick, and Deirdre here was going to empty the bank to get you back."

"Sorry," Gus said. "I'm really sorry, but the only reason

I'm here now is because, I suspect, the ransom was paid in some way, and I gave my word I'd not say anything more than that I was unavoidably delayed. Naturally, my word meant nothing to them, and they threatened in a good old-fashioned kidnappers' way to wreak vengeance if I spilt the beans. Unfortunately, I think they meant it. And now, Ivy, I'm sure you'll understand that I need to get back to the cottage. I called in briefly to pick up your present, and rescue Whippy from Miriam Blake. But both were out walking. Should be back by now, and I . . . well, you know. . . ."

Deirdre said that they all understood, and would everybody like to come up to Tawny Wings for coffee tomorrow, and get back to normal business for Enquire Within, which could now go ahead with their leader at the helm.

"Meaning?" said Ivy.

"Gus, of course! Who else did you think I meant, Ivy?"

AFTER GUS AND Deirdre had gone, Roy lingered on in Ivy's room, and they chatted for a while, recalling magical moments in the day. Then silence fell, and Ivy looked at Roy. He was frowning, and he seemed to be fumbling again in his jacket pocket.

"Are you all right?" Ivy said anxiously. Had all the excitement been too much for him? She put out her hand, and he took it quickly. Then, to her alarm, he kissed it.

"Ivy," he said breathlessly, "dear Ivy."

"Are you sure you're all right?" asked Ivy, and now her heart had begun to pound.

"Never better," Roy said. "There's just one more thing I wanted to say on this day of days. May I say it, Ivy?"

Ivy was silent for what seemed to Roy like hours, and then she gave a small cough and said, "Nobody's stopping you."

This was such an unromantic answer, and so like his Ivy, that Roy chuckled. "I love you Ivy Beasley," he said. "I've never met anyone like you, and I thank my lucky stars that you came to live here. You've changed my life, my dear, and I just want to know whether you could consider changing yours, just a little?"

Ivy, back in charge of herself, said briskly, "Well, get on with it, Roy."

Now he produced the small box and opened it. A single and quite large diamond twinkled in the light. "I'm not up to going down on one knee, my dearest," he said shyly, "but would you do me the great honour of marrying me?"

This was said so gently and with such feeling that Ivy melted, for only the second time in her life. "Oh, Roy, my dear, dear Roy," she said. "Before I give you my answer, can I just tell you something about what happened to me once? I would like you to hear it so that you'll understand a bit more about me."

"I could listen to you all night, my love," Roy said. "Please go ahead."

Ivy began hesitantly but soon got into her stride. "It when I was in Round Ringford, and had a lodger named George. He was always pleasant and helpful, and I grew quite fond of him."

"I'm jealous already," said Roy with a fond smile.

"Yes, well, in due course he suggested we get married. Asked me one summer's day when we'd gone on a picnic. I couldn't believe it, Roy. All my life, ever since Mother died, I'd lived alone. Suddenly I could see a totally different future opening up. A man about the house, company on long winter evenings. Me with a husband!"

She paused, and a shadow crossed her face.

"So what happened, dearest?" Roy said in a whisper.

"It was on our wedding day," Ivy continued. "I was all dressed up, pale blue it was, and then he didn't turn up. Just didn't . . ." Her voice petered out, and the hand that was still holding Roy's suddenly gripped hard.

"So he did a runner?" Roy asked gently.

Ivy nodded mutely, her lips clamped together to hold back tears.

"He must have been out of his mind," Roy said, quite fiercely now.

They sat in a tense silence for a few minutes, and then Ivy took a huge breath and said that was the story, and she'd vowed never to trust a man again.

"But my dearest Ivy," Roy said lightly, "even supposing it was remotely likely, I don't think I'd get far in my shopping buggy." He looked at her closely, and when he saw the beginnings of a smile, sensed a cloud had lifted.

"Then you'd better not even think of it," Ivy said. "I'd catch you before you'd turned the corner!"

"Is that a yes, then?"

Again Ivy paused. "Um, well, if we could wait a while before we actually . . . you know . . ."

"Until you make sure I am not limbering up for doing a runner? Of course, my love. You shall fix the date when you're ready. So is that a yes?"

Ivy beamed. "No, it's a yes please!"

Roy took her left hand and carefully placed the ring on her finger.

"Oh, look, Roy! It's a perfect fit!" Ivy turned her hand round and round, the light catching the fiery sparkle of the diamond. Then she kissed him shyly on the cheek, and for a while, all was sweetness and joy, until Roy said, "Ooops! Ivy, don't look now, but Tiddles is . . . I think she's . . . Oh dear, too late. Never mind, let's hope Katya's still on duty. We'll ask her to clear up, and then maybe . . . ?"

"Yes," said Ivy firmly, "she shall be the first to know!"

Thirty-four

DEIRDRE LAY AWAKE in her large bed, and could not sleep. She had tried all the usual methods, counting sheep—useless—relaxing from the top of her head through every muscle of her body to her toes—equally useless. By the time she got to her toes, her neck muscles had tightened up again, and whichever way she turned she could not find a comfortable position. In the end, she got out of bed, made herself a cup of tea and returned to listen to the World Service on the radio.

The usual mixture of warring African countries and political stories from far-off lands slowly relaxed her. This usually worked, especially with the sound so low that she could barely hear. She could then abandon the attempt at making sense of it and slowly drift into sleep.

But tonight it did not work. She relaxed, certainly. But then the whole extraordinary day began to replay in her mind. Mrs. Spurling had really turned up trumps, hadn't she? With a generous donation promised by Deirdre, Springfields had certainly given Ivy a birthday to remember. And Tiddles was the crowning moment, until, that is, the surprise appearance of Gus.

Gus! Why did she bother with him, when she was pretty sure Theo Roussel would take her to the altar with alacrity? She was no fool, and was perfectly well aware that not only did he still fancy her, but he fancied her bank balance even more. But why would she want to do that? Acceptance into the charmed circle of the county aristocracy? She knew better than that. That lot would be brilliant at a cool polite-ness judged appropriate for a garage owner's widow! No, no, stuff them and their cut-glass voices. As the good old saying went, she knew her place, and was happy with it.

Marry for love, her mother had always said, and when Bert popped the question, her father had given his bless-ing and said that although love wouldn't pay the bills, it went a long way towards making poverty bearable. Of course, in the end she and Bert had made money, lots of it, and poverty never came into it. And she had loved Bert with all her heart. But her heart had not ceased beating along with his, and now she was pretty sure she loved that stupid idiot, Gus Halfhide. And, if necessary, his skinny little dog, too.

So, Gus it was, and she needed to know a great deal more than he was so far prepared to tell them. What did she already know? That he had been kidnapped and held against his will. A ransom had been demanded, and she had been prepared to pay it, but in a fugitive message he had said she was not to. Now he'd said he thought some-one did pay it but claimed he had no idea who.

And then there was Alwen Wilson Jones. There was the real mystery. If the woman had actually been able to influ-ence his release, how on earth had she done it? Perhaps she had settled the ransom, as she had hinted. But why should she? There had been that brief aside to Alwen from Gus as he sat down beside her. What had he said that cleared the miserable expression from her face?

"Oh, sod it!" Deirdre said aloud, as she heard the

grandfather clock in the hall below strike three o'clock. She reached for her sleeping pills, not touched for many months, and took one with a slurp of water. "Sod them all," she muttered, as sleep finally overtook her.

"I LOVE THESE blustery days," Roy said as he steered his buggy skilfully round the potholes in the pavement on the way up to Tawny Wings next morning. "Reminds me of my farming days, Ivy. It was a great time of the year, when the harvest was all in, the stock sleek from summer grazing and ready to be brought into shelter for the winter."

"What about all those summers when it rained and ruined the crops?" Ivy said, walking beside him and whacking encroaching nettles with her stick. "And when whole herds had to be slaughtered because of mad cow disease? I seem to remember there were plenty of disasters. Farmers' wives used to come to Ringford Women's Institute complaining that their husbands were even more gloomy than usual. Most farmers are gloomy. Have you noticed that, Roy?"

"I wasn't, Ivy. Nor was my Dad. But then, we weren't really living on the edge, like a lot of farmers. Grandad had salted away plenty of reserves, and one bad harvest didn't matter all that much to us. And Mum, she had inherited money of her own, bless her. Never stinted us for anything."

"Pity I didn't meet you years ago," said Ivy with a smile and an affectionate pat on his shoulder. "My Dad always said I should marry money. Sadly disappointed, he was."

They were turning into Tawny Wings when they were hailed from behind. "Hey! Wait for me!" It was Gus, and a sprightly Whippy by his side. "I swear you two get younger every day," he said.

"Must be love," said Roy. "You should try it, Gus."

Gus looked at him and frowned. "Am I missing something?" he asked, seeing the grin on Roy's face. And Ivy, too, was smiling broadly, and held out her left hand for inspection.

"You two?" Gus asked, scarcely believing what he saw

on Ivy's ring finger. "You've been and gone and done it! So he's popped the question, Ivy?"

Ivy nodded, and said if anybody asked her, she would say that was obvious.

DEIRDRE WAS WAITING for them, and had set out coffee in the drawing room, thinking that after yesterday's festivities the old ones might not manage the stairs. But when she saw them coming up the drive, Ivy striding along with her stick, Roy doing a three point turn to park his vehicle and Gus standing smiling at them, Whippy at his side, she picked up the tray and took it up to the Enquire Within office.

Gus sat in his usual chair and waited until the others were settled. Then he said that he knew he had to give them an explanation for his absence, but he hoped they would bear with him if there had to be gaps. "But first," he said, "Ivy has much more interesting news for us. Go on, Ivy— or you, Roy!"

Then Deirdre insisted on opening a bottle of champagne, and they were suitably mellow when the business of the meeting got going.

"Why?" said Deirdre. "Why can't you tell us the whole truth, Gus? After all, I think we three went through a nasty time, and you owe it to us."

Gus did not answer but looked down at his shoes, as if considering the matter. Ivy broke the silence.

"Now wait a minute, Deirdre," she said. "We know Gus was taken against his will and kept a prisoner for a while. We know money was demanded, and we don't know whether it was paid. And now he has come back, all in one piece. That must have cost something, even if not money. Don't you think we should leave him alone to get over his ordeal? He'll tell us, all in good time. Isn't that right, Gus?"

He looked at her gratefully. "Absolutely right, Ivy. But I can give you a brief account of what happened. I walked away from my prison. I got out once, and they caught me before I could get away. But then the next thing that happened was that one of my captors appeared and gave me a warning. I think it was a real warning, not an empty one. I was to be freed, provided that I made no attempt to trace them, nor gave anyone information which might lead to their discovery." He stopped and looked around at their solemn faces. There was no comment, and they waited for him to continue.

"More importantly," he carried on, "I was to make sure Enquire Within gave up all attempts to find out about demands made on Alwen Jones. For the sake of the safety of us *all*, I must keep my promise. If this does not satisfy the other members of Enquire Within, I shall be willing to resign and leave the decisions to you."

Max had actually put it more bluntly. "Forget it, forget the whole business, Halfhide. Stick to lost dogs and missing cats, or else you'll regret it, all four of you." He had gone on to say he personally wished he'd never set eyes on Gus, but the boss—whose name he did not reveal—set up the whole kidnap thing to find out if Enquire Within was onto them. To go to all that trouble, Gus had thought, Max and company must be involved in something big.

But now there was a chorus of "No, no, don't resign!" and Ivy suggested that with a tactful approach and Gus's agreement, and bearing in mind Alwen had been mentioned and was obviously involved in something much more serious than they had thought, they should continue to keep her and her problems in mind. "And at the same time," she added, not entirely convinced that there was any real danger to Enquire Within, "we can get on with the case of the old man in Measby and hear what Deirdre discovered on her visit there."

Gus sighed and said he, too, was reluctant to knuckle under to a blackmailer's threats, but added that he thought Deirdre going on her own to Measby had been a bit rash, hadn't it?

"Of course not," said Deirdre. "I was sick of waiting around with no word from you, and as it happened, I had a real stroke of luck." She told him about the For Sale notice in the shop window, and how the shopkeeper introduced her to his boss, who was handling the sale. "She showed me round the actual cottage where the man died," she said, and shivered at the remembrance. "She didn't seem at all anxious to sell, fortunately. More keen to put me off."

"It was all a bit strange, Gus," she continued. "This woman, Doris May Osborne, was clearly well-heeled. She had all the signs of wealth. Designer clothes, great haircut, expensive scent—same as mine, actually—and when we parted, she grudgingly said that she lived at Measby Manor, behind the trees of what looked like extensive parkland."

"She might have lured the squire into marriage. It does happen," said Ivy, looking pointedly at Deirdre.

"Maybe she'd been a kitchen maid and the lord of the manor seduced her?" Gus offered.

"All right, all right," said Deirdre. "That's quite enough of that. But I think it is odd, anyway. Honestly, Gus, that cottage was a wreck, a stinking wreck. Wouldn't you think that if it had belonged to the manor estate they'd have smartened it up a bit before putting it on the market?"

"Was there any furniture left in there? Nothing to see as evidence of a brutal murder, I suppose?" Roy liked a gruesome story, and the idea of Deirdre confronted with the scene of the crime was promising.

"More to the point," said Gus seriously, "did she say anything about the old man's death? Or didn't you talk about it?"

"I asked, but she didn't say anything much more and never once mentioned the word murder. She didn't seem to think it was very important. I tell you, Gus, it was really odd."

Roy had not had his question answered, and he persisted. "Was there any furniture, Deirdre? Any interesting clues?"

Deirdre reached across for her handbag. She unzipped it, and brought out the foxed and crumbling gambling book. "Not much furniture," she said, "only a few sticks. But I stole this. I don't suppose it's important."

Gus almost snatched it from her. "Oh, yes it is!" he said. "This is a very important find, Deirdre. I am ashamed to say I am no stranger to this particular book. It is an illustrated account of all the ways of cheating at gambling, ostensibly to open the eyes of those who are being cheated. Everything a serious gambler should know."

"How is that important, though?" Ivy said, wrinkling her nose at the musty smell.

"Well, think back, Ivy. Money in all its glorious guises. Investment, gambling, extortion, whatever you like to call it. And all preying on old, vulnerable people. Maybe like the old man who died. Could mean revenge, and you can take it from me, the world of gambling is full of cheated people out for revenge."

Deirdre had begun to see a glimmer of light. "Maybe like Alwen? Has she been one of these vulnerable victims? I do wish you could be more forthcoming, Gus."

"Sorry, can't help you there," Gus said quickly, and changed the subject. He asked more questions about Doris May Osborne, and said he thought Deirdre had done very well. "We might have a return visit to that interesting village," he said. "But this time, I go with you. Now, who wants this book? The very sight of it gives me the creeps."

"I'll have it," said Ivy. "Might help me beat our newest recruit at pontoon."

The ghost of a smile crossed Gus's face, and he said quickly, "Goodness, look at the time. If we've nothing more to discuss at the moment, I must be off to the shop before it closes. Come on, Whippy girl, let's be making tracks. Oh, and Ivy, I must tell you again how pleased I am about you and Roy. It's the best news I've had for a long time. Bye, Deirdre, thanks for coffee."

After he had left, there was an uncomfortable silence. Then Ivy said that it was quite possible that Gus did not know anything more about Alwen Jones, but as this was part of their investigation, perhaps they should carry on for a bit without him and plan what they would do next in that direction.

"Excellent," said Roy.

"If I'm right," said Deirdre, "when Gus sees how determined we three are to continue our enquiring, he will not be able to keep away from joining the team."

"Thank you for that, Deirdre," said Ivy. "And now who's for one more cup of coffee?"

Thirty-five

"WHERE DO YOU think you're going?" said Bronwen, staring at Trevor. He was wearing a loud check sports jacket that she had not seen before. Clearly new, then. Added to that, he was carrying a new leather briefcase, stuffed with papers, and was accompanied by a strong smell of aftershave.

"Out," he said. "I've got a meeting with an important client. He can only manage this evening, in the County Hotel."

"And I'm expected to believe that, am I? And what about the new jacket and briefcase? I suppose you think now that Mother intends to put right some financial problems, you can spend, spend, spend, just as before? Well, you can't, Trevor my lad. I haven't had an extra penny direct, and what little I have left in my bank account is staying there. So you can just go and get changed and come back down and watch telly with me. Her at the County Hotel will just have to have a meeting by herself, won't she."

Trevor's face was an angry scarlet, and his developing boozer's nose took on a distinctly purple hue. "Don't you speak to me like that!" he said, but saw that she was smiling triumphantly and knew that he had lost.

"I have to make a call, then, to cancel the meeting. Probably lost us a good client with your stupid suspicions!" he added, but Bronwen merely turned up the sound on the telly and settled comfortably in her armchair.

"No need to use your mobile," she said over her shoulder, as he put his hand in his pocket. "You can use the phone over there. Then I can enjoy your feeble excuses."

IN BRONWEN'S SISTER'S house, the atmosphere was very different. Her children were safely tucked up in bed, and she and her mild husband Clive were listening to opera on the radio. Clive was absorbed in the latest choice from their reading group, and Bethan leafed through a catalogue of French children's clothes, much cheaper than the English equivalents, and with, as sister Bronwen would say, a certain je ne sais quoi. She had tidied up the scattered toys and put them in a big yellow box in the corner of the living room, and now she and Clive sat side by side on a sofa that had seen better days, with threadbare patches covered over with a cheerful tartan throw.

Bethan closed the catalogue, and said hesitantly that if Clive could have a pause from reading for a bit, she would really like to talk something over with him.

"Of course, chump. What's on your mind?"

"It's Mother. I had a call from Mrs. Spurling at Springfields this afternoon. She said she was a little worried about her. Nothing serious, she said, but she had been very quiet lately and seemed rather solitary."

"What about her card-playing friends?" Clive said. He had a small, pointed beard and had a habit of pulling it gently when puzzled. When his small son had asked why Daddy had hair on his face, he answered that it made up for losing it on his head, and for the moment that seemed to satisfy. The truth was that long ago a disillusioned girlfriend had said he had a weak chin, so he had taken action.

"I thought she was really happy with Ivy Beasley?" he continued. "Settled down well, we thought."

"Yes, well, that has cooled down a little. This deterioration is very recent, Mrs. Spurling said. But she thought that perhaps if we all went to see her as soon as possible it would cheer her up. She felt quite sure there was nothing wrong physically. It was depression, she feared, and this could be very debilitating."

"Right! That's easy enough. I'll take tomorrow afternoon off, and we'll all go. The boys will surely lighten things up."

"What about the garden centre?"

"Oh, that's okay. I'm owed a couple of days, so that'll be no problem. I'll go in early and leave at lunchtime. I can give the kids their jobs for the day, and Caroline will supervise the work."

Clive was in charge of a garden centre outside Thornwell. It was part of a workbridge setup for people with learning and physical disabilities, and under his management it had become a valuable resource for the young people, and also financially successful, which endeared it to the local authority under whose umbrella it existed.

Satisfied with the plan, Bethan found her own book, and with the music turned down so as not to disturb the boys, they relaxed.

NEXT MORNING, GUS turned up at Tawny Wings soon after nine and asked Deirdre if she fancied a run over to Measby to have another look at the cottage. She was still in her dressing gown and said she wished he had given her a little notice, but if he would wait in the sitting room, she would shower and be happy to go with him. Then she had second thoughts. She had been right about his change of heart, but what about his promise, and if he'd been warned off, was it safe for him to go?

He replied that he had lost count of all the warnings he had had over the years, and he had considered this one carefully. Now he was prepared to risk calling their bluff. He hoped the others would approve.

"So long as you're not on your own, I'm just pleased

to have you with me," Deirdre said, almost shyly. "Shall I ring Doris May Osborne first?" she said. "We don't want to go over and find she's not around. I think she's the only one with authority to show people the house. She actually made a point of that. She may even refuse."

"No, no, don't ring her. I've got a good idea from your description what the house is like. No, I'm more interested in the old man. You found that book in his cottage, and I know only too well the rotten core of the gambling scene. Ripe for blackmail and worse! If you remember the rumours that apparently flew around at the time of his death, a connection with a racket behind that and Alwen's nasty experience looks increasingly likely. After all, she's a dab hand at pontoon, as we know! Maybe we could speak to a few people in Measby? I'm learning that village folk don't forget easily. I'll try a bit of local research on your computer, while you're gilding the lily."

She sighed. "When you get to our age, Gus," she said, "you have to do a bit of gilding. But goodness," she added, cheering up, "what did you think of Ivy on her birthday? She looked almost pretty, with colour in her cheeks and her eyes sparkling! And that nice dress and matching shoes. No wonder Roy was bowled over! I've never seen her looking so fine. Probably Katya who insisted on smartening her up. That girl is very fond of Ivy."

"And Ivy's fond of her," Gus said. "I think she means to save her from Theo's evil clutches if it's the last thing she does."

"Yes, well, I'm with her there. The old devil is very persuasive, and I saw the way he looked at her at his cocktail party. I think he'd like her as a permanent fixture. But what a lousy life for a young girl in that great mausoleum with Theo's dreary friends all at least a generation older!"

"Glad to hear you say that, Deirdre," Gus said, and lightly patted her bottom. "Off you go and get ready to go enquiring. I'll be busy down here."

He waited until he heard the shower running, and then switched on the computer.

* * *

"WOULD YOU LIKE to drive?" Deirdre said, reappearing in a cloud of intoxicating scent. Under the shower she had been thinking, and had decided there was no time like the present to start on a campaign of wooing Augustus Halfhide, and she would begin straightaway by changing her image a little from the feisty, independent widow to a softer, more emotionally needy woman.

"It would certainly make a change from rusty old bangers," Gus said happily, as he climbed into the driving seat. "Wow, this is the life!" he chortled, as he cruised along. It wasn't quite as nippy as he'd expected, but the comfort factor was superb. "I feel like Mr. Toad in *Wind in the Willows*. . . . 'Poop-poop'!"

"Yes, well, when you've come down to earth, perhaps you'd like to tell me a bit more about your time spent incarcerated in London. Was it London?"

"Yes, I got there thinking I was meeting Martin, but a couple of nasties had other ideas," Gus said, quite serious now. "But Deirdre, I'd really rather not talk about it anymore. Let's concentrate on our mission to Measby, shall we?"

"Sorry. Shan't mention it again," she said. If she really wanted him, she did not want him to think she was a nagger. "Did you get anything useful from the computer?"

"Not much. There was the usual factual death notices, including several in Measby, but no details. Could have been anybody. No sensational story."

"Honestly? Well, that's interesting! So that explains Doris May's lighthearted dismissal of the tragedy."

"Not necessarily," Gus suggested. "She might have been concentrating on getting information from you, not giving it out."

"But why, Gus. Why should she bother? Oh, and if you don't mind my pointing it out, the hand brake is still on."

Thirty-six

"GOOD DAY, ALWEN," Roy said politely as he and Ivy were on their way across the lounge to the dining room. "We missed you at breakfast. Are you feeling well? Coming in to lunch?"

Alwen shook her head. "It's fish," she said. "Can't you smell it? I can't abide cod, and that's what it is. I'm fine with a sandwich."

"Why don't you bring it in and eat with us? We haven't had a chat for quite a while, and now Gus is back we need to fix a time for our next pontoon session. Mustn't let the old grey cells get rusty!" Ivy said firmly.

But Alwen again shook her head. "I'll give it a miss at the moment," she said. "Just don't feel like it. But it's kind of you to ask."

"Well how about a walk after lunch? Ivy and me are going along to the church. They've got a flower festival on, and it's very beautiful, so Katya says. Won't you come with us?" Roy smiled kindly at her.

"No, I've got Bethan and her family coming to see me. Not that I wouldn't rather stroll along with you. They're a noisy lot, and the way I feel at the moment I prefer peace and quiet."

"Can't you put them off?" Ivy said.

"No. Bethan's husband has taken the afternoon off specially. Mrs. Spurling told me about it too late to change his arrangements. Don't worry, I'll get rid of them as soon as possible. I might stroll up to meet you, if I can find the energy."

Ivy and Roy sat down at their table and began to eat cod in parsley sauce. "It's delicious," said Ivy. "The silly woman has got herself in a state. I suppose it's up to us to find out why."

"Obviously something to do with Gus and his escape," Roy said indistinctly, attempting to extract a fish bone from between his teeth.

"And her part in it, d'you mean? I doubt if we'll get anything about that from her. She knows how to keep her trap shut."

"Her trap? That's an old Ringford Juniors expression, if I'm not mistaken!"

"And a perfectly good one," she answered, wiping the corners of her mouth with her napkin. "You must have seen plenty of rat traps in your farming days. Snap! Nothing more final than that. And Alwen ain't going to talk. We'll have to find out some other way. She's not a bad old thing, and a good one, if she really did play a part in Gus's release. We'd like to help her, wouldn't we?"

"Maybe we could have a word with her daughter when they leave. Bethan, isn't it? She seems like the nicer one. Don't care for that Bronwen at all."

WHEN IVY AND Roy came out of the dining room, Alwen had disappeared. Miss Pinkney was on duty, and she said Mrs. Wilson Jones had had a sandwich in her room and was resting before her visitors arrived.

"Right-o," said Roy. "Miss Beasley and I are going for a stroll down the High Street to have a look at the flower festival in the church. It's on for a week, and will still be fresh from the weekend."

Ivy nodded agreement. "Flowers always stay fresh in church," she said. "God's blessing, probably."

Roy thought of disagreeing, pointing out that it was always cold in church and the temperature was what kept them fresh. But he knew Ivy had a hotline to her Maker, and would have mentioned the flowers in her prayers. If she trusted God to keep them fresh, who was he to doubt?

It was a chilly morning, and Miss Pinkney advised wrapping up well. She had had many years' experience looking after old people, and knew that they could very quickly lose heat. "Coats and hats, and possibly scarves and gloves as well," she said, keeping her voice light. She knew only too well the need to approach Miss Beasley carefully. If she thought she was being told what to do, it was most likely she would choose the opposite.

Finally Roy and Ivy were ready. They set off at a good pace, Ivy keeping up with Roy in his shopper. If he went too fast, she allowed him to get ahead, and then he would slow up. Neither would imply that the other was failing.

"Oh, lor, there's Miriam Blake heading in the same direction," Ivy said. "Shall we walk on past the church up to the river, and then look in on our way back? Give her time to be gone?"

"Now, Ivy, there's nothing wrong with Miss Blake. She's lonely, that's all."

"I don't see how you can say that," Ivy replied huffily. "She works in the shop several days a week, and must see plenty of people then."

"Not the same as having a person living with you in the house. I know that from experience, and before you can say it, my love, I know you do, too. But now we have each other, haven't we?"

"And a host of other dopes alongside, especially Mrs. Worth," Ivy said tartly. "She was the only one who voted against my having Tiddles, didn't you say? And I know why. That time she was screaming and creating, I faced up to her and told her straight. I mean to go and have another word with her. She's not nearly so gaga as she pretends, you know. If you ask me, she could tell us a thing or two about her early days with her husband gardening for William and his wife. Have we ever asked Alwen about that?"

Roy turned into the churchyard, and steered his vehicle along the narrow path between fading lavender bushes and the odd late rose. "Well, I haven't," he said, as he bumped along. "It isn't easy to introduce the subject of her husband. Does she go and see Mrs. Worth? Surely she must know the old thing is bedridden upstairs?"

"Something else to ask," Ivy said. "Still waters run deep, as my mother used to say, and Alwen don't like the surface disturbed!"

"Oh, very neat, my love," said Roy, chuckling. "Now, I'll park in the porch and we can take things slowly inside the church."

As Ivy had expected, the flowers were mostly chrysanthemums, from small multiheaded buttons to huge shaggy blooms that reminded Ivy of an Old English sheepdog. She said so, in a loud voice, and several of the flower arrangers tending to their creations glared at her. Almost more beautiful than the flowers were the sprays of leaves in all shades of yellow and red and orange, lit up by rays of sunlight streaming in through the ancient plain glass windows.

"Now look at those Michaelmas daisies, Roy," Ivy said, pointing to a perfectly symmetrical arrangement at the foot of the pulpit steps. "Those are really lovely. Not a trace of mildew. At home in Ringford, I always got mildew. I wonder whose these are?"

"Mine," said Miriam Blake, coming out from behind a pillar. "And my gardening secrets are not for passing on!"

"Huh!" said Ivy. "Well, Miss Blake, since I no longer have a garden, I can't see the harm in telling me. But for the same reason, I have no desire to know, thanks very much." She turned to Roy. "Come along, let's go and look at that pedestal arrangement by the altar."

But Roy knew that every so often he had to stand firm.

"I would be interested to know, even though I'm not a gardener anymore, Miss Blake," he said.

Miriam looked a little mollified. "Oh, all right, then. I'll whisper my secret, Mr. Goodman," she said with a murderous look at Ivy.

"Good morning, Miss Beasley! And how are we this morning? Well wrapped up, I'm pleased to see. It's a cold wind, I'm afraid." The vicar was pleased with himself this morning. He had just been interviewed for promotion to rural dean, and fancied he had done rather well.

"Seasonal," grunted Ivy. "You don't expect balmy winds now. Only barmy people," she added, glancing sideways at Miriam Blake bending close to whisper in Roy's ear.

BETHAN AND CLIVE and the two boys had arrived promptly, and were now sitting with Alwen in a corner of the lounge. Clive decided the most useful thing he could do would be to keep the boys occupied, leaving Bethan to talk tactfully to her mother to see if she could discover the cause of her depression.

Certainly the old thing did look pale, Clive decided, and seemed unlike her usual composed self. Once or twice, when the boys shouted suddenly, he noticed Alwen gave a start, and looked nervously at the door.

"I'll take these terrors into the garden, Mother," he said. He always called her Mother, unaware that this irritated her. She wasn't his mother, and Alwen felt that if he had been her son she would have tidied him up and found him a proper job.

Left alone, mother and daughter looked at each other and found they had nothing to say. Bethan sighed. "You don't look so happy, Mother," she said finally. "Is anything wrong? You know you can tell me, and Bronwen and I will do our best to put it right."

"There's nothing wrong with me except old age and decrepitude," Alwen said crossly. "And I don't want you suggesting anything of the sort to Bronwen! You know what she is. She'll be in here reorganising the place, offending everyone in sight and causing more trouble than there was before."

"Is there trouble, then?" Bethan interrupted.

"No! And if that's all you came to ask, you'd better collect the boys and Clive, and go home."

"Mother! There's no need to be nasty," Bethan said, and Alwen could see her nice, gentle daughter was near to tears.

"Oh, I'm sorry, love. The truth is I *have* been feeling a bit off-colour. It's just the usual arthritis and rheumatism and the general frustrations of old age. After years of being a bossy head teacher, I am finding it hard to cope with being told I must be cared for now. Oh, how I hate those words, Bethan. 'Cared for' must be the most unwelcome words in the language for people like me."

Bethan gave her mother an impulsive hug and said that she quite understood. Would Alwen like to come over to lunch next Sunday? Maybe she needed to get out of Springfields a bit more. "I could ask Bronwen and Trev to come, too," she added, and was surprised when her mother shook her head violently. "Not yet, dear," she said. "I'd better stay here and get used to it before I venture out again. Besides, I do go for little walks with Roy and Ivy, my friends here. No, don't worry about me, Bethan. I have a great deal to be thankful for." And a great deal to worry about, she said to herself.

She was still sitting in the lounge, her family having departed with assurances that any time she wanted to visit them they would be delighted, when Ivy and Roy returned.

"You look the picture of misery," Ivy said bluntly, sitting down next to Alwen. "Come on, Roy, let's do some cheering up."

"Right," said Roy. Pink-cheeked from the nippy wind, he looked full of life and his clear blue eyes twinkled at Alwen. "What you need, Mrs. Wilson Jones, is an exciting evening gambling away a fortune in matches. Ivy, give Deirdre a ring, and Gus, and fix it up. I'm sure they'll be only too pleased. It will be just like old times."

Thirty-seven

ALWEN HAD PROTESTED at first, but under the full force of Ivy's and Roy's persuasive powers, she agreed, and even seemed to brighten at the thought of a distracting interlude.

"It's a bit short notice," Deirdre had said. She had been planning a quiet evening watching telly, but Ivy had said it was a cheering-up emergency. In the end, Deirdre said she would ring Gus and not allow him to refuse to come. "He is fairly malleable at the moment," she had added. "We've been over to Measby, and some interesting things have come up. We'll tell you all about it."

"Wait a minute, Deirdre," Ivy had said, frowning. "If you ask me, I think we'd be wise to keep Enquire Within business to ourselves at the moment."

"In other words, not in front of Alwen?"

"Yes, that's it. We do need to ask her some questions, but me and Roy can do that anytime. I think we should just concentrate on cheering her up this evening. Maybe we can come up to Tawny Wings tomorrow, and hear how you got on at Measby?"

"Fine," said Deirdre, glad of an excuse to see Gus again. He obviously fancied her, but she was not at all sure of his willingness to commit. When he had been grumbling about his damp cottage, and she answered that she was thinking of taking a permanent lodger, although she had winked and made it sound like a joke, he had stiffened and visibly backed away from her. So, gently does it, she had decided.

"We'll just have some fun this evening, then, Ivy," she continued. "God knows we can do with it, after all we've been through."

Now they were gathered in the interview room, and Miss Pinkney had smuggled in a vase of tiny chrysanthemums for the card table. Mrs. Spurling was off duty, and while the coast was clear, Miss Pinkney—now generally called Pinkers by Enquire Within—had offered sandwiches and hot chocolate halfway through the evening. "Perhaps one evening I could join you!" she said, not entirely joking. They seemed to enjoy themselves so much that she had felt occasional pangs of envy. And she loved being Pinkers, sensing a certain affection in the name.

"Of course!" said Gus, quite sure that her sense of duty would not allow it.

Alwen won a hand or two and began to cheer up. Colour came into her cheeks as she accused Gus of cheating, and he cheerfully admitted it. "I learnt some terrible tricks at the casinos," he confessed. "Watch this, everybody," he added, and palmed a couple of cards from the top of the pack to the bottom. "What did I do?" he asked Ivy.

"Nothing, as far as I could see," she said doubtfully.

"Right, now, let's try again. Look at the top card," he instructed, and showed her a six of hearts. Then he put it back to where he had taken it from. He changed the pack from one hand to the other, whilst the rest watched closely. "So what was the top card, Ivy?" he said.

"Six of hearts," Ivy said confidently.

He turned the top card over, and it was the six of diamonds. Ivy gasped. "How did you do that? I could swear . . ."

"That's an old one," said Roy. "Let me have a go, Gus."

"Certainly not!" said Ivy. "I forbid it, Gus. You may cheat as much as you like, but my Roy is not to be corrupted!"

Gus laughed. "Never mind, Roy, you can have a read of the book Deirdre found—"

Before he could continue, Deirdre butted in quickly, remembering Ivy's strictures about not discussing EW matters in front of Alwen. "I can see this going on all night," she said. "Can we please get on with the game?"

When Miss Pinkney came in with refreshments, the players relaxed and began to talk idly.

"How's Miriam next door, Gus? Was she sorry to hand over Whippy?" Ivy said.

"She said she was, but I know from what Whippy said that she is not the greatest dog lover."

"For God's sake, Gus! That's a bit twee. Animals can't talk." Deirdre grinned at Alwen, who, she knew, shared her indifference to the talents of dogs in general and Whippy in particular.

Tiddles, curled up asleep on Ivy's lap, suddenly started awake and hissed. "Hush!" Ivy said and stroked her back to sleep. "She's only little, but quite capable of being offended, Deirdre."

"To change the subject," said Roy manfully, "has any-one noticed we've not heard anything this evening from the madwoman upstairs in room five?"

"Mrs. Worth?" Ivy said. She looked at her watch. "Early yet," she said. But just then, on cue, a piercing shriek filtered through into the interview room.

"Uh-oh, spoke too soon," said Roy. To his amazement, Ivy got to her feet.

"I'll just nip up and make sure she's all right," she said. "Give Pinkers a break. As a thank you, sort of, for these flowers. Back very soon," she added, and left the room.

The others looked at each other. "Ulterior motive?" said Gus.

"You bet," said Deirdre. "My dear cousin is not one for acts of charity, unless there is some benefit to herself.

And before you protest, Roy, I've known her longer than you have!"

"Not much," Roy said, frowning. "And how many of us here can claim to be totally unselfish? No hands raised? Then I suggest we have a quick game of snap. I happen to know Alwen has a pack in her handbag, all ready for grandchild invasions."

Alwen really laughed then. "You're a national treasure, Roy," she said, and duly delved into the capacious bag, bringing out a pack of animal snap.

UPSTAIRS IN ROOM five, Ivy sat down beside Mrs. Worth's bed and put out her hand. She gently stroked the withered one in her grasp, and said quietly that there was nothing to be alarmed about. She was Ivy Beasley, she said, and nothing bad was going to happen.

"Was it the same nightmare?" Ivy continued. "The one where your Joe is about to fall into the beer?"

Mrs. Worth opened her eyes wide. "How did *you* know?" she said.

"You told me the other day."

"Never seen you before in me life!" the shrill voice shouted.

"Hush, you'll wake the children," Ivy said, a cunning note creeping into her voice.

"What children? I ain't got no children."

Ivy put out a soothing hand. She had done some serious thinking about Daisy Worth and Mr. William. Daisy's Joe was obviously a steady but perhaps boring old husband. Juicy Jellies every Friday! Mr. William was the spoilt younger son, and rumours of him being seen drinking with his secretary had filtered through from the gossips in the lounge. So he liked the women. Wife too bossy? Joe busy sowing carrot seed in the boss's garden, and his pretty young wife left alone, but waiting for a visitor. Then, sure as eggs is eggs, a bun in the oven and a handout of brewery money to keep it all quiet. It hadn't taken Ivy long to put it all together and come to a conclusion that would have made her Ringford chums proud.

"That's what Mr. William wanted, didn't he? Wanted you to get rid of it?" Ivy said carefully. "But what did Joe say?"

There was a moment's silence, and then Mrs. Worth said in a perfectly rational voice, "He didn't know, did he. My Joe and me were married and Joe thought the babe was his, right from the beginning. Nothing was said, not then nor later, when the little 'un was the spitting image of the Joneses. Joe might have noticed, but he never said nothing. Mind you, Miss Beasley, it cost Mr. William a packet, I can tell you! I made sure of that."

"He was a generous man, was he, your Mr. William?" Ivy continued to stroke Mrs. Worth's hand, and her tone was soft and slippery.

"Not so's you'd notice!" Mrs. Worth said. "But he didn't have no option, did he! That Jones family would have run him out of town. Still, by the time he went, me and Joe had a nice little nest egg. How else d'you think I got in here? Mind you," she confided, "I always thought it was Mr. George's money. He'd stump up for anything to save the family name. Them Joneses were always above the rest of us. If it got known that precious William had got the gardener's wife in the club, the local papers would have been onto it like dogs on a rat."

"So you have visits from your son—or daughter? That's nice, isn't it?"

There was a pause, and then Mrs. Worth heaved herself up into a sitting position. She stared at Ivy. "Who are you?" she said.

"Ivy Beasley."

"Never heard of you. You come in 'ere, pretending to be my friend, and you don't even know my Sammy died when he was eleven! Knocked down by a brewery lorry, what's more."

She collapsed back onto her pillows, and her eyelids flickered. Ivy sat quietly for a couple of minutes, then stood up. "Night, night," she said, and waited.

"Did I ever tell you?" Mrs. Worth whispered. "Don't tell a soul."

Ivy held her breath.

"My Joe," Mrs. Worth continued, so softly that Ivy could hardly hear. "My Joe, he used to bring me Juicy Jellies every Friday." And she cackled loudly as Ivy made her way back downstairs.

"AH, THERE YOU are, little love," said Roy. "We were beginning to worry you had been spirited away by the legendary Joe Worth."

"Being spirited away is not my favourite subject for conversation at the moment," said Gus. "Now, unless Ivy wishes to play snap instead of losing her shirt on a real game, can we get on?"

"Shirt? Shirt?" said Ivy. "If you ask me, Augustus Halfhide, your mysterious absence has addled your brain." She smiled all round, and said she was glad they had not wasted time, but could they now get back to business.

"You look very pleased with yourself, Ivy," Deirdre said sharply. "Visiting Mrs. Worth's room is not usually a ball of laughs, is it?"

"Ah ha," said Ivy. "You never know what's round the corner, my old mother used to say. Now, no cheating, Gus. Let's make a start. Oh, and by the way, how are you feeling now, Alwen?"

"Much better, thanks. Never a dull moment, as my old mother used to say."

Thirty-eight

AS SOON AS Roy walked into the breakfast room, he sensed a strange atmosphere. It was very quiet, for a start, and then he realised nobody looked up from their cornflakes and nobody said, "Good morning, Mr. Goodman."

What had he done? Was he being sent to Coventry for some gross lapse of polite behaviour? Of course not. He sat down at his usual table, and looked anxiously into the hall for a sight of Ivy coming to join him. Had something happened to her, and he had not been told? He was about to get to his feet to investigate, when Mrs. Spurling hurried in and made straight for his table.

"Ah, Mr. Goodman," she said. "May I sit down for a moment, just until Miss Beasley joins you?"

So it wasn't anything to do with Ivy. Roy said of course she was welcome to sit with him. He looked at her enquiringly. "Is there something I should be told?" he asked.

"Well, yes. I have some sad news for all residents at Springfields. The others have been informed, and are naturally rather shocked. I am afraid that in the night Mrs. Worth died very peacefully in her sleep. Young Katya was on night duty and was with her. Holding her hand, the girl reported to me this morning." Mrs. Spurling sniffed, and Roy could see she was genuinely upset.

"I'm so sorry, my dear," he said. "I believe she had been in your care for a long time?" The noisy old thing had been at Springfields for as long as Roy could remember, though he had never actually met her. She had been like Mrs. Rochester, upstairs in her room and never seen. She had certainly been heard, though! He recalled many a night when he had awoken to hear her bellowing for attention.

"Thank you, Mr. Goodman," Mrs. Spurling said, visibly pulling herself together. "I suppose it is the nature of my job to lose friends now and then. Springfields is my family, you know."

Roy could not quite reconcile this with the number of times he had overheard Mrs. Spurling cursing under her breath and vowing to give in her notice the very next day. But then, he reasoned, who wouldn't do the same, put in charge of this lot? He glanced round the dining room and was relieved to see Ivy approaching from the hall.

"Perhaps you could break the news to Miss Beasley, Mr. Goodman?" Mrs. Spurling said, getting up rapidly from the table. "And thank you so much for your support. Mine is not always an easy billet, you know."

She nodded a greeting to Ivy, and then crossed the room to answer a beckoning finger from another table.

"Good morning, my love," said Roy, struggling to his feet. He reckoned that when he ceased being able to keep up the little courtesies, he would give up. But then he looked at Ivy's smiling face, and knew she would not let him give up, whatever befell him.

"Bit quiet in here, isn't it?" she said, looking round. Her voice sounded louder than usual in the silent room.

"There's a reason for that, my dearest," Roy said, and explained to her gently and considerately what had happened to poor Mrs. Worth in the night.

Ivy raised her eyebrows, shook out her table napkin and arranged it neatly on her lap. To Roy's extreme surprise, when she looked at him across the table, her eyes were twinkling, full of mirth.

"Ivy!" he said, hoping to forestall any indiscretion. "You did hear what I said? The poor old lady died in the night."

There was a kind of smothered snort from Ivy, and then she took a deep breath and said that she hoped that where Mrs. Worth had gone there would be a plentiful supply of Juicy Jellies.

Roy passed her the milk jug, and asked if her hand was steady enough to pour the tea. "How had she seemed when you looked in on her last evening?" he said, hoping to sober up his unaccountably cheerful beloved.

"Awkward as ever," Ivy said matter-of-factly. "Mind you, I thought she was a bit more breathless than usual. Didn't stop her shouting at me as I went back downstairs, though. Maybe it was what they call a last gasp."

"Katya was with her, apparently," Roy said.

This sobered up Ivy immediately. "Where is she? Gone off duty, I suppose?"

Roy nodded. "I expect Mrs. Spurling will give her time off today. Probably the first time she has witnessed the grim reaper coming to collect his harvest."

"I'll find out as soon as I've had breakfast. The girl might need to have a little weep."

Roy marvelled once more how little he actually knew of his Ivy. Tough as old boots at the announcement of a death in Springfields, and then full of compassion for a young girl far from home and doing her best to make life more pleasant for a bunch of oldies, who, it had to be said, were most of the time full of complaints.

"Would you like me to come with you?" he asked, but knew the answer before Ivy spoke. She shook her head. "No thanks," she said.

"No? Right, well, I'll be in the lounge with the newspaper,

ready to go up to Tawny Wings. At your disposal, madam," he said, and smiled very fondly.

GUS WAS ALREADY in the Enquire Within office, and greeted Ivy and Roy with a cheerful smile. This was not returned, and Deirdre, who had answered the door and accompanied them up the stairs, knew at once that something was wrong.

"Now then, Cousin Ivy," she said, sending a warning look at Gus, "you and Roy could use a good strong cup of tea. Right?"

"Thanks, Deirdre," Ivy said, and Roy said that he would appreciate that. The wind had been cold as they made their way to Tawny Wings. "And added to that," he said, before Deirdre left to make the tea, "we had a bit of sad news at Springfields this morning."

Deirdre sat down at once. Her mind flew around the various possibilities, but strangely enough, considering it was an old folks' home, she did not consider a death of a resident, not even Alwen Jones, who had certainly looked a bit middling lately.

Gus asked the question for her. "Who was it, then, Roy?" he said, as sympathetically as he could manage.

"Mrs. Worth," Ivy said baldly. "The old trout who yelled a lot, and whose husband was gardener for Mr. William Jones, and who got pregnant from a secret assignation with the said William Jones. Joe Worth never knew the boy wasn't his, and William, or, more likely, George Jones, paid up to keep Mrs. Worth quiet. And knowing what we know about her, he must have paid a lot."

There was a stunned silence, broken finally by Deirdre saying that if there had been a son, why on earth were there never any visitors for poor old Mrs. Worth?

"The boy, named Samuel, aged eleven, was run over by a brewery lorry and killed outright."

Roy looked at Ivy in astonishment. "Did she tell you that, Ivy?" he said.

Ivy nodded. "Last night, when I went up to see why she was yelling again. She was quite lucid, for once. Sometimes happens, so I'm told, just before the end. My mother did the same. Sat up in her bed, straight as a die, and announced that she wanted to live. Then she lay down again and breathed her last. Odd, really."

Gus was puzzled by Ivy's apparent indifference to what must have been something of a shock to Springfields. Then he noticed Roy surreptitiously handing her a clean white handkerchief. Ivy turned away, as if to look out of the window, and Gus saw her pat her cheeks swiftly and hand back the handkerchief. So, thank goodness for that! He could not believe the old thing was so completely stonyhearted.

When Deirdre returned with the tea, Ivy said it was time they got down to business, and she personally was anxious to hear how they got on in Measby.

Gus looked at Deirdre. "Will you start?" he said.

"No, you."

"Right-o, but feel free to correct me if I get anything wrong."

"Oh, for goodness' sake, get on with it!" said Ivy.

And so Ivy and Roy listened with interest to an account of a visit that had turned up some very strange facts.

"First of all," Gus said, "we had great trouble finding Doris May Osborne. We tried at the shop, but the shopkeeper was no help. In fact, he did his best to persuade us to forget all about the cottage for sale, and hinted that it was already sold."

"O'course, we didn't believe him," chipped in Deirdre. "Nor did we accept that his boss had gone on holiday to New York and hadn't said when she'd be back! He was clearly making it up as he went along, wasn't he, Gus?"

Gus nodded. "Which, of course, made us all the more keen to find out what was going on," he added. "In the end, Deirdre reminded me that Doris May had said she lived at the Manor, and we decided to call there. So off we went, up the long drive, to a very impressive manor house of Tudor origin, if I'm not mistaken."

"Is that relevant?" said Ivy shortly.

"Could be," Gus replied defensively. "In my experience, Ivy, every little detail can be relevant. So, as I was saying, the house was very impressive and very expensively maintained, Deirdre reckoned."

"Yep, just like Doris May herself," Deirdre said, taking over the narrative. "Talk about manicured lawns! And the flowerbeds immaculate. We pressed the bell, and waited."

"Yes?" said Roy, who was beginning to side with Ivy in wanting them to get to a few important points.

"After a while," Deirdre continued, "we heard footsteps coming towards the door."

"And it opened slowly with a terrible creak, and there stood Adams the butler, with only one eye and a menacing leer on his sallow face!" This was from Roy, and spoken with a completely straight face.

Silence. Then Gus gave a shout of laughter. "Point taken!" he said, and patted Roy on the shoulder. "Come on, Deirdre, let's be brief."

Deirdre was looking distinctly offended, but she shrugged her shoulders and said that Gus should carry on.

It was an interesting account. Doris May had finally opened the door and invited them in. She had been pleasant and polite, but firm in her confirmation that the cottage had been sold. She was sorry, but had gained the impression that Mrs. Bloxham had not been seriously interested in it, and so she had accepted an offer from a subsequent approach. She had apologised if they felt they had wasted their time in coming over to Measby.

"So we left. Nothing much else we could do. Then, as it was nearly lunchtime, we went to the local pub for a bite to eat. And that was when it got really interesting. Go on, Deirdre."

"Well, we got into conversation with the publican, and naturally we mentioned the sad business of a possible murder and that nasty stuff about the old man's demise." She looked at Gus.

"And he said," Gus carried on slowly, determined not to be done out of his moment of drama, "he looked at both of us as if we were barmy, and said, 'What murder? You got the wrong village, mate.'"

"That's right," said Deirdre, "that's what he said. 'What murder?'"

Thirty-nine

DOWN THE LONG Measby farm track, Max and Margaret huddled over a small fire which Max had lit on their return to base, the run-down cottage once occupied by a misguided artist.

"This place will be the end of us," Margaret said gloomily. "Damp through and through, no matter how many fires we light. Look at the paint peeling off the ceiling! And there's our Doris, rich as Croesus, with her designer outfits and smelly scent. You'd think she would at least slap a coat of paint on this hovel before she rented it out. She owes us, after all we did for her when we worked in the casino."

Maxwell sighed. "Maybe," he said. "But remember how much we owed her. Both of us gambling away as if there was no tomorrow! She says she wrote it off, but would you trust her? And think how little we pay in rent. We wouldn't get anywhere else as cheap as this."

"But why don't we just pay a bit more? After all, we should soon have money in the bank when she gives us our share, and the strong possibility of more to come. Doris has got a list, y'know. Surely we could shell out for a bit more comfort?"

"There is another thing you seem to have forgotten," he said coldly. "We are not exactly anxious to be known around here. Keep our heads down. That's what we agreed. The next thing you'll want is to join Measby WI! For God's sake, woman, be thankful for small mercies. When the job's done, that will be the time to enjoy the fruits of our labours. And miles away from here."

"Oh, shut up, Max!" she said, and threw another log on the fire.

A shadow passed by the window, and then a knock at the door sent Max scuttling upstairs. "It's that farm bloke," he said as he went out. "Get rid of him."

The farmer touched his cap politely, and said he was sorry to disturb Margaret, but he had a message for her. Well, for her husband, actually.

"Sorry, he's not here," she said blandly. Lying came as naturally as breathing to Margaret.

"Well, perhaps you could pass it on. A visitor was here looking for you. A woman, in a big black car. She seemed disappointed to find that you were away, and I said I would tell you she had called. Didn't leave a name, I'm afraid."

"Thanks," said Margaret. "I'll tell my husband when he returns. Probably some old business associate," she added and shut the door firmly in the man's face.

When he judged it was safe, Max crept downstairs. "What did he want?" he asked.

"Some woman called while we were away," she answered, shrugging her shoulders. "I expect it was you-know-who. I saw in the paper the brewery's been taken over. Maybe she's out on her ear, and skint. Who could blame them? Snooty bitch. Thank God we weren't here."

"No good antagonising her," Maxwell said. "She's part of the plan, ducky. Just watch what you say."

"I'm getting sick of watching what I do and say all the time! Why can't we take what we've got and cut and run? You're just being greedy, *Martin*!"

"What do you mean?" he said angrily.

"I mean greedy, always wanting more! Just like when you couldn't wait for that shaky old Smithson to fall down stairs by himself, which he certainly would've done after the pressure you put on the poor old bugger. Pay up, Bernie, or else! How many times did you threaten him? No, you couldn't wait for nature to take its course. You had to pull that mat out from under his feet, didn't you? Proud of that, weren't you."

Max took a step towards her, but she put out her hand as if holding him at bay. "Don't touch me," she said. "You'd be nothing without me."

Max subsided onto a chair, and Margaret continued her tirade. "Poor old Bernie. An' then those kids coming in and messing everything up around the cottage and covering up any traces you might have left. *And* taking the rap. Jammy old Max! But we won't always get away with it, y'know!"

"Oh, sod off," he said wearily. "How many more times are you going to rake over all that? And next time you want three weeks' luxury holiday in the Bahamas, just remember which of us is the greedy one."

THE MEETING OF Enquire Within had broken up, and Ivy and Roy went their way slowly back to Springfields.

"Funny old day," said Ivy eventually, after a long silence between them.

"Certainly is," Roy said. "First that poor lady dies in the night. Then we hear that odd report from Gus and Deirdre. What on earth is going on over at Measby, Ivy?"

For once, Ivy was not sure. "We've got to find out more about that old man who was found dead. Not murdered, said that publican. I reckon he was lying, for a start. And he told them that the old boy died of falling downstairs, and some evil yobs got into the cottage and splashed red paint about? Does that seem likely to you, Roy?"

He shrugged. "Could have happened, I suppose. But if it was true, why was Doris May so cagey with Deirdre the first time she went?"

"We should have talked about all this straightaway, instead of listening to Deirdre complaining of a migraine and ending the meeting before we had really started."

"Oh, don't be hard on her, dearest," Roy said, stopping his vehicle and looking up at her. "Didn't you see how pale she was, and those dark circles under her eyes? Poor love, she was obviously suffering."

"Mm," said Ivy. "And didn't you see how Gus stayed behind to comfort her? If you ask me," she added, her confidence returning, "they realise now they were taken in by a pack of lies and needed to think it all over. I reckon the whole thing, from the shopkeeper and his crafty boss to the man in the pub, was a crude attempt to get rid of a nosy pair of intruders for good."

"Or maybe they knew perfectly well who they were, and had a good reason for wanting them out of the way," Roy suggested.

They had arrived at the door of Springfields, and Katya rushed out to help Roy out of his vehicle. "You are sooner home than we expected," she said. "Now you can come in and have hot chocolate and freshly made cookies. Anya has found a new recipe, and I need you to road test them. 'Road test,' is that right?"

"It'll do," said Ivy, smiling kindly at her. "I can't think of anything more welcoming. Thank you, my dear. I must just go upstairs and collect Tiddles. She will be lonely, and I can keep an eye on her in the lounge."

The atmosphere seemed to have warmed up since breakfast. Residents were talking to each other, and Mrs. Spurling was arranging fresh flowers on the window ledges. She turned to see Ivy coming in with Tiddles cradled in her arms, and shuddered. She had never liked cats, and heartily wished she had not allowed Roy to persuade her.

"Has Tiddles been out in the garden this morning?" she asked, but Ivy was apparently deaf to her question. "No? Then later perhaps," she insisted, but thought that she might just as well have held her tongue. Ivy Beasley was really impossible, but what could she do?

"When's the funeral?" Ivy said to Katya as they sat down.

"Ivy!" said Roy, shocked at the baldness of her question. Ivy ignored him, and looked enquiringly at Katya.

"I do not know at the moment," the girl said. "There are so many arrangements to make, so I am told. As soon as we know, I am sure Mrs. Spurling will tell all the residents. Not many will be able to go, but I hope enough of us to send Mrs. Worth respectfully on her way."

"I shall go," Ivy said bluntly, gently stroking the curled-up kitten. "And so will Roy, I am sure. They say the parson here does a good funeral. At least there's not likely to be pop music and sentimental poetry. Mrs. Worth claimed she had no family, but you never know at funerals. All sorts of hopeful relations crawl out of the woodwork."

"Ivy!" repeated Roy.

"So now I shall fetch your chocolate drink and cookies," Katya said soothingly, and walked off towards the kitchens.

"Are you sure you want to go to the funeral, my love?" said Roy. He was anxious to protect her from herself. She had not liked Mrs. Worth, he was certain of that. And a funeral of any of their number would be a reminder of graveyards for them all. And now Ivy's strong sense of duty would force her to attend. Maybe he could dissuade her before the event.

"Of course I'm sure," Ivy said. "Goodness me, Roy, don't you see how important it might be? If Mrs. Worth was mixed up with the disappearing William Jones, there may well be people who are anxious to make sure she is well and truly out of the way. Never forget, my dear, that William Jones has had a second life somewhere, with who knows what ramifications?"

"I love that word," said Roy. " 'Ramifications.' It covers a multitude of sins. Very useful, Ivy. Very useful."

"Yes, well, don't change the subject. We shall both go to the funeral, with our eyes and ears open."

"Yes, Ivy," Roy answered meekly. She was a wonderfully strong woman, and he'd better get used to it.

Forty

ENQUIRE WITHIN HAD not met for a week, and apart from brief social visits from Deirdre to Ivy, and Gus calling in at Springfields to make sure both Ivy and Roy were not too distressed by the death in what was, after all, their home, there had been a tacit agreement that they needed a pause to consider all the facts they had collected before taking the next steps.

"Do you feel this is your home, Ivy?" Roy said to her one afternoon as they rested in her room after lunch. She did not talk much about Round Ringford, unless someone asked her questions about her former life, but he knew that she must miss it dreadfully. Maybe not all the time, but even he, who had been at Springfields much longer than Ivy, was occasionally saddened by a sudden picture in his mind of a sunny morning as he stepped out of his house into a yard busy with the life of the farm. In Ivy's case he could picture her working in her neat vegetable garden or sitting with her friends Doris and Ellen, drinking tea from her best cups.

"It's all we've got, isn't it?" Ivy said, looking at him in

surprise. In all the years of her spinsterhood, she had never dreamed that loving someone as she loved Roy could be so overwhelming. She took his hand and held it to her cheek.

"The thing is, Roy," she continued awkwardly, "if you ask me, I'd say that home is where the heart is. And mine is here with you . . . and that's home enough for me."

After that, they sat in companionable silence for a while, until there was a knocking and Katya popped her head round the door. "We shall be leaving in about half an hour," she said. "I expect you can hear the tolling bell? It is a little sad, isn't it?"

Ivy saw at once that the girl was upset by the mournful ringing of the single church bell. "Oh, don't let that worry you!" she said. "Our parson loves to make a meal of things. The tolling bell is not much used now, but it used to be. Told everybody in the village that there had been a death, I suppose. Anyway, we just need to get our bonnets on and then we're ready," she said, and rose to her feet.

"The day you get me into a bonnet, Ivy Beasley," said Roy, "is the day our relationship comes to an end!"

THE SMALL PARTY from Springfields filed into the church and took their places at the front. Ivy looked around curiously. One or two village people who had never met Mrs. Worth, but enjoyed a good funeral, sat at the back, and there was a lone figure of a woman in the front pew on the opposite side of the aisle.

"Who's that?" Ivy whispered to Roy.

He shook his head. "No idea," he replied. "One of the agency carers who come into Springfields, maybe?"

"Doubt if she'd sit in the front," Ivy said.

Roy put his finger to his lips as there was a shuffling noise from outside the church door. Then the parson's loud ringing tones filled the air.

"I am the resurrection and the life, saith the Lord: he that believeth in me, though he were dead, yet shall he live: and whosoever liveth and believeth in me shall never die."

Katya sniffed, and fumbled in her pocket for a tissue. Ivy opened her handbag and silently handed over a small, lace-edged handkerchief. The black-suited bearers carried the coffin slowly up the aisle, and the organist played softly Mrs. Daisy Worth's favourite tune, "On a Bicycle Built for Two," doing her best to make it sound like a funeral march. As the coffin passed by, Roy's eyes were suddenly riveted by the wreath of white chrysanthemums placed on top. There, nestling in the centre, was unmistakably a box of Juicy Jellies.

"Ivy!" he said in a stage whisper.

She looked at him with an innocent expression and smiled. Then the first hymn was announced and the service was under way.

As usual in these circumstances, Mrs. Spurling had asked the vicar to announce that there would be a cup of tea and light refreshments at Springfields after the service. Ivy had counted twelve mourners, and she watched with a sour look as the little group who had never met Mrs. Worth joined the others on their way back.

"Now then, Katya, back to work," Mrs. Spurling said briskly. "I am very anxious that there shall be no miserable faces in the lounge to depress our other residents. Bring in the refreshments and do your best to lighten the atmosphere."

"Yes, Mrs. Spurling," she replied. "Perhaps we could have a sing-song?"

Mrs. Spurling raised her eyebrows. "I didn't mean a knees-up, girl!" she said. "Off you go, now."

"Morning, Ivy," said a voice, and Ivy turned around to see Gus standing there with a cup of tea in his hand.

"Where did you spring from?" she said in surprise. "I didn't see you in church?"

"I was there in spirit," he said.

"And so was Mrs. Worth," muttered Roy. He offered a plate of tiny sausage rolls to Gus, who took a handful and conveyed them swiftly to his mouth. "Palming cards comes in useful sometimes," he said, bending down and whispering in Ivy's ear.

"So who's the mystery figure over there?" he continued, indicating the woman who had sat in the front pew.

"Why don't we find out?" said Ivy, and marched across the room, closely followed by Roy and Gus.

"How d'ye do," said Roy with his best smile. "A stranger round here, are you? It can be a sad time if you're on your own. Have a sausage roll, my dear."

The woman returned his smile gratefully, and said it was difficult holding a cup and saucer in one hand and a sausage roll in the other, and eat or drink at the same time. They all laughed, and the ice was broken. After introductions, Ivy discovered that the woman's name was Martha, and she had known the Worths when they were all young kids at the Junior School in Thornwell.

"We lost touch, as you do," she said apologetically. "Otherwise, of course, I'd have been over here to see Daisy while she was still alive. I happened to see the death notice in the local paper, and that's why I'm here. Poor old Daisy, she didn't have much luck. Looks as if I am chief mourner! No family members here, are there?"

"How d'you mean, she didn't have much luck?" asked Ivy casually.

"Well, I know she had a child who looked exactly like William Jones! Maybe I shouldn't speak ill of the dead, but everybody expected it, the way she carried on. Joe Worth was a bit simple, as they say, and not lively enough for Daisy.

"I'm lost," said Gus.

Roy laughed. "Tell him, Martha. Or shall I? The fact is, William Jones was a frequent visitor to the Worths, and always when Joe was out gardening."

"And it *was* William Jones's baby," stated Ivy clearly. "I had it from the horse's mouth."

There was a shocked silence, and then Martha nodded. "Did she tell you that? Daft old thing. Still, I suppose it doesn't matter now. William Jones went missing, presumed dead, and that poor little kid got run over. See what I mean about not much luck?"

"Have another sausage roll, Gus," Roy said.

"Don't mind if I do, squire," said Gus, putting on a funny voice. He was out of his depth, he decided. Couldn't keep up with Ivy. Better leave it all to her.

"How interesting, Martha," Ivy persisted. "And you said that William was presumed dead? Only presumed?"

Martha was enjoying herself, surprised that there was so much interest in her erstwhile school friend. She searched her memory, and said that after a while, some people swore they saw him skulking around dark corners in town. "But that died down, and the only reference I have heard since was when his wife, Mrs. Alwen Jones, put her house on the market and went to live in a home."

"This home, Martha." They all turned around to see who had spoken. It was Alwen Jones, and she was looking far from pleased.

Forty-one

"THAT WAS A sticky moment," Ivy said, as she sat at the supper table with Roy and Gus. Mrs. Spurling had invited Gus to stay, thinking it would cheer up Ivy and Roy, who, she mistakenly thought, were depressed by the day's events. Since Gus had sat with Mrs. Worth for only a couple of hours on two occasions and had spent the time reading the racing pages of the *Daily Mail*, the invitation was hardly justified. However, since steak and kidney pie and lemon sponge pudding were on the menu, he accepted gratefully.

"You mean when Alwen appeared? Where is she, by the way? Haven't seen her since then," Roy said.

"And she wasn't at the funeral, was she?" Gus had noted the mourners as they emerged from the church but had not seen Alwen Jones. "You'd have thought she would have wanted to be there to say farewell to her old gardener's wife?"

"You're joking, of course!"

"Yes, I suppose I am," said Gus. "But even so, all that was a very long time ago, and poor old Daisy did lose her only son under a brewery lorry."

Roy cleared his throat. "Um, we're not suggesting here that it could have been something more sinister than an accident, are we?"

There was a silence, as the horrifying possibility was considered.

"Did anyone get Martha's surname or address?" Ivy asked. "I reckon that could be the next step in our investigation. She would certainly have some more to tell us about those early days."

At this point, Alwen Jones could be seen entering the hall with her daughter Bronwen.

"Uh-oh, look out, folks," said Gus.

But Alwen did not even glance into the dining room. She received a peck on the cheek from her daughter and then went straight upstairs and out of sight.

"All clear," said Roy. "And yes, since you ask, Ivy, I always make a point of obtaining details of attractive women, as you know."

Ivy bridled. "Don't be ridiculous, Roy," she said. "Just remember what I said about trust. But did you ask her? Don't keep us in suspense."

"Her name is Martha Sparrow, she is a married lady with grandchildren, and she lives in a new housing development for elderly people on the outskirts of Thornwell. I heard her telling Mrs. Spurling that her number is in the phone book, should she be needed. I think maybe she was offering to be a volunteer visitor to Springfields."

"You're a marvel, Roy!" Gus said tactlessly. "Now, I suggest we look her up in the book, and ask if a couple of us can go over to have a chat."

"Me and Roy, then," said Ivy. "It'd make a nice little outing. You and Deirdre get out and about far more easily than us, so you can do something else. Maybe find out a bit more about those two who kept you prisoner, Gus?"

"If I may make a suggestion?" said Roy. "I have been wondering about that mysterious connection of yours, Gus. Martin, was it? He was the start of all this, and although I know you can't reveal your, um, secrets, don't you think you should check with him again to see if he's still wanting us to ferret out other cases of extortion and so on? I am really not too clear myself."

Ivy nodded. She had been thinking on much the same lines herself. Earlier on, Gus had led them to believe that the Measby old man's death was the most important, that it was a suspicious death, which meant murder, didn't it?

Then it had seemed that Alwen's panicked request for help concerning money taken from her under false pretences could in some way be connected to possible blackmail in the case of the death of the old man. But then Alwen had withdrawn her request in a false kind of way, saying she had retrieved the money.

"Do you think we've been a bit sidetracked by all the brewery goings-on?" she suggested now. But nobody seemed willing to answer that. Instead, Gus said that he would have another attempt at contacting Martin.

"The trouble is," he said, "he is quite difficult to get hold of. I am not sure I have his correct phone number. But I'll keep trying. As far as I am aware, we are still heading in the right direction. And so I suggest that Deirdre and I should make our way over to Measby again, and ask some more questions about the old man who died in his cottage, and why he should have had a well-thumbed book about serious gambling. My province, you know, and I have a hunch it may point us in the right direction."

"Who wrote that book, again, Gus?" Ivy asked. She had it safely inside her handbag but had a reason for asking.

"Weasel Murphy," he replied. "And he's an American, so no joy there, if that's what you were thinking, Ivy."

GUS HAD RETURNED home, and in his chilly, cheerless cottage he suddenly felt lonely. Funerals were like that. Not that he had attended, but at Springfields it was the topic for the day. The wake had been upbeat and full of noisy chatter, a kind of relief from the gloom, and then his supper with Ivy and Roy had been positive and useful. It was only on return to Hangman's Row that his thoughts turned to mortality and his spirits sank. Maybe he would telephone Deirdre and update her on developments.

"Hello, Gus? What's new?"

"Where were you today, Deirdre? The rest of us have been mourning the late Daisy Worth, and doing a bit of investigating on the side."

"Good," Deirdre said icily. "Are you going to tell me you've solved everything?"

"No, silly, I was only joking. But actually, we did get some things confirmed." He filled her in on the Martha Sparrow meeting, and their plans for the next steps. "So looks like you and me trudging around Measby again. Shall we meet and work out something more productive than calling on Doris May or going to the pub?"

"Sounds fine by me," Deirdre said. And then Gus heard a man's voice in the background, calling her. He could tell she covered the phone with her hand and answered the call in muffled tones that he could not decipher. "But not now, Gus." She returned with a clear voice. "I plan an early night. How about tomorrow morning? Coffee time?"

"I'll be there," Gus said. "And just watch it, Deirdre. You know you can't trust the aristocracy, don't you?"

She cut off the call without so much as a good-bye.

MRS. SPURLING WAS happy to pass on Martha Sparrow's address and telephone number. She had liked the woman and intended to cultivate her. She had a nice cheerful manner and would be just the kind of person to visit one or two of her residents who had no family visitors and tended to settle into a distressed limbo, waiting for the final exit.

"We shall be calling on her, as invited," Ivy said. "I might give her a ring now and see if she's free tomorrow. We can order ourselves a taxi. I'll let you know if we're in for lunch."

How good of you! Mrs. Spurling wondered if she would ever get used to being treated like a paid subordinate by Miss Beasley, and she decided she would not. Still, between them they seemed to have declared an unspoken truce, and things were going reasonably well. When she attended meetings of staff from other retirement developments in the Oliver Luxury Retirement Homes chain, none of the other managers had residents even remotely like Ivy Beasley, and were quite envious when she described what a lively place Springfields had become with Ivy's arrival.

"A cold wind is forecast for tomorrow," she said now. "Do make sure you and Mr. Goodman are well wrapped up if you venture forth," she advised, and left them to make their way upstairs to Ivy's room.

Ivy went straight to her telephone and dialled Martha Sparrow's number. "Hello? Is that Mrs. Sparrow? Oh, good. Yes, it's Miss Beasley here. Yes, we met today at Springfields. I do hope you meant it when you said you'd be pleased to see us at any time? You did? Well, we, that is Mr. Goodman and me, will be in Thornwell tomorrow morning, and wondered if we could call. Oh, that's no problem. We have a taxi man who ferries us about. What time suits you? Oh, how kind. Yes, we'd love to have a cup of coffee with you and your husband. Right, well, we'll see you tomorrow! Good-bye until then."

"No sooner said than done, Ivy," Roy said admiringly.

Ivy put her hand on his cheek and daringly darted a kiss onto his smiling lips. Then she reached for her handbag. "Now, I think it's time we had a look to see what Mr. Weasel Murphy has to say about cheating at cards. I have a feeling this is the way we should be going. Draw up your chair, Roy, and we can read it together. But remember," she warned, "this is for research purposes only."

Forty-two

ALWEN JONES HAD had an uncomfortable night. She had spent yesterday afternoon with her daughter Bronwen, visiting places she would never have chosen on her own. Bronwen had been in a strange mood, very tense and snappy, and it had not been a happy outing. And then there had been that awful moment when the Sparrow woman had appeared in Springfields' lounge, gabbling away to Ivy and Roy, and, for heaven's sake, to Gus Halfhide, though what *he* was doing at a wake for Daisy Worth was beyond her.

She reflected that had she known that the blackmailing old widow of the simpleton gardener, Joe Worth, was living upstairs in Springfields, she would not have considered moving in herself. Still, as it worked out, there had been no danger of her having to confront Daisy, and as far as she could tell, nobody here knew of the connection. She had gathered from conversations in the lounge that Daisy was totally senile, and so would have been very unlikely to have remembered those distant humiliating days.

She was dressed and ready to go down to breakfast, but the thought of making conversation with Ivy and Roy, taking care with every sentence she uttered, filled her with gloom. Looking back on her days as a busy head teacher, with Bronwen and Bethan still living at home, and the three of them making such a success of their lives together, she decided that the whole thing had fallen apart when the girls got married. "We could have done without husbands, all three of us," she said aloud, not noticing that following a gentle tap at the door it had opened to reveal Katya, looking anxiously at her.

"I am so sorry, Mrs. Wilson Jones," the girl said. "I did not realise you were talking to somebody. Are you on the telephone?"

"No, no, come on in. Talking to myself, Katya, and you know what they say. Yourself is the last person you talk to before being taken off to the lunatic asylum."

"What is lunatic asylum, please?"

"Oh, don't trouble your head with my nonsense," Alwen said, taking a deep breath and pulling herself up straight. She reached for her stick, and made a big effort to smile. "Off to breakfast, dear," she said. "Do I smell smoked haddock? Again?"

Ivy and Roy were already seated at their table, and at the sight of Alwen both waved spontaneously and beckoned her over.

"Are you feeling better, my dear?" Roy said. "We were quite worried about you yesterday. Apart from whizzing in, grunting at Martha Sparrow, grabbing a sausage roll and whizzing out again, we hardly set eyes on you!"

"You're looking smart, anyway," Ivy said grudgingly. How could Roy say they were worried, when they had been relieved she hadn't joined them at supper time? Had mother been right about men? Traitors all, she had said, more than once. "Are you off out with your daughter again today?" she said, trying to make it sound a casual question, though she had been brooding overnight and had come to the conclusion that something serious was definitely going on between the two of them, and not just a loving mother and daughter relationship.

Alwen wished she had had breakfast in her room, but she did her best to answer the questions pleasantly. "No, not today," she said. "Bronwen insisted yesterday on taking me shopping for new shoes. She says my old ones look too scruffy even for the garden." Why did I mention the wretched garden? she asked herself. She had a mental flashback—all too frequent these days—of Joe Worth bent over his spade and slowly digging deep, preparing the soil for winter vegetables.

On an impulse, Ivy said that she and Roy were going over to Thornwell and would be having a coffee with Martha. Would Alwen like to come? Maybe she needed to get out and see people other than family?

Ivy and Roy were both stunned by Alwen's response.

"Why can't you leave me alone!" she said, pushing back her chair and standing up with difficulty. "All I need is a bit of peace," she added, and began to cry, sobbing bitterly and subsiding once more on to her chair.

Ivy, nonplussed, signalled for help to Roy. If anyone could handle this, it was him, dear, kind, gentlemanly Roy. As she had known he would, he rose to the challenge. Pulling a large handkerchief from the breast pocket of his tweed jacket, he handed it over to Alwen, and then, after she had blown her nose with a wonderful trumpet blast, he took her hand in both of his and gently stroked it until she had composed herself.

"I am so sorry," she croaked, sniffing loudly. "I don't deserve to have friends."

"A nice hot cup of tea is what you need," said Ivy briskly. She had no time for self-pity, and had to admit she was relieved when Roy relinquished Alwen's hand. As far as Ivy could judge, Alwen Jones had everything she could want. Wealth, daughters, as much good health as she could expect at her age, and several residents of Springfields perfectly willing to be her friends.

"So will you come with us to Thornwell?" Ivy continued. "After we've been to Martha's, we plan to try a new café that's just opened in the crypt of that big church in the middle of town."

Alwen was about to refuse again but thought suddenly that maybe she would go. It might do her good, and would certainly be better than sitting in her room worrying about Bronwen.

"Well, if you're sure, Ivy, that would be very nice. I don't want to play gooseberry, you know," she added with a wan smile. "But if you don't mind, while you are visiting Martha, I will stroll up the road to the cemetery and have a look at George's grave. I suppose the headstone won't be up yet, but there's bound to be lots of flowers still. It'll be balm to the spirit, maybe."

"My goodness!" said Ivy. "It's not where I'd choose to go to be cheered up! But if that's what you want, of course it's all right. Then we can all go and have lunch in town." She looked at her watch. "Better get some porridge into you, then, Alwen. The taxi's coming at half past ten."

As Ivy reached for her large handbag, there was tiny mewing sound.

"Ivy?" said Roy.

"Yes, Roy?"

"Is that a miaow I heard?"

"Yes, Roy."

"Tiddles?"

"Yes, Roy."

"Then we had better leave Alwen to her porridge and get out of here before La Spurling comes bearing down on us like a wolf on the fold."

"Yes, Roy," said Ivy, and walked out of the dining room with a seraphic expression on her face.

"COME ON IN! Coffee's all ready, and Stanley is looking forward to meeting you."

Martha Sparrow beamed at Ivy and Roy, and ushered them into a comfortable sitting room where an elderly man was standing, smiling a welcome.

Roy had failed to persuade Alwen to come in with them, and had said they would pick her up at the cemetery gates in an hour. When he had seemed worried, Ivy said that Alwen Jones was perfectly capable of taking care of herself, and would he kindly forget her and concentrate on the task in hand, which was ferreting for any information likely to emerge in the conversation and be useful to Enquire Within.

Stanley Sparrow was a big, burly man with plenty of iron grey hair brushed back and grey eyes to match. He wore steel-framed half spectacles, which gave him a scholarly air, and with his grey cablestitch jersey and good grey cords, he blended in nicely with the largely muted tones of Martha's sitting room.

Roy took to him at once. "Sparrow?" he said. "That's a good old Thornwell name, I know. I'm sure my father had a friend called Sparrow. Sid Sparrow, that was it. Bred horses over Oakbridge way."

After that, with reminiscences lasting more than a half an hour, Ivy began to think they'd never get around to talking about Daisy and Joe Worth. Finally there was a lull in the conversation, and Ivy commented that it had been a good funeral yesterday. Had Stanley ever met the Worths? She was immediately alert when she saw Martha and husband exchange wary looks.

"Yes, I knew Joe vaguely," he said. "I seem to remember he came to us once or twice to do a bit of gardening, isn't that right?" he asked Martha.

She nodded and repeated what she had told Ivy and Roy already, that she had been at school with Daisy but had lost touch. "There was such a lot of unpleasantness around at the time of William Jones's disappearance. Quite frankly, Ivy, we felt that the less we had to do with them the better."

"Especially as rumours flew about that Joe Worth had blown the whistle on William's gambling debts, just before he disappeared," Stanley added.

"Seems Joe loved a flutter on the horses himself, and had watched William for years," Martha continued. "Oh dear, it does seem such a long time ago now. I was quite taken aback when Alwen Jones walked in yesterday. I think she was, too! She certainly didn't want a chat."

"But she recognised you," Roy said. He felt guilty. All those reminiscences with Stanley had been so enjoyable, but now he remembered what Ivy had said about why they were here.

"Oh, yes," Martha replied. "I expect she'd have seen me at brewery Christmas parties, and things like that over the years."

"I worked at the brewery," Stanley explained. "Half of Thornwell did at that time. They were good employers, too. Sad what happened with those brothers. The brewery suffered, I reckon. Never was the same place after the gambling scandal. And now the Joneses have all gone. I expect they'll turn the place over to nasty fizzy lager."

"There's still a Bronwen Jones at the brewery, I believe?" said Ivy innocently. "She works in Public Relations, whatever that is."

Again that wary look between the Sparrows.

"Not anymore, she doesn't," said Martha. "Now, more coffee, anyone? I can easily make some fresh." There were no takers, and Roy looked at his watch.

"We should be going, Ivy," he said. "We have to pick up Alwen in a couple of minutes."

"Alwen?" said Martha. "Alwen Jones?"

"Yes, she's up at the cemetery, paying her respects to her brother-in-law," Ivy said. "Now he's gone, I suppose Bronwen is, or was, the last link to the brewery?"

Martha did not answer straightaway, but as they said their farewells at the door, she looked up the road towards the cemetery and said, "Just keep your eye on Alwen, Ivy. And on her smart daughter Bronwen. Don't let them fool you. Mother is devious, and the daughter is the spitting image of her father. They'll run rings round you. Known for it! Don't get involved," she added, and Stanley nodded his agreement.

Forty-three

"WELL, I DON'T know, I'm sure," said Ivy as she and Roy settled into the back of the taxi. "But it sounds like we were right to feel that we should keep our investigations secret from Alwen."

"What about Gus's abduction? Alwen knew all about that. Rescued him, if the little we know about that is true."

"We *must* get some more information from Gus. He can't expect us to carry on if he doesn't explain more about *why* he was kidnapped, and then released with a warning. It doesn't really make sense. He must know, Roy."

"Perhaps Deirdre can get it out of him. They're off to Measby again tomorrow, aren't they?"

"Oh, look, there's Alwen, waiting outside the gates. She looks twice as miserable as she did before she went in. You've got your work cut out cheering her up this time, my dear," said Ivy.

"WELL, WHERE IS she?" Bronwen said. She and Trevor were having a drink in the bar of the Kings Arms in

Thornwell, and Bronwen had tried several times to get hold of her mother. The phone in her room was not answering, and Miss Pinkney knew only that Mrs. Jones had left with Miss Beasley and Mr. Goodman in a taxi.

"Gone shopping, I expect," Miss Pinkney said. "I'll find Mrs. Spurling, and put her on. I am sure she will be able to help."

"Do that!" snapped Bronwen. But then her mobile lost the signal, and she put it back angrily into her handbag. "Mother's not paying those astronomical fees to be allowed to drift off out into the unknown with a couple of senile old idiots."

"From what I hear, Miss Beasley is far from senile." Trevor had his ear to the ground. It was his business to engage clients in conversation, and he heard more than one wife explaining to her husband, as they came to commission him to sell the now redundant family house, that Mother or Father would be fine in Springfields. Look at that Miss Beasley we heard about, one had said. Full of life and always off out in taxis.

"I don't know why you're in such a hurry to talk to her," Trevor said. "Won't it wait until you get home?"

"I'm worried about her. She seemed very down when I left her yesterday. I thought a trip out would do her good, but she seemed anxious from the moment we set foot in the place."

"No wonder," said Trevor nastily. "Not exactly a picnic for her, was it?"

"No, no. But you needn't worry. I was sensible."

"Thank God for that. We don't want any more trips over to Measby to face the music, do we. Not that it's my business, really. But contrary to what you may think, I do still have some husbandly feelings when my wife needs protection."

"There's no answer to that," said Bronwen, and she climbed off her bar stool with difficulty. She had not given up power dressing, even though she had no job, and her tight skirt made it a tricky operation. "Come on, we'd better get going." Trevor followed her out, watching appreciatively as she stalked out on her high heels, head held high and not a strand of her dark, shiny hair out of place. He had found himself thinking often lately that she was a valuable asset, and he would do well to hang on to her. He noticed several men's eyes following her as they left the pub.

"Well, back to work for me," he said, giving her a peck on her scented cheek. "But hey, wait a minute, Bron, isn't that your mother over there, the other side of the square, with a couple of oldies?"

Bronwen looked over the square. It was a busy market day, and she peered through the stalls. "Can't see her," she said. "Anyway, it doesn't matter. If she's with friends, what I have to say to her will keep until we can have a private conversation."

THE CRYPT CAFÉ was empty. It was early, and Ivy, Roy and Alwen had a choice of tables.

"Let's sit in the corner," said Alwen. "Then we can watch people as they come in. They've made it look very nice in here, haven't they?"

"Were you a churchgoer when you lived in town?" Roy asked. He had decided the best thing to cheer up Alwen was to talk about her good times as head teacher and important citizen in Thornwell.

"Oh, on and off," she said. "We used to take the children to special services like Easter and Christmas. Two by two, we walked through the town. Plenty of helpers amongst the parents, and we didn't have any stupid health and safety regulations in those days."

"Must have been a pretty sight," Ivy said, catching on to what Roy was up to. "Did the children have a uniform?" She remembered with a pang the children in the village school at Round Ringford. Smart blazers and grey skirts and shorts. She had watched generations of them walk through the school gates.

"Yes, they did. Scarlet and grey. I always loved the babies, as I called them when they first arrived in the school. Jerseys too big, with room for growing, and brand new shoes for the new term. And if they cried for their mothers, we would give them a cuddle on our laps. Can't do that now, you know." The colour had returned to Alwen's cheeks, and she smiled at Roy. "This is a nice idea," she added, "and lunch is on me."

"We'll see about that," Roy said. "Now then, what shall we have to eat? Let's go mad, shall we, Alwen? Take our minds off graveyards? How about a smoked salmon omelette, Ivy?"

Ivy said a ham sandwich on white bread, without mustard, would be fine for her. She could see that Alwen had responded, as always, to Roy's gentle charm, and she tried hard not to feel jealous. And she did feel sorry for the poor woman. She certainly had something on her mind, and it wasn't graveyards. Why had she wanted to watch people as they came into the café? Was there someone she would rather not see?

"Well, it's the omelette for me," Roy said firmly, and Alwen nodded. "I'll have the same," she said. "Thanks, Roy. You're a star, as my grandchildren say."

Forty-four

DEIRDRE HAD WOKEN early. She saw sunshine streaming through a gap in her bedroom curtains, and got out of bed. Drawing back the curtains to see the day, she opened the window wide, and heard the piercing sound of the rooster that lived with his wives in an old wooden henhouse on the allotments over the road. His voice had a crack in it, and Deirdre found herself wondering how long chickens lived. Two, three years? That cockerel had been there for longer than that.

It had rained in the night, and the air was clean and fresh. She turned back into the room and pulled the bedclothes back. No Theo last night, after all. She decided she was glad. Yesterday, when Gus had come up for coffee and a planning meeting for just the two of them, she had sensed a coolness in his voice. Well, for God's sake, what did she expect? He had heard Theo's voice in the background when he phoned, and no doubt he assumed the worst.

Gus had made it plain that he was very fond of her, and would be happy to take things further, but was not interested in sharing. She had hesitated. Theo had also declared his fondness. The trouble was that neither of them appeared willing to be more closely involved.

But Deirdre Bloxham! Wasn't this exactly what she wanted? She shook herself and went back to the window. "Oh, blast it all!" she said aloud, and her tame blackbird, perched on the window ledge waiting for his raisins, flew off with an alarmed squawk.

The telephone rang, and Deirdre picked up the bedside extension.

"Deirdre? Ah, I'm glad to hear you're awake. Have you seen the lovely morning?"

"Hello, Ivy. Yes, I am awake. Just. And yes, I have seen the lovely morning, and am about to have a shower, breakfast and make myself look equally lovely for a trip to Measby with Gus. What's on your mind so early?"

"For a start, Deirdre," Ivy said, "I don't call this early. And secondly, I was wondering whether it wouldn't be a good idea for all of us to go to Measby together? Four heads are better than two."

"We'd hardly be inconspicuous, Ivy! Isn't that what we usually aim at? I bet Measby doesn't often see four assorted strangers appearing out of a Rolls!"

"Ah. Well, I suppose you're right. But I have been thinking."

Deirdre groaned.

"I have been thinking," repeated Ivy firmly, "that it is time Gus told us more about his abduction and why exactly he was taken. And who those two mysterious kidnappers are. And don't forget to find out if he's phoned that Martin, and what came of it."

"In other words, Cousin Ivy, you don't want me to forget this is an Enquire Within trip, and not just a jolly outing to the other side of the county with friend Gus?"

"That's right," said Ivy. "You'd better get yourself prepared. I shall ring Gus to remind him of one or two things now. Report back on Monday. Meeting at Tawny Wings? Fine. Good-bye."

* * *

AS THE ROLLS purred along the road to Measby, Gus was silent. When Deirdre spoke he answered in monosyllables.

"All right, then, what is it?" she said in the end, thinking he might be brooding about Theo, and this was her punishment.

He sighed. "It was Ivy's call this morning. She made it quite plain that she thinks I am not pulling my weight with Enquire Within. She says I have to explain a lot more, and report back on my contact with Martin. Is she right, Deirdre? Are things falling apart?"

Deirdre thought for a moment, then said that on the whole she agreed with Ivy. "As you know," she said, "it wasn't exactly a picnic for the rest of us when you went missing. Don't you think you owe us something, Gus? Okay, so maybe you do still have to keep up some kind of secret agent image, but frankly I'm not convinced. If you want my opinion—"

"—not sure I do, Dee-Dee," he interrupted quietly.

"Well, you're getting it, anyway. I think it is a bit of a game for you. I think you know perfectly well who those two kidnappers were and what it was all about. And I am beginning to wonder if the mysterious Martin actually exists."

"Right!" he said, straightening up in his seat. "Well, here goes. I used to work for a government department, and still have a retainer from them. If they think I can now and then be useful, then I have to jump to it."

"Why aren't you still working for them full time, then? You're not retirement age, for sure."

"No, not in the usual way. But once your cover's been blown in that kind of work, you cease to be useful on most occasions. Sounds dramatic, I know, but that's how it was. Not exactly a secret agent, Deirdre. Investigating, as I have quite honestly told you before."

"Does that mean you could be in danger?" Deirdre said.

He was serious now, she could tell. Or was he just telling a good story?

"As for those kidnappers, I did *not* know who they were. One object of the exercise was the ransom money. They threatened me with what they knew about my past life. One or two hints about unpaid debts, suspicions of cheating at cards, that kind of thing. Enough, Deirdre my dear, to convince me they were not joking. Someone, if not you, then probably Alwen Jones, paid the ransom, and I was allowed to go, but not without renewed threats of retribution if I tried to find out more about them. They had a gun, and I decided they would use it if necessary. They might have missed the target then, judging from the way they handled it, but next time they might get the bull's-eye."

"But you *are* still investigating them, aren't you?" Deirdre refused to be frightened off.

"Not just them. That is what we have to find out. We need to know whether there is any connection between that uncomfortable episode and the assignment given to me by Martin."

"And have you—"

"I have tried to speak to him. I think to save time, I'll tell all when we meet on Monday. Can't have Ivy feeling left out, can we?"

They drew up in a lay-by on the outskirts of Measby, and Deirdre switched off the engine. "A little walk will do us good," she said. "This car sticks out like a sore thumb, and I suppose the less we draw attention to ourselves in this village the better."

"I have a secret agent's false moustache in my pocket, if you'd like that? And I could pull my cap down over my face?"

"Any more of that," said Deirdre, "and I'm going home, and you can find your own way back."

"Pax, Mrs. Bloxham," Gus said, taking her arm. "Let's step out. What did we plan to do first? Oh, yes," he said hastily, seeing her expression harden, "call at the vicarage.

Ask about a distant relation who used to live in the ruined cottage. Right, best foot forward!"

The village street was empty. Deirdre guessed that most people would have gone into town to do supermarket shopping. As they passed the village shop, she glanced into the open door, and saw the shopkeeper standing in the shadows, staring out at them. She bent down and took off her shoe. "Stone in it," she said to Gus. When she straightened up, the man had gone. "Straight to phone his boss, I bet," she said.

The vicarage was a large, turreted house, built at a time when the vicar was one of the most important men in the village. They knocked gently on the smart front door, and Deirdre noticed that the paint was fresh. In fact, considering vicars were so poorly paid, the whole place had a surprising air of prosperity about it. Neat garden, closely mown lawns, weed-free gravel drive. It was certainly a more impressive place than the new utility model vicarage in Barrington.

The door opened. "Yes?" A tall, bearded figure with a dog collar peeping out looked at them suspiciously.

"Good morning," said Gus. "So sorry to trouble you, but we were wondering whether you could help us. We are trying to trace a relative of my wife here."

Deirdre dug him fiercely in the back with her handbag. Wife, indeed!

The vicar sighed. "Oh, dear," he said. "We get so many people. . . . You'd better come in, but I can't give you much time. I have a meeting I must attend."

They followed him into a very pleasant study. He had obviously been working on his sermon, thought Deirdre, seeing papers and books spread out on his desk.

"Now, who are you looking for? Name?"

"Well, that's the problem," said Gus. "We don't exactly know. Could be Smith or Jones. Two sides of the family, you know. All we do know is that he lived in an old cottage in this village. He died relatively recently, and we are anxious that he should have a decent memorial. It is possible that he had no close relations. Never married, apparently."

"Are you sure you are looking for *Smith*? We had a Bernard Smithson, died quite recently," the vicar said. When Gus said that yes, of course it was Smithson he had meant to say, the vicar continued.

"Easily found. His cottage, now tumbling down, is in the High Street, and he is buried in the churchyard. No headstone as yet. In fact, we were hoping a relative would come forward to take care of that. Why don't you go along and have a look? The new cemetery is just up the Oakbridge road, and his is the newest grave. Marked with a wooden cross at the moment, as are all graves until the ground settles. Now, if you'll excuse me, I must dash."

He began to gather his papers together, and stacked the books into a neat pile. Deirdre watched him, thinking he certainly seemed a very busy man, and well organised, for a vicar. Maybe a bit too smooth? Then he picked up a paperback book that had been open facedown on the end of the desk. He closed it and slipped it underneath the pile, but not before Deirdre had noticed the name of the author. Weasel Murphy. *Weasel Murphy?* She couldn't wait to tell Gus.

Forty-five

GUS'S REACTION WAS disappointing. "Well," he said, "I don't suppose he'd be the first man of the cloth to have a flutter on the gees."

"But Weasel Murphy is not about having a few bob on the Tote. It's big stuff, isn't it? Ivy's got it now. Maybe we should take another look."

As they walked slowly up the road towards the cemetery, Gus once more took Deirdre's arm. "On reflection, Dee-Dee," he said, "you may be right, and the sad truth is that I really don't want to know."

She looked into his face, and was shocked at his despairing expression.

"On the face of it," he continued, "there's nothing wrong with an old man and a reverend gentleman having an interest in gambling. Lots of people enjoy the excitement, and don't get fleeced. But there is another side to it, as I know only too well."

He stopped and turned to face Deirdre. "Sod it!" he said loudly. "I really thought I'd left all that behind!"

They stood without speaking for a moment, and then

Deirdre took his arm. "Poor old thing," she said. "So do you want us to duck out of this case?"

Gus laughed. "Not likely," he said. "Never fear, Gus is here!"

"Even if it turns out to have nothing to do with your Martin's investigation?"

"Even so."

"Right, well, let's find Bernard Smithson's grave and see if we can pick up any clues."

They stepped out again purposefully, and Gus squeezed Deirdre's hand. "And don't worry about Weasel Murphy," he said. "I know him off by heart."

The cemetery was shaded and chilled by a row of tall, aged yew trees, gnarled and twisted, their gloomy grave-yard green turned into black by the heavy rain clouds now gathering over Measby. The iron gate stuck fast, and Gus put his weight behind it to force it open. A rusty watering can stood under a tap, and the rubbish bin was overflow-ing with dead flowers and discarded cellophane wrappings. Beside the bin, lying where its killer had thrown it, was a dead fox, its fiery coat soiled with smears of liquid mud.

"God, what a place to be laid to rest!" said Gus. "Let's find the old man's grave and get out of here as soon as poss."

Deirdre was surprisingly unmoved. "Foxes are vermin, so we're told," she said. "Theo has a lot of trouble with the anti-hunt lot, but he says local farmers lose lambs and chick-ens to the fox every year. They have to be culled, he says."

Gus had no interest in what Theo had to say about any-thing except a little matter of increasing the rent on his cot-tage. He ignored Deirdre's remark, and stepped forward to a clearly recent grave. A wooden cross had only the name Bernard Smithson and his dates of birth and death. Two wreaths of long-dead flowers remained.

"Not much to go on here," he said.

"Wait a minute," Deirdre said, leaning forward and picking up one of the wreaths. A label still clung to the wire frame, and she peered at it closely. "Have you got your glasses, Gus?" she said. "Didn't think to bring mine." She handed the wreath to him, and he began to read. " 'With fond remembrances. Bill and Jean next door.' Neighbours, obviously."

"What about this one?"

" 'Bernie—Gone but not forgotten. D.M.O.' Any good?"

Deirdre frowned. "D.M.O.? Oh my God, Gus. Doris May Osborne. That's who it is. Not the usual loving message, is it?" She shivered. "Come on, let's go. I reckon that's enough for one day."

"Not really, Deirdre," he said, replacing the wreath carefully. "What about the second item on our plan? Investigate the Reading Room. Remember? We noticed it on our first visit. The notice in the window about an archive that could be seen on applying to the caretaker for the key?"

"I need a drink," Deirdre said, without much hope.

"Stiffen the sinews, wife," Gus said. She took a deep breath, but he did not allow her to reply. "Now, do you remember where the Reading Room is? I think it's up that side road near the church."

THE CARETAKER LIVED conveniently close to the Reading Room and answered the door at once. Deirdre had the feeling that behind every cottage window was a pair of watchful eyes, following their progress round the village.

"Just a minute," the woman said. "I'll get the key. My name's Betty, by the way. And yours?"

"Brian and Maureen," said Deirdre quickly. "Nice to meet you, Betty."

They were ushered into the Reading Room, a pretty nineteenth-century building restored by public subscription five years ago. The roof gables were edged with carved wooden boards, and the windows decorated with a latticed frieze of coloured glass.

"Nice and dry in here," Deirdre said. "Good for your archive material. Damp is death to old documents, isn't it."

Betty nodded proudly. "Was it something particular you was looking for?" she said.

"Yes, we're trying to trace some information on the Smithson family," Gus answered. "We've seen old Bernard's grave. So sad. I'm a distant relation, and never met him. But I'm interested in researching the family. Lots of people do it these days. Maybe we're living in an insecure age where we need to find our roots!"

Betty looked at him blankly. "I suppose so," she said. "Research, did you say?" She was clearly impressed. "Well, help yourself. It's all in that filing cabinet over there. It's this small key. I've got work to do, so I'll leave you to it. Bring the key back to me, please, and then I'll come and lock up."

"You're very busy, I'm sure," said Deirdre. "Do you work in the village?"

"Oh, yes, I clean at the school, and I do some cooking for Mrs. Osborne at the Manor, when she's got dinner parties, an' that. I've got a steak and kidney pie in the oven right now! She'll not be pleased if the pastry's burnt!"

After she had gone, Deirdre and Gus got to work. They looked up Osborne first of all, and found a fat file full of details of the local squires, resident at the Manor since the conquest. They had lived in some style, it seemed, and a couple of generations back, one Geoffrey Osborne had used the family money, plenty of money coming from coal mines in Derbyshire, to install main drainage and water supply for the entire village.

"So Doris May married into the right family." Deirdre remembered that for all her airs and graces, Doris had seemed not quite top drawer. "Mind you, she struck me as a very determined lady. Perhaps the late Mr. Osborne didn't stand a chance!"

Gus didn't answer, and she saw that he had crouched down and was absorbed in an old photograph in the bottom drawer. She looked over his shoulder, and saw a wedding group. She peered closely at the bride. "Hey, that's our Doris May, isn't it?" she said.

Gus nodded. "And read the caption," he said.

Deidre read through the names and details of the wedding party. "Ah, here it is," she said. "This is Doris May's maiden name. Oh my God, it says 'nee Wilson'! Ringing bells, Gus?"

"Oh, yes," he said. "Loud and clear. How about you?"

"Alwen *Wilson* Jones," they chorused.

Forty-six

"I'LL GO AND sit in the car, Gus," Deirdre said, "and you can go to the shop and get something for us to eat. A couple of cans of something alcoholic wouldn't come amiss."

"Sure you don't want to come?"

"No, the old man will recognise me and that's probably not a good thing at the moment."

"Right-o. See you in a couple of minutes."

Gus strode off down the road to the shop, and Deirdre retraced her steps to the car. She sat in the driving seat and switched on the radio. Measby was giving her the creeps, and so she put on some loud jazz to cheer herself up. She did not hear the approach of footsteps, and was startled when a face appeared at the window next to her. With great presence of mind, she hit the locking button, and mouthed, "What do you want?" to the woman's face.

"Open the window," the woman shouted.

Deirdre switched off the radio, and lowered the window, but not very far, leaving enough open for a conversation.

"Mrs. Bloxham?" the woman said. She smiled, but

Deirdre did not return the smile. How did this woman know her name?

"What do you want?"

"Just a little chat. It's an awfully cold wind, isn't it. Do you think I might sit in the car for a second or two? I'm doing a survey on the recent outbreak of swine flu, and would be most grateful if you could answer one or two questions?"

"How did you know my name?"

The woman did not answer but walked round to the passenger door and knocked gently on the window there. Deirdre sighed. She supposed the car was well-known. After all, Bert had been a public figure in the county. The woman seemed genuine enough, and it was important to get as much information as possible on swine flu.

She had her finger on the unlock button when she heard a great shout from down the road. She could see Gus approaching, and he was waving his arms about in a crazed semaphore. "Don't open!" she heard as he came closer. She turned to speak to the woman, but she had disappeared.

"For God's sake, Deirdre! That was her, the woman who kidnapped me!" Gus was level with the car now, and Deirdre unlocked the doors. Gus jumped in beside her and said in the time honoured phrase, "Follow that car!"

"What car?" said Deirdre.

"Oh, yes, sorry. Got carried away. She ran off down that track. But Deirdre, I did recognise her. She calls herself Margaret. What did she say to you?"

"Said she was doing a swine flu survey, and asked to sit in the car to talk to me for a minute. I was just going to let her in when you shouted. Are you sure that was the Margaret woman? This one seemed genuine to me."

"Very convincing, I'm sure. She was very convincing in the train that day. No, I'm quite sure, Deirdre. I had plenty of time to get well acquainted with her. Are you up to following down that track? Might be a bit hard on the Rolls's paintwork."

"I'll go if you think we must, but if the man is down there, too, and it's likely to be a dead end, we might be in danger. What do you think?"

"I think a dead end might be exaggerating, but at the same time we don't know how many more of them there are. You're probably right. So why don't we just note where it goes and leave our visit to them for another day?"

"I can see a muddy sign over there, pointing down the track. Can you read it?"

Gus peered through the window. "Hollings Farm, it says. Remember that. Now, let's eat. There was a young girl in the shop. No sign of your old shopkeeper. Here you are, ham and mustard or cheese and pickle?"

MARGARET PUFFED INTO the house, and Max looked up expectantly. "Well?" he said.

"No good," she said. "Doris wasn't quick enough with her call. Bloxham was in the car, and about to let me in, when our mutual friend returned from the shop with supplies. He saw me and went mad, shouting and waving his arms about, so I beat it as quickly as I could."

"Ah, well, it was a long shot. Worth a try, though. Nothing like a personal warning to make them realise we mean business. We have to get them off our case, Margaret, just until we finish the job. Then it's away to the sunshine and a life of Riley."

"Who was Riley?"

"God knows. But he obviously knew how to have a good time." Max folded up his newspaper and walked over to where Margaret stood, still red-faced and breathing fast.

"How near are we to the end?" she said as he put his arms around her.

"Close, I would say," he replied. "Last time I caught sight of the old woman, she looked very peely-wally, very peely-wally indeed."

"I hope that means something bad," Margaret said sharply. "We can do without Alwen fighting fit!"

"Take it from me," he said, giving her a hug, "peely-wally will be much too mild to describe her by the time we take off."

GUS AND DEIRDRE sat in the car until the windows steamed up and Deirdre said she supposed they'd better be getting back.

"One more call to make," Gus said. "I can do it by myself, or you can come, too. Not too spooked by our day out so far?"

Deirdre shook her head. "I'm not going to be left alone here, though," she said. "Wherever you go, I go, too, Augustus Halfhide."

"Even to the Manor House?"

"Oh, no, not Doris May! Do you think it's wise?"

"What can she do to us? She'll probably be expecting us, anyway," he said. "Come on, sooner we get this one over, sooner we can go home."

It was raining gently when they got out of the car. Deirdre took an umbrella from the backseat and then locked up. "Straight there, then," she said. "What are we going to say? She'll know me again, I'm sure. I reckon the shopkeeper contacted her the minute he saw me pass by."

"And then rang Margaret? Is it a village network we're looking for? Small beer, in investigating circles, but may be dangerous, nevertheless. Is that umbrella fixed with a sharp point on the end?"

"Okay, okay. Enough of your sarcasm. I don't care how small the network is, it could still be lethal. And I am *not* exaggerating. Depends on how high the stakes are, doesn't it?"

"A very appropriate gambling phrase, Deirdre," Gus said. "Now, here's the entrance to the Manor. We might as well be consistent, and carry on with our family researches into the late unlamented Bernard Smithson."

They walked briskly up the long drive, Gus determined and Deirdre reluctant, until they were within sight of the house.

"Come on, Dee-Dee," Gus said, aware that she was slowing down.

"But Gus," she said, "look at the windows. The blinds are down on every single one. There's nobody there, surely. Why don't we go back and try again another day? This is just a waste of time."

Gus hesitated. "You may be right," he said. "But then who made the call to Margaret, telling her you were in the village?"

"The old man in the shop?"

"But he wasn't there, either, when I went in. That young girl was serving."

"Doesn't mean he wasn't there. He could have been lurking in the back of the shop. Or gone to ground with his devious boss. Just because the blinds are down, it doesn't mean they aren't in the house. Oh, no, why am I saying this? I know what you're going to suggest. Keep going and see what's happening round the back?"

Gus smiled at her and nodded. "That's my girl," he said. "Best foot forward."

They walked on, agreeing that they were probably under observation from behind the blinds. "Still, we're not doing any harm. We have a perfectly good reason for being here. We shall say we understand Bernie was at one time a handyman at the Manor, and hope that Mrs. Osborne might have some information to give us on his wider family."

"Glib, that's what you are, Gus," Deirdre said. "I can see why your secret department keeps you on a retainer. I bet you were top agent at one time?"

"Never mind about that," he replied. "Isn't that a fig-ure standing in the shadows by the entrance to the stable yard?"

Deirdre gulped. "Yeah, it is. She's sure to remember me. So can we turn and run, please?"

"Nope, carry on. It's a woman. Maybe Doris May."

As they drew near, the figure emerged from the trees and stood in the middle of the drive, confronting them. It was indeed Doris May, Deirdre saw, and she watched them approach with no trace of a welcoming smile.

"What do you want?" she said. "I am about to go out. I have to catch a train to London, and have very little time."

Gus apologised for bothering her, and began to explain about Bernie Smithson. He was cut off almost immediately by Doris May.

"I have no time for that rubbish now," she said. "And if you have any ideas about breaking and entering, I can assure you that the Manor is safely secured, with a direct line to the police if the alarms go off. So just go away, and I will do nothing more. If you insist on snooping around here suspiciously, I shall report you. I know who you are, and where you can be found, so you would be well advised to go away and not return. Now, I intend to see you off the premises before I leave."

Forty-seven

THE VILLAGE WAS quiet, as always on a Sunday morning, and Ivy and Roy made their slow way along the High Street towards the church, the chill wind causing Ivy to shiver. Katya had warned them that it was a beautiful day, so long as they were well wrapped up. Now Ivy was glad of her fur tippet, even if it did smell of mothballs, and had a malevolent looking fox's head at one end. She bent down and gently adjusted Roy's thick woolly scarf, and he looked up at her from his vehicle and smiled. "It's only because I love you, Ivy, that I am breaking the habit of a lifetime and coming to church with you this morning. I do hope the vicar won't be too warm in his welcome, in case I never darken his door again."

"Oh, you will, Roy. Once you see how much good it does you to have a little talk with Him, you'll be a regular. And in any case, I have no intention of going with you to a dingy registry office in Thornwell when the time comes. If you're still keen on taking me to the altar, then the altar has to be there in front of us!"

It had rained in the night, and the church path was

slippery. "Hold on to the back of my seat, Ivy," Roy said, delighted that she was thinking positively about marriage. "Can't have you hobbling up the aisle."

The churchwarden had seen them arriving, and rushed out to give a hand. Roy said that he would manage perfectly well, but Miss Beasley could do with a supporting arm until they were safely in the church. This did not go down well with Ivy, but she swallowed a sharp comment and took the churchwarden's arm with good grace.

There were the usual half dozen elderly parishioners, and two helpers from the home for autistic young people escorting the lad whose face lit up when the organ played. Ivy took Roy's hand and led him to her front pew, and they sat down.

"Vicar's away on retreat," Ivy whispered. "Don't know who's coming instead. Hope it's not that retired one who's deaf as a post and loses his place in the book."

At this point, the vestry door opened and the replacement clergyman appeared, tall and bearded and clad in a chalk white surplice.

"Looks as if he's been rushing, Ivy," whispered Roy. "We're late starting, anyway."

The service was conducted with great efficiency and, in spite of the delayed start, seemed to Ivy to finish at least ten minutes before the usual time. As they made their way to the church door, she saw the vicar was using the "passing on" technique. This had been explained to her by a nice young curate at Round Ringford as a firm moving-on motion as hands are taken for a farewell at the church door. Apparently it was recommended by the church for avoiding long chats with certain people known for delaying the rest of the congregation after a service.

"Wait a bit, Roy," she said. "We'll let the others go first." When they were the only ones left, and the vicar's smile had become rather fixed, Ivy led Roy to the door and extended her hand.

"Very nice service, Vicar," she said. "We haven't seen you here before, have we? Where do you come from?"

"Oh, from the other side of the county," he said, smiling genially. "And am I right in thinking you are Miss Beasley?"

Ivy confirmed this, and was surprised that he knew her name. Perhaps their usual vicar had warned him! Ivy chuckled and said, "And you're from Oakbridge? Such a pleasant town."

"Well, not the town itself," the vicar said. "A village, actually. A few miles into the country. Measby is the name. You know it, I expect?"

"I have heard of it," said Ivy enigmatically. "Can't think why. Something to do with some sort of scandal?"

"Good gracious me, no!" the vicar replied firmly. "Nothing so exciting happens in Measby. Now, if you'll excuse me, I must be going. Cares of office, you know!" he added lightly, and disappeared back into the church.

"Well, that was interesting, wasn't it, Roy?" The two made their steady way back to Springfields. "Funny coincidence that the man should come from Measby. And even stranger that he should know my name. We must tell Deirdre and Gus tomorrow."

Roy got out of his vehicle when they arrived at Springfields and took Ivy's arm. "You'll have to be careful with all this investigating, dearest," he said. "You're beginning to see spies round every corner. I am sure that vicar was as innocent as the day is long."

"Possibly," said Ivy, and unhooked her fur tippet, stroking the fox's head with an affectionate hand. "Do you think Tiddles would like to play with this?" she said.

Forty-eight

DEIRDRE HAD, FROM force of habit, since it was Monday and her mother had always washed on a Monday, put her small amount of washing in the noisy machine, and set it going. As a result, she did not hear the other team members at the door and was greeted by a frowning Ivy when she finally opened it.

"About time, too!" Ivy said, and marched in and straight up to the Enquire Within office. "Right," she continued, taking off her coat and folding it onto a chair. "Now we're all here, let's start."

The others quickly settled and, with Deirdre operating an unfamiliar coffee machine and attempting to take the minutes at the same time, the meeting got off to a shaky start.

"That's new, isn't it?" Gus said, attempting to lighten the atmosphere. "The coffee machine, I mean, Dee-Dee."

Ivy noted the affectionate version of her cousin's name but said nothing. She was not at all sure of Gus's reliability, but Deirdre was a toughie herself, and it was no good worrying about their relationship.

"Yes, well, it was reduced at the kitchen shop in Thornwell, and I reckoned it would be just the thing for our meetings. Second cups, and all that."

Ivy lost patience. "For goodness' sake! This is not a mother's meeting, you know. Who is going first? You two have lots to report, I expect and hope, from your visit to Measby?"

"Quite right, Ivy," said Gus firmly. "Shall I report, Deirdre?" She nodded, and he continued. "When we arrived, we parked a little way outside the village. We had agreed a plan, which took in visiting the vicar, the graveyard, the Reading Room archive and the Manor. We hoped to speak to Doris May."

Roy had perked up when the vicar of Measby was mentioned. "Did you talk to the parson?" he said.

"Let him finish, Roy dear," said Ivy.

"Well, yes, we did. He wasn't all that helpful, but we discovered that the old gambler's name was Bernard Smithson, and he had no known relations. The vicar was quite pleased in the end that we'd turned up, actually. He was clearly hoping we'd pay for a headstone."

"Your fault, Gus," Deirdre interrupted. She turned to the others. "Our Gus came up with this story that we were Bernie's long-lost relations, researching the roots of the Smithson family."

"Well, it worked," Gus continued. "The vicar sent us round to the graveyard to see the grave."

"Very creepy and shivery," said Deirdre, ignoring Ivy's frown. "And there were two really mangy little wreaths of dead flowers."

"One was from a Bill and Jean, the old boy's neighbours, apparently. But the other had a most interesting label." Gus was now determined to stick to his task. "It said 'Bernie—Gone but not forgotten. D.M.O.' " He paused, waiting for Roy and Ivy to catch on. He hadn't long to wait.

"Doris May Osborne," said Ivy. "Go on, Gus."

Gus then described how the kidnapper Margaret had tried to ambush Deirdre in the Rolls, and he added their discovery of Doris May's wedding details in the Reading Room.

"And guess what?" Deirdre could not resist the punch line. "Her maiden name was Wilson!"

Ivy and Roy looked at each other. "Alwen," Roy said. "Oh, dear."

"So then I wanted to come home," Deirdre said. "But Gus said that our plan had included a visit to find Doris May. He was going to use the same story about tracing Bernie's family, and said I could stay in the car. But I was really spooked by then, and went with him up to the Manor."

Gus took over. "This is probably the most important thing we discovered. Doris May knew exactly who we were, where we lived and how to find us. She gave us a nasty, vicious warning that unless we stopped snooping it would be the worse for us."

The silence that followed this revelation seemed to go on forever. Finally, Ivy said could she have another coffee, and this triggered second cups all round. Then she cleared her throat and said that she thought it had become clear that their next move would be vital to their investigations.

"So, what shall it be?" Roy said, gazing at Ivy with admiration.

Ivy looked at Gus, and said, "*You* know what it is, don't you?"

"Yes," he answered. "You are quite right, Ivy. We must find out right away what is going on in Measby that is so sensitive to discovery. They are quite clearly operating a scam of some sort, and Bernard Smithson was a victim. But one impoverished old man is not going to be worth their while. It's a ring, involving some we already know. Doris May, Margaret and hubby—"

"—and possibly the vicar," said Roy. "Go on, Ivy, tell them about church yesterday."

"That vicar you called on," she said. "He took the service yesterday. After the service, we had the usual word at

the church door, and he addressed me by my name. Then
he tried seeing what we knew about Measby. It wasn't
much, but enough to make me suspicious. Now," she continued, "Roy says I'm seeing spies round every corner, but
don't you think it's a bit of a coincidence that he turned up
here? I've enquired around, and apparently he's never been
to our church before."

"But how would he know our vicar was away, and how
would he get to replace him?" Deirdre was frowning.

"I expect there's a list of vicars willing to fill in," Roy
said. "He was probably a last-minute volunteer. And from
what you said about Doris May, she probably knows about
Ivy and me, and the likelihood of our being in church. You
bet she's got her hooks into that vicar and he was obeying
orders."

"Oh my God!" said Deirdre, running her hands anxiously through her apricot curls. "Do you mean Doris May
has an informant here in this village?"

"I'm afraid that's probably so," said Gus. "Which
means, as I'm sure Ivy has concluded already, that we have
to act quickly. So what do we do, Ivy?"

"You know perfectly well, Gus. And who better to do it?
We visit a gambling den, and the nearest is Ozzy's Casino
in Thornwell."

Gus paled. "Must I?" he said.

"Why not?" Deirdre said. "You're not trying to tell
us there's any danger for you in going to a crummy little
casino in a provincial town like Thornwell. You'd never
even been to the place before you moved to Barrington."

"There's danger and danger," said Gus enigmatically.
"But so long as I have someone with me, I'm willing to
go. Are you up to it, Deirdre?" he added, and Ivy noticed
a pleading note in his voice. What was all this? A smooth,
sophisticated operator like Gus, apparently nervous of visiting a small-town casino?

Deirdre was thinking much the same, but then it clicked.
Addiction. She had forgotten but now realised this would
be difficult for him.

"I've got a better idea," she said. "I know Theo has been a gambler in his time, mainly up in London at the big casinos, but he probably knows quite a bit about the local one as well. Why don't I ask him to take me for an evening at Ozzy's? I'm almost sure he'd think it was a big laugh. A fun thing to do. What d'you think, Gus? I'm not doubting your experience, but—"

He interrupted her eagerly. "No, no. Great idea, Deirdre. Should have thought of it myself. Theo is our man. Can you organise it fairly swiftly?"

Deirdre looked at her watch. "He'll be in town until this afternoon," she said. "I'll ring him after lunch."

Ivy and Roy had listened to the other two without speaking, and now Roy looked across at Ivy and said, "So what shall we do? There must be something."

"Oh, yes, there is," she said. "We think of a nice, friendly outing for you, me and Alwen. Something that takes most of the day. Somewhere where she can't storm off in a huff, or in tears."

"A day out together, when we can have a nice long chat?" said Roy, his old face creased in smiles. "I can think of just the place, my love."

Forty-nine

NEXT MORNING, ALWEN was already at the breakfast table when Roy and Ivy came into the dining room. She turned and looked at them, and nodded without smiling. "Good morning, both," she said in a voice that sounded as if it had emerged from some dark dungeon beneath.

"Good morning, Alwen!" said Roy. On an impulse he leaned over and planted a small kiss on her pale cheek. "And how are we this fine morning? 'The sun is shining to welcome the day, and it's hey, ho, come to the fair!'" He produced a quavery tenor voice and sang the last encouraging line.

This was too much for Ivy. "That's quite enough of that, Roy," she said. "Really, Alwen," she said confidingly, "you'd think he'd been at the brandy bottle before breakfast!"

"Just trying to cheer up this young lady here," Roy said, winking at Ivy. He was growing more sure of her, and had decided that a little gentle teasing would be good for their future relationship.

Earlier on, they had worked out a plan for persuading

Alwen to go with them on an outing for the day. Fortunately Mrs. Spurling had gone to visit an ailing sister, and Miss Pinkney was in charge. Roy had had a word with her, and she had agreed that both she and Mrs. Spurling had been worried lately about Mrs. Wilson Jones. She had seemed so depressed, and nothing would lift her out of it. Yes, she said with enthusiasm, it would be a very good idea if Roy and Ivy could persuade her to have a day out with them.

"It would take her out of herself," Pinkers had said, and she agreed to do what she could to persuade the poor soul.

Now the three sat at the table and Ivy and Roy tucked into scrambled eggs and bacon, while Alwen toyed with a piece of dry toast.

"We were wondering," began Roy, "whether you'd be able to do us a favour today, Alwen?"

"Depends what it is," she muttered.

"Well, it's like this. Ivy and I have for some time wanted to pay a visit to Easterwold on the coast."

"Cold, wet and windy, that's Easterwold," Alwen said.

"Now, now, Alwen," Roy said, patting her hand. "Look out of that window. A beautiful blue sky likely to be so for a whole day, according to the weather forecast. We plan to have our special taxi to take us over and bring us back, and we want you to come with us. Don't we, Ivy?"

Ivy said there was plenty of room in the taxi, even with Roy's vehicle aboard, and it would be a comfortable ride.

"Why do you want me to come?" Alwen said suspiciously.

Roy was about to reply when Ivy got in first. "Because you could share the expense of the taxi," she said bluntly. "It'll be quite a bit, and Roy and me, well, we're not made of money."

Roy's heart sank. Ivy had really put her foot in it this time. But to his amazement, Alwen began to chuckle. "I like that, Ivy," she said. "There's a lot to be said for plain speaking." She looked across at Roy. "All right then. What time is the taxi coming? And if you take my advice, you'll put an umbrella in your bag."

* * *

THE DRIVE TO Easterwold was, as promised by Roy, comfortable and relaxing. The taxi was adapted to take Roy's vehicle, and there was plenty of room for the ladies to sit and gaze out of the windows. The last few miles took them through colourful heathland and marshes, where flocks of birds rose up as they passed, and Alwen proved to know their names, much to Ivy's annoyance. She had lived in the country all her life, and apart from knowing a sparrow from a robin, and a blue tit from a blackbird, she did not consider it necessary to join the loony company of bird-watching twitchers, who went from one end of the country to the other in pursuit of the greater spotted bobtailed whatsit.

"I saw a marsh harrier once," Roy said cheerfully. "Made my day, that did."

The taxi dropped them in the centre of the village, and Alwen looked around with interest. "My goodness, it's changed since I was last here," she said. "All these people! It was a shabby, empty little place then. But according to George, it had once been a busy trading port. Corn, timber and, of course, fish, so he said. Funny," she added, "I've not thought of Easterwold for years and years, and now I remember things like that. A real symptom of old age, that is."

"There's a nice little café for a coffee, girls," Roy said, at once assuming a jaunty holiday air, determined not to let Alwen's spirits sink. "Follow me, and I'll treat you to a toasted tea cake." He parked his vehicle outside, and they went in, selecting a table by the window.

"We'll probably have to settle for one of them muffin things these days," Ivy said, but had to backtrack when a pleasant girl in a frilly apron said of course they could have a toasted tea cake. "With jam or marmalade?" she added.

Alwen commented that there seemed to be an awful lot of tourists around, unlike when she was a girl, and was told that, on the contrary, it was near the end of the season now, and numbers were definitely down. "You should see the place when we have the sand castle championships!" the girl said. "Can't move for kids, young and old!"

Ivy looked at Alwen, and thought that if they did no more today than produce that amused expression on her face, they would have done a good deed. But there was more to do, and she suggested they have a stroll round the village, and then they found a place to sit in the sun and watch the boats until lunchtime. That would be the time to bring the talk round to Alwen's family, the Wilsons, and drop Doris May casually into the conversation. Meanwhile, she had to admit, it was a lovely day and she was enjoying herself no end.

They found a seat out of the wind, and chatted idly about this and that, mostly things that had happened to them in the past, and Ivy began to talk about her mother. "She did love me, I suppose, but not like people love today," she said and, to his delight, took Roy's hand. "My poor father could do nothing right, and it was the same for me. *She* was always right, of course, and there was no chance of a fair argument with her. She just came down like a ton of bricks, and if you knew what was good for you, you gave in and let her be right."

She paused, hoping for some response from Alwen about her own family, but there was nothing. She merely remarked that it made such a difference to children if they knew they were loved.

After a while, the wind seemed to change direction, and Roy suggested they move on. "Getting a bit chilly," he said. "Why don't we find the church and have a look inside. I know Ivy likes churches, and I find the history in them fascinating. What do you think, Alwen? Up to a stroll?"

Alwen said she was fine, but if it was too far and her hip became painful, she would rest and wait for the others. "I do appreciate what you're trying to do, you two," she said, and Ivy felt a moment's shame. After all, the real reason was to pump Alwen for more information about the Wilsons in general, and Doris May in particular. Still, if a day out was cheering up Alwen, that was a bonus.

Once out of the wind, the three wandered happily through the village, asking an elderly woman laden with supermarket shopping bags if she could direct them to the church and receiving far more information than they needed.

"If we'd looked around," said Ivy crossly, "we can see the church tower over there, behind that big hotel."

"Ah, but then we'd not have known that the first Queen Elizabeth slept in that hotel, and that helpful old thing's ancestors had emptied Her Majesty's chamber pot," Roy said.

"Don't be ridiculous," Ivy said. "Come on, Alwen, it's only a few steps further, just around the corner. Then you can have a rest in a pew. Let's hope the church is open."

"Bound to be," said Roy. "I read up on it, and it's very historic with lots to see. With all these tourists around, it'll certainly be open, with a collecting box well to the fore."

It was open, and Roy drove slowly up the ramp into the dark interior. Inside they were welcomed by a spruce grey-haired man who, when exchanging pleasantries with Roy, announced himself as chief volunteer. "Anything you need to know, just ask me," he said. "And madam," he added to Alwen, "if you would like a tranquil corner with a comfortable seat, we have reserved the side chapel over there for the purpose."

After having had most of the objects of interest pointed out to them, Roy and Ivy had had enough, and joined Alwen in the chapel.

"She's gone to sleep!" Ivy whispered.

"No I haven't," Alwen said, her eyes popping open. "It has been so nice just to sit here and think. Are you ready to go?"

"Nope, it's our turn to rest now. And maybe ask for a bit of guidance," Ivy said humbly. "I always do that in churches. You never know who's listening. It can be quite helpful, I find."

They were quiet for a few minutes, and then Roy nudged Ivy. "Needs help!" he mouthed at her, and then looked at

Alwen. She had taken a handkerchief from her handbag and held it in front of her face. Muffled sounds quite clearly indicated that she was once more in tears.

Ivy shook her head at Roy. "Wait," she whispered.

They waited until the sounds stopped and Alwen mopped her eyes. "Sorry," she said.

"Tell us," said Roy. "We might be able to help."

"It's your Bronwen, isn't it," Ivy said. "Is there trouble there?"

Alwen nodded and sniffed. "It's money, I'm afraid. Always has been with Bronwen. Always wanted more than she could afford to pay for. Now it's out of control, and I can't help. I couldn't help her father, and now I can't help her. But don't worry, Ivy, I'll find a way. It just gets me down sometimes. If she had a good husband to rely on, it would be different. But he's useless. Vain and stupid. But don't worry," she repeated. "I shall find a way."

She rose to her feet, tried a tremulous smile, and said they should be looking for somewhere to have a snack. "Must be the sea air," she said bravely. "I feel quite hungry. How about you two?"

AT THE TIME specified, the taxi was ready to collect them, and once they were all inside, Roy asked the driver not to go too fast. He was well aware that they had not managed to extract any Wilson family details from Alwen, and this would be their last chance today.

"It's such a lovely drive," Roy added. "And with the sun out on the heath, we want to get the benefit."

"My mother used to say that," said Alwen suddenly. "You know, if it was cold and we were wrapped up, and then went indoors, maybe to a café, she'd always make us take off our coats and said otherwise we'd not feel the benefit."

"You weren't an only child, then?" Ivy said casually.

"No, there was me and Doris. Just like my two girls, except there were more years between me and Doris. I was big sister, and had to look after her a lot. She was an awkward little cuss, right from the start."

Ivy held her breath. She could see Roy was doing the same, and prayed for him not to say anything. She looked out of the window, and waited.

"Of course, she went her own way, once we were both married," Alwen continued quietly, almost as if thinking aloud. "Doris married for money, me for love. I don't know which was worse. We both lost our husbands, hers because he was very old, and mine in a stupid accident. Mind you, William had left us by then."

Still Ivy said nothing, and Roy took his cue from her, smiling gently but keeping quiet.

"Money's the root of all evil, they say." Alwen had her eyes closed now, and her hands folded neatly in her lap. "Depends where the money comes from, I suppose. Wilson money in my case, loot from her husband's casino in Doris's. So she ended up Lady of the Manor, and I earned my keep teaching unwilling schoolchildren. Funny how things turn out. . . ." Her voice tailed away, and Ivy could see that she had drifted into sleep.

Roy raised his eyebrows, and Ivy shook her head. "Leave her," she whispered. "That's probably all we'll get today. Poor old thing," she added, and Roy nodded. "She's had a nice day out," he whispered, "thanks to you, my love." He leaned over and kissed Ivy's cheek, and the taxi was silent until they reached Springfields.

Back inside the hallway, Alwen thanked Ivy and Roy warmly for the day out, and when Miss Pinkney asked if she had enjoyed her trip to the seaside, she said that it was the best day out she had had for a long time.

"Then you'll have to go again soon," Miss Pinkney urged. She would have something really good to tell Mrs. Spurling tomorrow. Mrs. Wilson Jones seemed to her to be much more cheerful, though when she had tactfully questioned Ivy and Roy, they had agreed that Alwen looked a lot better for getting away from Barrington, but they thought there might still be a serious problem worrying their friend.

"I don't see what more we can do," Ivy said when she and Roy were relaxing in her room after supper. "It's up to Deirdre and Theo to see what they can find out at the casino."

"Thanks to your clever handling, my love, I think we probably confirmed the most important factor in the whole of this sorry business," Roy said. "Our Alwen is Doris May's sister. Do you remember what she said?"

"'Doris was always an awkward little cuss,'" Ivy answered. "And added to that, her husband died because he was very old! What does that tell us? That Doris married some poor old bloke who owned a casino and was very rich. She probably slipped something in his coffee."

"Ivy! You have no reason to suppose that. We must be careful what we say, my dear, otherwise we might get ourselves into hot water. I believe that there is an informer in our midst, keeping the Measby villains aware of our every word."

Ivy looked nervously up at the light fixture in the ceiling. "You don't mean we're *bugged*, surely!" she said.

Fifty

A VERY DISGRUNTLED Doris May Osborne trudged up the track leading to the cottage she had secured for Margaret and Max. She had exchanged her smart high heels for little-used green Wellington boots, and cursed as she stepped into a deep rut that splashed mud up to the bottom of her skirt. She had ordered her two lackeys, as she thought of them, to come up to the Manor, and they had refused point-blank. Max had suggested that if she wanted an urgent word, she could come to them. They were at home, trying to keep an approaching flood of rainwater from entering the back door.

Their reaction to her order was so shocking to Doris that she had for once been lost for words. She had slammed down the phone and set off straightaway. Two could play at that game, she decided, and meant to catch them unawares, unprepared for the ultimatum she intended to issue. The cottage was in sight now, and she kept to the side of the track, close to the hedge, out of sight of the windows where one of them might be lurking.

Inside the cottage, a council of war was in progress.

Margaret sat one side of the smouldering fire, and Max the other. Max had a glass of whisky in hand, and had snarled at Margaret when she suggested it was Dutch courage, and useless. "She'll nail us to the wall," he had said. "You underestimate her, Marg."

Margaret explained now what she planned they should do. "There's no hope of our getting any more money from this job," she said. "I feel it in my bones that the end is in sight, and unless we clear out very quickly, we shall be in the mire. And, by the way, I don't underestimate the old bag. She's very cunning, and we're not the only ones she has had over a barrel. Poor old Bernie fell to his death— with a little help from you."

"Doris had softened him up, made him nervous and shaky, with her constant demands and threats. You know very well it was her idea. Didn't take much to finish him off." Max's face was full of self-pity.

"And now, if I'm not mistaken, our very reverend vicar is in her clutches. Don't ask me how she does it. But again, I don't underestimate her. Ozzy's has a blameless reputation in the area. Clean as a whistle, according to my sources."

"What sources?" said Max, filling up his glass.

"Oh, here and there," she answered. She got up and fetched her handbag. "Here," she continued, "these are our flight tickets, and we leave in six hours' time. I've packed, and we can take the old banger to the airport and leave it there. It's worth nothing, except to us."

Max was still holding the tickets in his free hand when the door burst open and Doris May faced them with an icy expression that chilled the room.

"No you don't!" she said. "Don't even try to hide those tickets! Hand them over!"

"Bugger off!" said Margaret, advancing towards Doris's outstretched hand. "This is a private house, and you're trespassing! Go on, get out, and don't come back! Or else I'll, I'll . . ." She stuttered to a halt, seeing what Doris had now pointed straight at her.

"You'll what?" said Doris contemptuously. "Now, Max,

or whatever you call yourself, give me those tickets. You two are going nowhere, except possibly to hell if you don't do what you're told." She waved her hand, and Max saw the small, neat pistol. He knew absolutely that she would not be afraid to use it. Self-defence, whatever. She would have her defence all prepared.

He threw the tickets towards her, and they landed on the floor at her feet. "There you are," he said. "You can pick them up, if you want them."

Doris laughed, and Margaret shivered. "I don't fall for that old one!" Doris said. "I bend down to pick them up, and you pounce, knocking this little protector out of my hand. Oh, yes, I'm sure you'd love to play the hero, but you're not cut out for it, you idiot. Your only hope, both of you, is to stick with me. I shall make sure we all complete our mission successfully, and then I shall be glad to see the back of you. As far away as possible," she added, kicking the tickets to one side. "Where were these going to take you? All the way to Lanzagrotty?"

She looked at them for a full minute, and then said, "Well?"

Margaret sank down into her chair. "You win," she said. "Sit down, Max. She's got us tied up whatever we do now."

"Very sensible," Doris said, and put the gun back in her handbag. "Now, listen carefully. This is what we are going to do next. Have you heard of one Theo Roussel, squire of the village of Barrington?"

UNAWARE THAT HE was being discussed, Theo strode along the corridor to the kitchen, where he found Noreen sitting by the Rayburn, her feet up on a stool, reading the morning newspaper. She looked up at him, gave him a beaming smile, and said that her feet were killing her this morning, and was it really coffee time already?

"Never mind about coffee!" he said crossly. "It will soon be lunchtime, and as I told you yesterday, Mrs. Bloxham will be having lunch with me and I particularly want it to be delicious."

"Even nicer than I usually do?" Noreen asked, struggling to her feet. "And anyway, I haven't forgotten, Mr. Theo. There's a nice cottage pie in the oven, and I've opened a tin of baby carrots. Would you like one of sweet corn as well? That would make it a bit special, wouldn't it? And, before you can ask, I got a nice treacle tart from the shop yesterday, and it's warming up in the bottom oven. I think a nice slice of that, with a dollop of vanilla ice cream, will be just the ticket. All right?"

Theo groaned, and Noreen looked sympathetic. "Not suffering with the rheumatics, too, are we? I've got a tube of good stuff to rub into my legs. Smells like horse linament, but it does the trick. Like a squeeze, would you?"

Theo turned on his heels and left, hurrying into the drawing room and opening all the windows. I mustn't throw up, he said to himself several times. Deirdre will be here any minute. When the nausea had subsided, he once more vowed to get rid of Noreen within the next two weeks. He had had enough. No man could have been more patient, he comforted himself, but the time had come. He would approach little Katya and however much money it took to lure her away from Springfields, he was prepared to stump up.

By the time Deirdre arrived, the table had been hastily laid, and Theo had taken it upon himself to shine up a couple of glasses for preliminary gins.

"Hi, Theo!" Deirdre said, giving him a warm kiss. "How's everything? I looked in on Noreen on my way in, and made sure she was expecting me." She sniffed. "There is a strange smell around the house this morning, Theo. Strongest in the kitchen . . ."

"Don't mention it," Theo said, and groaned again. "It's the dreaded Noreen's horse linament. She puts it on her rheumatics. Shall we go out to the terrace with our drinks? At least the air's fresh out there."

They walked out and Theo relaxed. "How are you, my darling?" he said. "You're looking fabulous, as always. I do hope the little talk you wanted is not going to be serious?"

"Far from it," said Deirdre. "I do have a request, but it should be fun. Something you'll love, and an opportunity for you to teach me new tricks."

Theo brightened. "New tricks, Deirdre Bloxham?" he said waggishly. "Shall we go upstairs now, or wait until after lunch?"

"Not *those* kinds of tricks," she answered. "You're incorrigible, Theo! No, I want you to escort me to the casino in Thornwell. I've always wanted to see what goes on, and I have a fancy for a flutter. I'm not the addictive kind, so I won't get hooked. My Bert loved an afternoon at the races, but he used to say casinos were dens of iniquity, and that made me want to see for myself. How about it? Just for a bit of fun?"

Theo frowned and looked closely at her. "What are you up to, Deirdre?" he said.

"Up to?" she asked innocently. "Nothing, of course, except a desire for a bit of excitement. Not much of that at Tawny Wings these days. Except when the squire comes visiting," she added hastily.

"All right," Theo said, smiling indulgently at her. "I haven't been at the tables for some time now, but I'm sure it will come back to me. As you know, I have very little spare cash, but I am sure I can empty my money box and find enough to teach you how to lose."

"Oh my, how bitter!" Deirdre said. "And don't you worry, gambling money will be provided by me, and I am always lucky. I don't intend to lose, and nor will you. It will be such fun, Theo! When can we go?"

Noreen appeared at the terrace door, wiped her hands on her apron, and said luncheon was served. Theo whispered in Deirdre's ear that to call it luncheon was an offence as set out in the Trades Description Act. "Just do your best, my dear," he added. "I've opened a bottle of very good Bordeaux, so we can wash down the food without tasting it."

After manfully tackling the cottage pie and treacle tart, Theo told Noreen that after she had cleared away and washed the dishes, she could go home. He would be dining out this evening, and he would see her tomorrow morning. "And I do hope your feet are feeling better soon," he added kindly. The Bordeaux had been followed by a very precious Château d'Yquem, and these had done their work. He was full of bonhomie, as was Deirdre. After they had had coffee and a fine old brandy, they heard the back door slam shut and knew Noreen was on her way home.

As she followed Theo up the wide stairs, a little unsteadily here and there, Deirdre repeated her question. "When can we go, Theo?" she said as they turned towards his bedroom.

He began to take off her jacket, and kiss her fondly, gently following a downward path. "You've always been a goer, my darling," he said in muffled tones. "None better."

"No, silly," she said, guiding him with difficulty towards the bed, "I mean, when can we go to the casino? Tomorrow?"

"Mmm," he muttered. "Anything you say, my lovely girl."

Fifty-one

THE LOUNGE AT Springfields was almost empty. It was the hour when residents were encouraged to retire to their rooms, "for a little shut-eye," as Mrs. Spurling put it. "Then we shall be fresh as daisies to come down for a cup of tea and a spot of socialising," she would add, privately hoping that eyes went on being shut for long enough to allow her to get on with administration and one or two telephone calls of a private nature.

This afternoon, Ivy and Roy did not go upstairs after lunch but sat in comfortable chairs in their corner of the lounge. They had a token nap, and then ordered tea and spent some time discussing Alwen Jones.

"There's an awful lot we don't know about her," Ivy said, presiding over the teapot. "She hasn't come downstairs today, and Miss Pinkney said she had breakfast and lunch in her room. I wonder if yesterday was too much for her? She came out with some useful stuff, especially details of her sister Doris, the millionaire casino owner."

"I don't think it was too much for her, dearest," Roy said. "A few more days out with us and she'd be as right as rain.

No, it's being alone with her thoughts that's doing the damage, I reckon. Oh, and by the way, Deirdre left a message for us," Roy added, pouring second cups of tea, and saying reassuringly that there was no danger of ginger twins for the pair of them, even when they were married. "She said that she and Theo are going to Ozzy's Casino tomorrow. Perhaps we should tell them what to look out for?"

"Good idea," said Ivy. "As we know," she added primly, "there's only one thing on their minds when those two get together."

"Let's ring Gus and Deirdre to see if they can come here after supper this evening. No chance of the squire coming, too. But we could maybe have a game of cards after we've talked about tomorrow at the casino."

"Another good idea, my dear," said Ivy, blowing him an awkward kiss. "Shall I make the calls? Better be upstairs in my room. I sometimes think Spurling has got this lounge bugged. I've found one in my bedroom and covered it up with sticky tape."

"Where was it?" Roy asked in alarm.

"On the ceiling, of course. Nasty looking thing. Still, I fixed it."

"How did you get to it?" Roy said suspiciously. He was beginning to wonder if Ivy was confusing dreams with reality. Nothing new there, he thought. He did it himself sometimes.

"Stood on my bed, naturally," said Ivy smugly. "You don't believe me, do you? Well, next time you're in with me, I'll show you how I stepped on the little stool that Katya gave us, and then onto the bed. I've complained about that hard mattress, but this time it stood me in good stead."

Roy stared at her. "Ivy," he said in a measured voice. He would have to put this tactfully. "That's the smoke alarm you've covered up with sticky tape. I really don't think there are listening bugs in Springfields. . . ."

He was going to say more when he noticed that Ivy's face had an unusual expression. Then she began to splutter, and the splutter grew to a chuckle and the chuckle grew to a rip-roaring bellow. "Got you there, Roy Goodman!" she burbled. "I know I'm good for my age, but climbing onto a bed?" And then she was off again. Finally she calmed down, and said that she was really touched that Roy could think her capable of such a feat.

"So shall we get back to making those calls, Ivy my love?" he said, and reflected that every day he learnt something new about his beloved.

GUS WAS READING the morning newspaper when the phone rang. He did not immediately recognise Ivy's voice, as she seemed to be smothering a giggle. Ivy giggling? Pigs might fly, he said to himself. But there she was, asking him to go down to Springfields this evening. Deirdre, but probably not Theo, would be there, and they could discuss strategy for the visit to the casino. As she knew Gus had experience of gambling dens, she was sure his expertise would be vital. Gus was aware that by including him in the meeting, she was trying to make it easier for him to tolerate the idea of pairing Deirdre and Theo, and he felt a glow of affection for the old thing.

"Right-o," he said. "I'll be there about seven. Nothing to report from this end, but I am sure the discussion will be useful." He put down the phone and considered that in view of his failure ever to make any profit out of gambling, his expertise would not necessarily be of much use. But at least he knew the seamier side of that world, which might prove to be a considerable asset.

Deirdre was not quite so cooperative. She took offence at the idea that she and Theo needed instruction on what to look out for at the casino. They were interested in Doris May, weren't they, and by careful questioning intended to find out more about her operation. She knew most casinos were owned by big companies, but the one in Thornwell was privately owned. And, as they knew, inherited and run very successfully by Doris May Osborne.

"Mind you," Deirdre said knowledgeably now to Ivy in the interview room at Springfields, where the four had gathered, "with online gambling so widespread and successful, actual casinos might well have taken a knock in numbers playing the games."

"I suppose cheating the public is more difficult online?" Roy said.

"Something we shall find out," Deirdre replied confidently.

"And will you find out more about Doris herself?" Ivy said. "There's bound to be rumour and gossip amongst her staff. From the sound of it, she's a smooth operator, and probably a con artist into the bargain!"

Roy smiled. It amused him to see his Ivy, a former pillar of conservative respectability, using the jargon expected of an experienced investigator. My goodness, he thought, how all those years in Round Ringford were wasted! With such a sharp brain, she could have ruled the world, and made a much better job of it than the present lot.

Tiddles uncurled herself from Ivy's lap and jumped down, miaowing at the door.

Gus got up to open it and let her out. Miss Pinkney had, with some difficulty, persuaded Mrs. Spurling to have a cat-flap in the rear cloakroom door that led into the garden, so that Tiddles could come and go. She was still too small to go far, but with great bravery and resourcefulness managed to push her way out of the flap and back in again. This saved Springfields staff the unwelcome job of emptying a litter tray, and the little cat was now fully accepted.

"I expect I shall recognise somebody who I know from the past. I could ask a question or two," Deirdre said.

"Not sure if that's such a good idea," said Ivy. "Wouldn't it be better if you went incognito?"

Roy laughed delightedly but refused to explain why.

Deirdre was beginning to feel irritated. "Ivy Beasley!" she said. "Do you really think that I, Deirdre Bloxham, widow of one of the best-known men in Thornwell, could go incognito anywhere in town? And that landowner and scion of a long line of local squires, Theo Roussel, would not be recognised immediately? And why would it matter?"

Ivy raised her eyebrows and shrugged. "Perhaps you two aren't the right people to go. Maybe Roy and me, looking for a risky game of bingo, would be more successful?"

"Now, now, Ivy dear," Roy said. "You know we wouldn't have a clue how to go on in a casino. Deirdre and Theo will be fine for the job, I'm sure. It seems to me that the most important part of their visit will be to keep their ears and eyes open. And the simple fact that you and I both have hearing problems would rule us out."

Ivy bridled. "Nothing wrong with my hearing," she said crossly.

Gus had been silent through this exchange, and now cleared his throat. "Perhaps I should go," he said, with considerable reluctance. "On my own. Not instead of Deirdre and Theo. We should all three go, those two together and me separately. We can keep in touch with simple signals, and might that way pick up more than one interesting observation. By the way, Deirdre," he added. "Have you *read* the Weasel Murphy book?"

"Cover to cover," she lied. "So you can be sure that nothing will get past me."

Fifty-two

UPSTAIRS IN HER room, Alwen Jones sat hunched in her chair, staring out of the window at the pleasant garden below. If the ground had suddenly opened up in the middle of the rose bed, and Lucifer himself had emerged, glowing with fire and smelling strongly of rotten eggs, she would not have noticed. In her mind she saw another picture, a familiar one, of her handsome young husband standing beside her in a church full of flowers, smiling down at her and declaring that he would love and cherish her until death did them part. And so he would have, if a terrible compulsion had not overtaken him.

Alwen thought back, going over in her mind those dismal memories. Her sister Doris, although the younger of the two, had married first. Her husband was part of a well-calculated plan. More than twice her age, Geoffrey Osborne was already frail and long past anything much in the way of marital delights. But he owned the local Ozzy's Casino and was reputed to be a millionaire several times over. Doris, younger and prettier than Alwen, quite soon became a merry widow, and had in due course set her sights on stealing her sister's husband, William.

All right, Alwen told herself, shifting uneasily in her chair, so William was weak, and easy prey. He had been the baby of the family and was duly spoilt and indulged by his mother. His every want had been anticipated and provided. When he married her, he had recognised a strong character on whom he could depend, someone just like his mother. At first all had gone well with their marriage.

Alwen glanced at her watch. Too late to go down now, and her thoughts had not finished with her yet.

They had been blissfully happy, and the babies were unplanned but welcomed with delight. But then Doris had moved into step two of her plan. Soon after she was widowed, she had invited Alwen and William to spend an evening at her casino, where they could have a meal and a couple of flutters on the spinning roulette wheel. Just a bit of fun, she had assured them, and no expertise needed. She was positive that neither had played before.

Alwen had found it boring, but William was hooked. So hooked that when Doris knew he had moved on to blackjack and games where luck was mixed with skill, she checked in her records that he was in debt and casting about for ways of making money, including rumours of fiddling the books at the brewery. She then generously offered to advance a loan, provided he sampled her considerable charms on a regular basis. If he had said no, she would have had no hesitation in putting her sister Alwen, unaware of his debts, fully in the picture.

Poor William. He struggled for a while with a bad conscience but then in desperation took the easy option and fled from all his transgressions. Needless to say, after he had disappeared out of reach, Doris had put Alwen in the picture in ruthless detail.

Now she took up a photograph from her bedside table. William's smile, in spite of everything, still warmed her. She replaced it and reached in the little drawer of her desk for a letter newly arrived this morning. It was dated two weeks ago but had taken until early this morning to arrive from Australia, first at her old address and then duly forwarded to Springfields.

She read again the bald words, holding the letter with a shaky hand.

Dear Mrs. Jones. We are writing as William Jones's solicitors to inform you of his demise in this town on the twenty-third of this month. He contacted us only once, on a matter of claiming compensation for an unsatisfactory purchase. We have now made preliminary enquiries, and are informed that there was an inaccurate rumour many years ago in another part of the country that he had died as a result of a bungee jumping accident. However, we can confirm that he has lived here in Junee for a number of years, though we cannot be sure when he first arrived.

You may not know of his circumstances here. He has lived quietly, almost a recluse, with the local church being his only source of friendship. He was apparently reluctant to give any information about himself or his background, but we have discovered from records that you and he were divorced. To our knowledge he never remarried.

No will has been found, but it is thought he had little in the way of possessions or wealth. We shall be in touch with you further on this matter.

With our sincere condolences, we are, yours faithfully . . .

By now, tears were running down Alwen's pale cheeks. So she must once more go through all those good and bad years since he had promised to love her forever, but now she knew that he had lived on, alone and probably lonely. Why hadn't he got in touch and come home? Too scared to face the music. What a terrible price he had paid! She folded the letter carefully, and put it back in the drawer.

Now she thought of the girls. She must tell them, and

Bethan would be sad but brave, since she had been too small to get to know her father well. But Bronwen was a different matter. Alwen realised she had no idea how Bronwen would react. She had always thought that in many ways, her elder daughter was stonyhearted, caring only for herself. Perhaps it was because she had had no children, and her husband had turned out to be such a disappointment. But she might remember how William had doted on her, and still comfort herself with those few years when she had come first in his world.

There was a knock at the door and Katya came in. "Do you feel like coming down for a cup of tea before bedtime? Your friends are playing cards, and would, I know, welcome you among them."

"Cards?" said Alwen. "I think not, Katya. Tomorrow, perhaps. Now I am ready for sleep."

Fifty-three

THEO HAD BEEN walking for half an hour around the two largest chestnut trees in the Hall park, tracing as he went a large figure of eight, something he had done when solving a problem since he was a child. It was not that there were any magical properties to the number eight, but because the trudge round and round presented no sudden distractions, and he found he could concentrate. He was not even aware that he had fallen into this old habit, and had earlier set out to check the sheep. But then he had become lost in thought, wondering how he could get out of taking Deirdre to Ozzy's Casino in Thornwell that evening.

He had been careless, he decided, that in the heat of passion, he had agreed to Deirdre's request without thinking, but now he knew that he could not possibly be seen with Bert Bloxham's widow in amongst the riffraff who made up the motley crew of gamblers in Thornwell.

Still without a solution to his problem, he broke out of his reverie and set out across the park towards the Hall, thinking that perhaps a strong coffee might help. As he approached the gravelled courtyard at the front of the house, he saw a familiar figure. It was Augustus Halfhide, his tenant from Hangman's Row.

"Good morning!" he called. "Are you looking for me?" He did hope it was not another complaint about faulty plumbing or dangerous electrical wiring. Those old cottages should really be pulled down, but he relied on the rents to supplement his meagre bank balance.

"Not really," said Gus, restraining Whippy from an overenthusiastic greeting to Theo's dog. "It was just such a fine morning, I thought I would walk this way and perhaps take a few photographs of the Hall, if you don't mind. It's such a magnificent old building, and positively glows with sun on the ironstone." He hoped Theo didn't spot that he was improvising as he went along. He had had no intention of taking photographs, but luckily had his camera in his pocket.

No, he had come this way in the hope of catching Noreen in the kitchen. He intended to warn her that it was all round the village that Theo was going to replace her with the Polish girl from Springfields, and she had better smarten herself up if she wanted to stay. Added to concern for the old slattern, he was fond of Katya and hated to think of her shut up in the gloomy old Hall with the predatory Theo.

"Splendid!" said Theo. "Do carry on. Perhaps I might see them later? Haven't thought to take pictures of the old place for years. Anyway, now you're here, why don't you come in for a coffee? I could do with a bit of intelligent male conversation!"

"Ah," said Gus. "That would be very nice. Thank you."

Theo led the way past the kitchen and put his head round the door to ask Noreen for coffee, frowned when he saw the breakfast dishes still unwashed, and took Gus up the stairs to his study. "It's the only warm room in the house," he said. "Quite a chill in the air this morning, don't you think?"

The conversation proceeded pleasantly enough. Both had from time to time lived in London, and one or two names of mutual friends emerged. "Were you ever at the Ritz Casino?" Theo asked. "I'm sure I've seen your face around."

Gus shrugged. "Only too likely, I'm afraid," he said. "Finished with all that now, though," he said, and Theo suddenly saw the answer to his problem. Heaven sent!

"Now, Gus," he said. "I may call you that, mayn't I? I wonder if I could ask a terrific favour? I have promised an old friend that I would take her to Ozzy's Casino this evening, just to look around, and now I find it impossible to make it. Could you take my place, and save my life? Hell hath no fury, and all that. Do say yes!"

Gus was silent for a whole minute, and Theo's heart began to sink. "Gus?" he asked anxiously.

"As it happens," Gus said finally, "I am going there this evening myself. May I make an intelligent guess as to who your friend is?"

Theo nodded, looking a little guilty. He had forgotten Enquire Within and the four members of its team.

"Deirdre Bloxham?"

"Of course. You knew that, didn't you, Gus. Colleagues, and all that. Do hope I haven't blown it with the dear girl. I'll give her a ring and explain."

"Do that," said Gus, and, making excuses that he must take advantage of the clear light and see what he could do with snapping some good shots of the Hall, he left.

"WHY DON'T YOU come up to Tawny Wings for an early supper, and then we could go on to Ozzy's together?" Deirdre asked. Gus had given Theo time to make his call, and then he rang her himself, saying that although it was a change of plan, he thought they could do some useful observation together.

He walked through the village slowly, aiming to be with Deirdre around six o'clock. He had a niggling dread brewing in the pit of his stomach, and told himself this was just being unnecessarily dramatic. But he could not deny that he feared walking through the casino door. What would happen when he saw the dimly lit room filled with gaming tables, some people with poker faces, concealing their reactions at the contents of their hands of cards, others seated in attitudes of excitement or despair? Would there still be that old smell of stale, fear-induced sweat mixed with heady alcohol fumes? And would he be drawn in, the temptation proving too great?

He was at the gates of Tawny Wings now, and took a deep breath. He reminded himself that he would be with Deirdre, the most sane, confident woman he had ever met, one with her feet firmly on the ground. With Deirdre beside him, with any luck he would see Ozzy's through her clear-eyed objective view.

Nevertheless, he was unusually silent during supper, and Deirdre took a good look at him. "You okay about all this?" she said, setting down a large helping of sticky toffee pudding in front of him.

"Fine," he said. "I don't have to watch my weight, as I'm sure you have noticed."

"Idiot," she said and reached out to put her hand over his. "You know perfectly well what I mean. Not too late to back out, Gus. I can go by myself, make up some excuse about doing research for my work for social services with compulsive gamblers."

Gus was silent for a few moments, and then he began fumbling in his pocket. He pulled out a handful of silver coins and a battered old leather wallet. He emptied the wallet of two twenty pound notes and added it to the coins. Then he pushed the whole lot over the table to Deirdre.

"Please put that in your handbag, there's a love," he said. "Don't ask questions, just be sure that you'll be doing me a favour."

Deirdre was going to ask him if he'd like her to harness him to her belt with Whippy's lead, just in case, but then she saw the tension in his expression and knew that it was no joke. Her heart went out to him, and she went to stand behind him, planting a kiss on the top of his head. "Come on, Augustus Halfhide," she said. "Let's go and do a job of work. And that's all there is to it."

"WELL, I NEVER!" said Deirdre cheerfully as she approached the desk in the casino. "If it isn't my old pal Mandy! The girl who lived next to me when we were all kids playing hopscotch in the street!"

A heavily made-up woman smiled with genuine pleasure at seeing Deirdre. "Good God, girl," she said. "What are you doing here? Bert would turn in his grave!"

Deirdre roared with laughter. "That's all you know, Mandy Wise," she said. "My Bert loved a Saturday afternoon flutter on the gees. Anyway, now I'm here, just tell me how I should choose a surefire winner."

Gus marvelled at her composure. She had manoeuvred herself to shield Gus, and made no attempt to introduce him. She listened carefully as Mandy explained what she should do with her twenty pounds' worth of chips, and directed her to the roulette table. "Start there. Easy peasy, that is," Mandy said. "All you need to do is cross your fingers. And I'm always here if you need more chips. Have fun, you two." She raised her eyebrows at Gus and asked if he was Deirdre's brother. But giving him no time to answer, Deirdre marched off towards the roulette wheel, perfectly relaxed.

With beginner's luck, Deirdre won at the first spin, and she looked round at Gus, standing behind her. "Shall I have another go?" she said, and then her expression changed. She stood up abruptly, and whispered to him to follow her. She retreated into a shadowy corner where there were a few empty chairs for onlookers.

"Gus, look over there, by the desk. Keep out of sight and don't make a sound. Thank God they keep this place so dark."

"It's so nothing distracts the punters, and nobody sees the dealer fiddling the cards," Gus whispered into her ear. His heart was pounding, but he put both hands in his empty pockets and sat down. He looked over towards the desk, peering through the gloom.

"Oh, my," he said as he watched a smartly dressed woman turn and walk towards the roulette wheel. She stood there with the accustomed ease of someone who'd been there many times before. Gus caught sight of her face, and knew at once, without question, that he was looking at an addict.

"It's her, isn't it?" said Deirdre.

Gus nodded. "Alwen's pride and joy. Wonderwoman Bronwen, God help her."

Fifty-four

DEIRDRE AND GUS waited in the shadows until they could see that Mandy Wise was, for the moment, surrounded by a group of punters newly arrived. Then they sidled out with their faces averted. Outside, they walked swiftly to Deirdre's car and drove out of the car park and sped off towards Barrington.

They were in total agreement. There had been no point in staying longer. What they had seen was so important that no gossip or rumour could match it. And they needed to get out before Bronwen Evans saw them. Two other pairs of eyes watched them leave, but they were not aware of these.

"So there we have it," Gus said as they left the outskirts of town and took the shortcut to the village through dark, overhanging tunnels of trees. "Alwen's beloved daughter, so sophisticated and successful, is a compulsive gambler, and has probably worked her way through her own and her mother's savings, and any other source of income she could get her hands on. Oh, yes, Deirdre, that's how it works, believe me. The only thing that matters is the conviction that you will scoop a fortune with the next game. Game! What a misnomer, my dear. Never think of it as only a game. To quote our Ivy, it is the work of the devil."

"But not everybody gets addicted," Deirdre said, though she believed every word that Gus had said.

"True," he replied but added that until you tried it you wouldn't know. And then it would be too late. "Mind you," he continued, "some of the best casinos offer helpful advice on how to recognise the signs of a growing addiction."

"Quietening their bad consciences?"

Gus shrugged as they drove into Tawny Wings gateway. "Bad consciences are soon smothered, Dee-Dee, when there are larges sums of money involved."

Deirdre turned off the engine and looked at her watch. "You know what I'd like to do now?" she said, and Gus's spirits rose.

They were soon dashed. "I'd like to go down and see Ivy and Roy. It's early yet, and a bit of Ivy's sharp commonsense would be welcome just now."

"Supposing Alwen is with them?"

"Well, we could risk it. If she was there, we could say we were just passing and decided to look in and say hello."

"Sounds a bit lame to me," Gus said.

Deirdre started the engine again, and began to back out of the drive. "Oh, come on, let's just go. Please, Gus."

"Personally," he answered, "I would rather go to the pub and have a large, strong drink. But each to his own. I'll come, if you promise to take me back to Tawny Wings and give me a generous tot of whisky to help me sleep."

"Done," said Deirdre, and she pulled up outside Springfields. They got out and looked up at Ivy's window.

"Light's on," Gus said, "so chances are that it's just Ivy and Roy. In we go, my lovely."

MAX AND MARGARET had been sitting at the casino bar for some time, perched on high stools, drinking coffee as instructed. "So they weren't here long," Margaret said.

She was talking about Deirdre and Gus, but both kept their eyes on Bronwen. Her face had lit up as the wheel spun and she was in luck again.

"But it wasn't Theo Roussel, was it. It was our friend Halfhide. Can it be that Doris is slipping? Or have her many informants finally turned, like us."

"Well, we tried. And I haven't given up yet," Margaret said. "Just give me a little more time."

"Oh, God," said Max. "Look, she's risking all, the little fool." They watched as the wheel spun. Bronwen's luck had run out, and she went swiftly over to the desk, her face expressionless.

"You watch," Margaret said. "Another loan. Special privileges, being part of the family? Or perhaps not," she added as she heard a raised voice. It was Bronwen, and she could see Mandy's red face as she tried to calm her down.

"Get on to my aunt!" Bronwen shouted. "Is she in her office? I'm going straight up to see her, and you'll be out of a job by the time I come down!" With that, she marched off and disappeared.

"Ooops!" said Margaret, smiling. "I'm right, you know, Max. Things are changing, and with any luck not for the good for our Doris."

"So what do we do next?"

"Report back to Doris that Deirdre Bloxham came in, but not with the squire. A very uncomfortable-looking Gus Halfhide was her escort, and they left as soon as they clapped eyes on Bronwen. That should put the wind up her knickers."

"And then?"

"Trust me, Max. There's more than one way of killing a cat."

IVY AND ROY were watching television on the small set Ivy had installed opposite her bed. From vowing never to watch the horrible thing, she had become something of a fan of one or two programmes. Once more, Roy marvelled at her ability to switch off if the programme did not suit. She would address it in a stern voice, warning that if it did not pull up its socks it would be banished to the dustbin. Soap operas were her favourites, and even among these she was very picky. No violence, no overt sex, and drunkenness was treated to a lecture on temperance.

The result was that Ivy and Roy watched very little television, and even in the lounge, where it was on constantly, they turned their backs with great deliberation. Roy sometimes wished he could see something Ivy had rejected, but he managed to catch up when she was upstairs resting.

"We've not seen Alwen again," Ivy remarked, using the remote to switch off as two youngsters collapsed in ecstasy on an unmade bed.

"True. Something's up, I reckon," said Roy. "I'll have a word with Pinkers tomorrow. She's more approachable than Mrs. Spurling. Maybe we could help in some way."

There was a gentle tap on Ivy's door, and she and Roy looked at each other questioningly.

"Is that her, do you think?" Ivy got up and opened the door. "Oh," she said, "it's you two. What on earth is it that couldn't wait until tomorrow?"

"It's important, Ivy," Deirdre said. "Can we come in for a bit? It's about Ozzy's and Bronwen. It's not that late, you know. Fortunately Miss Pinkney was on duty, so we managed to break through the blockade."

Fifty-five

ALWEN HAD ONCE more had breakfast in her room, and now sat gazing blankly out of the window. She had had an early call from Bethan, who said she was very sorry but she would not be able to visit this afternoon, as they had no water. The men were coming to investigate but could not give her a time. She would ring later, and fix to come over tomorrow instead. There was good news, she said. Alwen's house was finally sold, and all looked simple and swift. The buyers were not in a chain, and had ready cash.

At first, Alwen had thought it was Bronwen. The two girls' voices were much the same, although they were in all other ways so different. Bronwen was on her mind all her waking hours. She was so tired of trying to think up new ways to help her but always came back to the most drastic option. It would be worth it, wouldn't it, especially now the house was sold?

She heard footsteps coming along the corridor, and wondered whether it would be Ivy. She knew that sooner or later Ivy Beasley would not be able to curb her curiosity. Probably Roy, too. Nice man, that. And old Ivy was not so bad, once you got to know her. Pity they had got mixed up in that ridiculous enquiry agency! She knew, of course, that it had been Augustus Halfhide's idea. The man should have known better. If he knew what was good for him, he would lie low. Strange that he should turn up in Barrington, when her sister's contacts had remembered him as a young fool at the gaming tables. Then she had heard more of him when Max and Margaret had traced him working alongside Martin Reeves, who had been one of the gambling gang all those years ago. Those two idiots had used Martin's name but made a real mess of that kidnap, and she had had to bail them out, paying the ransom money much reduced by skilful bargaining on her part.

The footsteps stopped outside her door. A sharp rap caused her to look round in alarm. "Who is it?" she said quickly.

There was no reply, but the door opened wide.

"Doris! What on earth are you doing here?"

"I can visit my big sister, can't I?" Doris said, shutting the door firmly behind her. "I haven't heard from you lately, and I was worried. Can't have one of my important sources of information drying up! Besides which, there are urgent things we need to talk about." Her voice was dry and chilly, and Alwen shivered.

"What things?"

"Well, your precious daughter for one. In fact, for one, two and three. It is time you rode to the rescue, Alwen. I've given her a long rein, but it has to end. It was sensible of you to pay the so-called ransom money, no doubt in the hope that all would be hushed up. No telling what those two idiots were planning to do after the mess they made of my kidnap idea. All designed to make Halfhide talk, and he said not a word!"

Alwen looked at her sister's smirking face and felt chilled. "I don't think you can blame me for their failure, Doris," she said. "I played my part. You had all the information I could gather."

"Oh, I don't blame you," Doris said carelessly. "No,

that's all in the past. *But,* I'm afraid Bronwen's gambling debts are very much in the present, and I need to have them settled. Immediately, Alwen. So what do you intend to do?"

"ROY! WHO IS that woman? Look, over there, talking to Mrs. Spurling."

"No idea, beloved. Should I know her? She's a very smart lady, whoever she is."

Ivy gently put Tiddles down to the floor and reached for her second pair of glasses. "You're right, Roy. Very smart indeed. Money oozing from every pore."

"Oh dear, I hope not," said Roy, feeling queasy. "I expect she's been visiting."

"We know all the regular visitors by now. I've not seen her before. But she reminds me of somebody. Have another look, Roy. Isn't she familiar?"

He peered across into the hall, where Doris was giving a stern lecture to Mrs. Spurling. "Yes, you're right. Now who is it, Ivy?"

They were both quiet for a moment, staring unabashed. Then Ivy said suddenly, "Got it! If she were twenty years younger, she'd be the image of Alwen's daughter Bethan."

Roy nodded. "I don't know about the exact image, but there's definitely a look of Bethan about her. So who is she?"

"Doris," said Ivy. "It's Doris May Osborne, nee Wilson, younger sister of Alwen Jones and owner of Ozzy's Casino in Thornwell. I'd put money on it."

"How apt," said Roy. "Well I never. Fancy her coming here. She's not bothered before, has she? Why now, Ivy?"

"Think, Roy," said Ivy as they both watched Doris strut out of the entrance hall on her expensive high heels. "Remember what Deirdre and Gus told us last evening? He said he could see by the look on Bronwen's face that things were bad with her at the casino, and that could mean Doris needing to take action." She shuddered. "Someone walked over my grave," she said.

Roy frowned. "Don't say things like that, Ivy. I don't like it, my dear, not at our age."

"Just a saying. No, what I mean is, I've got a horrible feeling that it's all coming to a head. We need to move fast, Roy."

"If only we knew which direction to take," he said.

IVY SAT ALL afternoon in her room, thinking. She had told Roy she hadn't slept well the previous night and would be having a good sleep. This was not true, but she wanted time to be by herself and think without interruptions.

At last, just before the summons for tea, she stroked the little cat curled up asleep on her bed and went out of the door. She walked along the corridor until she came to Alwen's door. She put her ear to it but could hear nothing, so she tapped. No reply, so she knocked more firmly. Still nothing, so she tested the door and opened it gently.

"Alwen? It's Ivy. Are you coming down for tea?" She pushed the door wide open and walked in.

Alwen was stretched out on the bed, her hands clasped on her chest. Sleeping peacefully, thought Ivy, and she prepared to leave. But then something made her turn back. The room was deathly quiet, and Alwen's mouth hung open.

"Oh, dear God," said Ivy. She went across to the bed and stroked the cold, rigid hand. "Poor soul," she muttered and sat down quietly by the bed. "I'll just sit here for a bit, my dear, to keep you company on your journey."

After half an hour, she got up and walked slowly out of the room, shutting the door carefully. With a slow tread, she made her way downstairs and along to the office. Miss Pinkney sat at the computer and looked up at Ivy with a smile. "Can I help you?" she said.

"No, not me. Nor Mrs. Jones, I'm afraid. But you'd better go and take a look. I shall be in the lounge with Roy when I'm wanted."

Fifty-six

THE WAILING SOUND of the ambulance spread alarm throughout Springfields. When it pulled up outside the gates and paramedics rushed in and up the stairs, hearts were beating dangerously faster, and Katya and daily carers were busily occupied reassuring residents that it was not really an emergency, but something that had to be dealt with straightaway.

In a sense, they were telling the truth. It was not an emergency, because Alwen was already dead, and all efforts to revive her had failed. It had to be dealt with at once, because there were rules to be followed when a death occurred in the home. Mrs. Spurling supervised the whole thing with efficiency and long experience of such happenings. It went with the job, as she had told her husband before he ran off with the cook.

Other residents were manoeuvred into the dining room for their tea, so that they should not see Alwen being carried out with her face covered, and by the time they had had their cake and as many cups of tea as they liked, all was quiet and the television switched to a cheerful quiz programme.

Ivy and Roy went quietly with the rest, speaking in low tones to each other, and most of the time holding hands.

"I saw an empty pill bottle on the table by her bed," Ivy whispered, and Roy nodded. "But where did she get it from? We're not allowed to have pills permanently in our rooms, not even painkillers."

"I suppose she brought them in with her. Do you remember how she guarded her handbag as if it carried a gun? Well, sleeping pills can be equally effective. I bet that's what happened. But what on earth possessed her?"

"Worry," said Roy flatly. "That poor woman was consumed with worry. She's been up in her room brooding alone ever since we came back from our outing. And we know what she was so anxious about, don't we, my dear? Daughter Bronwen, deeply in debt and being squeezed by her Auntie Doris."

"I think it was Alwen who was being squeezed," Ivy replied. "After all, she was the one with the money. We don't know how much. Maybe Bronwen knew, and was putting pressure on her mother. So Alwen was getting it from her sister Doris and her daughter as well."

Roy shook his head, as if trying to rid himself of thoughts of a desperate Alwen. Ivy took his hand again, and moved a little closer.

"Let's think, Roy," she continued. "When Alwen came here, she seemed a straightforward sort of woman. Retired teacher, good position in the town. Proud of her daughters, and secretive about their father. But nothing suspicious about her at all. Good family background over at Measby, comfortably off. Then we find out husband William was an adulterer and a gambler, and went through his own money, some of the brewery's, and probably Alwen's as well. She made it plain she had to work to bring up the girls."

"Ah, but there's the mystery," Roy said. "We don't really know. She may have tied up her own money safely so William couldn't get at it. Probably inherited a fair bit from her parents, as did Doris. Alwen must have had savings, Ivy, to afford to come and live here."

"So now that Bronwen has no job and no means of raising money on her own to pay her debts, she's a pawn in Doris's cunning little game of blackmail and extortion? All carefully planned in order to get Alwen to shell out all she has to rescue her daughter," she continued. "Oh my dear Roy. It doesn't bear thinking about."

"I agree," Roy said, patting her hand. He could not help contrasting his Ivy now, visibly deeply upset, and the Ivy who reacted with mirth at the death of Daisy Worth. A complicated little person, his beloved. He said he could see how trapped Alwen was. But why should she decide to end her life? After all, she could have released her money, rescued Bronwen, told Doris to go to hell, and found a nice state-run retirement home where she could end her days, couldn't she?"

Ivy was silent for a couple of minutes, then shook her head. "No, I don't think she would have been able to face that. And anyway, she was probably past thinking straight, poor soul. Escape must have looked like the kindest way out."

They looked across at the entrance hall, where the door had opened and Alwen's two daughters appeared.

"And there they are," Ivy said. "And if I'm right, one as innocent as the day is long and the other as guilty as hell. It will be a nasty business, Roy, and I'm afraid we shall be deep in it."

Fifty-seven

TREVOR EVANS HAD tried hard to get a word out of Bronwen ever since she came back from Springfields. She would not look at him but went through the motions of making supper. "I'll do that," he had said, but she pushed him out of the way without a word.

They sat now at the table in the kitchen, eating baked beans and sausages. Trevor had cleared his plate, but Bronwen had managed only half a sausage and then moved her plate to one side. She sat looking down at her hands, her shoulders hunched, and Trevor could take it no longer. He got up and came round to her, leaning forward and putting his arms around her.

"Come on, Bron," he said. "Let's go into the sitting room and have a cuddle on the sofa. We'll not bother about talking. I can't bear to see you so alone."

She allowed him to pull her to her feet, and take her hand. They sat like young lovers on the sofa, except that there was none of the lovers' spark. After about half an hour, Bronwen moved her head away from his shoulder and looked at him.

"I murdered her," she said, and silent tears streamed down her cheeks and plopped onto her clenched hands.

BETHAN AND HER family were in a huddle, crouched on the floor and lamenting in a loud, uninhibited wail. There was a sudden knock at the door, and Bethan went to open it. It was her neighbour, looking anxious.

"Are you all right, dear?" she said. "We heard this awful noise, and had to come and see what has happened. I do hope you don't think me nosy and interfering."

Bethan reached out a hand. "Come in, Marjorie," she said. "My mother has died, and we are grieving together. I know she met you once or twice and liked you very much. She would be so touched that you cared. Come, join us for a minute or two."

Marjorie was acutely embarrassed, and perched on the arm of a chair. She muttered how sorry she was and how sad to lose your mother, and then said that she had left potatoes boiling on the stove and must go and check they hadn't dried out. "You know where we are if you need any help," she said, relieved to be out again and on her way home.

"Right," said Clive, as Bethan returned. "I think a warm drink for us all, and then we must get these boys into bed."

"But what about *Doctor Who* on the telly?" said Freddie.

"You can see the repeat on Tuesday," said Clive. "Just for tonight, lads, we are going to be quiet and think how much we loved Grannie."

"But she won't know," said Freddie, "she's dead."

"But our love will go winging its way to where she has gone, and comfort her," said Clive with a dreamy look.

"Where has she gone, then?" Freddie persisted.

"Be quiet, and get upstairs to your bedroom," said Bethan sharply. "And you, William. And no quarrelling in the bath. I'll be up in two ticks. Go on, get going, both of you."

Their mother's change of tone sent them scuttling upstairs, and Bethan gave Clive a hug. "Thanks, love," she said. "I'd better give Bronwen a ring and make sure she's all right."

"The woman's a murderer," Clive said, forgetting all about sweetness and light to all mankind. "No doubt about that."

DORIS MAY FELT quite pleased with herself. Everything was working out as she had planned. Bronwen was now completely under her control, and in due course would persuade her mother, already softened up by her sister's visit, to hand over some of the cash Doris was certain Alwen had salted away years ago. At least that would enable her to pay off some overdue wages at Ozzy's, and allow her to keep on the gardener for a while longer. She could see a time coming when she would not be able to stay on at the Manor, but not yet.

Business had been falling off for some years, with online gambling now so widespread that it was having a major effect on her profits. The big casino chains could draw on resources and widen their services to the punters. But Ozzy's was a small concern, and Thornwell an increasingly industrial town. Every family had a computer, and those who felt like a flutter had only to switch on.

No, she had done the right thing. She felt a sudden pang of regret at being so harsh with her sister but then consoled herself with memories of childhood when Alwen had treated her, the much younger sister, with a strict regime which in her opinion bordered on cruelty. It was her turn now, and after all, Alwen wouldn't miss the cash. She was old, and her wants were small. If she could no longer afford Springfields' fees, she could easily be moved into that place in Broad Street. It was quite adequate, people said.

So next she had to deal with Margaret and Max. They had worked for her for years, and she still had plenty of information about former indiscretions that they would rather not have made public, plenty enough to keep them loyal. They had been bluffing last time she saw them, she was sure of that. She wished she had picked up those tickets and checked the dates. Probably old ones. She had noticed they'd been turning out drawers. She had another job for them now, and intended to encourage them to work on a confiding relationship with the vicar. She had handled him gently up to now, but it was time to move things along. Vicars were poorly paid, she knew, but there were clear signs of family wealth there. She could see the evening sun streaming in through the coloured glass in the hall windows, and decided to walk up the lane and pay the pair a visit.

As she approached the cottage, she felt a sudden sense of foreboding. No car was visible, and although it was now twilight, there were no lights on in the house. She knocked several times, but nobody came.

"Evening, Mrs. Osborne," said a voice behind her. It was the farmer, and he smiled knowingly. "They're not there. They've gone," he said baldly.

"Gone where?"

"Gone for good, I should say," he replied. "They packed that old car of theirs, and made off down the lane. Went so fast it almost shook the old banger off its wheels! Anyway, they've gone. If you want a new tenant, I know somebody who'll take the cottage. At a reasonable rent," he added.

Doris was stunned. How dare they! She set off back down the track, and her mobile began to ring. She stopped and listened. It was Bronwen.

"Between us, Auntie, dear," the ice-cold voice said, "we have murdered my mother."

Fifty-eight

THE FUNERAL OF Alwen Wilson Jones took place in the parish church of Thornwell one week later. It was a big church, and Bronwen and a forgiving Bethan had made all the arrangements with a local undertaker. Mrs. Spurling had suggested that they might like to have a service in Barrington church with refreshments afterwards at Springfields. But Alwen's daughters had remembered the days when their mother was a notable figure in the town, when they could not walk with her down the High Street without at least half a dozen people smiling and saying hello. "I used to teach that girl, and her mother," she would say.

Trevor had said the church would be half-empty and echoing, whereas they could fill Barrington village church with no trouble. But the girls were adamant. Mother should have a decent funeral, and Trevor would be surprised how many turned up.

In the event, even Bronwen and Bethan were surprised. The big church was full, with extra chairs brought in. Men and women of all ages trouped through the big doors, greeting each other and exchanging memories of the teacher who had made their first experience of "big school" friendly and exciting.

Deirdre had offered to take Ivy and Roy, and Gus had surprised her by asking if he could cadge a lift, too. They sat towards the back of the church, and remained quiet, waiting for the entry of the coffin and mourners. As the vicar led the way up the aisle and the pallbearers gently set down their burden on trestles before the altar, Ivy watched the procession of family as they followed and filed into the front pews.

"There she is," she whispered to Roy. "She should have been banned from the church."

"Ivy!" Roy answered, deeply shocked. "She *is* her sister, my dear."

"So what? There's probably a word for—"

"Shhh!" hissed Deirdre, who had heard all of this, and knew what Ivy was about to say.

Gus was not watching Doris but had his eyes fixed on Bronwen. The woman was pale as a ghost, and hung on to her sister's arm as if she might faint any minute. As well she might, thought Gus. But alone amongst the members of Enquire Within, he felt compassion for her. He knew the alternating elation and terror of the compulsive gambler, and thanked God he had overcome it. But he knew that, like any addict, he could never again risk the smallest indulgence, not even an innocent little bet on a rural point-to-point race. Never again, he told himself.

The vicar delivered an excellent address, describing Alwen's valuable teaching career, and confessed that he himself had been for one year under her guiding hand. He commented on the full church and the warmth of feeling for this much-loved citizen of Thornwell.

Bethan read a passage from the Bible, and Bronwen got up to give a second reading. It was to be a poem by Christina Rossetti, and she got as far as "Plant thou no roses at my head" and then choked and stopped. Trevor immediately joined her, took her hand and finished the poem for her. Then he put his arm around her shoulders and gently shepherded her back to the pew.

Gus felt Deirdre's hand creep into his, and he gave it a squeeze. "Nearly done," he whispered.

When they finally emerged from the church through the chatting crowd, the sun had come out and shone cheerfully on the hearse and procession of cars taking the family to a private interment at the local cemetery, where Alwen would be buried next to her brother-in-law, George.

"I don't think she liked him much," Ivy said. "Still, who knows? They might not be going to the same place," she added enigmatically.

They drove back to Barrington in silence, until Deirdre turned into Tawny Wings, saying she had prepared lunch for them, and if that was all right with Ivy and Roy she would return them to Springfields later.

"That's very kind of you, Deirdre," said Ivy.

"Better give Pinkers a buzz to let her know," said Roy, and watched admiringly as Ivy fished her mobile out of her handbag and dialled the number using her thumbs, just like the kids in the village.

"We shall not be requiring lunch, Miss Pinkney," she said. "What did you say? Well, how could we let you know before? We've only just been invited. Yes, of course you can tell Mrs. Spurling. Time you stood up to that woman, you know. Good-bye, Pinkers."

"You could have used my phone, Ivy," said Deirdre as they got out of the car.

"No need," Ivy replied. "Oh, and Roy dear, remind me to top up my mobile at the shop. My balance is low."

"There's no answer to that," said Deirdre, and led the way into the house.

AFTER LUNCH, THE four sat in the pleasant room looking out into Deirdre's garden, and carried out a postmortem of their own.

"What did you mean, Ivy, when you said Alwen and George might not be going to the same place? Surely neither was destined for the nether regions?" said Gus.

"If you mean were either of them going to hell, then I couldn't even guess. But though Alwen was a good woman, a good mother and a good teacher, she was most likely the Barrington informant we talked about. A spy, if you like."

"What on earth do you mean?" Deirdre said.

"Think about it, Deirdre," Ivy insisted, "she was best placed to know all our movements, from the moment she arrived in Springfields and realised that we were investigators and on the trail of what turned out to be Doris's blackmailing activities."

"But who did she tell?" Roy did not believe in speaking ill of the dead and was not happy with this turn of the conversation.

Gus replied for Ivy. "I'm afraid it was Doris, who was no doubt more or less forcing her to help." He had worked out some time ago from conversations overheard when he was kidnapped that Doris had Alwen in thrall. "The twenty thousand story was clearly concocted by one or other of them and then dropped when it looked like we would be getting too close."

Ivy was nodding and the others waited for Gus to continue.

"Doris ordered my kidnap," he said. "That was quite clear. She needed to know how much we had found out about her schemes. I would be made to talk and then seriously warned with death and destruction if I spilled the beans. The ransom part of it was pure greed, and Alwen was dragged into all of it, I am sure."

"I've just remembered something," Deirdre said. "You and me, Gus, we must have made them more suspicious of us early on. Do you remember how Bronwen was standing in the newspaper queue that day? And us asking about her father? Couldn't have been a clearer warning to her, and no doubt she reported to her mother, who passed it on to Doris. Poor old Alwen," she added. "Talk about motherly love! She certainly did all she could. I bet she cursed her late husband more than once."

"*Late* husband?" said Roy. "Do we know that for certain?"

"We do," said Deirdre, picking up a pile of newspapers and leafing through them. "Look, here's a death notice. Alwen must have put it in."

"But I don't get it," said Deirdre. "Why kill herself? Now all the money will be divided between Bronwen and Bethan, and Doris will extract all that is due from her powerless niece."

Ivy looked at her watch. "We should be getting back. But before we go, I'd like to say that Bronwen ain't necessarily easy prey for Doris now. You can be sure that although Alwen paid up some, she still had plenty in the bank, tied up nice and tight so that Bronwen wouldn't inherit and be in Doris's thrall once more. She would have found a way to outsmart her sister." She paused and dabbed at her eyes with a handkerchief. "Something in my eye," she said crossly, but Roy knew better.

Ivy sniffed, and continued, "And now I can see," she said slowly, "that Alwen did pay more than the money ransom. She paid with her life."

There was a long silence until Gus cleared his throat. "I'd just like to add," he said, standing up and offering Ivy his arm, "that as I am probably the best person for miles around to help Bronwen kick her habit, I shall be in touch with her very shortly."

Deirdre smiled at him. She knew what this decision must have cost him, when he was still doing his best to forget the whole gambling scene. "So, all in all, and taking all things into consideration," she said, "have we actually achieved anything in this investigation? After Alwen's funeral today, I am inclined to think not."

"Oh, yes," said Ivy. "We're not done yet. I have made an appointment to see Inspector Frobisher on Monday. Blackmail and extortion are serious crimes, and if Doris hasn't skipped the country by then, she will certainly be receiving a visitor she would rather not see. And, with any luck, no more victims will suffer her evil attentions."

Roy stared at her. "Ivy, my love," he said. "You never cease to surprise me."

Fifty-nine

"YOU ARE CERTAINLY not going to that police station by yourself, Ivy," Roy said firmly.

"Why didn't the inspector offer to come here?"

"He did," said Ivy. "But can you imagine the commotion if a policeman came here asking to see Miss Beasley? And don't say he won't look like one, wearing plain clothes, because they always look like policemen, whatever they're wearing."

"An answer for everything, Miss Beasley!" Roy said, and blew her a kiss, provoking scornful jeers from four jealous old nasties playing Ludo in the corner of the lounge.

"You wanna watch 'im!" shouted one, but Ivy pointedly shifted in her seat so that her back was towards them.

"What time is the taxi coming?" Roy continued.

"Ten thirty."

"I shall be ready," Roy said, and went across to have a word with the demon Ludo players.

A BEMUSED INSPECTOR Frobisher scratched the top of his head, got up from his desk and went to look out of his first-floor window. There they were, Miss Beasley and Mr. Goodman, hopping into a waiting taxi like spring chickens. Well, the old boy wasn't so handy, but Ivy Beasley had rejected the small lift, and allowed the duty sergeant to use it for her fiancé—yes! fiancé!—in his wheelchair, while she climbed the stone stairs, punishing each one with her stick, with only a couple of pauses for taking a breath.

It was quite a tale they had to tell. Some of it he knew already. He had heard that Ozzy's Casino was on the slide. He had also seen the takeover at the brewery, and the consequent loss of jobs. His good friend Trevor Evans, a fellow Rotarian, was worried about his wife Bronwen, who had been sacked and now was having no luck finding a job.

Bronwen Evans! Frobisher turned away from the window and sat down. Why on earth hadn't Trevor mentioned the gambling problem? Well, it was pretty obvious why he hadn't. You don't tell a policeman that your wife is driving her mother to suicide. If it was suicide. She had not apparently left a note. At least, none had been found yet. And then all that stuff about Doris Osborne! Sister of the deceased, apparently, and a dab hand at blackmail and extortion. No telling with women, he thought to himself, not for the first time. One criminal sister putting on the squeeze, while the other innocent was at the receiving end, desperately trying to protect her daughter from demands she could not meet.

Where did they say Doris Osborne lived? Measby, that was it. They seemed to think an old man found dead in his cottage there was mixed up in gambling debts and his death was fishy. He remembered it well, and thought at the time that there was something not quite right about it. Accidental death by falling down stairs, wasn't it? Mm, well, perhaps they should take another look at all of that. Ghoulish yobs had got in and turned the place over, if he remembered rightly. Caught and punished, but still rumours flying about for months afterwards. Measby was not his patch, of course, but he would get in touch with their local constabulary. A lot of work to be done there.

He had remembered Ivy and Roy from their last adventure with Enquire Within, and did not underestimate the importance of what they had told him. There were two others in their team, weren't there? Bert Bloxham's widow, of course. She would be involved. Quite a girl, from all reports. Then a tall, stringy chap, kept in the background. New to the area.

He looked at his watch. Nearly lunchtime. Well, no time like the present. He lifted his phone and asked his secretary to get him Inspector Sanderson at Oakbridge police station.

Sixty

DORIS MAY OSBORNE was comfortably seated with her feet up on the velvet-covered sofa in her little sitting room, leafing through travel brochures. She had recovered from grieving for her sister. She had given it the whole day yesterday, and considered that was enough. After all, the old thing was clearly fed up with life, so why deny her a quick exit?

And now the money would be freed. It would, of course, be divided between the two girls, and it would be child's play to call in all Bronwen's debts. There wouldn't be much left! But then, that was the luck of the draw. She had had her fun at the casino. Time to pay up. And what her niece had left in her bank account would soon be trickling away at the roulette wheel. Doris knew a compulsive gambler when she saw one.

She flicked over the pages until she found a luxury hotel in the Maldives. There was already an autumn chill in the air, and she fancied a winter holiday in the sun. She deserved a treat, she decided, as a reward for all her hard work. She got up, intending to spend a happy half hour on her computer, booking tickets and dreaming of handsome young men on a golden beach.

Halfway up the wide stairs, she was halted by a firm knock at the front door. Damn! She did not feel like talking to anyone. Callers were never good news, and she had no wish to have her good mood dispelled. But then another knock, louder this time, made her sigh and return downstairs. She put the sheaf of travel brochures down on the hall table and unbolted the door, opening it only a fraction.

"What do you want?" she said crossly. "I'm very busy."

Inspector Sanderson offered his card, and said that he would like to have a talk with her. And no, he couldn't come back later. It was an urgent matter.

"Then you'd better come in," Doris said, and to her annoyance felt her heart begin to beat faster. What had that horrid Max said? Her luck was running out, he had blurted out the last time she had seen him. But that was ridiculous! Maybe he and Margaret had had an accident, wherever they were, and that was why this policeman had appeared. Maybe they were dead, she thought, and she could not suppress a sudden ray of hope.

She took the inspector into the morning room and seated him on a hard chair, while she sat opposite. "Now, what can I help you with?" she said, intending to keep the upper hand.

"I believe you are the sister of the late Mrs. Alwen Wilson Jones?" said the inspector. "We are investigating a possible suicide, and we are aware you will still be in shock and grief, and of course you have our every sympathy."

He had spotted the travel brochures, and added sternly, "We are anxious to clear this up as quickly as possible, as there could well be ramifications of a criminal nature. I should be glad, therefore, if you would answer a few questions now, and then we can continue our discussion down at the police station."

IN HIS SCRUFFY sitting room, Gus stood at the window, staring out at nothing very much. He had a great deal of thinking to do, but could not pin his mind down to tackling one of the several decisions he had decided must be made.

He looked down at Whippy, who, with the intuition of much-loved dogs, knew that he was troubled, and stood on her hind legs and licked his hand.

"Perhaps I should make a list?" he said to her, stroking her velvety head. "Ivy swears by a list, but in her case it is an aide-mémoire. Nothing wrong with my memory. In fact it is too good. I wouldn't mind forgetting a few things. Anyway, Whippy, I'll have a try at a list."

The word "list" sounded a little like "*bis*cuits" to Whippy, and she looked hopefully at the old tin labelled "Your Faithful Friend." "Later," said Gus, "after we've had a walk. First, where's my jotter?"

Armed with pen and paper, Gus began. One: had Enquire Within in any way caused the death of Alwen? If they had, he intended to wrap up the business at once. Two: if not, had she actually intended to die, or had it been an accident, as when old people forget how many pills they have taken and take a few more to be sure of a good night's sleep?

He caught sight of someone passing his window, and knew it was Miriam Blake, come to offer him tea, supper, breakfast, a picnic in the woods, or anything else he might fancy. He got wearily to his feet, opened the door to her and said he was working hard on a difficult assignment at the moment. He would give her a buzz later, and went back to his list.

Three: if, as he suspected, Alwen had meant to commit suicide, what had been so overwhelmingly insupportable that this was the only way out? He gritted his teeth and faced this one squarely. Gambling. A daughter who had huge gambling debts and a ruthless casino-owning sister who cared for nothing but money. But was this really enough? Yes, he decided, remembering how many similar cases he had witnessed over the years. And, he had to admit, his own marriage had come to grief partly because of his own addiction.

And four: could he sustain his impulsive decision to offer advice and support to Bronwen Evans, enabling her to kick the gambling habit? What about her husband? He might not take kindly to Gus's interference, as he would surely see it.

Whippy whimpered in sympathy as Gus put his head in his hands, temporarily defeated by the enormity of answering these questions. Then his phone rang.

"Hello? Gus? Deirdre here. Fancy a fish supper? I bought too much salmon from Kevin the Fish's van this morning, so you'd be doing me a favour."

How did she know? Gus said to himself. "Can't think of anything better, Dee-Dee," he said.

"Great. About six thirty? You can bring Whippy—if you must."

Gus replaced the phone and looked down at his little dog. "We'll convert her yet," he said with a smile.

"WE NEED A meeting," said Ivy. "Now the dust has settled. That Inspector Frobisher seems like a good man, and putting everything we know in his hands was the right thing to do."

"Certainly was," said Roy. "I was beginning to think we were getting in so deep we might all be murdered in our beds."

"There's murder and murder," Ivy said enigmatically. "We know that from poor beleaguered Alwen. So," she continued, "we need a meeting. I know Gus is all mixed up about the gambling side of it, and Deirdre is still smarting from being stood up by the Hon. Theo. She ought to know a leopard don't change its spots. The big question is," she continued with emphasis, "should we wrap up Enquire Within, forget about taking on any more cases, and think of something else to do? I think we're all feeling a bit guilty about Alwen, perhaps done more harm than good. But no, don't let's talk about it now. Wait 'til the meeting."

"What's your real feeling about it, my love?" asked Roy.

Ivy thought for a couple of minutes. "Beasleys ain't quitters, Roy," she said, and he laughed delightedly.

GUS SET OFF for a walk with Whippy but had gone only a hundred yards along Hangman's Row when his mobile rang.

"Is that Mr. Halfhide?" Gus did not recognise the man's voice, and from habit he was about to deny that he knew anyone called Halfhide, when the caller continued. "It's Trevor Evans here. I am Bronwen's husband. Bronwen is the daughter of the late Mrs. Wilson Jones. . . ."

"I know," said Gus. He could think of nothing more to say, and Trevor continued.

"This is rather a difficult call for me," he said. "You must have heard rumours of the reason for Mrs. Jones's death."

"Suicide?" said Gus baldly.

"Possibly," answered Trevor. "Well, as you can imagine, Bronwen is in a dreadful state. Blames herself, though goodness knows why."

"Gambling?" said Gus, who was now filled with confidence at the thought of a fish supper with Deirdre.

There was a long pause, and Gus wondered if Trevor had ended the call. But then he said that the best person to answer that was Bronwen herself. He would put her on.

"Hello? Mr. Halfhide?"

"Gus."

"Well, Gus, this is Bronwen Evans. Um, I was wondering whether I might come and see you? Well, the thing is, I need help, and I believe you might be the person who can do it."

"What makes you think that?"

"Just something my aunt's employees over at Measby said once. I remembered it, you see, because . . ."

As her voice tailed off, Gus cleared his throat and took a deep breath. "Give me a few days," he said, "and I'll let you know. I need to sort out some things but should be more certain about my immediate movements by then."

There was a choking sound from Bronwen, and Gus said she should cheer up. It was not the end of the world, though that's how it might seem at the moment.

"I'm so scared that that's how it seemed to my mother," she blurted out, and ended the call.

KATYA WAS CLEANING out the room that had last been occupied by Alwen Jones, ready for another resident. Mrs. Spurling said she wanted everywhere to be sparkling and welcoming. "And don't forget under the bed, please," she added.

Kneeling on the floor, Katya felt something touch the end of the cleaning brush, and hooked it out. It was a letter, addressed in a neat hand to Bronwen Evans, and it had not been opened.

"It must have fallen down the side of the bed," she said as she held out the letter to Miss Pinkney, who had come in bearing clean bed linen. They both looked at the small envelope as if it was radioactive.

"I must give it to Mrs. Spurling," said Miss Pinkney, and took it gingerly from Katya.

"Or I could just make sure it gets to the person for whom it was intended," the girl said.

Miss Pinkney stared at it for a moment, and then without a word, handed it back to Katya and walked away.

NEXT MORNING, GUS was surprised to see Bronwen Evans at his front gate. He watched her hesitate, then push open the gate and come in.

"Sorry to bother you," she said. "I know you wanted a few days to think over what I asked. But I have just been given this, and . . ." "This" was an envelope, and Gus could see that she was fighting for self-control.

"Come in," he said. "I'll get some coffee."

"No, no, please don't trouble. I just wanted to be with somebody when I open it."

Gus knew at once it must be from her mother, and wondered why she had come to him, and not to Bethan or Trevor. But then he realised that it was because he was *not* a family member. And because he had been a compulsive gambler. Like her.

"Sit down, then. Open it up."

But she was all fingers and thumbs, and her hands shook so much that he took the envelope from her, slit it open with a knife and handed it back. "You don't need to tell me what's in it," he said. "But go on, get it over with."

She unfolded the sheet of paper covered on both sides with small, neat handwriting, and began to read. It was as if she had been turned to stone. For what seemed to Gus like several minutes, she sat without moving a muscle, her face drained of all colour. Then she shivered, and silently handed the letter to him.

"*My dearest daughter,*" he read, and asked if she was sure she wanted him to read it.

She nodded mutely, and he carried on.

Forgive me for what I have done. I am afraid it is a coward's way out, just as your father's desertion of us was the same. Now it is my turn. Old age brings back early memories too clearly, and I have had enough. And this way I can have our revenge on my wicked sister. You will find I have put all my estate entirely in Bethan's hands, with instructions for a small allowance from your half of it to be paid regularly to you. Use it well. Do not think that I mean to be unfair. I have loved you both equally and with all my heart. Mother.

Gus handed the letter back to her. He shook his head sadly. "If only she had waited," he said, and took out his diary. "So can you come along tomorrow, and we'll make a start?"

Postscript

THE MOTORWAY WAS busy, and Max had been cursing the traffic for at least an hour. "What did you say?" he asked.

"I said, what's that knocking noise," replied Margaret.

"Which particular knocking noise?" asked Max. "This old banger's full of knocking noises." He laughed, and put his foot down harder on the accelerator.

"Don't go too fast, for heaven's sake," Margaret said. "The last thing we want is to be caught speeding. No licence, no insurance, and from the look of that petrol gauge, not much fuel left."

"We would've got going days ago if this old crate hadn't packed up. Lucky I had a contact."

"I wouldn't rate him very highly as a motor mechanic," Margaret said. "And for God's sake watch out! That woman in front is all over the place."

Planes were going over the motorway now, huge and close to the airport. "Not much further to go," Max said, and then it happened. The car began to judder, and slowly the engine died.

They were in the fast lane, and Margaret groaned. "That's it, then," she said, as cars all round them ground to a halt and a police siren sounded louder and louder. "End of story. For you and me, anyway."

ANN PURSER

THE

HANGMAN'S ROW INQUIRY

**The first book in the all-new
Ivy Beasley Mysteries**

Ivy Beasley may have been moved to assisted living, but she has more interest in assisting her new partners in an amateur-sleuth business. She teams up with Gus, a mysterious newcomer who can't resist a little excitement even as he strives to keep his past secret, and her own cousin, a widow with time on her hands and money in her purse. Together they're determined to solve a local murder . . .

In one of the houses on Hangman's Row, Gus's elderly neighbor has been found with a bread knife sticking out of her chest. Local gossip has it that there was no love lost between the victim and her daughter, but Ivy and her fellow sleuths soon discover no shortage of suspects—or secrets—in the small English village of Barrington . . .

penguin.com